It's Good to Tell You

IT'S GOOD TO TELL YOU
French Folktales from Missouri

Rosemary Hyde Thomas
Illustrated by Ronald W. Thomas

University of Missouri Press
Columbia & London, 1981

To all of the wonderful members of the
Old Mines area community, whose stories
these are, whose history this is, and
who were so generous in sharing with us
not only their cultural heritage but
also their friendship, their love,
and their sense of community.

Copyright © 1981 by
The Curators of the University of Missouri
University of Missouri Press, Columbia, Missouri 65211
Printed and bound in the United States of America

Library of Congress Cataloging in Publication Data
Main entry under title:
It's Good to Tell You.
    Translated into English by
Rosemary Hyde Thomas;
written in Missouri French dialect by
Joseph Médard Carrière.
    1. French-American tales—Missouri. I. Thomas,
Rosemary Hyde, 1939-. II. Carrière, Joseph
Médard, 1902-.
GR111.F73I86   398.2′09778   81-50530
ISBN 0–8262–0327–2   AACR2

The French stories are reprinted by permission of
Northwestern University. They first appeared in
Tales from the French Folk-Lore of Missouri, by
Joseph Médard Carrière, © 1937 by Northwestern
University, Evanston and Chicago.

Research for this book was partially supported with grants
from the National Endowment for the Humanities.

Preface

The major function of storytelling, which is one of our primary forms of entertainment, has passed to the television set. As adults, our command of "Tell us a story!"—one of the requests we most often hear from children close to us—is satisfied by watching the soap opera, the situation comedy, the spy story, the evening news, and the Westerns. These stories have well-known formulas, which impose a discipline and a frame of reference on the writer, cast, and audience. We generally know who are the villains and the heroes, how long evil will seem triumphant, and approximately when to expect righteous virtue to assert itself.

The stories told in this book, like the stories on television, illustrate the triumph of good over evil; the rewards of heroism and virtue; and the endurance of the human spirit when faced with tragedy and catastrophe. In addition, these fairy tales offer the thrills of exotic settings and of exciting adventures. They are spiced with humor, both focused and broad. Like other traditional stories, they provide an interesting mirror of cultural values that indicate western European influence. There is evidence that these tales and their direct ancestors have evolved from the ancient Sanskrit and Persian cultures to the European Middle Ages, from the Age of Enlightenment to the nineteenth and twentieth centuries, wherever oral cultures had flourished. They express a kind of universal human longing for things to come out right in the end, regardless of the dangers encountered along the way. We today know that many things can be explained rationally and thus can be controlled, rendering somewhat obsolete the idea of "forces of good" and "forces of evil." But, by no means, can we explain everything. When faced with forces beyond our control—nature, economics, diseases—we basically respond by hoping that somehow the forces of good will overcome the forces of evil. It is possible to argue both that our response is an inborn human behavior pattern or that it is conditioned by our cultural heritage. In either case, traditional fairy tales provide an insight into feelings and responses that we share with our children, as an expression of universal experience.

The French language is a crucial element both in the history of the Old Mines fairy tales and in the creation of this study. We discovered, while we were seeking opportunities to listen to and to speak Old Mines French, that some people indeed remembered some of the old stories that were told to them by their parents and grandparents and that these people enjoyed talking about them. This whole process demanded real cultivation, because the stories had not been told or heard for some twenty to thirty years, at least. Consequently, people needed time and encouragement to search them out from the dusty corners of their memories and to "put them back together" before they could be told again. Our interviews in the Old Mines area were conducted over a period of more than three years. They moved from general questions to detailed ones, until we arrived at a point where a whole series of these interviews focused primarily on the stories and their setting. In these final interviews, we learned many interesting details about the cultural and physical setting in which the stories flourished, about the people who told them, about the art of storytelling, and about the stories themselves.

We held our first interviews in the summer of 1977, after we decided that we would offer that September a free class for anyone who wanted to learn or to relearn the old French dialect. The purpose of the interviews was to enable us to find material for these lessons. We sought out people who spoke French in the Old Mines area and conversed with them in French, as well as was possible. Some of them knew the language fluently, while others remembered only disconnected words. For all these people, French, at one time, had been the primary language. Some of them had older relatives who spoke English either poorly or not at all, which necessitated that some French be spoken on a daily basis with them. These people were able to remember their mother tongue throughout their lives (in 1976 they were at least sixty years old). We found about thirty-five individuals in this category. Of these, about twenty lived close enough to Old Mines to be of significant assistance with the classes and with the ongoing research.

As we interviewed participants in French about modern-day topics, which were to form the basis for our Old Mines French textbook, we discovered that most people were more comfortable talking in French about "the old days" rather than about more modern events. We found it difficult to discuss current life because so many new inventions and situations have come about since Old Mines French stopped being used daily. As a result, we discovered that the use of Old Mines French in conversation was a kind of open sesame to people's memories of their youth. The discovery of archaic words that had been unused for years invariably led to a discussion of the circumstances surrounding those words.

Because of this natural tendency, we realized that our project had turned into an excellent opportunity to collect information on "the old days," as remembered by the people living in the Old Mines area today who had lived there most of their lives. People often referred to the good times they had had in the French years and derived much pleasure in sharing their experiences with us. We were intrigued by the frequent references in these conversations to square dances, bouillons, and "veillées," which were all neighborly or family gatherings in the community. It was by hearing about these various festivities that we became aware of the important role that the old stories collected by Ward Dorrance and Joseph Médard Carrière had played in the community's life.

In the fall of 1977, the community French classes started under the instruction of about eight native speakers of Old Mines French who served as assistant teachers. On many occasions, these classes turned into group reminiscing sessions in which situations and customs that many people remembered only vaguely were reconstructed. Different people's scraps of memory tended to supplement those of others. Soon, the long-ago past began to revive itself, as it were, and to take on life and color. It was on the basis of this long preparation that we decided, during the summer of 1980, to devote the whole summer's interviews to one topic, that of the old French stories. As a result, weekly series of "story meetings" were set up to which we invited the participants who had contributed the most in all of our previous interviews and classes. Each of the meetings was tape-recorded and then transcribed word for word on paper, as a way of studying people's thoughts and attitudes about the old stories. There were approximately thirty hours of tape-recorded conversations to deal with, which were collected over a period of three months, from June to September 1980. As our search for stories became more and more focused, we became much more familiar with the work of Carrière. One activity of the story meetings involved having the whole group translate one of his stories from French into English. Referring to his stories allowed us to see them in more depth: to know how they were likely to have varied in different tellings, how they could be combined with each other in different ways, and most importantly how they were worded by master storytellers who had the advantage of fresh and constant practice in the public forum. The people who had told these stories held them as symbols of the best that their culture had to offer and as memories of a time when life had been physically hard but emotionally and spiritually rewarding. Thus, it seemed important to preserve this kind of symbol at a time when the use of the Old Mines French language was diminishing, even though ethnic pride in the community was increasing. For this reason, it began to seem imperative to rescue the stories in Carrière's book, which he had so brilliantly captured in the 1930s, making them available once again not only to the children and grandchildren of his storytellers but also to the greater public today. *Rescue* is the proper word here, because Carrière had transcribed them exactly as he had heard them, in Missouri French dialect. At that time, there was no standard way to write down this dialect, so in addition to the unique words and constructions, he used unique spellings. Because the people within the community were not generally taught to read in French, Carrière's tales were not presented in a form that proved to be a useful vehicle to the people in the Old Mines area. While those fluent in standard French can understand about 75 percent of Old Mines French, there are enough peculiarities in the dialect to impede effective, in-depth understanding of the tales for even those who can read and speak French.

In addition to the twenty-one stories that we've included in this work for you to learn, read, enjoy, and perform, we will look at the community where these stories were collected, examine the ways in which the stories came to be preserved and the changing role that they have played in community life, and look at the people who told the stories and at the people who recorded them for posterity.

Acknowledgments

There are many people who deserve my deepest appreciation for their assistance with the various phases of the book. My thanks are extended first to the wonderful people of the Old Mines community who were such an integral part of this whole project. In a real sense, I feel that my role was to record their story on paper. Natalie Villmer and her mother, Eileen Villmer, worked closely with me as a team, arranging visits, meetings, classes, and interviews on which the book is based. The steadfast teacher assistants and storytellers were no less essential to the successful completion of the project: Annie Pashia, Pete Boyer, Robert Robart, Dennis Portell (deceased), Ida Portell, Genevieve Portell, Marguerite Politte, Mr. and Mrs. Matt Boyer, Walter "Lesin" Boyer, Charlie Pashia, Ethel Larue, and Rosie Boyer. The Rural Parish Workers of Christ the King, especially LaDonna Hermann and Natalie Villmer, were an inspiration and were also the patient workers who were mostly responsible for providing space, food, and publicity for project events. Their support has been invaluable to me and to the project itself. The Old Mines Area Historical Society provided the organizational backup and credibility that we needed in order to carry out the project. A generous group of people were kind enough to give preliminary suggestions or to read the manuscript, providing detailed suggestions prior to publication: Judith McCulloch, Monica Pashia, Judith Escoffier Politte, Jan Adkins, Natalie Villmer, and Debbie Boyer. It should be obvious, however, that the author is solely responsible for any inaccuracies or omissions. The Washington County Public Library in Potosi kindly provided us with a cool meeting place during an unusually hot summer. I likewise wish to thank Jack Cowart of the St. Louis Art Museum for his encouragement at an early stage of the drawings included in this book and for the opportunity to show them to the public at the museum; and Carol Shapiro of Carol Shapiro Gallery, St. Louis, for her ongoing interest in the artistic portion of the project. Barry Bergey of Missouri Friends of the Folk Arts was most helpful in sharing with me his bibliographic knowledge of the Old Mines area. Finally, I wish to thank Howard S. Miller for his encouragement to seek publication.

R. H. T. St. Louis, Missouri July 1981

Contents

Part II: Historical Background

Part I: The Stories

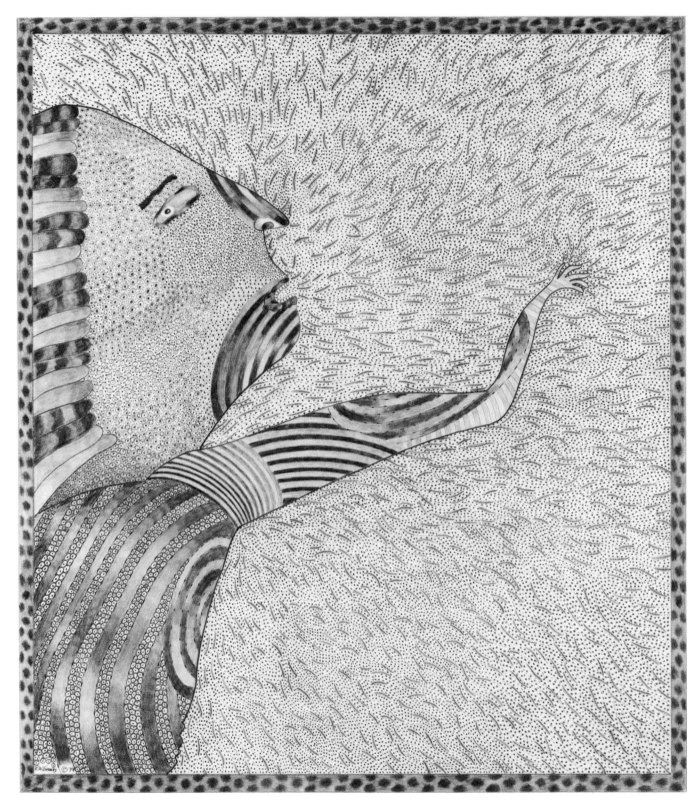

The thief in flight.

1.

Little John and His Animals

It's good to tell you that once upon a time there were an old man and an old woman. They had a little boy named Little John. When Little John grew up and got ready to leave home, he decided to go out and see the world. When he had gotten a good distance from home, he met an Ox. —"Hello, Little John," said the Ox. —"Hello, Ox," answered Little John. —"Where are you going, Little John?" —"I've left home to see the world." —"Would you like me to come with you?" Little John told the Ox, "You can come if you'd like, but I want you to walk behind me." A little farther on, he met a Sheep. He said, "Hello, Sheep." The Sheep answered, "Hello, Little John. Where are you going?" —"I've left home to go out and see the world." —"Do you want me to come with you?" —"You can come if you want, Sheep, but walk in back of me."

A little farther on he met a Cat that was sunning itself on a fence. The Cat said, "Hello, Little John. Do you want me to come with you?" —"You can come if you want to, but I want you to walk behind me." Yet a little farther down the road, they met a Skunk.— "Hello, Skunk," said Little John. —"Hello, Little John," answered the Skunk. "Where are you going?" —"I'm off to see the world," he answered. —"Can I come with you, Little John?" asked the Skunk. —"You can can come with me if you want, Skunk, but I want you to stay way behind me, because sometimes you don't smell so good."

As they all went on down the road, they met a Bumblebee. —"Hello, Little Bumble-bee," said Little John. —"Hello, Little John. Where are you going?" —"I'm out to see the world."—"Can I come with you, Little John?" —"Come along if you want to. You can sit on my shoulder, but you'd better not sting me." Farther on, they met a Rooster. —"Hello, Rooster," said Little John. —"Hello, Little John. Where are you going?" —"I'm going out to see the world." —"Do you want me to come with you?" —"You can come along if you want to, but walk behind me."

Late that evening, they came to a big house. Little John went in to look around, and no one was there. So he said to his animals, "Well, I guess this is a good place for us to sleep." He asked the Ox, "Where do you usually sleep?" The Ox answered, "Right inside my master's front yard fence." So Little John opened the gate and let the Ox go into the front yard. Then, he asked the Sheep, "Where do you usually sleep?" —"I usually sleep right outside the fence," answered the Sheep. —"Well, go on and go to bed. It's all ready for

The thief chased by Little John's animals.

you," answered Little John. He asked the Rooster where he was used to sleeping. —"I usually sleep right on the top of the roof," said the Rooster. —"Well, your bed is ready too. Go on and get up there," said Little John. Then, he asked the Skunk where he liked to sleep. The Skunk told him, "I like to sleep in a dark place." —"Well," answered Little John, "you can sleep under my bed, but you'd better not spray me!" Then, Little John asked the Cat about where he was used to sleeping. —"On the bed at my master's feet," answered the Cat. —"Go ahead and get on the bed, then," Little John told him. Then, he asked the little Bumblebee about the kind of place where he liked to sleep. —"I usually try to find a warm place to sleep in," said the Bumblebee. Little John told him, "Well, look over the fireplace

It's Good to Tell You

and see if you can't find a nice, warm little hole to sleep in." The little Bumblebee looked and found a nice, warm spot right away. Then, Little John got into bed and went to sleep too.

The house they had picked was a place where robbers met in the evening. One of the robbers came there that night with a big sack full of money. He threw the sack down on the floor in a corner and went to start a fire in the fireplace. But the little Bumblebee came out and stung him on the forehead. That hurt a lot, and he went to throw himself on the bed, but the Cat was there and scratched him with his claws. So he tried to hide under the bed, but the Skunk sprayed him. He left the house running as fast as he could to escape, but he ran into the Ox, who caught him with his horns and threw him over the fence. When he landed, on his hands and knees, the Sheep came up and butted him in the rear end. The robber got up and ran away as fast as he could run, until he had gotten pretty far away from the house, where he met his two pals. —"Where are you going in such a big hurry?" they asked him. —"Saints alive!" he answered. "I was just at the house, and the devil has gotten into it." —"What are you talking about?" asked the other two thieves. —"Well, I went to start a fire to make supper, and the awl poked me on the forehead. Then, I went to lie down for a moment, and the carding comb scratched me. When I went to get under the bed, the watering can was there and sprinkled me. I couldn't believe how much that hurt and how terrible it smelled. Then I tried to leave the house, and the farmhand was there with his pitchfork, and he pitched me over the fence. When I fell on the ground outside the fence, the wood splitter was there with his froe, and he just about split me in two. And on top of all those, there was another one, sitting up on the roof, shouting 'couroucoucou, bring him up here!' That one didn't have a chance to do anything to me this time, and I'm not going back to that house to give him another opportunity."

The next morning, Little John woke up and found the sack of money lying in the corner. "This will be enough money to last me for the rest of my life," he said to himself. He took the sack of money and all his animals and went back to his own house. He fed his animals and took care of them as long as they all lived.

P'tsit Jean

C'est bon d'vous dzire eune fouès c'étaient ein vieux pis eune vieille. 'L ontvaient ein p'tsit garçon qui s'app'lait P'tsit Jean. Quand P'tsit Jean 'l est v'nu à eune bonne âge pour partsir, 'l est partsi pour aller couparir dzu pays. Rendzu ein bon boute d'sa maisonne, 'l a rencontré ein boeu[f]. —"Bonjour, P'tsit Jean," i'dzit. —"Bonjour, l'boeu[f]." —"Où est-ce qu'tsu t'en vas, P'tsit Jean?" —"M'en vas courparir dzu pays." —"Tsu veux que j'vaille avec touè?" —"Viens, si tsu veux, maix marche derrière." Ein p'tsit boute plus loin, 'l a rencontré ein mouton. —"Bonjour, mouton," i' dzit. —"Bonjour, P'tsit Jean," i' dzit. "Où tsu t'en vas là, P'tsit Jean?" —"J'm'en vas courparir dzu pays."

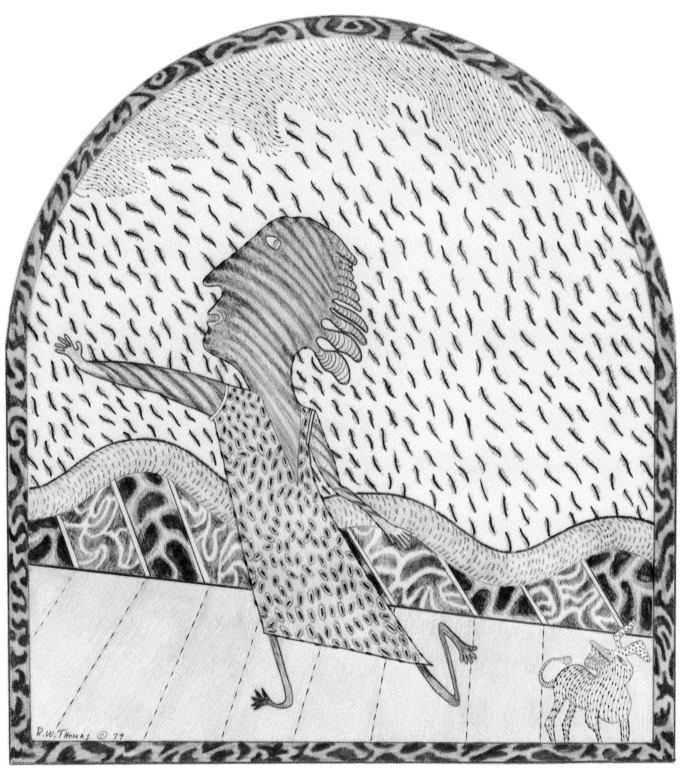

The thief searches for a place of refuge.

It's Good to Tell You

—"Tsu veux que j'vas avec touè?" —"Viens, si tsu veux, mais marche derrière." Ein p'tsit boute plus loin, 'l a rencontré ein chat qui l'était assis sus la clôtsure. —"Bonjour, P'tsit Jean, tsu veux que j'vas avec touè?" —"Viens, si tsu veux, mais marche derrière."

Ein p'tsit boute plus loin, P'tsit Jean a rencontré eune bête piante. —"Bonjour, la bête piante," i' dzit. —"Bonjour, P'tsit Jean, où tt'en vas, P'tsit Jean?" —"J'm'en vas courparir dzu pays," i' dzit. —"Tsu veux que j'vas avec touè?" —"Viens, si tsu veux, mais marche là-bas en errière, par rapport qu'des fouès tsu sens pas bon." Ein p'tsit boute plus loin, 'l a rencontré ein bourdon. "Bonjour," i' dzit, "p'tsit bourdon." —"Bonjour, P'tsit Jean, où ttsu t'en vas?" i' dzit. —"J'm'en vas courparir dzu pays," i' dzit. —"Tsu veux que j'vas avec touè?" i' dzit. —"Viens, si tsu veux; mets-touè sus mon épaule, pique-mouè pas, par exemp'." Ein p'tsit boute plus loin, 'l a rencontré l'coq. —"Bonjour, l'coq," i' dzit. —"Bonjour, P'tsit Jean," i' dzit. "Où tsu t'en vas?" i' dzit. —"J'm'en vas courparir dzu pays." —"Tsu veux que j'vas avec touè?" —"Viens, si tsu veux, mais marche derrière."

Tout tard l'souère, 'l ont arrivé à eune grande maisonne. P'tsit Jean 'l a été ouère dans la maisonne; 'l avait pas personne dedans. "Ben," i' dzit, "on va coucher icitte," i' dzit à ses bétailes. I' dzit au boeu[f]: "Oùsqu't'as coutsume d'coucher, touè?" —"Drétte en d'dans d'la barrière sus mon maître." Ben, i'a rouvert la barrière, pis i' l'a quitté entrer en d'dans. I'a d'mandé au mouton où i'avait la coutsume d'coucher. —"J'ai coutsume d'coucher drétte en dehors d'la barrière." —"Couche-touè," i' dzit, "ton lite 'l est paré." I'a d'mandé au coq oùsqu'i' avait coutsume d'coucher. "J'ai coutsume," i' dzit, "d'coucher sus l'faîte d'la maisonne." —"Ben, ton lite 'l est paré, monte sus la maisonne." 'L a d'mandé à la bête piante où 'l avait coutsume d'coucher. —"J'ai accoutsumé à coucher dans eune place nouèr'te." —"Ben," i' dzit, "tsu peux coucher sous l'lite, mais arrose-moin pas." I'a d'mandé au chat oùsce i' y'avait accoutsumé à coucher. —"Sus l'lite, sus les pieds d'mon maît." —"Ben, couche-touè là." I'a d'mandé au p'tsit bourdon oùsce i'avait accoutsumé à coucher. —"J'ai accoutsumé à coucher dans ein endrouè où i' fait chaud, moin," i' dzit. —"Ben," i' dzit, "eurgarde dessus la chum'née pour ouère si tsu pourras pas trouver ein p'tsit trou chaud." L'p'tsit bourdon i' s'a trouvé eune bonne place tout d'suite. P'tsit Jean i' s'a couché, lui aussite.

C'n était eune maisonne où i'avait des *robeurs,* des voleurs que s'rassemblaient l'souère. I' nn'a ein des *robeurs*-là qui a eursous l'souère avec ein sac plein d'argent. I' l'a j'té à terre dans ein coin. I'a été pour s'partsir ein feu dans sa ch'minée. L'p'tsit bourdon i' l'a piqué dans l'front, ça y'a faite mal. I'a été pour s'j'ter sus l'lite, l'chat était là, pis i' l'a cardé; i'a été pour rentrer sous l'lite, pis la bête piante a l'a arrosé. 'L a sortsi à la course pour s'sauver, 'l a été tomber sus l'boeu[f], l'boeu[f] l'a attrapé par ses cornes, pis l'a enwèyé par-dessus la clôtsure. Quand 'l a tombé, 'l a tombé sus ses mains pis ses g'noux; l'mouton 'l était là, pis i'est v'nu, pis i' l'a cogné dans l'gros boute.

'L a partsi à la course, s'a sauvé, s'est rendzu ein bon grand boute d'sa maisonne, 'l a rencontré ses deux associés. "Oùsqu'ttsu t'en vas, si pressé," i' dzisent, "Toussaint?" —"J'viens d'la maisonne," i' dzit, "l'dziab' 'l est là." —"Quocé qu'i' nn'a à la maisonne?" i' dzisent. —"J'ai été pour partsir dzu feu dans la chum'née pour faire á souper, l'alène a m'a piqué dans l'front; j'ai été pour m'j'ter sus l'lite, la cardeuse a était là, a m'a cardé. Après ça, j'ai été pour rentrer d'ssour l'lite, l'arrosouère 'l était là, i' m'a arrosé," i' dzit, "pis ça faisait mal, pis ça puait. J'ai été pour sortsir," i' dzit, "pis l'fourch'teur d'foin 'l était là avec sa fourche, pis i' m'a j'té sus la clôtsure. Quand j'ai tombé en dehors, l'fendeur d'perches 'l était là avec sa masse, pis i'a rasé d'tout m'défoncer. I' nn'avait ein aut'," i' dzit, "sus l'faîte d'la maisonne, i'a crié: "Couroucoucou, 'porte-lé icitte!" S'il a pas eu eune chance d'me cogner, i' m'cogn'ra de c'coup-là; j'eurtourne pus à maisonne-là."

L'lend'main matin, P'tsit Jean i' s'a réveillé pis i'a trouvé l'sac d'argent dans l'coin. "Ça va m'faire," i' dzit, "assez d'argent pour l'restant d'mes jours." 'L a pris l'sac d'argent, tous ses bétailes. I' s'a rentourné cheux lui, pis i'a ben eu soin d'ses bétailes tant 'l ont vi.

2.

The Seven-Headed Beast

It's good to tell you that once upon a time there were an old king and an old queen. They had a daughter who was married, and she had a little boy. In that town, there was also a man named Samson, who lived in the woods. No matter what the king did, Samson destroyed it. The king had lost many men trying to get rid of Samson. He offered a good sum of money to anyone who could give him an idea that would work to catch Samson.

Finally, his daughter thought up a plan. She said to lay a table with one hundred places, with different kinds of liquor. They should also make an iron chest with a lid controlled by a hidden spring. They should make a comfortable-looking bed in the chest and cut a window that could open and close in the chest near the head of the bed. Then they should haul in a big pile of wood, put it around the table, and set fire to it. When Samson would see the smoke, he would say, "My goodness! The king is up to something today." Then, he would come to see what was going on.

So sure enough, the king had the big table all set with one hundred places, and he set fire to the pile of wood. When Samson saw the smoke, he said, "My goodness! The king is up to something today. I'd better go see what's happening." When he got there, he saw this beautiful table all set with a feast, and he began to sample everything that was on the table, saying, "The king won't enjoy this before I do!" When he had eaten his way all around the table, he was full. He looked around and saw the beautiful bed and said, "Oh! The king won't get to sleep there before I do!" He got into the bed, the lid closed automatically, and he fell asleep. The king's men came then and opened up the little door at the head of the bed, so that they could see Samson's hair. They cropped it close to his head. When Samson's hair was cut short like that, he was no stronger than any other man, and the king's men took him then and put him in prison. The king said that anyone who set Samson free would be hanged.

Samson was in prison for quite a while, and his hair was beginning to grow back. He was starting to jump around and shake the whole prison. Little John had a golden ball and was playing near the prison. One day, his ball fell inside the prison walls. He begged Samson to give it back to him, and Samson said to him, "Well, I'll give it back to you this time, but don't come back around here any more." Little John left with his ball. He started coming back again after awhile and finally started playing with the ball again. The golden ball fell inside the prison once again, and Little John begged Samson to give it back to him. This time Samson said, "I'll give you back your ball if you get me out of here." Little John answered, "How can I get you out of there? I don't have any key." Samson said to him, "Go to your mother. She's the one who has the key, in the pocket of her dress. Start scratching your head and tell her that you want her to check your hair to see if you have any lice. Put your head on her lap and sneak your hand gently into her pocket. When you've gotten the key, tell her that your head doesn't itch any more, and she doesn't need to look for anything any more in your hair. Then come out to play and come let me out."

When Little John had gotten the keys, he went to let Samson out. Samson and Little John played for a while outside, then Little John said, "It's time to go back in there, Samson. If my grandfather sees you out of prison, he'll have me hanged." —"I'm not going back in there at all, Little John," said Samson. "I'm leaving here." Little John got scared and began to cry, and Samson asked if Little John wanted to come along with him. Little John answered, "I'd rather go with you than stay around here. If I stay here, my grandfather will have me hanged." —"Well, get up on my back," said Samson.

They traveled until they got to a town where there was another King. Samson said to Little John, "Do you see that house over there? It belongs to an old woman who is very poor. All she has to eat is beans. But you can stay with her, and whenever you need me, all you have to do is come to this place and call me three times. I'll come to help you out." Little John went and knocked at the old woman's door. She came to answer it, and he said, "It's me, grandmother, Little John." He went in and asked if he could stay with her. She told him that he could, but that she was so poor all she ever had to eat was beans.

In that country, there lived a beast, that was called the Seven-Headed Beast. Every year, they had to give him a fifteen-year-old girl to eat. When Little John got up the next morning, he went out and looked all around and noticed that the whole town was in mourning. He asked the old woman what the trouble was. She said, "You know, my little boy, there's a Seven-Headed Beast in the forest not far from here, and every year we have to give him a fifteen-year-old girl to eat. This year, the only girl in the whole town who is fifteen is the King's daughter." Little John asked the old grandmother why they couldn't just get rid of that beast. She said that the King had lost one hundred men in trying to get rid of it, and that it hadn't done any good.

Little John watched the King and his army set out to deliver his daughter to the beast. He went to find Samson. When he called three times, Samson came running. —"Ah," he said. "So you want to deliver the Princess?" He put Little John on a black horse. He was all dressed in black armor and had three black dogs and a black sword. He rode out to catch up with the Princess after her father had left her off. He asked her to ride on his horse with him. She said, "Oh, no! It's enough for me to go and be eaten up without you coming

along too!" —"The beast will have to earn the right to eat us!" answered Little John, and the Princess climbed up on his horse with him.

When they got to the beast's den, the beast came out, with flames coming out of its nostrils. It said, "Hey, Little John, instead of one meal, I'm going to have six!" —"You'll have six if you earn them!" answered Little John. —"I can do that," sneered the beast. —"Well, let me know then when you're ready," said Little John. —"I'm ready now!" So they began to fight. Little John called to his dogs, encouraged his horse, rode up to the beast, and cut off one of his heads with his sword. The beast cried out, "Time out for an hour!" and went back into its den to lick its wounds.

The Princess took this chance to wipe the sweat off Little John's face and to give water to his dogs to drink. She took the gold necklace she had around her neck and made three collars out of it to put around the necks of Little John's dogs. At the end of the hour, the Seven-Headed Beast came out of its den again. It roared, "Hey, Little John! I'm seven times stronger with six heads than I was with seven!" —"Good for you!" answered Little John. "When I'm done with you, you won't have any heads left at all." He called to his dogs and told his horse to be brave. Then, he swung mightily with the sword and cut off another of the beast's heads. The beast cried out, "Time out until tomorrow!" Little John took out his knife and cut the tongues out of the two heads he had cut from the beast. The Princess gave him her silk handkerchief to wrap the tongues up in, and he stuck them in his pocket.

They left together, but when they got to the fork in the road, Little John had the Princess get off his horse. The Princess wanted him to go with her, but he said, "No, not tonight." When the Princess got back home, the King was surprised. "What? Didn't the beast eat you up?" The Princess answered, "No, it wasn't hungry today. It told me to come back tomorrow." So the next morning, the King set off with his company to bring the Princess back to the edge of the woods. Today, Little John had on a suit of red armor, with a red horse, red dogs, and a red sword. He went and caught up with the Princess and took her up on his horse with him.

When they got to the beast's lair, the Seven-Headed Beast roared out, "Hey, Little John! I'm five times stronger now with five heads than I was with seven!" —"Good for you!" said Little John. "When I'm done with you, you won't have any more heads left at all. Tell me when you're ready." The beast answered, "I'm ready right now, Little John." Little John encouraged his animals: "Be brave, my dogs! Hold steady, good horse!" He gave a mighty blow with the sword and cut off two of the monster's heads. The beast asked for time off until the next day and went back into its den to lick its wounds. The Princess

The Seven-Headed Beast

gave her silk handkerchief to Little John, and he wrapped the two new tongues in it. Then, they turned around and went back. When they got to the fork in the road, the Princess wanted Little John to go home with her. He answered, "Oh, no, Princess, I couldn't go back with you. I have to get back home."

When the Princess got back to her own house, the old King was surprised again. "The beast still didn't eat you up?" he asked. "No, Father," answered the Princess. "He still wasn't hungry. I have to go back there again tomorrow." So the next morning, the old King set out once again with his whole company to bring his daughter back to the edge of the woods. Little John went to find Samson again, and Samson dressed him all up in white, with a white horse and three white dogs. He rode off to catch up with the Princess. When he got to the spot where he had found her the two other days, she was there sitting on a stump waiting for him. She got up behind him on his horse.

When they got to the den of the Seven-Headed Beast, it came out and roared at Little John, "I'm seven times stronger with three heads than I was with seven!" Little John answered, "Well, good for you! When I'm done with you, you won't have any more heads at all. Tell me when you're ready." —"I'm ready right now," answered the beast. Little John encouraged his horse and dogs to be brave, and then they fought for about half an hour. Finally, with one blow of his sword, he cut off the beast's other three heads. He got down off his horse, took the Princess' silk handkerchief, and wrapped these three tongues up in it, before putting them in his pocket.

They turned around and started back. When they got to the fork in the road, he helped the Princess down off his horse. She didn't want to get down and begged Little John to go back home with her so that they could get married. But, no, Little John was too young to get married. He said, "Maybe I'll be able to find others to save, as I've saved you." So the Princess walked off crying, really upset that she couldn't bring Little John back home with her.

Not long afterward, she came face to face with a charcoal burner. He said, "Well! How come the beast didn't eat you up?" —"The beast is dead," answered the Princess. —"Who in the world could have killed it?" —"I don't know. It was a very nice young man." The charcoal burner took out his pistol and stuck it in the Princess' face. "If you don't swear," he said, "that I was the one who killed the Seven-Headed Beast with my shovel and my rake, I'll blow your brains out." The Princess was really scared, and she swore. The charcoal burner said to her, "Get into my wheelbarrow and show me where those seven heads are." When they got to where the beast's den had been, he loaded the seven heads into his wheelbarrow, with the Princess perched on top of the pile.

Little John's Princess with the heads of the Seven-Headed Beast.

The charcoal burner then went back to the King with his wheelbarrow, shouting, "You lost so many people trying to kill this beast, and I was able to kill it all by myself with my shovel and my rake! I'm not lying either. Here's the seven heads and the Princess to prove it!" The King said, "Well, if you killed the beast, you will have to marry my daughter." The Princess didn't want to marry the charcoal burner and said to her father that first she wanted three big feasts, three days in a row, and the charcoal burner would have to be scrubbed good and clean to come to the dinners. The charcoal burner wanted to get married before the dinners, but the Princess said that she was too young and wasn't in any big hurry to get married. She wanted everyone in the town invited to her three big dinners.

The first day, Little John and his grandmother weren't invited to the feast at the King's house. Little John said to her, "The King is proud. He didn't invite me, but we're going to taste his feast anyway." He called in his dog called "Fast-as-the-Wind" and said to him, "Go to the King's house. Go on in to the dinner and put your paw on the Princess' lap. She'll know who you are and will feed you well. After you've eaten your fill, get up on the table, and bring us back a loaf of bread and a bottle of wine. So the dog went and put his paw on the Princess' knee. She looked down and saw who it was and fed him well. She said to herself, "Ah! Little John can't be far away." When he had eaten enough, he jumped up on the table and grabbed the white bread and white wine and disappeared with it. The woodsman said, "Kill that thieving dog." The Princess, however, told her father to give orders not to harm the dog, because it was not a thief. She said that there were still some people in the town who had not been invited to the dinners, and she wanted everyone to be invited.

The next day, the charcoal burner asked the King, when everyone had sat down at the table for the second feast, to lock all the doors and windows, so that no dogs could come in. The King did this for him. Little John said to his grandmother, "We weren't invited again today." He called in his second dog, "Goes-Anywhere," and told him, "Go to the King's house. All the doors are locked today, but I want you to go through the door and go under the table. Put your paw on the Princess' knee. She'll know who you are and she will feed you well. When you've eaten enough, jump up on the table and bring us a little suckling pig." When that dog got up on the table, the woodsman began to holler, "There's that thieving dog again! I want him killed!" But before they could get the doors opened, the dog had disappeared.

The charcoal burner was getting really impatient to get married before the three days were up. "That's too long to wait," he said. But the Princess answered that no, she wasn't in any hurry; she was still young, and he could wait till after the three dinners. The next day, everything went the same way. Little John and his grandmother still weren't invited. Little John called his third dog, "Iron-Breaker," and told him, "Go to the King's house. The doors are all locked, but I want you to go through them and lay at the Princess' feet under the table. Put your paw on her foot. She'll know who you are, and she'll feed you well. After you've eaten, jump up on the table and get us a cake. But this time come home slowly enough so that some of them can follow you from a distance."

The dog left and went to the King's house. When he jumped up on the table, the woodsman hollered, "Kill that thieving dog!" The Princess said they should do no harm to the dog but should follow him, to see where he went. The people in that house should be invited to dinner the next day. When they came to the house to invite Little John and his grandmother to the King's dinner, Little John told them that if the Princess wanted them at her dinner, she should send the King's best horses and finest carriage to pick them up. They should drive the carriage right up to the porch, so that his old grandmother would not have to set a foot on the ground. The man who had followed the dog answered, "You should just be happy to be invited, without demanding the best horses and carriage." — "Well, tell the King what I said anyway," answered Little John.

So the messenger gave Little John's message to the King, and the Princess overheard him. She said, "I want the best horses harnessed up to the best carriage to go get them tomorrow morning." So Little John and his grandmother came to the King's house. The Princess said to Little John, "All you have to do is tell a little story after dinner." So after the dinner had been eaten, it was time for each person there to tell a little story. Since the old grandmother was the oldest person, she had to tell the first story. She said, "I don't have much to tell you. I never get out, and this young man keeps me good company." After that, it was the charcoal burner's turn to tell his story. He said, "The King lost whole companies of soldiers to get rid of the Seven-Headed Beast, and I was able to kill him all by myself with my shovel and my rake. To prove that I'm not lying, the seven heads are hanging on the King's porch."

Then it was Little John's turn to tell his story. He said, "Sire, I don't have much to tell. But which is the true hunter, the man who has the tongues, or the man who has the heads?" The King answered, "Well, it has to be the one with the tongues." Suddenly, the woodsman didn't feel good and wanted to be excused from the table. The King told him to lie down in the corner until he had finished his dinner. Then, the Princess told her father what the charcoal burner had done. She said, "This is the young man who freed me from the Seven-Headed Beast, not that woodsman." They hanged the charcoal burner, and Little John and the Princess got married. They had a big wedding, but they didn't invite me to come.

La Bête à Sept Têtes

C'est bon d'vous dzire eune fouès c'étaient ein vieux rouè pis eune vieille reine. 'L ontvaient eune fille qu'était mariée et qui l'avait ein mouèyen p'tsit garçon. Pis dans c'te ville-là, 'l avait ein homme qui s'app'lait Som'pson. I' restait dans l'bois, lui. I'avait pas d'dzifférence quoi l'rouè faisait, i' l'détruisait, lui, i' l'démanchait. L'rouè avait fait perdre ein tas des hommes pour essayer d'faire détruire Sam'son. Il a offert eune bonne somme d'argent pour n'importe qui y'aurait donné ein avis pour attraper Sam'son.

Sa fille alle a jonglé ein plan. A dzit d'mett' eune tab' d'cent places, et d'mett' dzifférentes liqueurs tout autour d'la tab', pis faire faire ein coff' de fer, fermé par ein eursort qui rentrerait d'dans, et qu'i' mettent ein beau lite là d'dans, et laisser eune p'tsite f'nêt' à la tête qui peut rouvert, pis après, charrier ein gros tas d'bois tout près d'la tab', pis l'mett' en feu. "Sam'son i' va ouère la boucane et i' va dzire: 'Pargué! l'rouè est après faire queud' chose aujourdz'hui.' Pis," a dzit, "vous savez, i' va v'nir ouère."

Comme de faite, l'rouè 'l a faite arrranger la tab' tout parée et il a mis l'feu au tas d'bois, et quand Som'psone 'l a vu la boucane: "Pargué! l'rouè est après faire queuque chose aujourdz'hui. Faut que j'vaille ouère." Quand il a arrivé, 'l a vu c'te belle tab', pis i'a commencé à manger entour d'la tab', dzisant: "L'rouè i' goûtera pas ça avant moin." Quand il a eu fini d'faire l'tour d'la tab', 'l était plein. 'L a eurgardé, pis 'l a vu c'te beau lite. "Oh!" i' dzit, "l'rouè l'essayera pas avant moin." Quand il a rentrè, la porte s'a fermée, pis i' s'a endormi. Les hommes sont v'nus pis i'ont rouvert la p'tsite f'nêt', i'ont coupé les ch'veux à ras d'la tête. Sa force a était tout dans ses ch'veux. Quand ses ch'veux étaient coupés courts, 'l avait pas plus d'force qu'ein aut' homme. Ils l'ont pris, pis ils l'ont mis en prison. L'vieux rouè 'l a dzit ceul qui mettait Sam'son dehors d'prison, l'aurait pendzu.

'L avait eune bonne escousse Sam'son 'l était d'dans les prisons. Ses ch'veux sontaient après eurvenir grands. Il sautait pis i' brandait tout la prison. P'tsit Jean il avait eune boule d'or, pis i' allait vouère entour d'la prison. Eune journée, sa balle a tombé dans la prison. I'a *bégué* Sam'son qu'i' y rende, pis lui y'a dzit: "J't'la rendras aujourdz'hui mais eurviens pus." I' s'a en allé, l'P'tsit Jean. Deux, trois fouès après, 'l est eurv'nu encore, pis 'l a eurcommencé à jouer encore. La boule d'or 'l a eurtombé dans les prisons encore. I'a *bégué* Sam'son pour qu'i' la rende. "M'as t'la rend' ta boule, si tsu m'mets dehors." —"Comment moin, j'peux t'mettre dehors? J'ai pas d'clef." I' dzit: "Va à ta mère, c'est elle qui a la clef. Alle l'a dans sa poche d'robe. Commence à t'gratter, pis dzi[s]-y qu'tsu as des poux, qu'a charce dans ta tête. Mets ta tête sus ses g'noux, mets ta min tout douc'ment dans sa poche, pis après qu'tsu vas avouère la clef, dzis à ta mère qu'ta tête a démange pus, qu'a t'laisse tranquille, tsu veux t'en aller jouer, pis après tsu pourras v'nir m'mett' dehors."

Après qu'il a eu les clefs, il a été lâcher Som'sone. Som'sone 'l a joué eune bonne p'tsite escousse en dehors. P'tsit Jean voulait qu'i' rent'. "Si mon grand-père, i' t'vouè en dehors, i' va m'pendre." —"Non," i' dzit, "moin, j'rent' pus là d'dans, j'm'en vas." P'tsit Jean i' s'a mis à brailler, i'avait peur. Sam'son y'a eurd'mandé si i' voulait aller avec lui. "Mais," i' dzit, "j'aime mieux aller avé touè qu'rester icitte. Si j'reste icitte, mon grand-père i' va m'pend'." —"Ah!" i' dzit, "monte dans mon dos."

I'ont trav'lé jusqu'à eune ville, où i'avait ein aut'rouè. I'a dzit: "Vous vouèyez p'tsite maisonne là-bas. C'est eune vieille grand'mère qui reste là. Alle est pauv', i' dzit, "a mange ien qu'des fèves. Vous pourra rester avec elle, et quand vous va avouère besoin d'moin, v'nez icitte et dzites trois fouès: 'A moin, Sam'son.' M'as êt à vot' s'cours." I'a été cogner à la porte d'la vieille grand'mère; a était là, elle, la vieille. "C'est moin," i' dzit, "ma vieille grand'mère, P'tsit Jean." Il a rentré, il a d'mandé à la vieille grand'mère pour rester avec elle. Alle a dzit; "Vous pouvez rester avec moin, mais j'sus pauv', j'mange ien qu'des fèves."

Dans c'pays-là, nn'avait eune bétaille qu'i'app'laient la bête à sept têtes. Tous les ans, i' fallait qu'alle aye eune fille d'quinze ans à manger. L'lend'main matin, quand P'tsit Jean i' s'a l'vé, i'a eurgardé à l'entour, pis la ville était tou[t] en deuil. I'a d'mandé à la vieille quocé c'était l'trouble dans la ville. A dzit: "Vous savez, mon p'tsit garçon, i'a eune bête à sept têtes dans la forêt pas ben loin d'icitte, pis tous les ans i' faut qu'alle aye eune fille d'quinze ans à manger. C't'année, c'est la princesse dzu rouè qui, seule, a quinze dans la ville." I'a d'mandé à sa vieille grand'mère si i' pouvaient pas faire détruire c'bétaille-là. A y'a dzit qu'le rouè avait fait détruire cent personnes pour la fair détruite, mais i'avaient pas pu.

P'tsit Jean a eurgardé partsir l'rouè avec sa princesse pis son armée qui la conduisait. I' s'en a allé trouver Sam'son. "A moin," trois fouès, "Sam'son." Som'son est v'nu à la course. "Ah!" i' dzit, "P'tsit Jean, tsu as envie d'délivrer la princesse." I'a mis P'tsit Jean sus ein joual nouère, tou[t] ein habit nouère, trois chiens nouères, ein sable tout nouère. P'tsit Jean a été l'attraper la princesse après qu'son père l'a eu laissée. I'a d'mandé qu'alle excepte la croupe d'son ch'fal. "Oh! non," a dzit, "i'en a ben assez d'moin qui s'en va s'faire manger sans qu'vous vienne."—"Faudra qu'a nous gagne avant qu'a nous mange." La princesse 'l a excepté la croupe d'son j'val.

Quand 'l a arrivé à la ouache d'la bête à sept têtes, alle a sortsi pis l'feu sortait par ses narines dzu nez. "Hé!" a dzit, "P'tsit Jean, alieurs d'ein eurpas, j'vas en vouère six." —"Tsu vas en avouère six, si tsu les gagnes."—"J'peux faire ça." —"Quitte-moin connaît' quand tsu s'ras parée." —"J'sus parée à c't'heure." Ah! i' commencent à s'batt' à c't'heure. P'tsit Jean dzisait: "Hardi, mes chiens! Quiens bon, mon joual!" En dzisant ça, i' ôte eune tête d'ein coup d'sable. "Quarquier pour ein heure," a dzit, "j'vas m'bagner." Alle a rentré dans sa ouache, la bête à sept têtes.

La princesse a commencé à ôter la sueur d'ssus la figure à P'tsit Jean, donner d'l'eau à ses chiens dans ses mains. Alle a pris son collier d'or alle avait dans son cou, pis a en faisait des colliers pour mettre dans l'cou des chiens à P'tsit Jean. La bête à sept têtes alle a sortsi au bout d'son heure. "Hé! P'tsit Jean," a dzit, "j'sus sept fouès meilleurte avec six têtes qu'j'étais avec sept." —"Tant mieux pour touè," i' dzit P'tsit Jean. "Quand j'auras fini avec touè, t'en auras pus d'têtes." Dzisant: "Hardi, mes chiens! Quiens bon, mon joual!" i'a donné ein coup d'sable, pis i'a ôté ein aut' tête. "Quarquier d'icitte à d'main." I'a pris son couteau, 'l a l'vé les deux langues. La princesse alle y'a donné son mouchouère d'souè alle avait avec l'nom d'son père et l'nom d'son armée d'ssus. 'L a env'loppé ses langues d'dans, pis les a mis dans sa poche.

I'ont partsi, pis quand 'l ont arrivé à la fourche d'ch'mins, 'l a mis la princesse à terre. La princesse a voulait qu'i' va avec elle. "Ah! non," i' dzit, "j'vas pas avec vous à souère." Quand alle a arrivé cheux eux, l'vieux rouè i' s'a trouvé surpris. "Quocé c'est?" i' dzit. "La bête t'a pas mangée aujourdz'hui?" —"Non, mon père, a n'a pas voulu d'moin aujourdz'hui, alle avait pas faim. I' faut qu'j'eurtourne d'main." L'lend'main matin, l'rouè 'l a partsi avec sa copagnée pour eurconduire la princesse jusqu'au bord dzu bois. P'tsit Jean i' s'a chanzé tou[t] en rouge, ein j'val rouge, trois chiens rouges. I'a été rattraper la princesse. La princesse alle était montée sur eune chousse après l'attend'.

Quand 'l ont arrivé, la princesse pis P'tsit Jean, la bête à sept têtes y'a dzit: "Hé! P'tsit Jean j'sus cinq fouès meilleurte avec cinq têtes qu'j'étais avec sept." —"Tant mieux pour touè," a dzit P'tsit Jean. "Quand j'auras fini avec touè, tsu en auras pus en toute. Dzis-moin quand tsu vas êt' parée." —"J'sus parée à c't'heure, allons," a dzit. —"Hardi mes chiens! Quiens bon, mon j'val." I' donne ein coup d'sab' pis i'a ôte deux aut's têtes. "Quarquier jusqu'à d'main." Lui, a pris la princesse, pis la bête à sept têtes alle a rentrè dans sa ouache, ça, pour s'bangner. La princesse alle a donné son mouchouère d'souè à P'tsit Jean. I' s'ont rentournés. Arrivés à la fourches de ch'mins, la princesse

voulait qu'i' va avec elle. "Oh! non, j'pourras pas aller avec vous, ma princesse, i' faut que j'me rentourne."

Quand alle a arrivé cheux aut's, l'vieux rouè s'a trouvé surpris encore. "Est-ce qu'la bête a vous a pas mangée acore aujourdz'hui?" —"Non, mon père, alle avait pas faim encore aujourdz'hui. I' faudra qu'j'eurtourne d'main." L'lend'main matin, l'vieux rouè 'l a eurpartsi avec sa copagnée pour eurconduire sa princesse. P'tsit Jean a été trouver Sam'son. I' l'a habillé tou[t] en blanc, ein joual blanc, pis trois chiens blancs. I' s'en va rattraper la princesse. Arrivé à place qu'i' l'a eurjouègnée, la princesse était placée sus eune chousse pour l'attend'. Alle a monté derrière sus son ch'val.

Quand il[s] ont arrivé à la bête à sept têtes, alle a sortsi, pis alle a dzit à P'tsit Jean: "J'sus sept fouès meilleurte à matin avec trois têtes que j'sus avec sept." P'tsit Jean y'a dzit: "Tant mieux pour touè. Qund j'auras fini avec touè, tsu en auras pu d'têtes en toute. Dzis-moin quand tsu vas êt' parée." —"J'sus parée drétte à c't'heure," a dzit. —"Hardi mes chiens! Quiens bon, mon choual!" I' s'sont battsus la moquié d'ein heure. Tout d'ein coup, il a eu ein bon coup d'sable, i'a ôté trois têtes. I'a descendzu d'son ch'val, i'a pris l'mouchouère d'la princesse, i' l'vé les trois langues d'la bête à sept têtes, les a mis dans l'mouchouère d'la princesse qu'avait l'nom d'son père et l'nom d'son armée d'ssus.

I' sont partsis pour s'rentourner. Quand 'l ont arrivé à la fourche de ch'mins, i'a mis la princesse à terre. A voulait pas descend', a béguait P'tsit Jean pour qu'i' va avec elle, i' s'auraient mariés. Ah! non, i'était trop jeune pour s'marier. "Peut-êt' qu'j'en trouv'ras des aut's qu'j'pourras délivrer comme j'ai faite avec vous." La princesse a partsi en braillant, chagrine d'pas pouwère emm'ner P'tsit Jean.

Ça l'a pas été ben longtemps, a s'a trouvé face à face avec ein charbollier. "Bougre!" i' dzit, "ma princesse, la bête a vous a pas mangée encore aujourdz'hui?" —"Non," a dzit la princesse, "la bête alle est morte." —"Qui dans l'monde qui l'a tsuée?" —"Ah!" a dzit, "j'connais pas, c'est ein p'tsit jeune homme." I' 'hale son pistolet à la figure d'la princesse. "Si vous prètez pas serment qu'c'est mouè qu'a détruit la bête à sept têtes avec ma pioche pis mon râteau, j'vous flamb'ras la cervelle." La princesse alle a eu peur, alle a fait serment. "Montez dans ma bourouette, vous va m'montrer où sont les têtes." I'a mis les sept têtes dans sa bourouette, la princesse par-dessus.

I' s'en va chu l'rouè, en criant: "Voute qui a faite détruire tant d'monde pour faire tsuer c'te bêtes, mouè, j'l'ai tsuée avec ma pioche pis mon râteau. 'Marquez qu'j'mens pas, vouèlà les têtes pis la princesse pour l'prouver." —"Ah!" l'rouè a dzit, "si vous a détruit la bête, i' faut qu'vous s'marissent, vous pis la princesse." La princesse a dzit qu'a s'mariait pas, qu'i' fallait qu'il[s] ayent trois dzîners, trois jours d'suite, fallait qu'charbognier souèye écuré ben net. Charbognier voulait s'marier, lui, avant les dzîners. La princesse a dzit non, alle était jeune, elle; alle était pas pressée pour s'marier, a voulait tout l'monde d'la ville êt' invité.

La première journée, P'tsit Jean pis sa vieille grand'mère i'étaient pas invités. I'a dzit à sa grand'mère: "L'rouè i'est fier, i' m'a pas invité mais," i' dzit, "on va goûter d'son dzîner toute la même chose." I'a app'lé son chien Vite-comme-le-vent. "Tsu vas aller cheux l'rouè, pis tsu vas rentrer; tsu vas mett' la patte sus l'pied d'la princesse, a va t'eurconnaître, pis a va ben t'souègner, pis après qu'tsu vas avouère eu mangé d'ça qu'tsu voudras, saute sus la tab', 'porte-nous ein pain pis eune bouteille d'vin blanc."

I'a arrivé, i'a pilé sus l'pied d'la princesse, alle a eurgardé, pis alle l'a vu. "Ah!" a dzit, "P'tsit Jean i'est pas loin." Alle l'a ben souègné. Quand il a eu mangé assez, i'a sauté sus la tab' pis i'a pris son pain blanc pis sa bouteille d'vin blanc. Charbognier a crié: "Tsuez c'chien voleur'là!" La princesse

"The Seven-Headed Beast"

a dzit à son père d'donner les ordres d'pas faire mal à c'chien-là, qu'c'était pas ein chien voleur. A dzit à son père qu'i' y'en avait queuques-anes dans la ville pas invités, qu'a voulait qu'toute la ville sèye invitée.

L'lend'main, Charbognier il a d'mandé au rouè après qu'toute la copagnie alle était rentrée, pis tout mis à la tab', d'tout fermer les portes à clef qu'i' n'y ait pas d'chiens qui peuvent rentrer. L'vieux rouè y'a accordé ça. P'tsit Jeana dzit à sa grand'mère l'lend'main matin: "On a pas été invité encore aujourdz'hui." 'L a app'lé son deuxième chien Passe-Partout: "Va sus l'rouè. Les portes sont tout fermées aujourdz'hui, passe en travers d'la porte, va d'ssour la table piler sur l'pied d'la princesse, a va t'eurconnaît', pis a va ben t'souègner. Quand tsu vas avouère mangé assez, saute sus la table, pis 'porte donc ein p'tsit cochon d'lait." Quand chien-là a sauté sur la tab', Charbognier a commencé à crier: "Chien voleur acore, tsuez c'chien voleur!" Mais avant qu'i' rouv' la porte, i' pouvait pus ouère l'chien.

Charbognier voulait s'marier avant qu'les trois jours finissent. "C'est trop longtemps pour attendre, ça," i' dzit. La princesse y'a dzit non, alle était pas pressée, alle était jeune, qu'i' attende après les trois dzîners. L'lend'main matin, c'était tout la même chose. I'étaient pas invités encore, P'tsit Jean pis sa vieille grand'mère. I'a app'lé son aut' chien Brise-fer. "Va sus l'rouè," i' dzit. "Les portes sont tout fermées, passe en travers, va en d'ssour d'la tab', mets ta patte sus l'pied d'la princesse, a va t'eurconnaît', a va ben t'souègner. Après ça saute sus la tab', pis apporte eune galette, pis viens douc'ment, laisse queuques-anes t'suire d'au loin."

'L a partsi pis i' s'a rendzu sus l'rouè. Quand 'l a sauté sus la table, Charbognier a crié: "Tsuez c'chien voleur!" La princesse a dzit qu'i' faisent pas d'mal à c'chien-là mais qu'i' l'suivent pour ouère où i' allait, pis qu'i' invitent c'monde-là où c'chien appartenait qu'i' viennent, alle leur aura donné à dzîner l'lend'main. Quand 'l ont v'nu les inviter, P'tsit Jean leu-z-a dzit comme ça si la princesse a voulait lui pis sa vieille grand'mère i' vonnent, qu'a envoèye le meilleur carrosse que le rouè 'l avait pis les plus beaux ch'vaux les qu'ri, pis d'placer l'carrosse tout près d'la gal'rie, sa vieille grand'mère n'aurait pas été à la peine d'piler sus la terre. L'homme qui a sui l'chien a dzit à P'tsit Jean: "Qu'tsu devras êt' fier d'êt' invité, sans app'ler pour l'meilleur carrosse!" —"Dzisez ça au rouè, toujours."

I' l'a dzit au rouè. La princesse l'a entendzu. "J'prétends que l'meilleur carrosse pis les plus beaux ch'vaux souèyent att'lés, pis qu'i' vonnent les qu'ri d'main matin," a dzit. P'tsit Jean pis sa grand'mère i' sont v'nus. La princesse a dzit à P'tsit Jean: "Tout c'que vous avez à faire, c'est d'conter eune p'tsite histouère après manger." Après qu'i' ont eu fini d'dzîner, i' fallait qu'tout chaquin i' raconte leus p'tsites histouères. Ben, la vieille grand'mère, c'était la plus vieille, i' fallait qu'a sèye la première à raconter sa p'tsite histouère. A dzit: "J'ai pas grand'chose à vous conter. J'grouille jamais, moin. C'p'tsit jeune homme, c'est eune bonne copagnée pour moin." Après ça, ça a été à charbognier d'conter son histouère. Charbognier i'a dzit, lui: "L'rouè a fait détruite des bandes d'monde pour faire détruire la bête à sept têtes et, moin, j'l'ai détruit tout seul avec ma pioche pis mon râteau," i' dzit. " 'Marquez que j'mens pas, v'là les têtes d'pendzues sur la gal'rie dzu rouè."

A c't'heure, c'est v'nu à P'tsit Jean à conter son histouère. "Sire, j'ai pas grand'chose à conter, mouè, mais queul est l'bon chasseur, l'homme qui 'porte les langues ou ben les têtes?" —"Ah!" l'vieux rouè, i' dzit, "c'est celui qui 'porte les langues qu'est l'bon chasseur." Charbognier i'était pas ben, lui, i' voulait s'excuser d'la table. L'rouè y'a dzit qu'i' s'couche dans l'coin jusqu'à il ait fini d'dzîner. La princesse a déclaré à son père ça que l'charbognier y'avait faite. A dzit: "Ça, c'est l'p'tsit jeune homme qui m'a délivrée d'la bête à sept têtes, c'est pas Charbognier." I'ont pendzu Charbognier, pis P'tsit Jean pis la princesse s'sont mariés. 'L ont eu des grosses noces, mais i' m'ont pas invité à y aller.

3.

John the Bear

It's good to tell you that once upon a time there were an old man and an old woman. The old man was a Miller. One morning, he went out to open the spillway of his mill wheel and found a small box. In the box, there was a baby boy. The old man picked up the baby and brought it home to his wife. "We're poor," he said, "but it's better to raise the baby than to let it die in the river." John the Bear grew quickly. After awhile, he began to go to school with his stepbrothers and stepsisters. But one day his stepbrothers and stepsisters began to tease him, saying that he wasn't really their brother. He got mad at one of them and hit him, and he broke his jaw. That evening, the little boy told his father about this. The father scolded John the Bear, who said, "But they're after me all the time, saying that I'm not their brother. They got me mad, and I hit one of them." —"Well," said the Miller, "They're right. You're not their brother. You're an orphan. I found you in a box on the river, and we decided to keep you rather than let you die on the river." John the Bear answered, "Well, if you're not my father, I'll just leave you." He said good-bye to his father and mother, and went to the blacksmith, and had him make an iron cane weighing five hundred pounds. Then he went off traveling.

On his way, he met another man who was twisting walnut trees. "What are you doing, friend?" asked John the Bear. —"I'm just twisting up those little walnut trees to tie my gate shut." —"Leave your gate alone and come with me," answered John the Bear. After they left together, John the Bear asked the man his name and said, "My name is John the Bear." The other answered, "I am called Oak Twister." As they were walking along, they met another man who was throwing millstones so they skipped on the surface of the water. John the Bear asked him, "What are you doing, my friend?" The other one answered, "I'm playing with these little stones." —"Leave your little stones there and come with us," answered John the Bear. "Well, all right," answered the man, "I'll come with you." —"What's your name?" John the Bear asked him. The man told him, "My name is Stone Thrower." They traveled until late that evening and came upon a fine house with no one inside. John the Bear said to Oak Twister and Stone Thrower, "We'll spend the night here."

The next morning, no one had come yet, and John the Bear said to the two others, "Hey! Two of us will go out hunting. Oak Twister, you stay and make our dinner." When the others had been gone for a while, Oak Twister put some meat on the fire to boil in a kettle. All of a sudden, he heard "vroop" on the threshold. It was the Little Man with the Big Beard. —"What are you doing here, you worm?" he asked Oak Twister. "Who gave you permission to come into my castle?" Oak Twister answered, "No one did." —"What are you cooking there?" —"I'm cooking meat for dinner," answered Oak Twister. The Little Man asked, "Would you give me a little piece?" —"You can have it all if you win it," answered Oak Twister. —"Well, I'm all for winning it," said the Little Man with the Big Beard. So they started to fight. Then, the Little Man took one of the hairs out of his big beard and beat up Oak Twister with it. He said, "If I find you here tomorrow, I'll beat you up again."

When John the Bear and Stone Thrower came back, Oak Twister was sick in bed. John the Bear thought, "Maybe this is a place which is not healthy for us." But they made dinner and after awhile Oak Twister got up and ate a good meal. The next day, John the Bear and Oak Twister went out hunting. Stone Thrower started to make the dinner for them. The Little Man with the Big Beard came back and said, "What? Didn't I tell you that if I found you here today I'd really beat you up?" Stone Thrower turned around. "What do you want?" he said. —"What are you cooking?" asked the Little Man. —"I'm cooking some meat." —"Give me just a little piece." —"You can have it if you can win it." The Little Man said, "That's not hard to do." So they began to fight, and the Little Man made Stone Thrower sick, just as he had done to Oak Twister. The Little Man said that if he found Stone Thrower there the next day, this time he would kill him. When John the Bear came back, he said, "Oh, I see. Stone Thrower is in bed." So John the Bear and Oak Twister made the supper. Stone Thrower was able to get up and eat a good meal. John the Bear said, "It's my turn to stay here tomorrow. If I get sick, too, we'll have to leave. That will mean that this is an unhealthy place."

The next morning, Oak Twister and Stone Thrower went out hunting. They left John the Bear behind to cook the dinner. After they had gone a little way into the woods, Stone Thrower and Oak Twister looked at each other. "What made you sick? Was it a Little Man with a Big Beard, about that tall? Me too. Today he'll kill John the Bear." John the Bear, back at the house, began to make dinner. The Little Man came back and said, "Didn't I tell you that if I found you here again today I would kill you?" —"Kill?" asked John the Bear. "You look like you could kill someone, you worm." —"What are you cooking in my kettle this morning?" asked the Little Man. —"I'm cooking some meat." —"Let me have a little piece." —"No!" —"If you don't give me a little piece, I'll take the whole thing." —"You'll take the whole thing if you can win it." —"That," answered the Little Man, "is easy to do." So they began to fight. John the Bear got near the place where he had his iron cane. He hit

The Little Man with the Big Beard

It's Good to Tell You

the Little Man over the head with it and cut off his ear. The Little Man picked up his ear and ran away as fast as he could, with John the Bear right after him. He arrived at a place where there was a big rock. He moved the stone and jumped into a hole.

John the Bear came back to the house and finished making the dinner. When Oak Twister and Stone Thrower came back from their hunting, the dinner was all ready. John the Bear said, "Well, come and eat." While they were eating, John the Bear told them, "You know the Little Man with the Big Beard who made you both sick? I've been to the place where he lives." So after they had finished their dinner, they all went to look at the big rock. John the Bear said, "Oak Twister, I found you twisting oak trees to tie up your gate. Why don't you lift up that rock?" But Oak Twister couldn't budge it. Then he said, "Stone Thrower, you can play at throwing millstones, why don't you lift that rock over there?" But Stone Thrower couldn't lift up the rock either. Finally, John the Bear said, "Oh, I'll go lift it myself." And he picked it up with just one hand. There was a big deep hole there, where the Little Man with the Big Beard had gone down. They made a windlass, put it over the hole, and put a rope and a handle on it. "Well," said John the Bear to Oak Twister, "You go down first. Bring this bell with you. If you're afraid after you've gone down partway, then ring the bell, and we'll pull you back out." After awhile, Oak Twister began to think about the Little Man with the Big Beard and rang his bell, and they pulled him back up. So then, John the Bear said to Stone Thrower "Go ahead. It's your turn now." He said, "If you're afraid, ring the bell, and we'll pull you back up." Stone Thrower went pretty far, but then he began to be afrid of the Little Man, and he rang his bell. They pulled him up out of the hole.

Now John the Bear said to them that he'd go down, but without any bell. "I'm going now. If you don't see me after one year and one day, you can leave me. That will mean that I won't come back." They lowered John the Bear into the hole, and when he got to the bottom, he began to walk. It was like a whole different world. He saw a big brick house. In the window, a pretty Princess was sitting. She made signs to him to tell him to go away and not come any closer. He made signs to tell her that, no, he was coming the whole way. She was guarded by a lion, and when the lion saw him, he charged after him. John the Bear split its head open with his iron cane. The Princess was so happy she invited him to come in. She figured she would marry him. But he said, "Oh, no, Princess. I don't want to get married now. Maybe I'll be able to deliver other princesses too." —"Well, two of my sisters are also under spells farther along. One of them is guarded by a little black dog, and the other is guarded by the Little Man with the Big Beard." —"That's the fellow I'm looking for," answered John the Bear. So the Princess gave him her golden ball and her silk handkerchief, which had the name of her father and his army embroidered on it.

The next morning, he set out to deliver the Second Princess. When he got near to where she was, she made signs to him not to come any closer. But he made signs saying, "No." When he got there, the little black dog came after him, but he cut it in two. The Princess was really happy to be safe. She asked him to come in and said, "We must get

It's Good to Tell You

married." —"Oh, no," he said. "I may yet find another princess who is under a spell as you were." —"Well, yes, one of my sisters, the youngest, is guarded by the Little Man with the Big Beard." John the Bear said, "That's who I'm looking for." So, she gave him her golden ball and her silk handkerchief, as the First Princess had also done. He put them into his pocket, and the next norning he left early to find the Third Princess. The Little Man was walking back and forth on his porch. He went out to meet John the Bear at the gate. As soon as they met, they started fighting right away. John the Bear hit the Little Man on the head with his iron cane and split his brain in two. The Youngest Princess was so happy to be free that she came running out. She said, "Sir, look in his back pocket and take out the little can of salve he has in there. He'll grease himself up with that and come back as good as ever." She gave him her golden ball and her silk handkerchief, too, as her sisters had done. The next morning, John the Bear and the Youngest Princess started back to the hole where Oak Twister and Stone Thrower were waiting. When he got to the shaft, he tugged on the rope, and they let down a basket. He put the Oldest Princess into the basket, and they pulled her up. When she got to the top, Oak Twister shouted, "She's mine!" And Stone Thrower answered, "No, she's mine!" They started to argue and were getting ready to fight over the Princess, when she said, "Don't fight over me. There's a prettier princess than me waiting down there to come up." So they let the basket down again, and the Second Princess got into it. But when she got to the top, Oak Twister and Stone Thrower started to argue again. The Second Princess told them, "Don't fight over me. There's still another, more beautiful princess waiting at the bottom to be brought up here." So they let the basket down a third time, and the Youngest Princess got in. When she reached the top, the two men didn't want to send the basket back down to get John the Bear, but the princesses didn't want to leave without him. So Oak Twister and Stone Thrower winked at each other and lowered the basket again. John the Bear got in, and they pulled him up quite a way. But then they cut the rope, and he fell back to the bottom and broke his leg.

Oak Twister and Stone Thrower brought the princesses to the King. They made the princesses swear that they had been the ones who had rescued them. The old King told the two men that they could each choose one of his two older daughters to marry. But the princesses told their father that they would not marry these two men unless they had three golden balls made like that of their youngest sister. They told the King that the balls would have to be exactly like that of their sister or the two men should lose their lives. So the King told Oak Twister and Stone Thrower that they would have to make three golden balls exactly like the one that the Youngest Princess had, and that if they weren't able to do it, they would lose their lives. But if they did succeed, they would get a silver chest.

During this time, John the Bear was still stuck at the bottom of the hole with his broken leg. He thought about the little box of salve that he had in his pocket and put it on his leg. It got better right away. As John the Bear was wandering around, he passed a tree where a snake was climbing up to eat some baby eagles, and he killed the snake. One day, later on, he noticed, as he was still wandering around, that a beautiful eagle was flying

The Stone Thrower and John the Bear

It's Good to Tell You

around over his head, at the top of the hole. He said, "Oh, Beautiful Eagle. If I only had your wings!" She flew down to him right away and said, "What did you say, John the Bear?" —"I was just saying that if I only had your wings, it would not take me very long to get out of this hole," answered John the Bear. The Eagle answered, "Oh, I'll do everything I can to get you out of here. Go and kill a lot of animals and cut the meat up into small pieces. Tomorrow I'll come back." The next morning, she said, "Do you have the meat, John the Bear?" —"Yes, I think I have enough," answered John the Bear. —"Now, put it all on my back, and you climb on, too. Every time I holler, you give me a piece of meat." She flew up, but just as she was getting to the top of the hole, she hollered "quack," and he had run out of meat. Instead of going up, they started falling down. John the Bear opened up his knife and cut a piece out of his leg and gave it to the Eagle. When they got to the top, the beautiful Eagle looked at John the Bear and said, "Why is your leg bleeding?" —"Well," he said, "you were saying 'quack, quack' and I didn't have any more meat, so I cut a piece out of my leg to give to you." The beautiful Eagle said "Quack," and the piece of John the Bear's leg reappeared. He took it and stuck it back on where it belonged.

Then he left to go see the King. First, he went to an old Goldsmith, who told him why he didn't want to take on the job of making the three golden balls. "I can do good work, but I'm getting old, and I can't see as well as I used to. I'm afraid they'll hang me." John the Bear said to him, "Go take the job, and I'll make the golden balls for you." So the old man went to see the King and said to him, "Well, King, I'll take the job of making your golden balls." The King answered, "You're a true friend. But if you don't make them right, I will have to hang you." The Goldsmith answered, "Well, I'll take that chance."

That evening, John the Bear went to make the golden balls. He went into the room where the old man had his tools. He brought with him a big bunch of pecans, hazelnuts, and peanuts. He began to eat, and after awhile the Goldsmith's wife went to see how he was coming along. She peeked through the keyhole and saw John the Bear still eating his pecans and peanuts. At nine o'clock, she went back to look through the keyhole a second time. She came back and said to her husband, "Well, dear, he's still eating. You're going to be hanged! You're going to be hanged!" —"Oh, be quiet!" said her husband. "Maybe he's just a fast worker." At ten o'clock, the old woman went back to see how John the Bear was doing. He had made one golden ball and had put it on a pretty plate. She came back, clapping her hands. "He has one finished," she said. —"Well, I told you that you didn't need to worry," he said. "I told you he was a fast worker." At eleven o'clock, the old woman went back and peeked through the keyhole again. This time, John the Bear had finished. He had all three balls together on the plate. She came back and said to her husband, "Well, now, he's finished. We can go to bed and sleep in peace." They had no sooner gotten into bed than the old woman sat up and asked the Goldsmith what he was going to do with his money. —"Oh, go to sleep," he answered. "I'll tell you about that tomorrow."

The next morning, he brought the golden balls to the King. When the old King looked at the balls, he couldn't tell one from the others. The youngest daugher was there in the King's room, and she said, "Didn't you have a man help you do that, old man?" —"Yes, Princess, I did have someone help me," answered the Goldsmith. The Princess then said, "Will you please go and get the man who helped you and bring him back here with you." When John the Bear got to the King's palace, the Youngest Princess recognized him. She told her father that this man would be able to tell the golden balls from one another. So John the Bear took the three silk handkerchiefs out of his pocket and put one ball on each of the handkerchiefs. The old King said, "What? Are you the one who saved my daughters?" John the Bear answered, "Yes, I'm the one." Then the King turned to his daughters and asked them, "Why did you tell me that the two other men were the ones who had saved you?" —"They made us swear to tell you that they were the ones who had saved us, or else they would have killed us. To save our lives, we told you what they wanted us to." So the King took Oak Twister and Stone Thrower and had them hanged. Then, he gave John the Bear the privilege of choosing whichever of the three princesses he would like to marry. John the Bear chose the youngest, but the King wasn't too happy about that. It was his rule to marry his oldest daughters first. "But," he said, "since you freed all three of them, I'll let you marry the youngest." They got married and had a big dinner. But I don't know what happened to John the Bear after that.

Jean l'Ours

C'est bon d'vous dzire eune fouès c'étaient ein vieux pis eune vieille. L'vieux 'l avait ein moulin. Eune matsinée, il a été ouvert son étang. Il a trouvé eune p'tsite cassette sus la rivière. Dans c'te p'tsite cassette-là, i' y avait ein p'tsit garçon, ein bébé. L'vieux l'a ramassé, l'a porté à sa maisonne à sa femme. "On l'est pauvre," i' dzit, "mais i' faut ben mieux l'él'ver que l'laisser mourir sus la rivière." Jean l'Ours 'l a profité vite, 'l a commencé à aller à l'école avec ça 'l app'lait ses p'tsits frères pis ses p'tsites soeurs. Eune journée, ses p'tsits frères pis ses p'tsites soeurs 'l ont commencé à piquer après lui, dzire qu'i'était pas leu frère. Eune journée, i' s'a fâché cont' ane; i'a donné ane tape, i'a d'manché la mâchouère. L'souère, l'p'tsit garçon 'l a conté ça à son p'pa. Il a grondé Jean l'Ours. "Ben," i' dzit, "i' sontaient tout l'temps après moin, dzire qu'j'étais pas leu frère. I' m'ont faite fâcher, j'leu ai donné ane tape." —"Eh ben! non," i' dzit, "t'es pas leu frère. Vous êtes ein p'tsit-n-orphelin j'ai trouvé sus mon étang. On t'a él'vé plutôt que t'quitter mourir sus l'étang." —"Eh ben, si vous êtes pas mon père, j'vas m'en aller, j'vas vous laisser." 'L a dzit adzieu aux vieux, ça 'l app'lait son père pis sa mère. 'L a partsi, 'l a été à la forge, pis i' s'a faite faire eune can-ne d'fer qui pésait cinq cents. 'L a partsi à trav'ler.

En trav'lant, 'l a rencontré ein aut' homme. l'était après tord' des nouèyers. "Quocé donc tsu fais," i' dzit, "camarade?" —"J'sus après tord' ces p'tsits arb's d'nouèyer-là pour amarrer ma clôtsure."

—"Laisse donc ta clôtsure tranquille, pis viens avec moin." 'L ont partsi. I'a d'mandé quocé c'était son nom. I' dzit: "Mon nom, c'est Jean l'Ours." L'aut' i' dzit: "Mon nom, c'est Tord-Chêne." Mais, sus leu ch'min, i'ont trouvé ein aut' homme. I'était après jouer aux p'tsits palets avec des meules de moulin. Jean l'Ours y'a d'mandé: "Quocé tsu fais là, mon ami?" —"J'sus après jouer aux p'tsits palets." —"Laisse tes p'tsits palets tranquilles, pis viens-t'en donc avec nous aut's." —"Ah!" i' dzit, "ça m'fait pas d'dzifférence, j'vas aller." —"Quocé qui est ton nom?" i' dzit. —"Mon nom, c'est Joueur d'Palets." Il[s] ont trav'lé jusqu'à tard, l'souère, 'l ont trouvé eune belle maisonne, personne dedans. Jean l'Ours 'l a dzit à Tord-Chêne pis à Joueur d'Palets: "On va rester à coucher icitte."

L'lend'main matin, personne i'était v'nu. "Hein!" Jean l'Ours i' dzit, "deux d'nous aut's va aller à la chasse. Tord-Chêne," i' dzit, "tsu rest'ras, touè, à faire à dziner."Après qu'les aut's 'l ont été partsis ein bon boute d'temps, Tord-Chêne i' s'a mis d'la viande au feu dans eune marmite. Tout d'ein coup, 'l a entendzu "vroup" sus son pas d'porte. C'était l'P'tsit Bonhomme à la grand barbe. "Quocé qu'tsu fais icitte, ver de terre? Qui c'est qui t'a donné permission d'rentrer dans mon château?" —"Personne," i' dzit. "Quocé qu'tsu fais cuire là?" —"J'fais cuire d'la viande." —"Veux-tsu m'en donner ein p'tsit morceau?" —"Tsu peux tout l'aouère, si tsu la gagnes." —"Eh ben, j'sus pour la gagner." I' s'ont mis à s'abatt'. Alors l'P'tsit Bonhomme il a attrapé des crins d'sa barbe, pis il les a arranchés, pis il a taillé Tord-Chêne. I'a dzit: "Si j'te trouve d'main icitte, j't'en donn'ras plusse."

Quand Jean l'Ours pis Joueur d'Palets sont eurvenus, Tord-Chêne 'l était malade; il était dans l'lit, il avait la migraine. Jean l'Ours i' dzit: "P'tet' ben, c'est eune place qu'est pas si sain pour nous aut's." 'L ont faite à dzîner. Après ça, Tord-Chêne i' s'a l'vé pis 'l a ben mangé. L'lend'main, Jean l'Ours pis Tord-Chêne 'l ont été à la chasse. Joueur d'Palets 'l a commencé à faire son dzîner, lui aussite. P'tsit Bonhomme à la grand barbe 'l est eurvenu. "Quoi, j't'avais pas dzit si j'te trouvais icitte aujourdz'hui, j'te caress'rais pas mal?" Joueur d'Palets i' s'a eurviré. "Quoice qu'tsu charces icitte?" —"Quocé qu't'es après faire cuire?" —"J'sus après faire cuire d'la viande." —"Donne-mouè-z-en donc ein p'tsit morceau d'ta viande." —"Tsu peux tout l'aouère si tsu peux la gagner." P'tsit Bonhomme i' dzit: "C'est pas malaisé à faire." 'L ont commencé à s'abatt'; 'l a donné la migraine à Joueur d'Palets aussite. L'P'tsit Bonhomme 'l a dzit à Joueur d'Palets, si l'trouvait là l'lend'main, i' l'tsuerait. Quand Jean l'Ours 'l est eurvenu, i'a dzit: "Oui, j'vouès, Joueur d'Palets est dans l'lite." 'L ont faite à dzîner, Jean l'Ours pis Tord-Chêne. Joueur d'Palets i' s'a l'vé pis 'l a ben dzîné. Jean l'Ours i'a dzit: "J'vas rester, moin, d'main. Si moin, j'attrape la migraine, on va s'en aller d'icitte, ça s'ra pas sain pour nous aut's."

L'lend'main matin, Tord-Chêne pis Joueur d'Palets 'l ont été à la chasse. I'ont laissé Jean l'Ours faire l'dzîner. Ça s'fait qu'Tord-Chêne pis Joueur d'Palets, après qu'i'ont été ein p'tsit boute dans l'bois, i' s'ont eurgardés. "Quocé qu'ta donné la migraine à touè, l'P'tsit Bonhomme à la grand barbe, à peu près ça d'haut? Et moin aussite. I' va tsuer Jean l'Ours aujourdz'hui." Jean l'Ours i'a commencé à faire son dzîner. L'P'tsit Bonhomme il est eurvenu. "J't'avais pas dzit hier qu'si j't'eurtrouvais icitte aujourdz'hui, j't'aurais tsué?" —"Tsué? Tsu eursemb's à tsuer queuques-ane, touè, ver de terre." —"Quocé qu't'après faire cuire dans ma marmite à matin?" —"J'sus après faire cuire d'la viande." —"Donne-mouè-z-en ein p'tsit morceau." —"Non." —"Si tsu m'donnes pas ein p'tsit morceau, j'vas toute la prend'." —"Tsu vas tout la prend', si tsu la gagnes." —"Ça," i' dzit, "c'est pas malaisé à faire." I' commencent à s'batt'. Jean l'Ours 'l a passé oùsque c'est sa can-ne d'fer. Il a cogné après pis i'a coupé l'oreille. L'P'tsit Bonhomme i'a ramassé son oreille, pis 'l a partsi à la course, Jean l'Ours par derrière. Il a arrivé ane place où i' y'avait eune grosse pierre. I'a enl'vé la pierre, pis i'a sauté dans ein trou, l'P'tsit Bonhomme à la grand barbe.

Jean l'Ours 'l est eurvenu pis 'l a faite son dzîner. Quand Tord-Chêne pis Joueur d'Palets i' sont eurv'nus d'la chasse, l'dzîner était paré. "Ben," i' dzit, "v'nez dzîner." Padent i' sont après dzîner, "l'P'tsit Bonhomme à la grand barbe," i' dzit, "qui vous a donné la migraine, j'ai été ioùsqu'i' reste." Après qu'i'ont eu dzîné, i'ont été ouère à la pierre. I' dzit à Tord-Chêne: "Touè, tsu tords tes chênes pour arranger ta clôtsure, lève-donc pierre-là." Tord-Chêne a pas pu. "Joueur d'Palets, oh! tsu joues aux p'tsits palets avec des meules d'moulin, lève-la donc pierre-là." I'a pas pu la l'ver, lui non plus. "Ah!" i' dzit, "moin, j'vas la l'ver." Jean l'Ours i' l'a l'vée loin ien qu'eune main. C'était ein grand trou creux là où l'P'tsit Bonhomme à la grand barbe i'était rentré. 'L ont faite ein rouleau, pis l'ont mis sus l'trou. L'ont mis ein câble pis eune pognée après. "Ben," Jean l'Ours i' dzit à Tord-Chêne, "touè, va l'premier. 'Porte cloche-là avec touè. Si t'as peur, arrivé ein boute, eh ben, sonne la cloche, on va te 'haler en haut." Il a descendzu ein bon boute, 'l a commencé à penser au P'tsit Bonhomme, pis 'l a sonné la cloche. I' l'ont 'halé en dehors. Jean l'Ours i' dzit à Joueur d'Palets: "Va, touè, à ton tour." I' dzit: "Quand tsu vas aouère peur, sonne la cloche, on va te 'haler en dehors." I' a été beaucoup loin, i'a commencé à avouère peur dzu P'tsit Bonhomme, i'a sonné la cloche. I' l'ont 'halé en dehors.

A c't'heure, Jean l'Ours leu-z-a dzit qu'i'irait, mais qu'i' voulait pas d'cloche. "J'm'en vas. Si j'sus pas icitte au boute d'ein an et ein jour, vous pouvez m'laisser. J'eurviendras pas." Quand 'l a arrivé en bas, i'a partsi à marcher. C'était comme ein aut' monde. Il a vu eune grosse maisonne d'brique. Dans la f'nêt, i' y'avait eune jolie princesse. A y faisait signe qu'i' s'en va, qu'i' vienne pas. Lui, i'a faite signe qu'non, i' s'en allait tout l'long. Alle était gardée par ein lion, et quand l'lion l'a vu, 'l a foncé pour lui. I'a fendzu la tête avec sa can-ne de fer. La princesse a été fièr'te, a l'a faite rentrer. A pensait à s'marier. "Ah! non, ma princesse, j'veux pas m'marier, pas à c't'heure. P't'être qu'j'auras la chance d'délivrer des aut's." —"Mais j'en ai deux d'mes soeurs qui sont en esclave là-haut, eune d'gardée par l'p'tsit chien nouère, pis eune par ein P'tsit 'Bonhomme à la grand barbe." —"Ça, c'est l'beau gas qu'j'charce, l'P'tsit Bonhomme à la grand barbe." La princesse a y'a donné sa boule d'or pis son mouchouère d'souè. I'avait l'nom à son père et à son armé dessus.

L'lend'main matin, i'a partsi pour aller délivrer l'aut', la deuxième. Quand 'l a arrivé tout près d'la princesse, a y'a donné l'sinal qu'i' s'en va. Lui y'a faite sine qu'non. Quand il a arrivé, l'p'tsit chien nouère 'l a foncé, pis i' l'a fendzu en deux. La princesse a été fièr'te d'être délivrée. A y'a d'mandé qu'i' rent'. "I' faut s'marier." —"Oh! non," i' dzit, "p't'être qu'j'en trouv'ras des aut's, des princesses en esclavage comme vous." —"Ah! oui, j'en ai eune aut' d'mes soeurs, la plus jeune, a y'est gardée par l'P'tsit Bonhomme à la grand barbe." —"Ça," i' dzit, "c'est l'bonhomme j'charce." A y'a donné sa boule d'or pis son mouchouère d'souè, elle aussite. I' l'a mis dans sa poche. L'lend'main matin, il a partsi d'bonne heure. Il a arrivé tout près d'la maisonne dzu P'tsit Bonhomme. L'P'tsit Bonhomme, il était après marcher sus sa gal'rie. Il a partsi pour aller rencontrer Jean l'Ours à la barrière. Quand i' s'sont rencontrès, i'ont commencé à s'batt'. Jean l'Ours y'a donné ein coup d'can-ne de fer sus la tête, i'a fendzu la cervelle. La plus jeune princesse a était si fièr'te d'êt' délivrée, alle a sortsi à la course. "Monsieur," a dzit, "eurgardez donc dans sa poche d'en errière, i'a ein p'tsit potte d'enguent. Otez-yi. I' va s'graisser avec ça, i' va eurv'nir aussi bon qu'ja-mais." A yi avait donné sa boule d'or, elle aussite, pis son mouchouère d'souè.

L'lend'main matin, i'a partsi avec sa princesse. Quand il a arrivé à la gueule dzu trou, i'a escoué l'câb' et i'ont descendzu l'pagnier. La plus vieille des princesses, alle a monté dans l'pagnier, pis i'

John the Bear

l'ont 'halée en dehors. Et quand 'l ont arrivé en haut, Tord-Chêne i' dzit: C'est la mienne." Joueur d'Palets i' dzit: "Non, c'est la mienne." C'était eune quérelle, i' sontaient parés à s'batt pour la princesse. "Ah!" a dzit, "quérellez-vous pas pour moin. I'en a eune plus jolite qu'moin." I'ont eurdescendzu l'pagnier. La deuxième des princesses alle a monté dans l'pagnier. Et quand i' sont arrivés en haut, c'était ein aut' quérelle. "Querellez-vous pas pour moin, i'en a eune plus jolite qu'moin encore." I'ont eurdescendzu l'pagnier. La plus jeune alle a rentré dans l'pagnier, et quand 'l ont arrivé en haut, i' voulaient pas envouèyer l'pagnier à Jean l'Ours. Les princesses i' voulaient pas s'en aller sans qu'i'envouèyent l'pagnier à Jean l'Ours. I' s'sont faite chaquin ein clin d'oeil pis i'ont eurdescendzu l'pagnier. Jean l'Ours il a monté d'dans. I' l'ont 'halé ein bon grand boute pis il[s] ont coupé l'câb'. I'a tombé au fond pis i' s'a cassé eune jambe.

Les deux aut's i' s'en vonnent emm'ner les princesses au rouè à c't'heure. Pis i'ont faite faire serment aux princesses comme ça qu'c'étaient ces deux hommes-là qui les avaient délivrées. Quand i' ont arrivé chu leu père, 'l ont dzit qu'c'étaient les deux hommes qui les avaient délivrées. L'vieux rouè les a dzit qu'i' pouvaient marier n'importe lesqueules des deux plus vieilles. Les deux princesses 'l ont dzit à leu père qu'i' s'mariaient pas avec les hommes-là hormis d'avouère trois boules d'or faites jusse comme la celle d'leu p'tsite soeur. Mais 'l ont dzit au rouè qu'lui s'enterpeurnait d'faire l'ouvrage, s'il la fésait pas jusse comme la celle d'leu p'tsite soeur, fallait qu'i' perde la vie. L'vieux rouè 'l a dzit que eux aut's qui 'l auraient faite les trois boules d'or, fallait qu'i' les faissent jusse comme la celle d'leu p'tsite soeur, pis lui qui les faisait, il aurait eune châsse d'argent.

En eurvenant à Jean l'Ours, lui, i'était toujours dans son trou avec la jambe cassée. Il a pensé à son p'tsit potte d'enguent qu'il avait dans sa poche. Il a graissé sa jambe pis alle a été mieux. Quand Jean l'Ours 'l était après trav'ler, il avait passé oùsqu'i'avait ein serpent qui était après monter dans ein arb' pour manger les p'tsits d'eune aigle, et pis i' l'a tsué. Eune journée, i'était après marchailler dans sa souterrain et ce qu'il a vu, eune belle aigle qui était après voltiger en d'ssus d'lui. "Eh! belle aigle, si j'avais tes ailes!" Alle a voltigé à lui; alle a rentré dans la souterrain tout d'suite. "Quocé qu't'étais après dzire," a dzit, "Jean l'Ours?" —"J'étais après dzire qu'si j'avais tel ailes, j'aurais bétôt eu sortsi d'icitte." —"Ah!" a dzit, "Jean l'Ours, j'vas faire tout ça j'pourras pour t'sortsir. T'as aller et pis t'as tsuer ein tas d'viande, pis coupe-la tout par p'tsits morceaux, pis d'main, j'vas eurvenir." L'lend'main matin, a dzit: "Jean l'Ours, t'as ta viande?" —"Ah! oui, j'crouès j'en ai assez." —"Mets-la tout sus mon dos à c't'heure. A c't'heure," a dzit, "monte par-dessus. A chaque fouès j'vas dzire: Couac! donne-mouè-z-en eune bouchée." Alle a arrivé tout près d'la porte dzu souterrain; a dzit: "Couac!" Mais c'est qu'il avait plus d'viande pour y donner. Aulieurs d'monter, i' descendait. I'a ouvert son couteau, i'a coupé ein morceau après sa cuisse à lui, Jean l'Ours, pis i'a donné. Quand il[s] ont arrivé en haut, belle aigle y'a d'mandé; "Qu'est'ce qu'vot' jambe l'a à saigner?" —"Ah!" i' dzit, "vous dzisiez: Couac! couac! pis j'avais pus d'viande, j'ai coupé ein morceau d'ma cuisse pis j'vous l'ai donné." La belle aigle alle a faite: "Couac!" pis alle a renvouèyé. I'a pris l'morceau d'viande, pis i' l'a collé sur sa cuisse.

Là, il a partsi pour s'en aller sus l'rouè. Il a été sus ein vieux orfévier. I'a dzit pourquoi i' prenait pas ouvrage-là d'faire les boules d'or. L'vieux orfévier y'a dzit: "J'peux faire d'la bonne ouvrage, mais j'sus après v'nir vieux et j'vouès pas ben clair comme j'avais coutsume, et j'ai peur de m'faire pend'." —"Eh ben," i' dzit, "allez prend' l'ouvrage pis, moin, j'vas les faire les boules d'or pour vous." L'vieux a été trouver l'rouè. "Ben, mon rouè, j'prendras l'contrat à faire vos boules d'or." —"Ah! mon vieux," l'rouè i' dzit, "vous êtes mon bon ami. Si vous les faites pas ben, vous va êt' pendzu." —"Ben," i' dzit, "j'vas prend' eune chance." L'souère, Jean l'Ours 'l était pour les faire à la veillée. Il a rentré dans la chambre làsque c'est l'vieux 'l avait ses outsil pour travailler. I' s'a emporté ein tas des pacanes, des nouèsettes, des pistaches. Il a commencé à manger et la vieille dzu vieux orfévier alle allait vouère par l'trou d'la serrure d'porte. Jean l'Ours 'l était toujours après manger ses pistaches et ses pacanes. Neuf heures est v'nu. La vieille alle a eurtourné ouère. "Eh! mon cher vieux," a dzit, "i'est toujours après manger; t'as t'faire pendre, t'as t'faire pendre." —"Ah! tais-touè donc," i' dzit, "c'est ein homme qui travaille vite, 'te-ben." A dzix heures, la vieille alle a eurtourné ouère. I' nn'avait faite eune, pis i' l'avait mis dans ein joli p'tsit plat d'vaisselle. Alle est eurvenue en tapant dans ses mains. "I' en a eune de faite," a dzit, "mon vieux." —"Ben, j't'ai dzit, ma vieille, qu'c'était pas nécessaire qu'tsu t'troubles. J't'ai dzit n'homme-là travaillait vite." A onze heures, la vieille 'l été ouère encore. I'avait fini; il les avait mis tout les trois ensemb' dans son p'tsit plat d'vaisselle. —"Ah! mon cher vieux, i' les a finies. On pourra s'coucher pis dormir tranquilles." I' sontaient pas plusse que couchés, la vieille alle a commencé a yi a d'mandé quocé 'l aurait faite avec son argent. "Ah! dors," i' dzit, "j'vas t'zdzire d'main matin."

L'lend'main, 'l a été porter les boules d'or sus l'rouè. Quand l'vieux rouè 'l a vu les trois boules d'or, i' pouvait pas les dzire eune cont' l'aut'. La plus jeune des filles alle était là, d'dans la chamb' dzu rouè. Alle y'a d'mandé: "Est-ce qu'vous avez pas ein homme pour vous aider à faire ça, mon vieux?" —"Ah! oui, ma princesse, j'avais d'l'aide." —"Si ça vous plaît, allez donc qu'ri l'homme pis emm'nex-lé icitte." Quand Jean l'Ours 'l a rentrè dans l'palais dzu rouè, la princesse a l'a eurconnu. A dzit à son père ce n'homme'-là pouvait séparer les boules d'or, i' connaissait l'eune cont' l'aut'. Jean l'Ours 'l a aveindzu les trois mouchouères d'souè 'l avait dans sa poche, 'l a separé les boules d'or, les a mis ane sur chaque mouchouère d'souè. L'vieux roué y'a dzit: "Quocé, c'était vous qui a délivré mes princesses?" —"Oui, sire," i' dzit, "c'était moin qui a délivré vos princesses." L'rouè i'a d'mandé à ses filles: "Comment ça s'fait vous m'avez dzit c'étaient les deux aut's hommes qui vous avaient délivrées?" —"I' nous ont faite faire serment qu'c'étaient eux aut's qui nous avaient délivrées ou ben i' nous auraient tsuées. Pour sauver not' vie, on vous a dzit ça i' voulaient." 'L ont pris Tord-Chêne pis Joueur d'Palets, les ont pendzus. Pis, l'vieux roué a donné à Jean l'Ours l'privilège d'ramasser n'importe queule des princesses i' aurait voulu. Jean l'Ours 'l a chouèsi la plus jeune des trois. L'vieux rouè 'l aimait pas beaucoup ça. Son *roule* c'était d'marier la plus vieille avant. "Mais," i' dzit, "comme tsu les a délivrées tous les trois, j'vas t'donner la plus jeune." I' s'sont mariés, pis 'l ont eu ein gros dzîner. Ça, c'est tout Jean l'Ours. J'sais pas c'qui est d'venu d'lui après.

4.

The Ogre with No Soul

Well, it's good to tell you that once upon a time there were an old man and an old woman. They had two sons, named Peter and James. The boys lived alone with their mother, and it was not easy to make ends meet. One day Peter, James, and their mother were talking things over. Peter said that if James and his mother could stay alone for a while, he would go out and get a job and make good wages, so he could save some money for winter. James said to him, "Well, go ahead and get out of here. You're not doing anyone any good by staying." So the next day, Peter said good-bye to his mother and brother and left the house. After awhile, he came to a river. There was a little canoe there on the bank, but there wasn't anyone around to take him across. He thought to himself, "I don't know whether to get in, or what." Suddenly, he heard a voice saying to him, "Get in!" So he got in and paddled across. When he got to the other side, he tied up the canoe and started walking again. He found a village where he could get a job. He worked hard and saved up a lot of money. Finally, he said to himself, "Now, I'm going to go back and visit my mother and James." So he stopped working and left to go back home. On the way, he passed by a big brick house in the woods. He looked in the window and saw the most beautiful Princess he had ever seen in his life. When he got back to the river, the little canoe was still there waiting for him. "What should I do?" he asked himself. "Should I get in or not?" He heard the voice telling him, "Get in!" So he got in and paddled across the river. When he got to this side, he got out and tied the canoe back up.

When he got back to his own house, it was starting to get dark. He leaned on the door frame with his hands and looked in. His mother was getting old and couldn't see too well any more. James was busy making corn bread in the skillet, in the fireplace. His mother said, "James, isn't that Peter standing there?" When she said that, James burned his finger on the skillet and shouted, "Why don't you stop bothering me about Peter? I don't know anything about Peter." Peter, in the doorway said, "It *is* me, Mother. I'm so happy to see you again." The old lady was delighted that her son had come back. Peter said, "But I won't stay very long here with you. I will give you money so that you and James can buy food for the next few months. I have to leave again tomorrow. On the way back home, I saw the most beautiful Princess that I've ever seen. I'm almost sure that she's under a spell. I intend to set that Princess free and will never stop trying until she is free or else the earth swallows me up." His mother wished him good luck, and then he said good-bye to her and to James and left.

He went to the blacksmith and had him make a flint stone for him. Then he took the flint stone and left. When he got to the river, his little canoe was still there waiting. He wondered if he should get in or not, and then he heard the voice again, saying to him, "Get in!" So he got in and paddled across the river and, then, went on his way. The sun was setting when he got to the castle where he had seen the Princess. He found a ladder and leaned it up to the window where the Princess had been. Then, he climbed up through the window. The Princess was lying in bed asleep. He took out his flint stone and struck sparks on it. He was doing it so fast, and the Princess looked so beautiful that he forgot what he was doing, and a spark fell on the girl's stomach. It burned her, and she awoke suddenly. She cried out, and he said, "Don't make any noise, Princess."

The Princess was guarded by an Ogre, and when he heard her cry out, he went to the bottom of the stairs that led up to her room and asked her what was the matter. —"It was nothing," she answered. "It was just a dream. Go back to bed." —"Well," said the Ogre, "you shouldn't dream like that. You startled me." Then, the Ogre went back to bed, and Peter asked the Princess, "What would it take to get you out of here?" She answered, "Well, I don't know. I've never asked." —"What's keeping you here?" —"It's an ogre," answered the Princess. So Peter said to her, "Tomorrow, ask the Ogre what it would take to set you free. I'll come back tomorrow night."

The next morning, the Princess brought the Ogre his soup and asked him what it would take to set her free. She said, "I don't think it will do me any good to ask you, but it can't do any harm, either." The Ogre answered, "No, it won't do any good, because you will never be set free. Many leagues from here, there is a mountain of yellow copper, and a mountain of silver. These mountains are guarded by a Porcupine. To kill that Porcupine, it takes a Lion as strong as seven lions, and he must be strangled. Inside the Porcupine is a hare. To catch the hare, it would take a Dog as fast as seven dogs. Inside the hare is a dove, and it would take an Eagle that flies as fast as seven eagles to catch it. Inside the dove is an egg. That egg is my Soul. Before I can be killed, the egg has to broken against my forehead." —"Well," answered the Princess, "I can see that it didn't do me any good to ask you about it." That night, Peter came back to see the Princess. She told him all the things that would have to be done to set her free. Peter answered, "Well, I'll spend the night here with you, and tomorrow morning, I'll leave to find the mountains and the Porcupine. I'll keep going until the earth swallows me up or I find a way to save you."

The next morning, he went to the store and bought a big, strong hunting knife. Then he left. One day, he arrived on the top of a big hill. He practically bumped into a Lion, a Dog, an Eagle, and little Yellow Ant. They had caught a big ox and were fighting over how to divide it up. The Lion said to Peter, "Hello, kind sir. Would you do me a little favor?"

—"I'll do you a favor if I can," answered Peter. —"Please cut up that ox for us," said the Lion. —"Well, I can divide it up, but the way I do it might not please you," answered Peter. The Lion said, "It doesn't make any difference how you do it. We'll be satisfied."

So Peter began to divide the ox. First, he cut off all the big pieces of meat and put them in a pile. Then, he took the bones and put them in a second pile. After that he took the innards, the heart, and the liver and put them in a third pile. And finally, he put the head off to one side by itself. Then, he called the animals and said to the Lion, "You like to gulp down big mouthfuls, so you can have that pile of meat." To the Dog he said, "You like to gnaw, so I made the pile of bones for you. There's a lot of good meat left on them." Then, he told the Eagle, "You don't have any teeth, so the innards and the heart and the liver will be good for you." Finally, he turned to the little Yellow Ant and said, "You can have the head. When the weather is nice, you can eat on the outside, and when it's raining and stormy you can stay inside."

When he had finished, Peter left the animals, who began eating. He had gotten quite a distance away from them, when the Lion said to the Dog, "We're very impolite. We never said thank you to that man." The Dog answered, "Well, I never even thought about that. You can shout really loud. Why don't you holler after him to come back?" So the Lion roared at the top of his voice, "Sir, come back here. We want to see you!" Peter heard him and said to himself, "I guess they're not satisfied with the way I divided up the ox and are going to eat me up. But I guess I'll go back anyway and see what they do want." So he went back to the animals and said to the Lion, "What's the matter? Didn't you like the job I did?" —"Yes, dear friend, we are more than happy. But we were very impolite and didn't thank you." He turned around and pulled three hairs from his tail, and said, "Whenever you want to turn into a lion, call me three times, and you will become a lion seven times stronger than me." Then, the Dog also pulled three hairs out of his tail and gave them to Peter, saying, "Whenever you want to be a dog, call me three times, 'Beautiful Dog,' and you will be a dog who can run seven times faster than me. And I can tell you that I move pretty fast." Then, it was the Eagle's turn, and she took a feather from her tail and gave it to Peter. She said, "Whenever you want to turn into an eagle, call me three times, 'Beautiful Eagle,' and you will instantly turn into an eagle who can fly seven times faster than me." The little Yellow Ant pulled off one of her feet and gave it to Peter, saying, "When you want to be a little ant, call me three times, 'Beautiful ant,' and you will turn into an ant seven times smaller than me."

Peter thanked the animals very much and started off again down the road. He hadn't gone very far when he called on the Lion. As a strong lion, he could tear up all the brush that was in his way. Then he turned into a dog and was able to run seven times faster than any dog. Finally, he turned into an eagle, and as he was soaring far over the earth, he could see the mountains of silver and copper where the Porcupine lived. He went and landed right next to a house near the mountain. "I'd better go see if anyone is home," he said to himself. He went up and knocked on the door, and a woman opened to him. She looked surprised and said to her husband, "A man!" During the whole thirty years they had lived in that house, they had never seen a man come there before. The were really happy to see Peter. They had him come in, and they fed him a good supper. Peter stayed there for two or three days, and finally he asked them if there wasn't some work he could do for them. They answered that they never worked, so there was nothing for Peter to do. But then the man said, "Take my hogs and go watch them while they eat in the forest. But don't go across the river. The land on the other side belongs to the Porcupine. My land is on this side of the river." Peter answered, "Oh, no. I'll never cross the river. I don't want to put your hogs in any danger." After awhile, the old woman looked out, and Peter was crossing the river with all the hogs. She turned to her husband and said, "Well, come and see. He's taking all your hogs across the river!" —"Let him go," answered the old man. "I'm not going to go after them over there!"

When Peter got to the other side, the Porcupine met him. "Hey," he said. "Instead of one meal this morning, I'll have several." —"You'll have to earn your meals if you want them," answered Peter. The Porcupine said, "I can do that easily." —"Let me know when you're ready," said Peter, and the Porcupine said, "I'm ready right now." Peter said three times, "Come to me Beautiful Lion," and turned into a lion. The lion and the Porcupine started to fight. The old man and the old woman were watching them from the other bank of the river. The lion caught the Porcupine and strangled him to death. Then he called to the old man, "Come here, old man." The old man came over and said to Peter, "Can you really change yourself into a lion?" Peter answered yes and then said to the old man, "Take my knife and open up the Porcupine, while I change into a dog." The old man looked at him, "Can you really change yourself into a dog?" —"Yes," said Peter. "Inside that Porcupine is a hare, and I have to catch him." So he changed himself into a dog and waited. As soon as there was a little hole in the Porcupine, the rabbit sprang out and ran away, with the dog running after it. The dog caught the hare right away. He brought it back to where the old man was standing and said, "Now I'm going to change myself into an eagle." The old man was still more surprised. "Can you change into an eagle too?" —"Yes," answered Peter. "Inside that hare there is a dove. Cut the hare in two." As soon as there was a little hole in the hare's skin, the dove flew out, with the eagle right after it. The eagle lost the dove from view, but finally saw it land on big dry stump. Peter wished himself as a little yellow ant right by the dove's foot. When he got there, he turned himself back into an eagle and brought the dove back to where the old man was waiting. He turned back into himself and cut the dove in two to get the egg.

At this point, the Ogre began to feel sick. The Princess went in to him with his dinner, and he said to her, "Get out of here, you witch. You have found a way to be set free!" The Princess thought to herself, "Is it possible that Peter is going to be able to save me?" At that point, Peter was saying to the old man, "I'll give you the mountain of yellow copper and

The Princess gains her freedom by breaking the Ogre's Soul on his forehead.

It's Good to Tell You

the mountain of silver. You can do as you like with them, until I ask for them again." He turned back into an eagle and flew into the window of the Princess who was waiting for him. —"Did you really find a way to set me free?" she asked him. Peter answered, "Yes, I have the Ogre's Soul right here with me." The Princess answered, "Well, give it to me. I want to break the egg on his forehead myself." She got a little plate of soup ready and brought it in to the Ogre, saying, "Try to eat little bit. It should make you feel better." The Ogre answered, "Go away, witch! You have my Soul in your hand." She went up to him and broke the egg right in the middle of his forehead. The old Ogre died. Peter brought the Princess back to his family's house, and they got married. I think they're living there still.

Corps-sans-Âme

Ben, c'est bon d'vous dzier eune fouès c'étaient ein vieux pis eune vieille. 'L ontvaient deux garçons. I' les app'laient Pierre pis Jacques. I' restaient tout seuls avec leu mouman; i' nn'avait pas grand argent à faire là. Eune journée, i' sont après charrer, Pierre pis Jacques pis sa mère. Pierre i' dzit à sa mère pis à Jacques s'i' pouvaient rester tout seuls ein qu'leu deux il aurait été s'charcer d'l'ouvrage où 'l ontvaient des bonnes gages, s'sauver d'l'argent pour l'hiver. "Ah!" Jacques i' dzit, "sac' donc ton camp, tsu fais rien d'ben icitte." L'lend'main, Pierre 'l a dzit aguieu à sa mère pis Jacques. Partsi à trav'ler 'l arrivé à eune rivière. 'L avait ein p'tsit *conou* là, mais 'l avait pas personne pour l'traverser. "J'connais pas si j'vas embarquer ou ben quoi." 'L a attendzu eune vouè qui y'a dzit: "Embarque!" 'L a embarqué, pis 'l a traversé. Arrivé d'l'aut' bord, 'l a amarré son p'tsit *conou*, pis 'l a partsi à trav'ler. I'a été à ein p'tsit village où 'l a eu d'l'ouvrage. I' s'a sauvé joliment d'l'argent. "A c't'heure," i' dzit, "m'as vouère à ma mère pis Jacques." 'L a arrêté son ouvrage, pis 'l a partsi. En eurvenant, il a passé là oùsqu'i'avait eune grande maisonne de brique dans l'bois. 'L a eurgardé d'dans, pis 'l a vu la plus belle princesse 'l avait jamais vue d'sa vie. 'L a arrivé à sa rivière. Son p'tsit *conou* 'l était toujours là. "Quocé m'as faire?" i' dzit. "Embarquer ou pas embarquer?" I' a attendzu eune vouè qui y'a dzit: "Embarque!" I'a embarqué pis traversé la rivière. Arrivé d'ce bord-citte, 'l a amarré son p'tsit *conou*.

Quand 'l a arrivé cheux autres, 'l était après commencer à s'faire brin. 'L a mis ses mains eune chaque bord d'la porte. Sa mère a vouèyait pus beaucoup ben clair, a était après v'nir vieille. Jacques était après s'faire ein pain maï[s] dans eune *esquilette* dans la chum'née. Sa mère a dzit: "Jacques, c'est pas Pierre, ça?" Padent c'temps-là, Jacques 'l avait brûlé son douè, lui, sus son *esquilette*. "Vous d'vrez ben m'fricasser patience avec vot' Pierre," i' dzit. "J'connais pas Pierre, moin." Pierre i' dzit: C'est moin, ça, mouman. J'sus ben hureux d'vous ouère." La vieille était fièr'te que son garçon 'l était eurvenu. "Mais j'rest'ras pas longtemps avec vous," i' dzit, "ma mère. J'vas vous donner d'l'argent à vous pis Jacques pour ach'ter d'quouè manger pour plusieurs mois. D'main," i' dzit, "j'eurpars, moin. En eurvenant icitte, j'ai vu la plus belle princesse vous l'a jamais vue, ma m'man, pis," i' dzit, "j'sus presque sûr alle est en esclavage mais," i' dzit, "j'vas la délivrer c'te princesse ou ben j'vas marcher tant qu'la terre a va m'porter." Sa mère a y'a souhaité d'la bonne chance. I' dzit aguieu à Jacques pis à sa mère, pis i' part. Il a été sus l'forgeron, pis i' s'a faite faire ein batte-feu. 'L a partsi, là, avec son batte-feu. 'L a arrivé à sa rivière, son p'tsit *conou* 'l était toujours là. I' s'est d'mandé si i'allait s'rembarquer ou ben non. I'a attendzu eune vouè qui y'a dzit: "Embarque!" 'L a traversé la rivière, i'est partsi en marchant. L'soleil 'l était tout bas quand 'l est arrivé au château d'la princesse. I' avait ein échelle; i' l'a pris, pis i' l'a porté à la f'nêt; là oùsqu'i' avait vu la princesse. I' a rentré par le châssis. La princesse a était couchée après dormir. 'L a commencé à battre son batte-feu. I' était si annimé, i' trouvait la princesse si jolite qu'i' faisait pas entention quoi i' faisait. 'L a ch'té ein étincelle d'feu sus l'estomac à la princesse. Ça l'a brûlée, ça l'a réveillée. Alle a lâché ein cri pis i'a dzit: "Criez pas, ma princesse, c'est moin." 'L avait ein allogre qui gardait princesse-là. Quand 'l a attendzu la princesse crier, 'l a été jusqu'à l'escalier d'la chambre d'en haut, 'l a d'mandé à la princesse quocé qu'alle avait. "C'n'était pas rien," a dzit, "justement ein rêve. Troublez-vous pas." —"Ah!" i' dzit, "i' faut pas rêver de même. Tsu m'as surpris." I' a eurtourné s'coucher. Pierre i' dzit à la princesse: "Quocé ça prendrait pour vous délivrer d'icitte?" —"Ah!" a dzit, "j'connais pas. J'ai jamais d'mandé." —"Ben," i' dzit, "quocé qu'c'est qui vous garde icitte?" A dzit: "C'est ein allogre." —"Ben," i' dzit, "d'mandé[z]-y donc d'main quocé ça prend pour vous délivrer." I' dzit: "M'as eurvenir d'main au souère."

L'lend'main, la princesse 'l a été porter la soupe à son ogre, pis a y'a d'mandé quocé ça aurait pris pour la délivrer. "J'pense," a dzit, "ça m'fait pas d'bien d'vous d'mander, mais ça fait pas d'mal non plus." —"Oh, non," i' dzit, "par rapporte tsu s'ras jamais délivrée. Tant d'lieues d'icitte," i' dzit, "i' nn'a eune montagne d'cuivre jaune pis eune montagne d'argent, pis," i' dzit, "c'est gardé, ça, par un porte-cupic. Porte-cupic-là, i' prend ein lion qu'est fort comme sept lions pour l'étrangler. Dans porte-cupic-là, i'y'a ein lièvre; i' prend ein chien qui court vite comme sept chiens pour l'attraper, lui, pis dans lièvre-là, i' nn'a ein pigeon; i' prend ein aigle qui voltige vite comme sept-z-aigles pour l'attraper, lui. Dans pigeon-là, i' nn'a ein oeuf. N'oeuf-là" i' dzit, "c'est mon âme. Faudra qu'n'oeuf-là i' souèye cassé dans mon front avant qu'j'meure." —"Ah ben," a dzit, "c'était pas nécessaire que j'vous en parle, ben sûr." L'souère, Pierre 'l est eurvenu charrer avec la princesse. A y'a tout dzit quocé i' peurnait pour la délivrer. —"Ben," i' dzit, "ma princesse, m'as veiller avé vous tout la nuit, pis d'main matin m'as partsir à trav'ler. M'as trav'ler tant qu'la terre a va m'porter pour que j'trouve eune monière d'vous délivrer."

L'lend main matin, 'l a été à ein magasin, pis i' s'a ach'té ein bon grand couteau. 'L a partsi à trav'ler. Eune journée 'l a arrivé sus ein grand crête de côte. I'a arrivé drètte sus ein lion, ein chien, ein aigle, pis eune p'tsite frémille jaune. Il[s] ontvaient attrapé ein gros boeuf, i' sontaient après s'quereller pour le séparer. L'lion y'a dzit: "Bonjour, monsieur, vous m'f'rez pas eune p'tsite faveur?" —"Ah! i' dzit, "j'te f'rai eune faveur, si j'peux, l'lion." —"Tsu devrais ben séparer boeuf-là pour nous autres," i' dzit. —"J'peux l'séparer, mais, teut' ben, ça vous plairait pas." —"Oui," l'lion y'a dzit ça y faisait pas d'dzifférence quouè il aurait faite, i'aurait été satisfait. 'L a commencé pis 'l a coupé toute la bonne grosse viande, pis i' l'a mis dans ein tas. I'a pris les ossailles, pis i' les a mis dans ein tas; 'l a pris la queue, les tripes pis les fouès, 'l a tout mis dans ein aut' tas. 'L a pris la tête, i' l'a mis à côté. "A c't'heure," i' dzit au lion, "touè, tsu aimes à manger par grosses bouchées, tsu pourras prendre tas d'viande-là icitte." I' dzit au chien: "T'aimes ben à ronger, tsu vas prendre les ossailles-là; i' nn'a ein tas d'la viande après." I' dzit à belle aigle: "T'as pas d'dents, tsu vas prendre les tripes, pis l'coeur, pis les fouès." I' dzit à la p'tsite frémille jaune: "Touè, tsu peux prendre la tête. Quand i' va faire beau, tsu pourras manger en dehors. Quand i' va faire mauvais, tsu pourras manger en d'dans."

A c't'heure, Pierre i' part. Les bétailles 'l ont commencé à manger. Pierre 'l était rendzu ein bon grand boute, l'lion i' dzit au chien: "On a été des ingrats, on n'a jamais eurmercié c't homme-là," i' dzit. L'chien i' dzit: "Tsu voués, j'ai jamais pensé à ça. Touè, tsu peux crier fort. Crie-y donc qu'i' vienne." L'lion 'l a crié: "Ah! monsieur, v'nez donc icitte, on veut t'ouère." Pierre i' dzit: "J'pense qu'i' sont pas satisfaits, pis i' vont manger moin; ça fait rien, j'y vas." 'L a arrivé sus eux autres. "Quocé?" i' dzit, "l'lion, t'es pas satisfait?" —"Ah si, cher ami, j'sus trop satisfait. On a fait les saf's, on t'a pas eurmercié, I' s'a eurviré, 'l a arraché trois pouèles après sa queue. "Ah!" i' dzit, "quand tsu voudras être ein lion, appelle après moin trois fouès: beau lion! tsu vas ein lion sept fouès plus fort que moin." L'chien 'l a arraché trois pouèles après sa queue pis i'a donné, lui aussite. "Quand tsu voudras êt' ein chein, appelle après moin trois fouès: beau chien! tsu vas être ein chien qui va courir sept fouès plus vite que moin, pis va, j'ten assure, j'marche pas douc'ment, j'peux grouiller vite." La belle aigle alle arraché eune pleume après sa queue. "Quiens," a dzit, "quand tsu voudras êt' ein aigle, appelle après moin trois fouès: belle aigle!, tsu pourras voltiger vite comme sept aigles." La p'tsite frémille jaune a s'eurvire, pis a arrache eune d'ses p'tsites pattes. "Quand tsu voudras êt' eune p'tsite frémille jaune, appelle après moin trois fouès: belle frémille jaune! tsu vas êt' sept fouès plus p'tsite que moin."

Pierre 'l a ben eurmercié ses bétailles, pis 'l a eurpartsi. 'I a pas été ben loin, 'l a app'lé sus l'beau lion. I' pouvait tout déchirer les chêneaux. Il a app'lé l'beau chien ça; ensuite, 'l a app'lé la belle aigle. Il a voltigé aussi haut comme il a pu. Il a eurgardé pis il a vu la montagne d'cuivre pis la montagne oúsque l'portsupic i' restait. Il a été s'poser drètte à ras d'ça, pis il a eurgardé pis il a vu eune p'tsite maisonne drètte à ras. "Faut que j'vas ouère," i' dzit, "si i' nn'a dzu monde qui reste là." Il a été pis il a cogné à la porte. I' nn'a' eune femme qui a v'nu y rouvert. 'L a dzit à son mari: "Ein homme!" Trente années i' restaient là pis 'l ontvaient jamais vu ein homme avant. Sontaient fiers d'vouère Pierre. I' l'ont faite rentrer, pis i' l'ont ben traité. Pierre 'l a resté à l'entour deux, trois jours. I' leu-z-a d'mandé si 'l ontvaient pas queuque chose pour lui faire. "Non", i' dzit, i' travaillaient pas là, i' nn'avait rien à faire. "Prends mes cochons," i' dzit, "pis va les garder dans la forêt. Traverse pas la rivière. Ça qui est d'l'aut' bord, c'est au portsupic, ça, dzu bord-citte, c'est à moin." —"Ah! non," i' dzit, "m'as pas traverser. J'veux pas emm'ner tes cochons dans eune place d'meme." Taleure, la vieille a eurgarde. Il était après traverser la rivière avec tous ses cochons. "Mais," a dzit, "viens donc vouère, mon vieux, i'est après traverser la rivière avec tous tes cochons." —"Laisse-lé aller," i' dzit, "moin, j'vas pas les qu'ri."

Quand il a eu arrivé d'l'aut' bord, l'portsupic i' l'a rencontré. "Hèye!" i' dzit, "à la place d'ein eurpas, à matin, m'as en aouère plusieurs." —"Faudra qu'vous les gagne les eurpas, si vous veut les aouère." L'portsupic i' dzit: "J'peux faire ça." —"Laisse-moin acconnaît' quand est-ce tsu vas être paré." L'portsupic i' dzit: "J'sus paré drètte à c't'heure." I' dzit: "Viens à moin, beau lion!" 'L ont commencé à s'battre. L'vieux pis la veille sontaient sus l'aut' bord d'la rivière après les guétter faire. Il a attrapé l'portsupic, pis i' l'a étranglé. I'a crié après l'vieux: "Viens icitte, mon vieux!" L'vieux i'est v'nu. "Tsu peux t'mettre en lion, mon jeune homme?" i' dzit. "Oui," i' dzit, "à c't'heure prends mon couteau, pis rouvre portsupic-là, j'vas m'mettre en chien." —"Oh!" i' dzit, "tsu peux t'mettre en chien?" —"Ah! i'dzit, "oui, j'peux m'mettre en chien. Dans portsupic-là," i' dzit, "nn'a ein lièvre, faut que j'l'attrape." I' s'a mis en chien pis il a guétté. Juste comme i' nn'avait ein p'tsit jour là, l'lièvre 'l a sortsi, l'chien par derrière, pis i' l'a attrapé tout d'suite. I' est eurvenu oùsqu'i' est l'vieux. "A c't'heure," i' dzit, "j'vas m'mettre en aigle." —"Oh!" i' dzit, "tsu peux t'mettre en aigle?" —"Ah! oui," i' dzit, "j'peux m'mettre en aigle. I' nn'a ein pigeon," i'dzit, "dans n'aigle-là." Fend l'lièvre, i' l'a rouvert en deux. Ah! i' nn'a ein p'tsit jour, pis l'pigeon i'a sortsi, belle aigle par derrière. A l'a perdzu d'vue. Alle a voltigé là-bas en l'air; i'a eurgardé, pis i' l'a vu poser sur ein gros chicot sec. I' s'a souhaité eune p'tsite frémille jaune après la patte dzu pigeon. Après ça i s'a eursouhaité en son aigle. 'L est eurvenu, 'l a pris son couteau, pis i' a fendzu l'pigeon en deux.

En eurvenant à vieille n'allogre, alle a commencé à êt malade. La princesse alle a été pour y porter son dzîner. "Va-t'en d'icitte, ma méchante. T'as trouvé eune monière pour t'délivrer." —"Ça s'rait-i' possib'," a dzit, "qu'Pierre i' m'délivrerait? Là, Pierre i' part pour s'en v'nir eurtrouver sa princesse. Pierre a dzit au vieux: "J'te donne la montagne d'cuiv' jaune, la montagne d'argent. Fais c'que tsu veux avec jusqu'à quand j'appelle pour." I' s'a eursouhaité en belle aigle, i' a voltigé dans la f'nêt' d'la princesse. "Ben, Pierre," a dzit, "t'as trouvé eune monière pour m'délivrer?" —"Oui," i' dzit, "j'ai son âme dans mon corps icitte." —"Ben, donne-moin-la, j'vas y casser dans l'front moin-même." 'L a pris eune p'tsite assiette d'soupe, 'l a commencé à dzire: "Assayez donc d'manger ein p'tsit brin, p'teut' ben qu'ça vous f'rait dzu bien." —"Va-t'en, ma méchante," i' dzit, "t'as mon âme dans ta main." Alle a été drétte à ras d'lui, pis a y'a cassé l'oeuf-là drétte dans l'front. La vieille allogre a était morte. Pierre a pris la princesse, pis i' l'a remm'née sus son père. I' s'ont mariés, pis j'crouès i' sont là encore.

5.

Teigneux

It's good to tell you once upon a time there were an old man and an old woman, and they had a lot of children. They had a new baby to baptize, and they couldn't find anyone to be the Godfather. Finally, they found an old man and asked him if he would be Godfather. He told them he would, if they would give him the baby when he should reach the age of reason. So when Teigneux reached the age of seven years, they gave him away to his Godfather. The old man raised him until he was getting to be a young man. One day, his Godfather went away for two or three days. He asked Teigneux to stay by himself. "During the day," he said, "you should do your work, and in the evening you can go and get some of your friends to spend the night with you." He gave Teigneux all the keys to the buildings on the place, but there was one little key that he told Teigneux he couldn't use.

After his Godfather had been gone for a while, the boy said, "I have to see what is in that building!" He went in and found a spring that was all yellow. When he dipped in the tip of his little finger, it turned golden. The old Godfather, who was a sort of magician, already knew that Teigneux had gone into the little building. He turned around, after he got back, and told Teigneux, "Bring me my book from the mantel." Teigneux was afraid that his Godfather would see his finger and wrapped it up. He gave the book to the old man with the other hand and kept his little finger sort of hidden. The Godfather said, "What is the matter with your little finger?" Teigneux answered, "Oh, I just scratched it a little bit awhile ago. It's nothing to worry about, just a little sore." —"Let me see," answered his Godfather. "Sometimes a little sore turns into a big one." Teigneux started to cry. —"Ah!" said the Godfather, "you went into the little building!" —"Yes, Godfather," answered Teigneux. "I went in there." The old man was angry with him and told him never to go in there again.

That old man had a Lion and a Black Mare, which he kept in his barn. He told his godson, "Go and feed the Mare with the meat, and the Lion with the hay." Teigneux went out and fed them as he had been told. But the Lion wasn't eating the hay, and the Mare wasn't eating the meat, and he said to himself, "I'm going to feed them as I usually do and give the meat to the Lion and the hay to the Mare." After he had changed around the hay and the meat, the Mare spoke to him, "Teigneux," she said, "while I'm eating my hay go and dip your whole head into that little spring, and your two hands as far as the wrists. Then go get a brush, a mirror, and a bar of soap, and bring along a loaf of bread and a bottle of wine as well. Put the saddle on my back, and we'll leave here. If your Godfather finds us here when he gets back, he'll kill us both." So Teigneux put the saddle on the Mare's back, and they left. It was getting close to noon, and the Mare said to Teigneux, "Pay attention, he's going to come up behind us. Be sure to notice when there starts to be a black cloud in a while." Teigneux answered, "There's already beginning to be a little black cloud." The Mare said, "Don't let it get too close without telling me." Teigneux replied, "That cloud is getting pretty close. I can already feel the wind starting to blow." —"Throw your brush out behind you, with bristles up in the air," said the Mare. "It will turn into a forest of thornbushes." When the Godfather got into the thornbushes, he grew angrier than ever. He was riding his Lion, and had to go through the thorns, and got his clothes all torn up.

After another while, the Mare said to Teigneux, "Be careful. You're going to see him coming again soon." —"I can see that cloud coming up pretty well," answered Teigneux. "It's turning purple." The Mare said, "Don't let it get too close." Teigneux answered, "It's getting pretty close." The Mare told Teigneux, "Throw out your mirror behind you with the glass facing up, and it will become a mountain of ice." When the Godfather arrived there, he found the mountain of ice. It took him a long time, but he finally managed to cross it. The Mare told Teigneux, "Don't let him get too close. You'll see him coming soon." Teigneux said, "I can see him coming pretty well. The purple cloud is turning blue and purple. I can feel the wind. It's hot."

"Throw out the bar of soap behind you," the Mare told him, "and it will become an ocean. Now I'm hungry. There's good grass for me to eat, and you have the bread and wine." When the Godfather got to the ocean, there was water everywhere, and he had to turn back. Teigneux and the beautiful Black Mare went to sleep at the foot of a tree.

The next morning, the beautiful Black Mare said to Teigneux, "We're going to go find the King, and you will hire on as a gardener. Whatever you plant today will be good to eat tomorrow. Whenever you need me, come to this place, and call. Say, 'Come to me beautiful Black Mare,' three times." Teigneux went to the King and asked for the job of gardener. The old Queen said to the old king, "Well, why don't you take him on? We haven't had anything good to eat from the garden for a long time." So they gave Teigneux the job.

The next morning, Teigneux began to work in his garden. He planted lettuce, radishes, onions, and beans. The morning after that, he went back out into the garden and brought back full baskets of vegetables for the table. When the old King and Queen came in to sit down at the table, they were surprised. They asked the cook where all the beautiful vege-

Baby Teigneux separated from his parents

It's Good to Tell You

tables came from. "Ah," he answered, "that comes from the garden. Teigneux brought all that in."

The youngest of the princesses said, "I can't believe that Teigneux can garden as well as that!" She began to watch Teigneux. Every evening she went to bathe in a spring that was at the back of the garden. One evening, the moon was especially bright, and the little princess watched Teigneux. She saw how his head and his hands were as bright as gold. "Ah! she said, "he doesn't have any sores on his head." Teigneux always wore a cap on his head and gloves on his hands. The young princess began to clean Teigneux's little house every day. She went into the King's kitchen and brought him back little dishes full of the best food from the King's table for Teigneux to eat. Every day she chatted with him in the garden.

One day, she went and picked a pretty white flower and put it right on Teigneux's little table, where he could see it from the garden. Then she went and talked with Teigneux in the garden. Teigneux said to her, "My princess, you will have to take that white flower off my table, because if the King sees that he will chase me away from here." The time came when the three princesses were to get married. The old King's rule was when his daughters were to get married he would have a big feast and would invite all kinds of important people so that his daughters could choose from among them. So the day was appointed for the feast. The big shots began to arrive with their white silk shirts and their white silk rosettes.

When the time came for each girl to choose her man, the oldest princess took her white flower and sat next to a big red-faced fellow. She gave him her flower so that he would be her husband, and the second princess took her white flower and chose a husband too. When it was the youngest sister's turn, she didn't want to get up. Her father said to her, "Little Marie, it's your turn now." So she got up with her white flower and said, "Father, will I marry the man that I give my white flower to?" The King said, "Yes, you will marry the man to whom you give your white flower." So the princess went all around the room and looked at all the men there three times. Then she ran through the door and into the garden and gave her flower to Teigneux. The old King was angry. "You can just go and eat with your Teigneux in your little room!" he shouted. They sent Teigneux and the princess to a little house that was on the far edge of the town.

Not long after, a war was declared against the old King. Teigneux sent his wife to visit her father and to see if he wanted his son-in-law to go fight for him. "Oh, yes!" said the old King. "I don't know what we can give him to fight with." Teigneux's brother-in-law said, "Give him the old three-legged horse in the yard, and the old rifle that doesn't shoot." The King said, "Oh, yes! Tell Teigneux, Marie, that he can take the old horse with the sore foot in the yard, and the rifle that doesn't shoot." Teigneux's wife went back home crying. Teigneux asked her what was the matter. "Well," she answered, "my father says for you to take the old horse with the sore foot in the yard and the old rifle that doesn't shoot. What can you do with those?" "Don't cry," said Teigneux. "Marie, I'm going to do more with that than all the others are going to do with their fine horses and beautiful swords."

So Teigneux went and got his old horse and rifle and left before the others. He soon got stuck in a mud puddle. When the old King left with his army, all the others were riding fine horses. The King passed by Teigneux who was stuck in his mud hole and slapped him on the back, saying, "Don't kill the whole enemy army before we get there!" When they had gone by, Teigneux called his Black Mare. The beautiful Black Mare came and dressed Teigneux all in black, with a sword that cut everything within a hundred yards around him. He took off at a gallop and rode by the King's whole army. With two or three blows with his sword, he destroyed the army that was preparing to fight his father-in-law. Then he turned around and rode back at a gallop, going by the King's whole army again. The old King shouted after him, "Stop, handsome, unknown prince!" But Teigneux didn't stop. He just kept on going.

When the old King and his army got to the battlefield, no one was left to fight them. Only the dead and the wounded were there. So the army turned around right away. Teigneux had let his Black Mare go, and had gone back to the old three-legged horse, and picked up his old rifle that wouldn't shoot. When they got to the place where he was, his brothers-in-law slapped him in the face and said, "It's too bad you didn't get at least halfway there. You would have seen a handsome prince." Teigneux answered, "Ah! he was no more handsome than I!" They hit him pretty hard while they were teasing him, and he said to them, "You'll pay for this!" The next day everything went the same way. Teigneux went out before the others. He went and got stuck in his mud hole with the lame horse, and his old rifle that wouldn't shoot.

When the King's army had passed him by, he called the Black Mare. He said three times, "Come to me, beautiful Black Mare!" He got on his beautiful horse, and very quickly he rode past the King's army. When he got to the battlefield, he had soon killed half of the enemy army and turned around right away, as he had done the day before. When he met the old King, as he was riding back, the King asked this fine unknown prince to stop. But he didn't turn his head. He kept right on riding. The King said, "Tomorrow if he comes back, I must find out who he is, dead or alive." When the King and his army arrived on the battlefield, there was no one left to fight. So the King and his army had to turn around and go back home.

On their way back, they found Teigneux sitting in his mud hole as he had been before, with his old lame horse and useless gun. One of his brothers-in-law said, "You should have come all the way. You would have seen a handsome prince." —"Ah!" said Teigneux. "That handsome prince wasn't any better looking than me!" The brother-in-law punched Teigneux's face pretty badly. "You really look like a prince, Teigneux," he sneered. Teigneux said to his brother-in-law, "You'll pay for this tomorrow!" The next day everything happened

"Teigneux"

It's Good to Tell You

the same way. Teigneux got on his old three-legged horse, and took his old rifle that wouldn't shoot, and went back to his mud hole.

When the army of the King passed him by, he called to his Black Mare. She said, "I'm going to change my color. It's the last day, Teigneux. I will be white, and I'll dress you all in white, and a white dog will follow you." Teigneux galloped off on his Mare. He arrived at the battlefield. Just as before, he cleaned up the enemy army in just a few minutes. The enemy called out to the old King to grant them peace. "Wait till the King comes and you can make peace with him," said Teigneux. Then, he turned around as usual and started riding back. When he met the King, the King told him to stop, but he didn't pay any attention. The King threw his lance at Teigneux, and it struck him in the thigh and broke off. Teigneux rode by his brother-in-law and cut off one of his ears. The dog was running along behind and picked it up.

Then, Teigneux went back and let his Mare go. The King went and made peace with his enemies. The enemy king gave his word in writing that there would be no more trouble caused by him. When the King got the promise in writing, he turned around with his army and came back home. When the brother-in-law passed by Teigneux sitting on his lame horse in the mudhole, he didn't say anything to him, because his ear hurt too much. Teigneux went back to his work in the garden the next day. He worked for two or three days, but his leg was beginning to hurt him a lot. He had to stop working. Marie had to go visit her father every day and ask him for help. He said, "How come Teigneux doesn't want to work in the garden any more?" —"He's sick," she said. —"What does he have?" asked the King. "Well," she answered, "he was wearing an old shoe the other day, and a piece of wood penetrated his foot."

It had been several days since Teigneux had gone to work in the garden. The Queen said to the King, "We would have pity on a dog, and we have to have pity on him." So the old King got his wife and the doctor, and they went to see Teigneux. The doctor began to ask him what the problem was. "Ah," Teigneux answered. "The other day I was wearing an old shoe, and this piece of wood penetrated into my foot, and my whole leg is hurting." So the doctor began to examine him. There was nothing wrong with his foot. He kept looking higher and higher until he got to the thigh. "Well," said the doctor. "There's a bruise here." He caught hold of Teigneux's leg and pressed on it, and the piece of lance flew out.

The King went to pick it up, but the princess was quicker than he was and got to it before him. She took it and stuck it on the end of the King's broken lance. It stayed there as it was before it had broken off. "Well, Teigneux," said the old King, "so you're the one who got us out of trouble." Teigneux answered, "You don't have to ask any questions, sire, your lance proves the truth." "Yes, it's true," replied the King. "Tomorrow we will really celebrate your marriage to my daughter." While they were waiting for dinner to be ready, Teigneux asked the King, "Would you recognize that handsome prince if you saw him again as he was dressed?" Teigneux went out, and after he had gone a little distance, he called his

Mare. She dressed him as she had the first time. Teigneux went and asked the King if he recognized him. —"Yes, I recognize you" said the King.

Then he went out again for a few moments and came back dressed as he had been the second time. He asked the King if he recognized him this time. "Yes, I recognize you," he said. The brother-in-law whose ear he had cut off began to feel really ashamed. When Teigneux came back the third time, he was dressed all in white, with his white horse and his white dog. The dog was carrying the brother-in-law's ear that had been cut off. He asked the King if he recognized him. "Yes, I recognize you," he answered. Then, he asked his brother-in-law if he recognized the ear. His brother-in-law was hanging his head with shame and said, "Yes, I recognize it." "Well," said Teigneux, "come back over here so I can put it back on. You don't look good with just one ear." Then, he left to bring his Mare back to the place where he had called her. She said to Teigneux, "You have saved me from the spell I was under. Now I'm going away and I won't see you any more." —"Well, I thank you very much," said Teigneux. "Because of you, beautiful Black Mare, I'm fine for the rest of my life."

Teigneux

C'est bon d'vous dzire eune fouès c'étaient ein vieux pie eune vieille, pis il[s] ont eu eune grande bande d'enfants. 'L ontvaient ein bébé à baptsiser, pis i' pouvaient pas trouver personne pour êt' parrain Il[s] ont trouvé ein vieux, pis i' l'ont d'mandé pour êt' parrain. I' leu-z-a dzit i' aurait été parrain au garçon si, par cas, i' y donnaient l'bébé à d'raison. Quand Teigneux est v'nu à l'âge d'sept, huit ans, i'ont donné. L'vieux l'a él'vé jusqu'à i'a été ein mouèyen p'tsit jeune homme. Eune journée, son parrain i' a partsi pour rester deux jours, trois jours. I'a d'mandé s'i' pouvait rester tout seul, lui. "Dans l'jour," i' dzit, "tsu vas faire ton ouvrage, pis l'souère, tsu pourras aller qu'ri quequos-ane d'tes p'tsits camarades pour coucher avec touè." I'a donné tous les clefs des bâtsiments, tout à part eune p'tsite clef; ien qu'ane qu'i' y a défendzu d'emplouèyer.

Aprés qu'son parrain 'l a été partsi eune bonne escousse, l'p'tsit garçon a dzit: "I' faut j'vas vouère dans p'tsit bâtsiment-là." Il a trouvé eune fontaine; alle était tout jaune. I'a mis l'p'tsit boute d'son p'tsit douè là, 'l était doré. Son vieux parrain 'l était manière magicien; i' connaissait ça, déjà, qu'Teigneux avait rentré dans la p'tsite maisonne. Il a eurviré, il a crié, après Teigneux. " 'Portemoin donc," i' dzit, "mon liv' qu'est sus la corniche." 'L avait peur qu'son parrain s'aperçouève, il a env'loppé son p'tsit douè. Il a donné l'liv' à son parrain d'l'aut' main, pis 'l a t'nu son p'tsit douè manière caché. "Quocé que vous a à vot' p'tsit douè?" —"Ah!" i' dzit, "je m'sus justement grafigné taleure ein p'tsit brin. Ah!" i'a dzit, "c'est pas rien. C'est ein p'tsit mau." —"Laissemoin ouère," son parrain i'a dzit, "ein p'tsit mau, ça peut causer ein gros mau." Teigneux i' s'a mis à brailler. "Ah!" i' dzit, "t'as rentré dans p'tsite maisonne-là." —"Oui," i' dzit, "mon parrain, j'ai rentré." L'vieux i'était ben fâché cont' lui, pis i' y'a dzit d'pas jamais eurtourner là d'dans.

'L avait ein lion pis eune jument nouèr'te, vieux-là, qui restaient dans sa grange. I' dzit: "Tsu vas donner l'foin au lion, pis la viande à la jument." Tingnieux i' les a souègnés d'même. L'lion i' mangeait pas l'foin pis la jument a mangeait pas, elle, la viande. I' dzit: "J'vas souègner ça comme j'ai coutsume, la viande au lion, l'foin à la jument." Après qu'il a eu chanzé l'foin pis la viande, la jument y'a parlé. "Tingnieux," a dzit, "padent que j'vas manger mon foin, va pis cale tout ta tête dans p'tsite fotaine-là, tes deux mains jusqu'au pognet, pis va qu'ri eune brosse, ein mirouère, pis eune barre d'savon, pis 'porte-touè ein pain l'vé, pis eune bouteille d'vin blanc, viens pis mets la selle sus mon dos, on va s'en aller d'icitte. Ton parrain si i' nous trouve icitte quand i' va eurvenir, i' va nous tsuer tous les deusses." Tingnieux 'l a mis la selle sus l'dos d'la jument, pis 'l ont partsi. Vers midzi, la jument a dzit à Tingnieux: "Fais-y attention, i' va eurvenir par derrière nous aut's. Fais ben attention quand i' va v'nir eune nué nouèr'te taleure." —"I' commence," i' dzit, "à en avouère eune p'tsite nuée nouèr'te." La jument y'a dzit: "Laisse-lé pas v'nir trop proche avant de m'le dzire." Tingnieux i' dzit à la jument: "La nuée a commence joliment à approcher, j'sens l'vent approcher." —"Jette ta brosse en arrière d'touè," a dzit, "avec les crins en l'air, ça va être eune forêt d'piquants." Quand son parrain 'l a arrivé dans les piquants, ça l'a faite fâcher pire qu'tout. 'L était monté sus son lion; 'l a passé en travers, a tout dechiré son linge.

Après ça, la jument a dzit à Tinyeux: "Fais attention, tsu vas l'vouère v'nir taleure." —"J'voués la nuée qui monte joliment ben. A est après v'nir violette, nuée-là." A dzit: "Laisse-la pas v'nir trop proche." 'L a dzit: "I'approche." —"Jette ton mirouère," a dzit, "avec la figure en l'air derrière touè, ça va être eune montagne d'vit'." Quand son parrain 'l a arrivé là, c'était eune montagne d'vit'. I'a pris beaucoup dzu temps, ça y'a pris longtemps, mais i' l'a traversée. "Laisse-lé pas arriver trop proche sans m'le laisser acconnaît'." I' dzit: "I'approche, la nuée violette alle est violette bleu. J'sens l'vent," i' dzit, "'l est chaud." —"Jette la barre d'savon en errière d'ton dos," a dzit, "ça va êt' eune mer." A dzit: "A c't'heure, moin, j'ai faim, i'a d'la bonne herbe; touè, tsu as dzu pain, tsu peux l'manger." Quand son parrain 'l est arrivé là, c'était tout d'l'eau, i' fallait qu'i' eurvire. Lui pis la belle jument nouèr'te 'l ont couché au pied d'ein arb'.

L'lend'main, la belle jument nouèr'te alle a dzit à Teigneux: "On va aller trouver le rouè, pis t'as t'engager jardigneur; ça on va s'mer aujourdz'hui va êt' bon à manger d'main. Quand tsu vas aouère d'besoin d'moin, viens icitte pis appelle: à moin, trois fouès, la belle jument nouèr'te!" Teigneux 'l a été trouver l'rouè, 'mander pour l'*djob* d'jardigneur. La vieille reine dzit au vieux rouè: "Ah! quiens, engage-lé donc. En v'là longtemps on a pas d'bons jardignages à manger." Ça fait 'l ont donné d'l'ouvrage à Teigneux.

L'lend'main matin, Teigneux 'l a commencé à travailler dans son jardin, s'mer des raves, pis d'la salade, des oignons, des fèves. L'lend'main matin, Teigneux 'l a èté dans l'jardin; 'l a 'porté des pleins pagniers d'jardignages pour la tab'. Quand l'vieux rouè pis la vieille reine s'en vont s'mett' à la tab', i' s'ont trouvès surpris; i' ont d'mandé au cuisinier d'où v'nait tout c'beau jardignage. "Ah!" i' dzit, "ça vient de d'dans l'jardin; c'est Teigneux qui l'a 'porté ça."

La plus jeune des princesses a dzit: "J'crouès pas qu'ça souèye Teigneux qui fait l'jardin si ben qu'ça." Alle a commencé à guétter Teigneux. Tous les souèrées, i'allait s'bagner dans eune fotaine qu'était dans l'fond dzu jardin. Eune souèrée, la lune 'l a éclairé ben. La p'tsite princesse a l'a guétté. Alle a vu sa tête pis ses mains comme i'éclairaient comme d'l'or. "Ah!" a dzit, "ça, c'est pas ein teigneux." Teigneux 'l avait toujours eune paire de gants pis eune tsuque sus la tête. La p'tsite princesse alle a commencé à nettèyer la p'tsite maisonne à Teigneux tous les jours. A allait dans la

Teigneux

cuisine dzu rouè, pis a 'portait des p'tsits vaisseaux à manger dzu meilleur qu'l'rouè 'l avait sus sa tab'. Tous les jours a allait charrer avec lui dans l'jardin.

Eune journée, alle a été pis alle a ramassé ein joli bouquet blanc, pis a l'a mis drétte sus sa p'tsite tab' à Teigneux là oùsqu'i' pouvait l'ouère de d'dans l'jardin. Après ça, 'l a été charrer avec Teigneux dans l'jardin. "Ma princesse, i' faudra qu'vous ôte c'bouquet blanc de d'sus ma table, pasce si l'rouè vouè ça, i' va m'chasser d'icitte." C'est v'nu l'temps les trois princesses dzu rouè sontaient bonnes à marier. Le *roule* d'vieux rouè-là, quand ses filles 'l étaient bonnes à marier, c'était d'avouère ein gros festin et pis d'inviter toute sorte d'gros monde haut, pis laisser ses filles chouèsir. La journée alle a été *appointée* pour l'festin. Les gros hommes 'l ont commencé à arriver avec des grandes ch'mises blanches d'souè, des grandes rosettes d'souè blanche.

Quand c'est v'nu l'heure pour chaqueune chouèsir leu-z-homme, la plus vieille alle a pris son gros bouquet blanc, alle a été s'assir là oùsqu'i' y'avait ein gros rougeaud. A y'a donné son p'tsit bouquet, ça a été son mari, et la deuxième alle a pris son bouquet blanc, a s'en a choisi ein, elle aussite. Quand c'est v'nu à la plus jeune, alle aimait pas d'se l'ver. Son père y'a dzit: "P'tsite Marie, c'est à ton tour." A s'a l'vée avec son bouquet blanc. A dzit: "Mon père, à l'homme que j'donne bouquet-là, c'est l'homme j'vas marier."—"Oui, l'homme vous donne l'bouquet, c'est l'homme vous marie." A a faite l'tour d'la maisonne, a a eurgardé les hommes trois fouès. Alle a enfilé la porte, alle a été dans l'jardin, alle a présenté son bouquet à Teigneux. L'vieux rouè i' s'a trouvé fâché. "Est-ce qu'tsu pourras manger avec ton Teigneux ton dzîner dans sa p'tsite chamb'!" l'ont mis Teigneux pis la princesse dans eune p'tsite maisonne au loin au bord d'la ville ein peu.

Ça l'a pas été ben longtemps, i' s'a déclaré eune guerre contre l'vieux rouè. Teigneux 'l a enwèyé sa femme vouère son père si i' voulait qu'lui vaille s'batt' pour lui. "Oh! oui," l'vieux rouè i' dzit, "j'connais pas quocé on va y donner s'batt' avec." Son beau-frère à Teigneux i' dzit: "Donnez-yi donc l'vieux ch'val à trois pattes dans la cour pis l'vieux fusil sans plaque."—"Oh! oui," l'vieux rouè i' dzit, "dzis-yi donc, Marie, qu'i' peut prend' l'vieux ch'val qui a la jambe cassée dans la cour pis l'vieux fusil sans plaque." La femme à Teigneux s'a rentournée en braillant. Teigneux y'a d'mandé quocé alle avait à brailler.—"Eh ben," a dzit, "mon père i'a dzit vous pouvez prendre l'vieux ch'val à trois pattes et vieux fusil sans plaque-là. Quocé qu'on peut faire avec ça!" Marie a dzit.—"Braille pas," i' dzit, "Marie, j'vas faire avec ça plus qu'i' vont faire avec leus beaux ch'vaux pis leus beaux sables."

Il a été qu'ri son vieux ch'val pis son vieux fusil sans plaque, pis 'l a partsi avant les aut's. I' s'a enfoncé dans ein p'tsit trou d'boue. Mais quand l'vieux rouè 'l a partsi avec son armée, sontaient tou[s] montés sus des beaux ch'vaux. L'beau-père i' passait oùsqu'est Teigneux 'l était dans son p'tsit trou d'boue. I' yi donnait des tapes, i' yi dzisait: "Détruis pas tout l'armée avant qu'on arrive!" Teigneux 'l a app'lé sa jument nouèr'te. Belle jument nouèr'te alle est v'nue, alle a habillé Teigneux tou[t] en nouère, ein sable qui coupait cent verges à l'entour d'lui. 'L a partsi l'galop, 'l a dépassé l'armée dzu rouè. Dans deux ou trois coups d'sable, 'l avait détruit l'armée des enn'mis d'son beau-père. 'L a eurviré l'galop, les rencontrés. L'vieux rouè i' criait: "Arrête, beau prince étranger." J't'en fous, i' s'arrêtait pas, lui, i' s'en allait.

Quand l-vieux rouè pis son armée 'l ont arrivé sus l'champ d'bataille, i'en avait pus personne pour s'batt', ien qu'les morts pis les blessés qui restaient. I' s'a en eurvenu tout d'suite. Teigneux 'l a été lâcher sa jument. I'est eurvenu monté sur son vieux ch'val à trois pattes, pis 'l a ramassé son vieux fusil sans plaque. Ses beaux-frères i' yi donnaient des tapes sus la yieule. "Ben dommage, t'es pas rendzu à moquié ch'min au moins, Teigneux, t'aurais vu ein beau prince."—"Ah!" i' dzit, " 'l était pas plus beau qu'moin." I' l'tapochaient pas mal quand i' dzisait ça. Teigneux a dzit à ses beaux-frères: "Vous va payez ça." L'lend'main matin, c'était tout la meme chose. Teigneux 'l a partsi au-d'vant des aut's. I'a été s'enfermer dans son p'tsit trou d'boue avec son vieux ch'val à trois pattes pis son vieux fusil sans plaque.

Après qu'l'armée dzu rouè a été passée, 'l a été app'ler vieille jument nouèr'te: "A moin," trois fouès, "belle jument nouèr'te!" I'a monté sus sa belle jument, i'a dans ben peu d'temps dépassé l'armée dzu rouè. Quand 'l a arrivé sus l'champ d'bataille, i'a bétôt eu détruit la moquié d'l'armée des enn'mis et il a eurviré drètte d'bord comme la matsinée d'avant. Quand il a rencontré l-vieux rouè, l'vieux rouè y a d'mande qu'i' arrête, beau prince étranger. I'a pas eurviré la tête, i' s'a en allé. L'rouè i'a dzit: "D'main, s'i' eurvient, faut que j'connais qui 'l est, mort ou en vie." Quand 'l ont arrivé au champ d'bataille, i'avait pus personne pour s'batt'. L'rouè a pris son armée, i' fallait qu'i' s'en eurvienne.

En eurv'nant, 'l ont trouvé Teigneux dans son p'tsit trou d'boue comme 'l avait coutsume d'être, toujours avec son vieux ch'val à trois pattes et son vieux fusil sans plaque. Ane d'ses beaux-frères y dzit: "T'aurais dzû v'nir tout dzu long, t'aurais vu ein beau prince."—"Ah!" i' dzit, " 'l était pas plus beau qu'moin, beau prince-là." Ah! son beau-frère y'a boursoufflé la gueule pas mal. "Tsu eursembles à ein prince, Teigneux!" Teigneux i' dzit à son beau-frère: "T'as payer ça d'main, touè." L'lend'main, c'n'était tout la meme chose. Il a eurmonté sus son vieux ch'val à trois pattes, 'l a pris son vieux fusil sans plaque, pis 'l a eurtourné dans son p'tsit trou d'boue.

Quand l'armée dzu rouè a été passée, 'l a app'lé sa jument. "M'as chanzer ma couleur," a dzit. "C'est la dernière journée, Teigneux. M'as être blanche pis j'vas mettre touè tou[t] en blanc, pis ein chien blanc va t'suire." 'L a partsi à toute course. 'L a arrivé sus l'champ d'bataille. Tout la même chose, 'l a nettèyé l'armée dans ben peu d'temps. L'vieux rouè, les enn'mis, 'l ont app'lé pour faire la paix. "Attendez qu'l'aut' rouè i' arrive, pis on pourra faire la paix avec lui." I' eurvient comme d'coutsume, l'rouè, pis, Teigneux 'l est partsi. Quand Teigneux 'l a rencontré l'vieux rouè, i'a d'mandé d'arrêter. I' nn'a pas faite d'cas. L'vieux rouè 'l a envouèyé sa lance après. I'a enfoncée dans la cuisse. La lance alle a cassé. Teigneux 'l a passé sus son beau'frère, i'a ôté eune oreille. Son chien i' s'a en v'nu en errière pis i' l'a ramassée.

Teigneux i' s'en va à c't'heure décharzer sa jument. Le rouè i' s'rend à son enn'mi pour faire la paix. Le vieux rouè enn'mi i' y'a donné ein billet écrit d'sa main qu'i' y f'ra plus dzu troub' davantage. A c't'heure, l'aut' rouè i'a eu son billet, lui, pis i' s'a rentourné avec son armée. Son beau-frère a passé où Teigneux 'l était dans son p'tsit trou d'boue. I'a pas parlé, son orielle a y faisait mal. Teigneux i' s'a enr'tourné à son ouvrage dans l'jardin l'lend'main. Il a travaillé deux ou trois jours. Sa jambe alle a commencé à y faire mal. Fallait qu'i' arrête d'travailler dans l'jardin. Marie allait sus son père tous les jours, i' fallait qu'a va y rend' ses visites, soupplier à lui. A avait pas marié l'homme qu'lui avait voulu qu'a marisse. "Comment ça s'fait," i' dzit, "Teigneus vient pus travailler dans l'jardin?" —"Il est malade," a dzit, "Teigneux." —"Quocé i'a?" i' dzit. "Ah!" a dzit, "I avait ein vieux souyer l'aut' jour, pis i' s'a enfoncé ein vieux chicot dans l'pied."

Ça faisait plusieurs jours Teigneux v'nait pus au jardin en toute. La reine alle a dzit au rouè: "I' faudra aller ouère à c't homme-là. On l'a piquié d'ein chien, i' faut aouère piquié d'lui." L'vieux rouè 'l a ramassé l'docteur pis sa vieille, pis 'l ont partsi. Quand 'l ont arrivé sus Teigneux, l'docteur a commencé à y d'mander des questions, quocé il avait. —"Ah!" i' dzit, "l'aut' jour, j'avais ein vieux souyer, j'me sieus enfoncé ein chicot dans l'pied, ma jambe a m'fait mal tout l'long." L'docteur a commencé à eurgarder. I'avait pas d'mal avec son pied. Ein p-tsit brin plus haut encore jusqu'à i'a arrivé à sa cuisse. "Comment," l'docteur i' dzit, "en v'là eune tache bleue icitte." L'docteur il a attrapé la jambe à Teigneux pis i' l'a pressée. L'bout d'lance 'l a volé en dehors.

L'vieux rouè 'l a été pour le ramasser, mais la princesse alle a été trop vif, a l'a ramassé avant

It's Good to Tell You

l'vieux roué. A l'a pris pis a l'a mis sus l'boute d'la lance dzu vieux rouè. A a resté collée comme avant qu'a sèye cassée. —"Oui," l'vieux rouè i' dzit, "pargué! Teigneux, c'est vous qui a tout fait c'te dédommage." —"Pas d'questions à d'mander, sire," i' dzit, "vot' lance a prouve la vérité." —"Ah!" i' dzit, "c'est ben vrai, d'main, on eurnouvellera les noces." Padent qu'i' sont apprès attendre l'dzîner i' sèye paré, 'l a d'mandé au vieux rouè: "Vous eurconnaîtra beau prince-là si l'eurwerrez comme il était habillé?" Teigneux 'l a partsi, pis il a été eune p'tsite distance. Il a app'lé sa jument, i' s'a habillé comme il était la première fouès. A d'mandé au vieux rouè s'il l'eurconnaissait. —"Ah! oui," i' dzit, "j'vous eurconnais."

I' s'a en est eurtourné ein aut' p'tsit boute, pis i' s'en a eurvenu comme i' était la deuxième fouès. Il a d'mandé s'il l'eurconnaissit encore. —"Ah! oui, j't'eurconnais." Son beau-frère, qui avait l'oreille ôtée, commençait à être malade, à avouère honte. Quand 'l est eurvenu la troisième fouès, i' s'a habillé en blanc, ein ch'val blanc, pis son chein blanc. Son chien i' 'portrait l'oreille à son beau-frère qu'i' y'avait ôtée là. A d'mandé au rouè s'il l'eurconnaissait. —"Ah! oui, j'vous eurconnais." 'L a d'mandé à son beau-frère: "Vous eurconnaît n'oreille-là?" Son beau-frère a baissé la tête avec la honte, en dzisant: "Oui, j'la eurconnais." —"Ben," i' dzit, "viens, j'vas t'la eurmettre. Tsu eurgardes pas ben ien qu'avec ein oreille." Il a été remm'né sa jument. "Tsu m'as délivrée," la jument a dzit, "d'être ein esclave. A c't'heure, j'm'en vas," a dzit, "pis tsu m'eurwerras jamais." —"Ben, en t'eurmerciant ben, belle jument nouèr'te; moin, j'sus ben pour l'restant d'mes jours."

6.

The Little Bull with the Golden Horns

It's good to tell you once upon a time there were an old man and an old woman. They had a boy whose name was Little John. When Little John grew up, he became a farmer. Little John's neighbor was Big Devil. Big Devil wanted to be a farmer, too, but he didn't know how, and besides he didn't have a team. One day, he went to see Little John about sowing a crop of wheat. Little John said, "That's fine. We can put in a crop of wheat together." The next spring when the wheat was ready to be cut, Big Devil went to ask Little John if the wheat was ready to harvest yet, because he didn't know anything about farming. When Little John thought the wheat would be ready, he went to see, and it was ripe. He said, "We're going to start cutting our wheat tormorrow, Big Devil. It's ripe."

They went into the field, and Big Devil wanted to know how they were going to separate the wheat. "Well," said Little John, "First, we cut it, and then we thresh it, and then we'll separate it." —"No!" said Big Devil, "I want to separate it right away." —"Well, if you want to separate it right away, go ahead. But how are you going to do it?" answered Little John. Big Devil said, "Well, I'll tell you what we'll do. I'll take the roots, and you take the tops." So Little John took the tops and went to thresh his wheat. He had all the grain and the straw, and Big Devil got all the roots. After a little while, Big Devil came back to find Little John, saying, "You stole all the wheat, Little John." —"But you're the one who separated it, Big Devil," he answered. —"Yes, but you knew better than that, Little John. You should have told me right away. You stole it all."

In the fall, Big Devil came to find Little John again, to put in some turnips. Little John said, "Well, that's fine. We'll put in some turnips together." So, they put in a big patch of turnips. When they were ready to pick, Little John said, "It's time to harvest the turnips. You said that I stole all the wheat. I want you to separate the turnips." —"Yes, but you'd better not trick me this time, Little John," said Big Devil. "This time I'm the one who's going to take all the tops." Little John answered, "That's fine. You take the tops and I'll take the roots." So, Big Devil went out into the garden, and cut all the leaves and stems off the turnip plants, and took them. Little John went along behind him and dug up the turnips and took them. Big Devil took all his turnip tops home with him. He tried to cook them and eat them, but it was impossible.

Of course, Little John was enjoying the turnips. Big Devil came back to his house and said, "Little John, you tricked me again! You stole all the turnips." —"I stole them? But you're the one who decided who would get what." —"Yes," answered Big Devil, "but you knew better than that." Little John said, "Well, Big Devil, so you're calling me a thief, are you? You mark my words. I am going to rob you, and then you'll see." Big Devil told him, "You'd better not try anything like that, or I'll eat you up like a grain of salt!"

Things went along quietly for a while, and Little John got tired of staying by himself. He went out and visited the King and asked if he could move in with him. The King answered, "Oh, yes, you can move in with me if you want to. I'd be really happy to have some company." The King's house was nice, and Little John was as happy as he could be, for a while. But then Little John began to get sad and sat around daydreaming all the time. The King asked him why he sat around all the time without saying anything. Big Devil had a little fiddle. Little John said to him, "I'm thinking about what a good time we'd have if we had Big Devil's little fiddle. We could have a party. Wouldn't that be nice?" The King said, "Leave Big Devil's fiddle alone, Little John. You're going to get yourself killed." —"Yes," said Little John. "I haven't tried anything like that. I only said that if we had it, we could have a good time."

One day, Little John said to the King, "I think I'm going to go visiting this evening." The King answered, "Yes, go ahead and visit the neighbors down the road." So, Little John went out visiting. He had to cross a wide river in order to get to Big Devil's house, and he did. He began to listen, and he heard Big Devil playing his fiddle. He thought to himself, "Now, if you could only just go to sleep." He crept right up to Big Devil's fence and hid behind a post. Big Devil played the fiddle for a while, but then he did fall asleep. The fiddle slid down onto the floor of the porch. Little John waited till Big Devil was sleeping soundly and then went up to him on tiptoes. He picked up the fiddle and the bow and ran away. After a while, Big Devil woke up and felt and looked all round him on the porch floor, to get his fiddle, but it wasn't there. "Well," he said, "Little John stole my fiddle." He ran after him to catch him, but Little John had already crossed the river, and it was too late.

Little John got back to the King's house and played the fiddle all night because he was so happy. But after he'd had the fiddle for a while, he began to get bored again and started daydreaming again. The King asked him, "What are you thinking about, Little John?" Little John answered, "Big Devil has a sun. If we could get that sun, we wouldn't need a lamp any more, and that would be wonderful." —"Please stop thinking about that," said the King. "You can't take that. You'll get yourself killed." So an evening or two later, Little John said he was going to visit the neighbors. The King said to him, "That's fine. Go and have a good time but don't go and steal Big Devil's sun, do you hear? You'll get yourself killed." When Little John got to Big Devil's house, Big Devil's wife was hanging out her wash. Little John sneaked up and hid behind a fence post. He thought to himself, "If she would only decide that she needs the sun to help her see the wash she is hanging up, I'd be

Big Devil watches as Little John steals his fiddle.

It's Good to Tell You

able to steal it." As it got near dark, the old woman said to Big Devil, "My wash is hanging up outside, and it's getting dark." The old man said, "Hang the sun on the end of the porch, so you can see, and go take in the clothes." So she went out, hung the sun on the end of the porch, and took in all her clothes. She ended up with too big an armful of clothes to be able to carry the sun, too, so she went in without the sun.

When she went into the house and left the sun outside, Little John took the sun down from the porch and left. When the woman had put her laundry away, she went back out to get the sun and bring it in, but it was gone, and all she could do was watch it shining in the distance. "Ah!" she shouted. "Someone has stolen the sun!" The old man got up and came out. He said, "This is one of Little John's tricks," and started out after him as fast as he could run. He stopped when he got to the river and shouted, "Little John, I know you're the one who stole my sun. I'll catch you, you can be sure."

Little John hung the sun up in the King's house when he got back. Then, he went and woke up the King to show it to him and said, "Come and see how the sun brightens up the house. It's just wonderful to have such a bright house." The old King and Queen got up, and they all spent the rest of the night admiring how pretty the sun was in their house. The King said, "That's very pretty, but you shouldn't do things like that Little John. You're going to get yourself killed." So for a while, Little John was just as happy as he could be at the King's house, because it was so beautiful.

But after a few months, Little John became sad again. The King noticed and asked him, "Little John, what's the matter?" —"Well," answered Little John, "I was just thinking about Big Devil's little bull with the golden horns, and how if we could have it here we would never need anything again." The King said, "Yes, Little John, that would be nice, but I've told you to stop thinking about things like that. You're going to get yourself killed." —"Oh," said Little John, "there's no danger."

So one evening, Little John told the King that he was going to go and visit the neighbors. The King said, "Go ahead but don't go after Big Devil's little bull with the golden horns. You're going to get yourself killed." —"Oh, no," answered Little John. "I won't go there." As soon as he went out, Little John went across the river. The little bull with the golden horns was sleeping right next to the fence. Little John waited until Big Devil fell asleep, while he tried to think of how to steal him. When Big Devil fell asleep, Little John grabbed the bull by his golden horns, but the little bull began to bellow. Weuh! Weuh! Weuh! That woke up Big Devil, who started running after Little John and the little bull with the golden horns as fast as he could. But he wasn't fast enough, and Little John and the bull were able to cross the river before Big Devil got there. Big Devil shouted across the river to Little John, "Now you've stolen everything I had in the world, Little John." —"Yes," Little John shouted back. "Not only have I stolen everything you had. I'm going to steal you too." —"You'd better not try to do anything like that," said Big Devil, "or I'll eat you up like a grain of salt."

So then, Little John went back to the King's house with the little bull with the golden horns and put him in a corner. He took out the sun, to light up the little bull. The King thought that it was the prettiest little bull he had ever seen. Then, they got out the fiddle and played the fiddle, all night long. Things went along calmly for a while, and Little John was as happy as he could be, but then one day he grew sad again. He was bored and had nothing to do in the house. The King noticed and suggested that he might go out in the neighborhood, to find something to do. There was a blacksmith shop not far away, and that would be a good place to go and spend the day.

So one day, Little John went over to the blacksmith shop to spend the day. He asked the blacksmith if he could make an iron coach. "Yes, I can make one of those," said the blacksmith. Little John went on, "I want it strong, and so heavy that it will take eight strong horses to pull it." Every day, he went back to the blacksmith shop, to see how the iron coach was coming along. When it was finished, Little John went to the King and asked him for his eight best horses. "What are you going to do with them?" the King asked him. "I'm not giving you my eight best horses unless I know what you are going to do with them." — "Well, if you don't want to loan me your horses, you can just keep them," answered Little John. —"I've never refused you anything, Little John," said the King. "If you want to get killed, go ahead and take the horses."

Little John went out and hitched up the eight best horses that the King had. He drove them to the blacksmith shop and hitched them to the iron coach. Then, he put on old clothes, and an old cap, and a big false beard, and got himself all disguised. He got on one of the horses pulling the iron coach and drove the coach by Big Devil's house. He left the door open so it would make noise, banging shut at every bump. When he got in front of Big Devil's house, he started to shout at the horses, "Whoop! Whoop!" The horses ran as fast as they could, and the door banged back and forth, "Vring, vrang." Big Devil came out to see what was going on. He couldn't imagine what in the world it was. He began to shout after it, "Hey, come back here!"

"Whoop!" Little John stopped the coach, turned around, and went back to Big Devil. "What in the world are you going to do with that?" he asked. He didn't recognize Little John at all. He went on, "I want to steal Little John. He has stolen everything I had in the world, and now I want to steal him and put him in that coach." Little John, in his disguise, said, "You don't say! He stole everything I had, too, and I'm going to tell you right where he is." —"Well, where is he?" asked Big Devil. "He's right on the other side of the river, at the King's house," answered Little John, disguised as the stranger. —"Do you think that will hold Little John?" asked Big Devil. "His power is so great, I'm afraid your coach won't hold him." The disguised Little John said to Big Devil, "You should be about as strong as he is. Why don't you get in to see if it will hold him?" Big Devil didn't want to get in, so he said, "I guess it will hold him, all right." But Little John answered, "Well, I'd like to be sure. Please get in so we can see." So Big Devil got in, and Little John closed the door behind him. Then he said to Big Devil, "Now try to get out. You should be about as strong as he is." Big Devil tried to get out and said, "Yes, it will hold him." But Little John called back, "You didn't push half hard enough. Try it again."

While Big Devil was trying out the iron coach, Little John took off his disguise. He took off the beard and the old cap and the old clothes, and when he was wearing his own things again, he went out where Big Devil could see him from inside the coach. Big Devil said, "Oh! Is that you, Little John?" Little John answered, "Yes, it's me. You said I was a thief, and I said I would steal you bodily, and now I have you." Big Devil said, "Hey, let me out of here, Little John!" But Little John answered, "No, I'm bringing you back to the King." He turned the eight horses around and went back toward the King's house. When they arrived in front of the King's house, Little John unhitched the horses and brought them back to the stable. Then, he came out, next to the iron coach, and shouted to the King to come out and see what he had in there.

The King came out to see. He was carrying an iron pitchfork. When he got beside the coach, he knocked the pitchfork against it, and a loud roar came out from inside. The King turned around and ran away. Little John called after him, "Come back, you coward, you don't need to be afraid." The King came back and thought he'd have some fun with whatever was inside, so he knocked his pitchfork against the side of the iron coach a second time. Big Devil let out a loud roar, and the King got scared again and ran away. Little John shouted to the King to come back. "Come back here, you coward. You don't need to be afraid. He can't get out." So the King came back again, and this time he looked inside the iron coach. Big Devil pleaded with Little John and said, "Little John, if you would only let me go, I would write you a promise that you would never see me again." —"You can cry all you want, Big Devil. I have you now in the place where you are going to spend the rest of your days!"

Le p'tsit boeu[f] aux cornes d'or

C'est bon d'vous dzire eune fouès c'étaient ein vieux pis eune vieille. 'L ontvaient ein garçon; i' l'nommaient P'tsit Jean. Quand 'l est v'nu grand, P'tsit Jean i' s'est mis à *farmer*. P'tsit Jean pis Grand Guiab' i' restaient ouèsins. Grand Guiab' 'l aurait voulu *farmer*, lui aussite, mais i' connaissait pas comment, pis il avait pas d'*team*. Eune journée, 'l a été vouère P'tsit Jean pour qu'i' sume dzu blé avec lui. "Ben," i' dzit, "c'est bon, on va sumer eune *croppe* de blé." L'printemps d'ensuite quand l'blé 'l a été bon à couper, 'l a été trouver P'tsit Jean, pis i' y'a dzit qu'i' fallait qu'i' y dzise quand l'blé aurait été bon à couper parce que lui connaissait pas rien dans la farme. Quand P'tsit Jean 'l a pensé l'blé 'l était bon, 'l a été ouère, pis 'l était mûr. I' dzit: "On va commencer à couper not' blé d'main, Grand Guiab', 'l est mûr."

'L ont été dans l'parc. Grand Guiab' voulait connaît' comment c'est i' l'auraient séparé. "Ben," i' dzit, "on va l'couper, pis on va l'faire batt'; après ça, on va l'séparer." —"Non," i' dzit, "j'veux l'séparer tout t'suite." —"Ben, si tsu veux l'séparer tout t'suite, sépare-lé, mais comment c'est tsu vas l'séparer?" —"Ben," i' dzit, "m'as t'dzire comment c'est on va faire. M'as prend' les racines," i' dzit. —"Ben, si tsu prends les racines, m'as prend' la tête." Ça s'fait P'tsit Jean 'l a fait batt' son blé. 'L a eu tout l'blé pis la paille, lui; l'aut' 'l a eu les racines. Il est v'nu trouver P'tsit Jean. "T'as tout volé l'blé," i' dzit, "P'tsit Jean." —"Heum," i' dzit, "C'est touè qui l'as séparé." —"Oui," i' dzit, "mais tsu connaissais mieux qu'ça, P'tsit Jean. Tsu aurais dzû m'dzire ça tout t'suite; tsu l'as tout volé."

Dans l'automne, 'l est v'nu trouver P'tsit Jean encore pour sumer des rabioles. "Ben," i' dzit, "c'est tout ben, on va sumer des rabioles." 'L ont sumé ein grand *patch* d'rabioles. Quand sont v'nues bonnes à arracher dans l'automne, i' y'a dzit: "Ben, i' faudrait arracher nos rabioles." —"Ben," i' dzit, "t'as dzit j'avais tout volé l'blé, ben à c't'heure sépare les rabioles." —"Oui, mais," i' dzit, "P'tsit Jean, tsu m'embêtes pas à c'coup-là." I' dzit: "M'as tout prend' les têtes à c'coup-là." —"C'est bon," i' dzit, "prends les têtes, pis m'as prend' la racine," i' dzit. Grand Guiab' 'l a été, pis 'l a tout coupè les feuilles sus les rabioles, pis i' les a pris. 'Tsit Jean 'l a été en errière, lui, 'l a tout arraché les rabioles, pis les a pris. 'L a apporté tous ses feuilles, tous ses têtes d'rabioles sus eux aut's. I' assayait d'les faire cuire, d'les manger, mais pas mouèyen d'faire.

Padent c'temps-là, P'tsit Jean, lui, 'l avait les rabioles. "P'tsit Jean," i' dzit, "tsu m'as embêté encore, t'as tout volé les rabioles," i' dzit. —"J'les ai volées? Mais c'est touè qui les as séparées; t'as pris tout ça t'as voulu." —"Oui," i' dzit, "mais tsu connaissais mieux qu'ça." —"Grand Guiab'," i' dzit, "tsu m'fais passer pour ein voleur, hein? Ben," i' dzit, "eurmarque quocé j'te dzis, m'as t'voler." —"P'tsit Jean, tsu f'rais mieux d'pas entreprend' des choses d'meme, m'as t-croquer comme ein grain d'sel."

Ça s'est passé de meume queud' temps. P'tsit Jean s'est tan-né d'rester tout seul. 'L a partsi, pis 'l a été trouver l'rouè. I' y'a d'mandé d'rester avec lui. "Oh, oui," i' dzit, "tsu peux v'nir rester avec moin; je s'rais ben fier, ça me f'rait d'la compagnée." L'rouè 'l avait eune belle maisonne, pis P'tsit Jean 'l était aussi satisfait comme i' pouvait êt'. Au boute d'quend' temps, 'l est v'nu triste. I' était après jongler tout l'temps. L'rouè y'a d'mandé quocé 'l avait à jongler tant. Grand Guiab' 'l avait ein p'tsit violon. I' dzit: "J'sus après jongler comment si on l'avait l'p'tsit violon dzu Grand Guiab' l'on aurait dzu bon temps, on pourrait s'assir, pis s'amuser. Comme on s'rait ben!" —"Oui," i' dzit, " 'Tsit Jean, mais c'est impossib', ça; laisse ça tranquille, t'as t'faire tsuer." —"Oh!" i' dzit "j'ai pas déjà été l'essayer, mais j'ai justement dzit, si on l'aurait, comme on pourrait ben passer not' temps."

Eune journée, i' dzit au rouè: "J'crouès, j'vas aller veiller à souère." —"Oui," i' dzit, "va donc, va donc veiller sus les ouèsins." Il a partsi pour aller veiller. 'L avait eune grande rivière à traverser. 'L a traversé sus l'aut' bord en allant sus l'Grand Guiab'. 'L a commencé à écouter, pis 'l attendait Grand Guiab' qui était après jouer dzu violon. "A c't'heure," i' dzit, "si tsu pourrais justement t'endormir." Il a avancé jusqu'à ras drètte la barrière, pis i' s'a caché derrière ein poteau. Grand Guiab' 'l a jouè dzu violon ein escousse jusqu'à temps i' s'a endormi. L'p'tsit violon 'l a tombé à terre sus la gal'rite. P'tsit Jean 'l a attendzu qu'i' s'endorme ben. Quand qu'i'l a ben été endormi, 'l a avancé tout doucement, 'l a ramassé l'p'tsit violon pis l'archet, pis i' s'a en allé. Taleure, Grand Guiab' i' s'a réveillé. D'abord i' s'a réveillé, il a tâté autour de lui pour vouère s'i' trouv'rait pas son violon, mais i' trouvait pas rien. "Ben," i' dzit, "c'est P'tsit Jean qui l'a volé, mon violon." 'L a couru à la rivière, mais i' était trop tard, il a pas pu le rattraper.

P'tsit Jean 'l a arrivé sus l'rouè. I' s'a mis à jouer dzu violon toute la nuit à force qu'i' z-étaient fiers. Comme ça eurparait la maisonne! Ça s'est passé queud' temps d'meme, pis P'tsit Jean 'l était pas satisfait, i' était après jongler encore. L'rouè i' dzit: "Quocé t'as à jongler, P'tsit Jean?" —"Grand Guiab', il a," i' dzit, "ein soleil." I' dzit: "Si on l'avait soleil-là, on aurait pus besoin d'lampe; comme on s'rait ben!" i' dzit. —"Mais laisse ça tranquille," i' dzit, "tsu peux pas voler ça. Tsu vas t'faire tsuer." —"Ben," i' dzit, "l'rouè, j'ai pas dzit qu'j'aurais été l'qu'ri."

The little bull with the golden horns

Ça s'est passé eune souèrée ou deux d'même, pis P'tsit Jean 'l a dzit i' irait veiller. "Oui," le rouè i' dzit, "va veiller, si tsu veux, mais t'attends, va pas voler soleil-là dzu Grand Guiab', tsu vas t'faire tsuer." Ça s'fait 'l a partsi pour aller veiller. La vieille dzu Grand Guiab' alle avait lavé c'te journée-là; alle avait tout son linge d'étendzu dehors. Lui, il a avancé, pis i' s'a caché derrière le poteau. "Ben, i' dzit, "si a pouvait mett' son soleil dehors pour étend' son linge, j'pourrais l'voler." —"Ah!" a dzit, "j'ai oblié mon linge dehors, pis i' fait nouère." L'vieux i' dzit: "Pends donc l'soleil sus l'boute d'la garlie, pis va charcer ton linge." A va, pis met l'soleil sus l'boute d'la gal'rie, pis a ramasse tout son linge. À nn'avait trop eune grosse brassé pour rapporter l'soleil dans la maisonne. Alle a partsi avec son linge.

Padent c'temps-là, lui, P'tsit Jean i' vient, pis i' attrape le soleil. Après qu'alle a eu serré son linge, alle a dzit: "M'as aller qu'ri l'soleil à c't'heure." Alle a sortsi pour aller qu'ri l'soleil. Tout ça a pouvait faire, c'ètait d'vouère l'soleil qui eurluisait tout loin là-bas. "Ah!" a dzit, "i' nn'a queuques-ane qui a volé l'soleil." L'vieux s'est l'vé, pis 'l a dzit: "Ça, c'est des tours à P'tsit Jean." I' s'a mis à courir aussi fort qu'il a pu par derrière lui. Quand il a arrivé sus l'bord d'la rivière, il a crié: "Eh, P'tsit Jean! c'est touè qui as volé mon soleil! Ah! j't'attrap'rai ben!"

P'tsit Jean 'l a partsi, pis 'l a pendzu l'soleil dans la maisonne, pis 'l a réveillé le rouè. I' dzit: "V'nez donc eurgarder comme ça eurpare la maisonne. C'est justement terrib', eune belle maisonne comme on l'a!" Ah! l'vieux rouè pis la vieille i' s'ont l'vés pis i' ont passé la nuit à eurgarder comme ça faisait ben. L'rouè i' dzit: "Oui, c'est ben beau, mais tsu devrais pas faire ça, tsu vas t'faire tsuer." Ça s'est passé queuque temps d'même, pis P'tsit Jean 'l était satisfait comme i' pouvait êt' dans la maisonne; comme c'était beau!

Mais queuques mois après, P'tsit Jean 'l a eurmenché à jongler encore; i' était jonglard comme i' pouvait êt'. L'rouè i' s'en a aperçu. "P'tsit Jean," i' dzit, "quocé vous l'a à jongler?" —"Ben," i' dzit, "jétais après jongler que Grand Guiab' a ein p'tsit boeu[f] aux cornes d'or, pis si on l'aurait eu icitte, i' y'a rien qui nous aurait manqué." —"Oui," i' dzit, "P'tsit Jean, ça, ça s'rait ben joli, mais," i' dzit, "j'te dzis, laisse ça tranquille, tsu vas t'faire tsuer." —"Oh!" i' dzit, "i' nn'a pas d'danger."

Eune souèrée, i' dzit: "J'crouès j'vas aller veiller sus les vouèsins." —"Tsu peux aller veiller sus les vouèsins, mais va pas charcer l'p'tsit boeu[f] aux cornes d'or, tsu vas t'faire tsuer." —"Oh! non," i' dzit, "j'iras pas là, j'iras pas là," i' dzit. Il a traversé la rivière. Le p'tsit boeu[f] aux cornes d'or i' couchait drètte à ras la barrière. Il a attendzu que l'Grand Guiab' sèye endormi; i'était après jongler. 'L a été pis 'l a attrapé l'p'tsit boeu[f] aux cornes d'or par la corne, pis l'p'tsit boeu[f] s'a mis à beugler: "Weu! Weu! Weu!" Ça l'a réveillé l'Grand Guiabe pis 'l a partsi par derrière. Il a pas pu l'rattraper. Il a traversé la rivière avant qu'i' ait pu l'rattraper. Grand Guiab' 'l a crié: "Eh! P'tsit Jean, t'as volé tout ça j'l'avais dans l'monde." —"Oui," i' dzit, "j'vas voler tout ça t'as, pis m'as t'voler, touè aussite." —"C'est mieux pas enteurprend' ça," i' dzit, "P'tsit Jean. M'as t'croquer comme ein grain d'sel, si tsu viens à l'entour d'moin."

Là, P'tsit Jean s'a en allé sus l'rouè avec son p'tsit boeu[f] aux cornes d'or, pis i' l'a mis dans ein coin. Il a réveillé le rouè. L'rouè 'l a vu le p'tsit boeu[f] aux cornes d'or. Oh! comme i' était fier! Il[s] ont mis l'p'tsit boeu[f] dans ein coin. P'tsit Jean 'l a sortsi l'soleil, pis il a éclairé l'p'tsit boeu[f]. L'rouè i' trouvait qu'i' était l'plus beau p'tsit boeu[f] il avait jamais vu. Ensuite i' ont sortsi le p'tsit violon, pis i'ont joué dzu violon tout la sainte grande nuite. Ça l'a été comme ça queud' temps. P'tsit Jean 'l était aussi satisfait comme i' pouvait être, pis ein jour, i' s'a mis à jongler encore. I' était tout jonglard, i' grouillait pas de dans la maisonne. L'rouè i' s'a aperçu d'ça, pis i' y'a dzit i' pouvait courailler à l'entour; i' nn'avait eune forge pas loin, i' pouvait aller passer la journée là.

Ça s'fait eune journée, P'tsit Jean 'l a partsi, 'l a été à la forge passer la journée. I' dzit au forg'ron: "Vous pourrez faire ein tomb'reau d'fer?" —"Oh! oui," i' dzit, "j'peux en faire eune." P'tsit

Jean i' dzit: "J'en veux ein fort, tout ça huit j'vaux pourront 'haler." —"J'vas te l'faire," i' dzit. Tous les jours, i' allait à la forge ouère comment i' avançait avec son tomb'reau d'fer. Quand 'l a eu fini, 'l est v'nu sus l'rouè, pis i' y'a dzit i' voulait huit d'ses meilleurs j'vaux il avait. "Quoi tsu veux faire, P'tsit Jean," i' dzit, "avec ça?" —"Ça fait pas de dzifférence," i' dzit, "quoi j'veux faire. J'veux huit des meilleurs j'vaux t'as." —"P'tsit Jean," i' dzit, "tsu peux pas aouère mes ch'vaux sans que j'connais quocé tsu veux faire avec." —"Ben, si tsu veux pas m'les prêter tes ch'vaux, tsu peux les garder." —"P'tsit Jean," i' dzit, "j't'ai jamais eurfusé rien. Si tsu veux t'faire tsuer, prends'lé, pis vat'en."

P'tsit Jean 'l a partsi, pis il a att'lé huit des meilleurs j'vaux l'rouè 'l avait. 'L été la forge, pis i' les a att'lés sus son tomb'reau. Là, i' s'est tout mis dzu vieux linge, ein vieux *cap*, d'la grande barbe, i' s'a tout défiguré, i' s'a tout chanzé autrement. 'L a monté sus ein des ch'faux il avait att'lés sus l'tomb'reau, pis 'l a été faire ein grand tour d'vant sus l'Grand Guiab'. Il avait laissé la porte rouvert pour qu'a mène dzu train, pour qu'a cogne. Quand 'l a passé sus l'Grand Guiab', 'l a commencé à brutaliser les ch'vaux: *Whoop! Whoop!* pis la porte 'l a battsu vrigne, vragne. Grand Guiab' 'l a commencé à eurgarder ça, lui. I' pouvait pas s'imaginer dans l'monde quocé ça c'était, quocé ça pouvait ê'. Il a commencé à crier après lui: "Heuye! Heuye! Viens donc icitte."

Whoop! il a arrêté. Il est v'nu jusqu'à lui. I' dzit: "Quocé dans l'monde tsu veux faire avec ça?" I' l'eurconnaissait pas en tout, i' connaissait pas qui c'était. I' dzit: "J'veux voler P'tsit Jean. Il a volé tout ça j'l'avais dans l'monde, pis," i' dzit, "j'veux l'prendre pis l'renfermer là d'dans." I' dzit: "Parle pas, i' m'a volé tout ça j'l'avais aussite, pis m'as t'dzire drètte où il est." —"Et où il est?" i' dzit. I' dzit: "Il est drètte icitte d'l'aut' bord sus le rouè." Là, i' dzit: "Tsu croués ça va l'quiend', ça, P'tsit Jean, Grand Guiab'?" —"Ah, oui," i' dzit, "ça, ça va l'quiend'." —"Tout ça j'ai peur," i' dzit, "il a ein si grand pououère, j'ai peur qu'ça l'quienne pas. Tsu d'vrais ê' aussi fort comme lui. A c't'heure, rent' là d'dans pour vouère si ça va l'quiend'." —"Oh, oui, ça va l'quiend'." —"Ben," i' dzit, "j'voudras ê' certain, monte donc là d'dans pour vouère." 'L a rentré là d'dans, pis 'l a fermè la porte. Après qu'il a eu fermè la porte, i' y'a dzit: "Assaye, touè; tsu d'vrais être aussi fort comme lui." —"Ah!" i' dzit, "ça, va l'quiend', ça, P'tsit Jean." —"T'as pas essayé à moquié assez fort. Essaye donc."

Padent 'l était après assayer l'tomb'reau comme ça, P'tsit Jean s'est chanzé, 'l a ôté sa grande barbe, 'l a eurmis son chapeau, *everything*, pis 'l a s'a eurdressé. Là, P'tsit Jean 'l a avancé làsque c'est i' pouvrait l'vouère. "Ah! P'tsit Jean," i' dzit, "c'est touè, ça?" —"Oui," i' dzit, "c'est moin. Tsu m'as fait passer pour ein voleur, pis j't'ai dzit que j't'aurais volé, pis j't'ai." —"Hé! Hé!" i' dzit, "P'tsit Jean, si j'peux sortsir d'icitte!" —"Oui," i' dzit, "mais j't'ai pis j't'emmène sus l'rouè." Il a eurviré ses ch'vaux, pis i' s'a en allé. Quand 'l a arrivé ein bon boute d'la maisonne, i' a dét'lé ses ch'vaux. Après qu'i' a eu fini d'tout serrer ses ch'vaux, 'l est eurv'nu *beck* au tomb'reau d'fer, pis il a criè au rouè qu'i' vienne vouère quocé 'l avait.

L'rouè 'l est partsi pour v'nir vouère. I' s'avait apporté eune fourche de fer, le rouè. Quand 'l a arrivé à côté dzu tomb'reau, 'l a piqué avec la fourche, pis ça l'a faite "Rreur" dans l'côté dzu tomb'reau, pis l'vieux rouè 'l a eurviré à la course. "Viens donc," i' dzit, "viens donc, beurdache, t'as pas besoin d'avouère peur." I' crouèyait d'avouère dzu plaisir avec ça, pis quand 'l a arrivé *next time*, i' l'a piqué, pis l'Grand Guiab' s'est enwèyé d'l'aut côté "Rrâwe. Rrâwe." L'rouè 'l a eu peur, pis i' s'a sauvé encore. P'tsit Jean a rapp'lé l'rouè qu'i' vienne ouère. "Viens donc, beurdache, t'as pas besoin d'aouère peur, i' peut pas sortsir d'là d'dans." Le rouè 'l est v'nu jusqu'à ras, pis 'l a commencé à eurgarder l' tomb'reau d'fer. "Eh, P'tsit Jean, P'tsit Jean, si tsu voulais m'lâcher, j't'écrirais ein billet qu'tsu m'eurwerrais jamis en face." —"Tsu peux brailler pis crier, mon Grand Guiab', j't'ai oùsque c'est t'as rester l'restant d'tes jours."

7.

Prince White Hog

It's good to tell you that once upon a time there were an old man and an old woman. They had only one son, and they were poor. When the boy grew up and had his twenty-first birthday, he said to his father, "Papa, I'm going to go out and try to get a job, to make some money." His parents didn't want him to go and said to him, "We've done all right up till now. We can keep on the same way." But they couldn't persuade him. He said good-bye and left.

He had been traveling for two or three days and hadn't seen anything on the road or met anyone. But, finally, one day he met an old fairy. She said to him, "Good morning, my son," and he answered politely, "Good morning, Grandmother." Now he was on a good path and could walk along quickly. But she was on a path that was littered with logs and all sorts of brush, and it was hard for her to go forward. She said to him, "My son, would you be willing to change paths with me?" He answered, "Where are you going, Grandmother?" —"I'm going to Paris," she answered. —"Since you're old, Grandmother, I'll change paths with you. I'm young," he said. So then, he was on a bad path and couldn't go forward at all. He had to climb over rocks and logs and all sorts of obstacles. He kept going until finally he got back in the good path again. "Well!" he said. "Here's the good path again. Maybe now I'll be able to make some progress." He had traveled hardly any time at all when he met another old woman. "Good day, my son," she said. —"Good day, Grandmother," he answered politely. "You're old to be out on the road like this." —"Yes, I'm pretty old, but I don't have a good path. Would you be willing to change paths with me, my son?" —"I've already traded paths once," he answered, "and I found myself in a path that was blocked, and I have a long distance to go, too. Where are you going, Grandmother?" —"I'm going to Paris," she answered. —"Well," he said, "since you're so old, I'll change paths with you, too. You're too old to be traveling on such rough paths."

So he traded paths with her and once again found himself on a terrible path. He said, "Well, I'm not trading paths any more, old or not. I have a long way to go, and this is terrible. I can't get ahead at all. There's nothing but logs, rocks, stones, and all kinds of things that I have to climb over. If I ever find the right path, I'm not changing any more with anyone." He kept on walking until he found the good path again. Then he said, "Old women can come along if they want to! I'm on the good path now, and I'm not giving it up again!"

So he started walking along the good path, and after a short time, he met another old fairy. She said, "Good day, my son." —"Good day, Grandmother," he answered politely. "You're old to be walking along the road like this." —"Yes," she answered. "I'm pretty old, and I have a long way to go." —"Where are you going, Grandmother?" —"I'm on my way to Paris," she answered. "My path is hard, and I'm not getting very far. Would you be willing to change paths with me?" —"Well," he said, "I've already changed paths twice, and I have a long way to go too. I said that I wouldn't change paths any more with anyone." —"So, you don't want to trade paths with me, my son?" —"No," he answered, "I don't want to trade with anyone any more, Grandmother." The fairy then said to him, "Well, I'm putting a spell on you. You will be a hog by day, and by night you will be the most beautiful prince anyone has ever seen."

So, there he was in the woods, changed into Prince White Hog. But, at night he turned into the most handsome prince the world had ever seen. He traveled along through the woods, toward his own house. He arrived at his own house, but no one recognized him. One night, he heard his father calling the hogs. He went where his father was feeding the other hogs. "Come and see!" the father called to his wife. "There's this beautiful white hog with the others." The old woman came and looked, and said, "That's the handsomest hog I've ever seen." Then the hog said, "Yes, a handsome hog. He could even be your son." The father said, "What? Is that you, my son, turned into a hog?" —"Yes, it's me," answered the hog. The father answered, "Well, I don't know what we're going to do with you, for sure. We'll have to build a stone pen and put you into it."

So the old man built a stone pen for his son and put him into it. Every day, he came out there to feed him. But one morning, he came out, and he found the stone pen knocked down. "What in the world have you done?" asked the father. "You've knocked down your whole pen!" —"Don't get upset," answered Prince White Hog. "I'm desperate to get married." —"But who would want to marry a hog?" —"Well, you'll have to try to find me a wife." The father went in and told his wife what had happened. She said, "But who would want to marry a hog?" He thought for a moment and said, "Well, my Aunt Blanche has three daughters. Maybe one of them would marry him." —"You don't think Aunt Blanche would let one of her daughters marry a hog, do you?" answered the old woman. But the father just said, "I'll go and see."

So he left to go see. When he got there, he called out, "Hello!" and the old woman came out. "Hello, my son," she said. "Good morning, Aunt," answered Prince White Hog's father. —"Come on in," said the old woman. —"No, I came on business," he answered. "Prince White Hog badly wants a wife this morning. I came to find a wife for him. You don't think one of your daughters would want to marry him, do you?" The Aunt answered, "Who in the world would want to marry a hog?" But her oldest daughter said, "It doesn't matter if he's a hog. I'll go." Her mother said, "Sure! I can just see you married to a hog."

But the girl answered, "I'm going, and you can't stop me!" So she got ready and left with Prince White Hog's father.

When they got back, they had a big wedding feast, and the girl married Prince White Hog. After the dinner, he went out and rooted all around in the mud. His nose got dirty, and then he took it into his head to come and kiss his new wife. She shouted at him, "Go away! Your nose is dirty!" So Prince White Hog turned away and went back out rooting in the mud. That evening, the old man said to the new bride, "Now, you have to go out in his pen and spend the night there with him. That's where he lives." But Prince White Hog was angry with her for turning him away, and he jumped on her and ate her up.

The next morning, the old man came out to bring them their breakfast. He went into the pen and looked around for his son's wife. He looked everywhere he could and then asked, "Where's your wife?" Prince White Hog answered, "Oh, I ate her!" —"Well, you can well be crazy over women, but if you're going to eat them up like that, I can't imagine who else would want to marry you!" said the father. Things went on for quite a while, and the father fed his son every morning. Then one morning, he went out and found the pen knocked down again. He asked his son, "Why in the world did you do that? Your whole pen is knocked down!" —"Don't ask!" answered Prince White Hog. "I need to get married again this morning." The father said, "Well, I don't know who will want to marry you, since you eat up your wives as you do."

But he went back in the house, and told his wife about it, and said, "Aunt Blanche still has two daughters. I guess I might as well go and see her." So he went, and when he got there, he called out, "Hello!" The old woman came out and invited him in. He said, "No, I can't stay. I'm in a hurry. I came on business. Prince White Hog wants to get married again this morning, and I'm looking for a wife for him. You don't think one of your daughters would want to come, do you?" —"Well," she answered, "they'd have to be crazy to go and marry him, just to get themselves eaten up." But the older of her two remaining daughters said, "I'll go!" Her mother answered, "Well, if you're silly enough to go and get eaten up like your sister, go ahead." So the girl got ready and left with the old man. When they got back, she got married to Prince White Hog and had another big wedding feast. After they had eaten, Prince White Hog went out rooting in the mud. he got his nose good and dirty and then decided to come in and kiss his wife. He went up to her and put his feet on her knees to kiss her. "Get out of here with your dirty nose!" she screamed at him. She slapped him and made him leave. So, he turned around and went back out and rooted around until night came. When it got dark, the old man told the new bride that she would have to go out and spend the night with Prince White Hog in the stone pen, because that

Prince White Hog tries to kiss his wife

It's Good to Tell You

was where he lived. But that night, Prince White Hog was angry with his bride. He jumped on her and ate her up.

The next morning, the old man went out to give them their breakfast. He started looking for the young woman, but he couldn't find her. He asked, "Where did your wife go?" Prince White Hog answered, "Well, I killed her and ate her." The father said to him, "Well, if you go on eating all your wives like that, you don't really want a wife!" But Prince White Hog answered, "As long as they're going to treat me like that, slapping me in the face and calling me 'Dirty-Nose' when I go to kiss them, I'm going to kill them and eat them." Things went smoothly for a while, and then one morning again the father went out to feed his son and found the stone pen all knocked down. The father said, "Why in the world did you do this? Your stone pen is all knocked down again!" Prince White Hog told him, "Don't ask! I want to get married again this morning." The father said, "I don't know where you're going to find a wife, since you eat them all up."

But he came back into the house and told his wife that Prince White Hog wanted to get married again. She said, "Well I surely don't know where you're going to find him a wife this time." The old man said, "Well, Aunt Blanche still has one daughter left. I'll go and see her. You never know. She might want to do it." He left to go see his Aunt Blanche, and when he got there, he cried out, "Hello!" The old woman came out and said, "Good day, my son. Come on in and visit." He said, "No, Aunt. I don't have time. I'm in a hurry. I came on business. Prince White Hog really wants to get married this morning, and I'm looking for a wife for him. You don't think that your daughter would mary him, do you?" —"Well, I don't know what she would be thinking," answered the old woman, "to marry a hog, especially one who eats all his wives." But her one remaining daughter said to her, "I want to go, Mama." —"No, you won't go," answered her mother. —"Yes, I am going," she answered.

So, she left with Prince White Hog's father, and they had another big wedding feast. After they had eaten, Prince White Hog did the same thing; he went out rooting in the dirt and got his nose all muddy. Then, he took it into his head to come in and kiss his wife. He came, jumped up into her lap, and put his paws on her. She grabbed him around the neck and kissed him. She caressed him for a while, and then he turned around and went out to root until evening. That evening, the old man said to his new daughter-in-law, "Well, now you'll have to go out and spend the night in the stone pen with him. That's where he lives."

They sat up together until nine o'clock, and then Prince White Hog turned into the most handsome prince the world has ever seen. She was as happy as she could be when she saw this handsome prince with her. But he told her, "You mustn't tell anyone at all about this. If you do tell someone, you will have to wear out a pair of steel shoes and a steel dress before you would find me again." One day, he said to her, "Aren't you a little lonely for your mother? You can go and visit her as much as you would like." So one morning, she said to him, "I think I will go and visit my mother." —"Go ahead," he said. So, she left to go to her mother's house. When she got there, her mother sent for her aunt to have lunch with them. But after they had eaten, at about four o'clock in the afternoon, the girl said, "Now, it's time for me to go back home." —"Is it possible that you would go back to eat dinner with a hog?" asked her mother. They laughed at her and got her angry, and she said, "Yes! He's a hog during the day, but at night he turns into the most handsome prince you've ever laid eyes on."

So Prince White Hog was found out. When the girl thought about what she had said, she ran toward her house as fast as she could. When she got there, she looked everyplace for Prince White Hog and called and called, but she saw that he was gone. She thought of what he had said, that before she could find him again she had to wear out a steel dress and a pair of steel shoes.

So she went to the blacksmith and had him make her a steel dress and a pair of steel shoes, and then she set out traveling. The first evening, she came to the house of an old fairy. The fairy said to her, "I know what you're looking for. If I didn't know so well, I'd eat you up. Your dress isn't very worn yet. Let me see the soles of your shoes. Hm! They're hardly used at all either. You still have a long way to go!" She said, "You're going to stay here with me tonight. But then tomorrow, with my power, you'll go a lot farther, and you'll be able to put a lot of wear on your shoes and your dress."

So the next morning, the girl set out again. She walked all day long, and that evening she came to the house of another fairy. This fairy said to her, "Well, if I didn't know what you are looking for, I'd bite you in two like a grain of salt! Show me your shoes. Your dress isn't too worn out yet." The girl showed her shoes to the old woman. They were getting pretty worn down. "Come on in and spend the night here with me," the old woman said to her. "By my power, your dress and your shoes will be pretty worn out when you get to where you're going tomorrow evening." So the girl stayed the second night with the old woman.

When the time came for her to leave the next morning, the old woman said to her, "By my power, you'll get there tonight. Prince White Hog is staying with a king and is getting ready to get married. I'm going to give you a magic wand. When you get to that king's castle, hire on as a cook. Whatever you have to make, just tap the table with your wand, and wish for the best dinner or supper they've ever had there, and you will have it." Then, the old woman gave the girl a beautiful silk handkerchief. It shone like gold. She said, "The Princess who is going to marry him will want this. There will be a little boy whom that Princess is using as a spy. He'll see everything you do and will tell the Princess about it. She'll send him to you to see if you want to sell her the handkerchief. You are to tell him that you won't sell it, lend it, or give it. She has to earn it. Tell her that if she lets you sleep with the prince that night, she can have it. She'll tell you that you can sleep with

him just for that night. You will be able to talk to Prince White Hog and let him know that you're his wife, and maybe get him back."

Just as the old woman had said, the little boy saw the beautiful silk handkerchief that the girl had. He went and told the Princess about it, that the cook had this beautiful silk handkerchief that shone like gold. She sent him to ask the girl if she would sell it. The little boy went running and said to the girl, "The Princess told me to ask you if you would like to sell that handkerchief." The cook answered, "I won't sell that little handkerchief, or lend it, or give it away. But she can earn it." The little boy ran back to the Princess to tell her what the cook had said. The Princess sent him back to the cook to find out what she would have to do earn the handkerchief.

The little boy came back and asked the cook what would have to be done to win the handkerchief. The cook answered, "If she lets me sleep with the prince tonight, I'll let her have the handkerchief." So that night, the Princess, to get the handkerchief, said to the prince, "You're going to have to sleep with the cook tonight." That night, the cook went in and got ready to sleep with the prince. But the Princess fixed up a cup of opium and said to the little boy, "Bring this to the prince and tell him to drink it so that he'll sleep well." The little boy brought in the drink, and the prince drank it up. No sooner had he drunk the mixture than he fell into a deep sleep. The cook waited for a while, and then finally she started poking and pulling the prince so that she could tell him her story. But she was never able to wake him up.

The next morning, she got up early and went out to make their breakfast. At noon, everyone came in to eat the dinner that the cook had made. The king was proud of her work and boasted about what a good cook she was. Then in the afternoon, the old fairy gave her a golden ball. She began to play with it, throwing it up in the air and catching it. The little boy who was playing spy was still there, and he went to tell the Princess about the beautiful golden ball that the cook was playing with. He said, "You should see that pretty ball that the cook has. It's the most beautiful thing I've ever seen!" The Princess said to him, "Go ask the cook if she would be willing to sell it to me." The little boy ran to the cook and asked her, but the cook said to him, "This ball is not to sell or to lend or to give. It has to be earned." The Princess told the little boy to ask the cook what would have to be done to earn the golden ball. The little boy went running back to the cook to ask her, and she said to him, "Tell the Princess that if she lets me sleep with the prince again tonight, she can have the golden ball." The Princess sent the boy back to the cook to tell her that she could sleep with the prince just one more time, but that she wouldn't sleep with him again after that! The cook gave the ball to the little boy, and he brought it to the Princess.

The three sisters who married Prince White Hog

When nighttime came, the Princess said to Prince White Hog, "You'll have to sleep with the cook again tonight." —"That's fine," he said. But when the time came for them to go to bed, the Princess fixed another glass of opium and sent it to the prince with the little boy. She said, "Here, bring this to the prince and tell him to drink it so that he'll sleep well." No sooner had the prince drunk the mixture than he fell sound asleep. The cook waited awhile. When she thought that everyone in the house must be alseep, she began to talk to him.

The little boy, after he had given the glass of opium to the prince, had hidden himself behind the door. He hadn't gone to bed. The cook began to poke Prince White Hog when he didn't answer. "Are you alseep?" she asked. "Don't you want to talk to me? What's the matter?" she said. "I have only one more night that I can sleep with you, and then, the day after tomorrow, my blood will be shed. You know what you told me, that I would have to wear out a pair of steel shoes and steel dress in order to find you again. Well, I wore them both out, and now you don't want to talk to me!"

The little boy hidden behind the door was listening and heard everything that she said. When she was quiet, the little boy left and went to his own bed. The next morning, the cook got up, and went out, and made breakfast for everyone. At noon, the same thing, she made dinner. After they had all eaten dinner, Prince White Hog said to the Princess, "I'm going to go out and take a nap by the spring, in the shade." The little boy followed him out to talk to him. Prince White Hog wanted the little boy to go away, but he said, "I've got to tell you something. I've got to tell you what the cook was saying to you last night." Then Prince White Hog got up and listened to the little boy. He said, "Well, what was she saying?" —"She said that she could only sleep with you one more night, and then her blood would be shed. She said that she'd used up a pair of steel shoes, and now you didn't want to talk to her." Prince White Hog said to the little boy then, "Go back to the house and don't say a word about this to anyone, do you hear?"

So the little boy went back to the house, and looked through the door, and saw that the cook was playing with a pretty gold ring. He went to tell the Princess about it, and she said, "Go and ask her if she would be willing to sell it to me." He ran to the cook and said, "Would you be willing to sell that pretty gold ring to the Princess?" The cook said, "Tell the Princess that this gold ring is not to be sold, or lent, or given. It has to be earned." The Princess sent him back to the cook to ask how it could be earned.

The little boy came back and asked the cook what would have to be done to earn the ring. She said to him, "Tell the Princess that if she lets me sleep with the prince one more time, she can have it." The Princess said, "Well, tell her that she can sleep with him just this one more time. But she can't do it any more after tonight, because tomorrow is our wedding day." He told this to the cook, and she sent him back to the Princess with the ring.

So, after supper, everyone stayed up until about nine o'clock. At nine o'clock, the Princess told the prince that he would have to sleep with the cook just one more time, but that the next day they would be married. When the prince was getting ready to go to bed, the Princess fixed another glass of opium and sent it in with the little boy. "Here," she said to the boy, "tell the prince to drink this so that he will sleep well." The little boy went in with the drink. The prince took the glass, turned around, and emptied it out behind the bed. When the cook thought that everyone must be asleep in the house, she nudged the prince. "Are you asleep?" she asked. No, he wasn't asleep. The cook asked him, "How come you didn't want to talk to me the other nights when we've slept together?" —"Well, those drinks they were giving me were putting me to sleep," he told her. Then, the cook said, "You remember, you told me that I'd have to wear out a pair of steel shoes and a steel dress before I could find you again?" The prince said, "Don't say any more. Tomorrow, we'll be together again."

The next day, the cook made the wedding feast. With her magic wand, she wished for the best dinner that they had ever had in that house. They were going to get married in the afternoon. When dinner was ready, she told them to come and eat. The king said, "I'd like nothing better than to tell stories before dinner." Everyone said to the old king, "Well, tell yours first, since you're the oldest!" So the old king told his story. Then it was the prince's turn. He said, "If someone brought you a big herd of horses and let you pick one out, and then told you that you could keep the one you had picked, what would you think if they didn't want to give you the one you wanted?" The king said, "That's just like me. If I picked one, I would want to have my first choice. I wouldn't want to let it go."

"Well," said the prince. "That's just like me, too. I would want to have my first choice. I was going to marry your daughter. But that cook is my first wife. She had lost me because she had betrayed me, and she had to wear out a pair of steel shoes and a steel dress before she could find me again. But she's my wife and my first choice. Today, she has found me again. I would like to go back with her." The king said, "Yes, you're right. If she's your wife, you should go back with her." They sent me here to tell you the story. I was all ready to have dinner with them, but they wouldn't let me stay there long enough.

Prince Cochon Blanc

C'est bon d'vous dzire, eune fouès, c'étaient ein vieux pis eune vieille. 'L ontvaient rien qu'ein garçon, pis i' sontaient pauv's, c'monde-là. L'garçon 'l a grossi jusqu'à 'l a attrapé vingt et ein ans. Quand 'l a attrapé vingt et ein ans, 'l a dzit à son p'pa: "M'en vas, p'pa. M'as assayer à attraper eune *djob*, faire d'l'argent." Les vieux i' voulaient pas qu'i' va en toute. "On l'a vi jusqu'à c'theure, on pourra viv' plus loin." I' n'avait pas d'cesse, i' fallait qu'i' va. Il a dzit ayieu, pis il a partsi.

I' nn'avait deux ou trois jours qu'il était après trav'ler. I' vouèyait pas rien, i' rencontrait pas rien au monde. Ane journée, 'l a rencontré eune vieille fée. "Bonjour," a dzit, "mon p'tsit garçon."

—"Bonjour," i' dzit, "ma grand'mère." Il était dans ein bon ch'min, i' pouvait trav'ler ben, pis, elle, alle était dans ein ch'min a pouvait pas trav'ler en toute. I' nn'avait des *logs* pis toutes sortes de choses dans son ch'min. "Mon p'tsit garçon," a dzit, "tsu chang'rais pas de ch'min avec mouè?" —"Oùsque vous va," i' dzit, "ma grand'mère?" A dzit: "J'm'en vas en Paris." I' dzit: "Comme vous l'êtes vieille, vieille, m'as chanzer de ch'min avec vous. J'sus jeune," i' dzit.

Là, i' s'a trouvé dans ein mauvais ch'min: i' pouvait pus avancer en toute, i' fallait qu'i' passe par-dessus des rochers, des pierres, des *logs* pis toutes sortes de choses. Il a marché jusqu'à i' s'a trouvé *beck* dans l'bon ch'min acore. "Quiens," i' dzit, "j'sus dans l'bon ch'min à c't' heure. Teut' ben, j'pourras avancer ein peu." 'L a pas trav'lé auquin temps, il a rencontré encore ane vieille grand'mère. "Bonjour, mon p'tsit garçon." —"Bonjour, ma grand'mère," i' dzit. "Vous l'êtes vieille pour êt' après trav'ler." —"Oui," a dzit, "mon p'tsit garçon, j'sus joliment vieille, pis," a dzit, "j'ai pas d'ch'min. Tsu chang'rais pas de ch'min avec moin, mon p'tsit garçon?" —"J'ai déjà changé eune fouès," i' dzit, "avec eune vieille, pis j'm'ai trouvé dans des ch'mins oùsque j'pouvais pas avancer en toute, pis j'ai loin à aller, moin aussite. Où vous va, ma grand'mère?" —"J'm'en vas en Paris," a dzit, "mon p'tsit garçon." —"Ben," i' dzit, "comme vous l'êtes si vieille, m'as chanzer encore avec vous. Vous l'êtes trop vieille pour trav'ler dans des mauvais ch'mins."

Il a chanzé avec elle, pis i' s'a trouvé dans des mauvais ch'mins. 'L a dzit: "Ah! j'chanz'rai pus d'ch'mins, vieille, pas vieille. J'ai loin à aller, pis c'est terrib', j'peux pus avancer en toute; i' nn'a rien qu'des rochers, des pierres, des *logs* pis toutes sortes de choses, pis i' faut que j'passe par d'ssus ça. Si j'eurtrouve jamais l'bon ch'min, j'changeras pus en toute." À c't'heure, i'a trav'lé jusqu'à i' s'a trouvé dans l'bon ch'min encore. Là, i' dzit: "I' peut v'nir des vieilles, si'i veulent! J'sus dans l'bon ch'min, à c't'heure, j'change pus."

'L a partsi à trav'ler dans l'bon ch'min. 'L a pas été auquin temps, 'l a rencontré eune vieille fée encore. "Bonjour, mon p'tsit garçon." —"Bonjour, ma grand'mère," i' dzit. "Vous l'êtes vieille pour être après trav'ler." —"Oui," a dzit, "mon p'tsit garçon, j'sus vieille, pis j'l'ai loin à aller." —"Oùsque vous va," i' dzit, "ma grand'mère?" A dzit: "J'm'en vas en Paris, pis," a dzit, "j'ai ein mauvais ch'min, j'peux pas avancer. Vous chang'rez pas d'ch'min avec moin," a dzit, "moin p'tsit garçon?" —"Ben," i' dzit, "j'ai déjà changé deux fouès d'ch'min, pis," i' dzit, "j'ai loin à aller, moin aussite. J'ai dzit j'aurais pus changer de ch'min avec personne. J'ai loin à aller, moin aussite." —"Ben," a dzit, "tsu veux pas chanzer d'ch'min avec moin, mon p'tsit garçon?" —"Non," i' dzit, "j'chanze pus d'ch'min avec personne, ma grand'mère." —"Ben," a dzit, "Prince Cochon, j'te souhaite," a dzit, "mon p'tsit garçon, le jour, l'plus beau prince dans la nuit l'monde 'l a jamais vu."

Ça s'fait i' s'a trouvé en Prince Cochon Blanc dans l'bois; dans la nuit, c'était l'plus beau prince l'monde 'l ont jamais vu. Il a trav'lé là d'meume dans l'bois. I' s'en allait d'ssus eux aut's pis i' connaissait pas. Eune souèrée, il a arrivé assez à ras de sus eux aut's i' attendait son père app'ler les cochons. I'a partsi pis il a été oùsqu'il était. L'vieux 'l était après souègner les cochons pis il a arrivé oùsqu'i' étaient les aut's cochons. I' crie après sa vieille qu'a vienne ouère. "Viens donc," i' dzit, "ouère c'beau cochon blanc qu'est avec les cochons." La vieille alle est v'nue pis alle a commencé à l'eurgarder, pis a dzit: "Ça, c'est l'plus beau cochon j'l'ai jamais vu." —"Oui, c'est ben," i' dzit, "ein joli cochon, i' pourrait ben être vot' garçon." L'cochon lui-meume i' dzit ça à son p'pa. —"Eh, quouè," dzit, "c'est touè, mon garçon, qu'es rendzu d'meume?" —"Oui," i' dzit, "c'est moin." —"Ben," i' dzit, "j'connais pas quocé on pourra faire avec touè," i' dzit, "ben sùr. Faudra t'faire eune mur de pierre pis t'mett' dedans."

L'vieux 'l a fait la mur de pierre pis i' l'a mis dedans. Tous les jours, i' l'souègnait là d'dans. I' y'apportait son eau, pis i' la mettait là d'dans. Ane matsinée, 'l a partsi pour aller l'souègner. 'L a tout trouvé la mur de pierre à terre. —"De quouè dans l'monde t'as faite?" i' dzit. "T'as ch'té toute ta mur de pierre à terre." —"Parlez pas," i' dzit, "mon père, j'sus fou pour m'marier." —"Quis qui voudrait marier ein cochon?" i' dzit. —"Ben," i' dzit, "i' faut vous l'assayez m'trouver eune fomme." Il a partsi, pis 'l a été trouver sa vieille, pis i' y'a conté ça. A dzit: "Quis qui voudrait marier ein cochon?" a dzit. —"Ben," i' dzit, "ma tante La Blanche alle a trois filles," i' dzit. "I' en aurait teut' ben ane qui l'marierait." —"Ah!" a dzit, "tsu crouèrais pas ma tante La Blanche a rest'rait ses filles s'marier avec ein cochon?" —"J'vas aller ouère," i' dzit.

Il a partsi pis 'l a été ouère. Il a arrivé, il a crié: "Allô!" La vieille alle a sortsi. "Beaujour, mon p'tsit garçon," a dzit. —"Beaujour, ma tante." —"Rent' donc," a dzit, "mon p'tsit garçon." —"Non," i; dzit, "j'sus v'nu par affaire." I' dzit: "L'Prince Cochon Blanc 'l est fou pour s'marier à matin. J'sus après y charcer eune femme. Vous crouè pas i' n'a ane d'vos filles qui voudrait l'marier?" A dzit: "Quis qui s'marier avec ein cochon?" La plus vieille a dzit: "Ça peut être ein cochon, si ça veut, moin, j'y vas." —"Oh! oui," a dzit, "j'pense t'as aller t'marier avec ein cochon!" —"Oui," a dzit, "j'vas, vous peut pas m'empêcher." A s'est préparée, pis alle a partsi avec le vieux.

Quand 'l ont arrivé, 'l ont fait des grosses noces, i' s'ont mariés Après dzîner, lui, 'l a partsi pis i' s'a en allé dehors fouiller d'ein bord d'l'aut'. Il a ben sali son nez, pis i' y'a pris idée de v'nir embrasser sa femme. "Va-t'en là-bas," a dzit, "nez sale!" pis a y'a emm'né ane tape, pis alle a pas voulu l'embrasser. Il a eurviré d'bord, pis i' s'a rentourné fouiller, pis, l'souère, l'vieux, lui, i'a dzit: "I' faudra t'renfermer dans l'mur de pierre avec lui; c'est là i' reste." Ça s'fait à la veillée i'ètait fâché cont' elle. I'a sauté d'ssus pis i' l'a mangée.

L'lend'main matin, l'vieux 'l a partsi pour aller leu-z-emporter à déjeuner. Il a arrivé là, pis i'a commencé à eurgarder pour sa femme là d'dans, d'ein bord d'l'aut', pis i' la vouèyait pas. "Oùsqu'alle est vot' femme?" i' dzit. —"Oh!" i' dzit, "j'l'ai mangée." —"Tsu peux ben êt' fou pour des femmes, si tsu les manges d'meume, j'sais pas qui c'est voudra t'marier davantage!" Ça s'est passé queud' temps d'meume. Tous les matins, i' allait y 'porter son manger. Eune matsinée, 'l a arrivé, 'l a tout trouvé la mur de pierre à terre encore. —"Dans l'monde," i' dzit, "quocé t'as faite? T'as tout fouillé la mur de pierre à terre." —"Parlez pas," i' dzit, "j'sus fou pour m'marier encore à matin." —"Ben," i' dzit, "j'connais pas qui c'est qui voudra t'marier, si tsu manges tes femmes d'meume."

Il est eurv'nu, pis i' y'a dzit ça à sa vieille. Prince Cochon Blanc 'l était fou pour s'marier encore. "Ben," i' dzit, "ma tante La Blanche alle a encore deux filles, pis j'vas aller la ouère." Il a arrivé, il a crié: "Allô!" La vieille alle a sortsi. "Rent' donc," a dzit, "mon p'tsit garçon." —"Non," i' dzit, "ma tante, j'ai pas d'temps." —"T'es ben pressé?" a dzit. —"Oui," i' dzit, "j'sus pressé, j'sus v'nu," i' dzit, "par affaire." I' dzit: "Prince Cochon Blanc 'l est fou pour s'marier à matin, pis," i' dzit, "j'sus après y charcer eune femme. Vous crouè pas," i' dzit, "i' nn'a eune d'vos filles qui viendrait?" —"Ah!" a dzit, "i' faudrait qu'i' souèyent bêtes pour aller s'marier avec lui d'meume pis s'faire manger." La plus vieille a dzit: "Moin, j'vas." —"Ben, a dzit, "si t'es assez bête pour aller t'faire manger touè aussite, vas-y donc." A s'est préparée, pis alle a partsi avec le vieux. Il[s] ont arrivé, elle pis Prince Cochon Blanc, i' s'ont mariés, pis il[s] ont fait des grosses noces encore. Après qu'l'a eu dzîné, 'l a partsi pour aller fouiller d'ein bord d'l'aut' dans la terre, dans la boue. Il a ben sali son nez pis i' y'a pris idée d'v'nir embrasser sa femme. 'L a v'nu, pis i'a sauté ses pattes sus ses g'noux pour l'embrasser. "Vat'en," a dzit, "nez sale!" A y'a donné eune tape, pis a l'a faite eurvirer. 'L a eurviré d'bord, i' s'a en allé fouiller d'ein bord de l'aut' jusqu'à l'souère. Quand ça l'a arrivé l'souère, l'vieux y'a dzit i' fallait qu'a s'en va avec lui dans la mur de pierre; c'est là i' restait et c'est là i' les aurait souègnés. 'L a partsi, pis 'l a été les mett' dans la mur de pierre. L'souère dans la veillée, 'l était fâché après elle. 'L a sauté d'ssus, pis i' l'a mangée.

It's Good to Tell You

L'lend'main matin, l'vieux 'l a partsi pour aller leu porter l'déjeuner. 'L a commencé à charcer sa femme, pis i' pouvait pas la trouver. "Oùsqu'alle est vot' femme?" i' dzit. —"Ah!" i' dzit, "j'lai tsuée, pis j'l'ai mangée," i' dzit. —"Ben," i' dzit, "si tsu manges toutes tes femmes d'meume, tsu n'en veux pas d'femmes." —"Tant qu'i' vont m'traiter comme ça, m'donner des tapes, pis m'app'ler nez sale quand j'veux les embrasser," i' dzit, "j'vas les tsuer pis les manger." Ça s'est passé queud's jours de meume. Eune matsinée, l'vieux i' va pour l'souègner. La mur de pierre alle était tou[t] à terre. "Quoice qu'dans l'monde t'as faite?" i' dzit. "T'as j'té tout ta mur de pierre à terre hier au souère." —"Ah!" i' dzit, "parlez pas, mon père. J'sus fou pour m'marier encore à matin." —"Ben," i' dzit, "moin, j'connais pas oùsque c'est on pourra t'trouver des femmes, si tsu les manges toutes de meume."

Il est eurv'nu, pis 'l a conté ça à sa vieille. Prince Cochon Blanc 'l était fou pour s'marier. "Ben," a dzit, "moin, j'connais pas oùsque c'est tsu pourras y trouver eune femme c'coup-là." —"Ben," i' dzit, "ma tante La Blanche en a encore eune fille. J'vas aller ouère; teut' ben qu'si a viendrait. Il a partsi, pis il a été trouver ma tante La Blanche. I' y'a crié: "Allô!" La vieille alle a sortsi. "Beaujour," a dzit, "mon p'tsit garçon." —"Beaujour, ma tante," i' dzit. —"Rent' donc," a dzit. —"Non," I' dzit, "ma tante, j'ai pas l'temps. J'sus pressé, j'sus v'nu par affaire." I' dzit: "Prince Cochon Blanc 'l est fou, fou, pour s'marier à matin, pis j'sieus après y charcer eune femme." I' dzit: "Vous crouè pas vot' fille a l'marierait?" —"J'vouès pas quoice que c'est a pens'rait, aller s'marier avec ein cochon, pis i' mange toutes ses femmes." La ceule des filles qui restait a dzit: "M'man, moin, j'vas." —"Non," a dzit, "tsu iras pas." —"Oui," a dzit, "j'me prépare, pis j'vas aller avec lui."

Alle a partsi, alle a été avec lui, pis il[s] ont faite des grosses noces encore. Après qu'il[s] ont eu dzîné, 'l a faite la même chose; il a partsi fouiller d'ein bord de l'autre, pis 'l a ben sali son nez. I' y'a pris idée de v'nir embrasser sa femme encore. I'a v'nu, pis i'a sauté sus ses g'noux avec ses pattes encore pour l'embrasser. Alle l'a attrapé par l'cou, pis a l'a embrassé. A l'a caressé ein bout d'temps, pis i' s'a eurviré d'bord, pis i' s'a en allé fouiller jusqu'à l'souère. Quand ça l'a arrivé l'souère, l'vieux y'a dzit à la femme d'Prince Cochon Blanc: "Ben, i' faudrait qu'tsu ailles là dans la mur de pierre avec lui; c'est là i' reste."

Ça s'fait 'l ont veillé jusqu'à neuf heures. Après neuf heures, i' s'a trouvé l'plus beau prince avec elle alle avait jamais vu. Ah! a était aussi fièr'te comme a pouvait êt quand alle a vu c'beau prince avec elle. I' y'a dzit: "I' faut pas tsu dzises rien d'ça à personne. Si tsu l'dzis à queuques-ane, i' faudra qu'tsu uses eune paire de souliers d'acier pis eune robe d'acier avant qu'tsu m'eurtrouves." Ane journée, i' dzit à 'helle: "Tsu t'ennuies pas d'ta m'man? Va t'prom'ner tant tsu voudras." Eune matsinée, a dzit à lui: "J'pense j'vas aller ouère ma m'man." —"Oui," i' dzit, "vas-y." Alle a partsi, alle a été sus sa m'man. Quand alle a arrivé, la vieille l'a envouèyée qu'ri sa tante pour qu'a vienne dzîner avec eux aut's. Alle a resté jusqu'à quatre heures dans l'après-midzi. Là, a dzit: "I' faudra que j'm'en eurtourne à c't'heure." La vieille a dzit: "Pas possib', tsu t'en eurtourn'ras pas dzîner avec ein cochon?" I' ont ri d'elle, i' l'ont ben fait fâcher. "Oui," a dzit, "c'est ein cochon dans l'jour, mais," a dzit, "si vous le ouèriez la nuit," a dzit, "c'est l'plus beau prince vous l'a jamais mis les yeux dessus."

Prince Cochon Blanc s'a trouvé découvert. D'abord, alle a partsi pour aller sus eux aut's, alle a pensé à quocé alle avait dzit. Alle a partsi à la course aussi fort, aussi fort comme a pouvait pour aller sus eux aut's. Quand alle a arrivé sus eux aut's, alle a eurgardé pour lui, pis alle a commencé à l'app'ler, à l'app'ler. A le ouèyait pus, il était *gonne*. Alle a pensé là à quocé 'l avait dzit. Alle a dzit:

"Prince White Hog"

"J'connais quocé i' m'a dzit i' faudrait que j'faise avant que j'l'eurtrouve, i' faudrait qu'j'use eune paire d'souliers d'acier pis eune robe d'acier."

Ça s'fait alle a été à la forge, pis alle a fait faire ses souliers pis sa robe. Alle a partsi, après, à trav'ler. La première souèrée, alle a arrivé sus ane vieille fée. A dzit: "J'connais quocé tsu charces." A dzit: "Si j'connaissais pas quocé tsu charces comme j'connais, j'te mang'rais. Ta robe alle est pas ben usée encore," a dzit. "Ben, laisse-moin ouère tes s'melles d'souyers," a dzit. "Hm!" a dzit, "i' sont pas usées boucoup encore. T'as loin à aller encore," a dzit. "T'as coucher icitte avec moin, à souère; d'main," a dzit, "par mon pouwère, tsu vas aller joliment plus loin, pis tes souliers vont êt' joliment plus usés pis ta robe."

L'lend'main matin, alle a partsi à trav'ler. Alle a trav'lé tout la sainte grand journée. L'souère, alle a arrivé sus ein aut' vieille fée encore. A y'a dzit: "Eh! si j'connaissais pas quocé tsu charces comme j'connais, j'te croqu'rais comme ein grain d'sel, mais j'connais c'est Prince Cochon Blanc qu'tsu charces." A dzit: "Restez-moin ouère tes souyers; vot' robe alle est pas ein tas usée." A y'a montré ses s'melles de souyers. I' sontaient après s'user joliment ben. "T'as rentrer, pis t'as coucher avec moin," a dzit. "Par mon pouwère, ta robe pis tes souyers i' vont êt' joliment ben usés oùsque c'est tsu vas arriver d'main au souère." Alle a couché là souèrée-là.

Quand alle est v'nue pour partsir, l'lend'main matin, a y'a dzit: "Par mon pouwère, tsu vas êt' là à souère, pis, " a dzit, "Prince Cochon Blanc il est sus ein rouè; il est pour s'marier," a dzit. "J'vas t'donner eune p'tsite baïonnette. T'as arriver là," a dzit, "pis tsu vas t'engager pour eune quisinière. Tout ça tsu vas aouère à faire, ien qu'cogner sus la tab' pis souhaiter l'meilleur dzîner ou souper qu'i' a jamais été dans quisine-là, pis t'as l'aouère." A y'a donné ein beau, beau mouchouère de souè; i' *shaïnait* comme d'l'or, son mouchouère. A dzit: "La princesse qu'est pour l'marier a l'voudra. I' nn'aura ein p'tsit garçon qui est à l'entour. I' va êt' après espionner; i' va tout vouère pis i' va tout y rapporter ça à la princesse." A dzit: "A va enwèyer l'p'tsit garçon ouère pour qu'tsu l'vendes. Dzis-li 'l est pas à vend', ni à préter, ni à donner, i'est à gagner. A va t'envouèyer d'mander comment c'est faire pour le gagner. Dzi[s]-y si a t'laisse à coucher avec l'p'tsit prince le souère a pourra l'aouère. A va t'dzire tsu peux coucher à souère mais pas d'main au souère." A dzit: "Tsu pourras y parler à Prince Cochon Blanc pis y laisser acconaît' qu't'es sa femme, pis tsu pourras le raouère p'tête d'meume."

Comme de faite, la p'tsit garçon 'l a vu l'beau mouchouère de souè qu'alle avait. I' est partsi, pis i' est allé dzire à la princesse comme c'était ein beau mouchouère la quisinière alle avait; i' *shaïnait* comme d'l'or. A l'a enwèyé d'mander si a voulait l'vend'. L'p'tsit garçon est partsi à la course, pis i' y'a dzit: "La p'tsite princesse a fait d'mander si tsu voudrais vend' c'p'tsit mouchouère-là." La quisinière alle a répond: "Mon p'tsit mouchouère il est pas à vend', ni à préter, ni à donner; i' faut l'gagner." Le p'tsit garçon 'l est eurtonurné a la princesse, pis i' y'a dzit le p'tsit mouchouère 'l était pas à vend' ni à préter, ni à donner, i' fallait l'gagner." A y'a dzit: "Ben, à c't'heure, va y d'mander quocé i' faudrait faire pour le gagner."

L'p'tsit garçon a été trouver la quisinière, pis i' y'a d'mandé comment c'est faire pour gagner l'p'tsit mouchouère. Alle a répond: "Si a m'laisse coucher avec l'p'tsit prince à souère, j'y donn'ras l'mouchouère." L'souère, la princesse, pour aouère l'mouchouère, a y'a dzit au p'tsit prince: "I' faudra qu'tsu couches avec la p'tsite quisinière." L'souère, quand i' sont v'nus pour s'coucher, alle a été pis a leu-z-a arrangé ein lite, pis i' s'a couché avec 'helle. Tout d'suite, après qu'i'ont été couchés, la princesse alle a faite arranger ein gob'let d'opium pis a y'a dzit au p'tsit garçon: "Quiens, va y porter ça au prince, pis dzi[s]-y qu'i' l'bouève, ça va l'faire dormir ben, ça." Quand le p'tsit garçon est v'nu avec, lui, i' l'a pris, pis i' l'a bu. Il a pas eu plusse que bu, il a tombé endormi. 'Helle, alle a attendzu ein bout d'temps, pis alle a commencé après lui pour assayer à y conter son histouère. Alle a jamais pu l'réveiller, alle a jamais pu y parler.

L'lend'main matin, a s'a réveillée d'bon matin, pis alle a sortsi pour aller faire à déjeuner. L'midzi, alle a fait son dzîner, pis i' sont tou[s] v'nus dzîner. Comme l'rouè i' la vantait! comme c'était eune bonne *couque!* Là, dans l'après-midzi, la vieille fée a y'avait donné eune boule d'or. Alle a commencé à jouer, alle a commencé à la j'ter en haut, pis l'p'tsit garçon était espionneur, i'était toujours là. I' a été dzire à la princesse comme c'était eune belle boule d'or la quisinière alle était après jouer avec. I' y'a dzit: "Tsu devrais ouère la p'tsite boule d'or la quisinière alle est après jouer avec, la plus belle d'or j'l'ai jamais vue. Alle l'enwèye en haut pis a la rattrape." La princesse a dzit: "Va y d'mander si a veut la vend'." L'p'tsit garçon 'l a partsi à la course, pis i' y'a dzit: "La p'tsit princesse a fait d'mander si tsu voudrais vend' c'p'tsite boule d'or-là." —"Alle est pas à vend', ni à prêter, ni à donner; i' faut la gagner."

L'p'tsit garçon 'l est eurtourné à la princesse, pis i' y'a dzit la p'tsit boule d'or alle était pas à vend', ni à prêter, ni à donner, i' fallait la gagner. A y'a dzit: "Ben, à c't'heure, va y d'mander comment faire pour la gagner." L'p'tsit garçon 'l a partsi, 'l est allé trouver la quisinière, pis i' y'a dzit: "La p'tsite princesse a fait d'mander comment i' fallait qu'a faise pour gagner la p'tsite boule d'or vous l'avez." Alle a répond: "Si a m'laisse coucher avec l'p'tsit prince encore à souère, a pourra l'aouère." Taleure, la princesse a renwèyé l'p'tsit garçon y dzire qu'a pourrait coucher avec, c'souère-là, mais qu'a couch'rait pas l'lend'main au souère, a gageait! Ça s'fait a y'a donné la boule. L'p'tsit garçon 'l a partsi pis 'l a été la porter à la princesse.

Quand ça l'a arrivé l'souère, la princesse a dzit à Prince Cochon Blanc: "I' faudra tsu couches encore avec la quisinière à souère." —"C'est bon," i' dzit. Quand 'l ont partsi pour aller s'coucher, la princesse a y'a arrangé son gob'let d'opium, pis a y'a envouèyé porter par l'p'tsit garçon. "Quiens," a dzit, "va y porter ça, pis dzis-yi qu'i' l'bouève; ça va l'faire eurposer ben." L'p'tsit garçon 'l est partsi, pis 'l a été. "Quiens," i' dzit, "la p'tsite princesse a t'envouèye ein gob'let. A dzit qu'ça t'eurpos'rait ben pis t'aurais ben dormi." I' l'a pas eu plusse que bu, i'a été endormi. 'Helle, alle a attendzu ein bout d'temps. Après qu'a pensait i' dormaient tou[s], alle a commencé à y parler.

L'p'tsit garçon, lui, après qu'i' a eu eurviré d'bord après qu'i' y'a eu donné son gob'let d'or, i' s'a caché derrière la porte; i' a pas été s'coucher. La quisinière 'l a commencé à pousser Prince Cochon Blanc encore quand i' y'a pas répond. "Tsu dors?" a dzit, "tsu veux pas m'parler ou ben quouè?" A dzit: "J'ai pus ien qu'eune souèrée à coucher avec touè, pis si tsu m'parles pas, tsu vas baingner dans mon sang après-d'main au matin. Tsu connais quocé tsu m'avais dzit, qu'i' aurait fallu qu'j'use eune robe d'acier pis eune paire d'souliers d'acier avant que j't'eurtrouve. Ben, j'ai usé eune paire d'souyers d'acier pis eune robe d'acier, pis tsu veux pas m'parler à c't'heure."

L'p'tsit garçon, lui, 'l était après écouter. I' était caché derrière la porte I' attendait tout ça quocé a dzisait. Après qu'alle a eu fini d'charrer, p'tsit garçon-là 'l a partsi, pis 'l a été s'coucher. L'lend'main matin, la quisinière a s'a l'vée, alle a sortsi, pis alle a fait son déjeuner. Il[s] ont tou[s] déjeuné. L'midzi, la meume chose, alle a fait son dzîner, pis il[s] ont dzîné. Après qu'l'ont eu dzîné, Prince Cochon Blanc 'l a dzit à la p'tsite princesse: "M'as aller m'coucher à la p'tsite fotaine sous la grosse ombrage, m'as dormir ein somme."

Ça fait l'p'tsit garçon 'l a été l'trouver pis commencer à charrer avec lui. I' voulait l'renwèyer, i' voulait qu'i' s'en va. "J'ai queud' chose à t'conter. J'veux t'dzire quocé la quisinière alle avait à dzire." I' s'est l'vé assis, pis i' a commencé à charrer avec l'p'tsit garçon. "Ben," i' dzit, "quocé alle a dzit?" —"Alle a dzit qu'alle avait ien qu'eune souèrée à coucher avec touè, pis si tsu y parlais pas, tsu baingn'rais dans son sang, qu'alle avait usé eune paire d'souliers d'acier, pis tsu voulais pas y parler." I' dzit au p'tsit garçon, lui: "Rentourne-touè, pis dzis pas rien d'ça à personne, t'attends."

Là, 'l a partsi pis 'l a eurgardé en travers la porte, pis 'l a vu qu'alle était après jouer avec eune belle bague d'or. 'L a couru en haut pis 'l a conté ça à la princesse, quelle belle bague d'or la p'tsit quisinière alle était après jouer avec. "Va y d'mander si a veut la vend'," a y'a dzit. 'L a partsi à la course pis i' y'a d'mandé si a d'mandé si a voulait vend' belle bague d'or-là. Alle a répond qu'non, c'te bague d'or alle était pas à vend', ni à prêter, ni à donner, alle était à gagner, elle aussite. L'p'tsit garçon 'l a couru, pis i' y'a dzit à la princesse qu'alle était pas à vend', ni à prêter, ni à donner, alle était à gagner. A dzit: "Va y d'mander comment c'est faire pour la gagner."

'L a partsi pis 'l a été y d'mander comment c'était faire pour la gagner. La quisinière a dzit: "Dzis-yi qu'si a m'laisse coucher encore avec l'p'tsit prince à souère a peut l'aouère." L'p'tsit garçon 'l a partsi, pis i' y'a dzit ça qu'si a la laissait coucher avec l'p'tsit prince a pourrait l'avouère. "Ben," a dzit, "va y dzire qu'a peut coucher avec, à souère, mais pas d'main au souère, parce que, demain, on s'marie." I'a été y dzire ça. Alle a pris la bague d'or, pis a y'a enwèyée. L'lend'main, i' s'mariaient, a dzit.

Ça s'fait, après qu'i' ont eu soupé, i'ont veillé jusqu'à neuf heures. Quand neuf heures 'l a arrivé, alle a dzit au p'tsit prince i' fallait qu'i' va coucher avec la quisinière encore c'souère-là, pis l'lend'main i' s'auraient mariés. Après qu'i' ont été couchés, la princesse a arrangé son gob'let d'opium, pis y'a enwèyé porter par le p'tsit garçon. "Quiens," a dzit, "dzi[s]-y qu'i' bouève ça, i' va ben s'eurposer, i' va ben dormir." L'p'tsit garçon 'l a arrivé avec. Lui, 'l a pris l'gob'let, i' s'a eurviré d'bord, pis i' l'a vidé derrière la couchette; i' l'a pas bu. Après alle a pensé qu'i' étaient tou[s] endormis, alle l'a poussé, elle, pis a y'a d'mandé si i' dormait. —Non, i' dormait pas. A dzit: "Comment ça s'fait tous les aut's souères qu't'as couché avec moin, tsu voulais pas m'parler?" —"Ben," i' dzit, "ça i' m'donnaient, ça m'faisait dormir." —"A c't'heure," a dzit, "tsu connais ça tsu m'avais dzit qu'i' fallait qu'j'use eune robe d'acier pis eune paire d'souliers d'acier avant que j't'eurtrouve." I' dzit à 'helle: "Dzis pas rien, on va s'trouver ensemb' d'main."

L'lend'main c'est encore elle qu'a fait l'dzîner d'noces. Avec sa baïonnette, alle a souhaité l'meilleur dzîner qu'i' s'avait jamais trouvé dans c'cuisine-là pour dzîner. Sontaient pour s'marier rien qu'dans l'après-midzi. Quand l'dzîner 'l a été paré, a leu-z-a dzit qu'i' viennent dzîner. I'ont rentré là d'dans, i' s'ont tou[s] mis à la tab' pour dzîner. L'vieux rouè 'l a dzit: "I' nn'aurait rien d'plus joli qu'chaquin conter ein histouère avant d'dzîner. Oh! oui," i' dzit. I' ont dzit au vieux rouè: "Conte la quienne avant, t'es l'plus vieux." L'vieux rouè i'a commencé, il a conté son histouère.

Après, l'rouè a dzit au p'tsit prince: "Conte la quienne à c't'heure." —"Ben," i' dzit, "si queud's-ane vous emm'nait eune grande bande de ch'vaux pis s'i' vous quittait en chouèsir, pis i' vous dzisait qu'vous peut les garder ch'vaux-là, eh ben! quocé vous dzirait si, après qu'vous l'aurez eu chouèsi vos ch'vaux, i' voulait pas vous les donner?" —"Ben," le rouè i' dzit, "ça s'rait jusse comme moin, quand j'auras eu chouèsi, j'aim'rais d'avouère le premier choué tout l'temps, j'voudras pas l'laisser aller."

"Ben," i' dzit, "c'est jusse comme moin aussite. J'aim'rais d'avouère l'premier choué, et pis," i' dzit, "j'étais pour marier vot' fille, mais ça, c'est ma femme, la p'tsite quisinière. Alle m'avait perdzu parce qu'a m'avait trahi, pis i'a fallu qu'a use eune robe d'acier pis eune paire d'souyers d'acier avant qu'a m'eurtrouve. C'est ma femme, c'est mon premier choué," i' dzit. "Aujourdz'hui, a m'a eurtrouvé. J'aim'rais m'rentourner avec 'helle." L'vieux rouè i' dzit: "Oui, vous l'est ben. Si c'est vot' femme, rentournez-vous avec." I' m'ont envouèyé conter ça icitte. J'étais paré à dzîner avec eux aut's, mais i' ont pas voulu que j'reste.

8.

The Little Boat That Could Sail on Land and on Sea

It's good to tell you that once upon a time there were an old man and an old woman, who had three sons. The old king had said that anyone who could make a boat that would sail on land and on sea would have his daughter in marriage. The oldest of the couple's three sons said to his mother, "I'm going to try to make one of those." He made some biscuits for himself in the ashes and went on his way. When he got into the woods, he met an old Grandmother. She said, "Good day, little boy." He answered, "Hello, old witch." —"Where are you going, little boy?" she asked. —"It's none of your business," said the boy. "I'm just going out to make wooden plates." The old woman answered, "Well, then, wooden plates is what I wish for you." The boy arrived in the woods and began to cut down some trees. But all of the chips that he got changed immediately into wooden plates. He chopped until around noontime, but all he had for his efforts was a pile of wooden dishes. So finally, he tucked one or two of his wooden dishes under his arm and left. When he got home, his mother asked him what he had gotten done. "I made some wooden dishes," he answered.

Then the second of the three brothers said, "I'm going to go out and try to make the boat tomorrow morning." The next morning, he fixed his little lunch and left as the first one had. When he got into the woods, he too met the old Grandmother. She said to him, "Good morning, little boy." But he answered, "Hello, you old hag!" —"Where are you going, little boy?" asked the Grandmother. —"I'm going out to make some wooden spoons," he answered. —"Well, wooden spoons is what I wish for you," she said. He got into the woods and began to chop down trees, but everything that he chopped turned right away into wooden spoons. After a while, he got tired of making all those wooden spoons. He took two or three of them and brought them to his mother and said, "Here's what I made today." The next morning, the youngest son said that he was going to go out and try too. He said, "But I don't know what I'll end up making." The next morning, he fixed his little lunch and left. He met the old Grandmother, too. She said to him, "Good morning, little boy." He answered, "Good morning, Grandmother." Then, she asked, "Don't you have any biscuits that you could let me have?" —"Ah!" he answered. "I do have some, Grandmother, but they are so unappetizing that I'm kind of ashamed to give them to you. I made them myself in the ashes this morning." He got out his little sack, and the old

The three brothers

It's Good to Tell You

Grandmother took a piece of one biscuit. The youngest son said, "But take a whole one, Grandmother!" —"Oh, no," she said, "I just wanted to see what you would do. Where are you off to, little boy?" —"Well, I'm going to try to make a ship that can go on land and on sea." —"Well, that's what I wish for you," she answered, "a ship that will go on land and on sea. You'll have it all made before the sun goes down."

All the trees that Little John cut down were already hewn, notched, and put in their place. Around three o'clock, Little John began to look at this ship. "I think it's done," he said. "I don't see anything left to do on it." The old Grandmother arrived where he was, while he was looking at his ship. "Have you finished, Little John?" she asked. —"I don't see anything else that it needs, Grandmother," he answered. She said, "All it needs now are the sails. We can't finish those tonight," she said. "Go and collect all the old rags you can find in the town," she told Little John. "Put as many as you can carry on your back and bring them here. Tomorrow morning I'll come back to help you finish your ship."

So the next morning, Little John brought all the old rags he could carry on his back. The old Grandmother came back to help him, and they spread the rags out on the ground. She took her little magic wand and touched the rags with it. They all turned into beautiful sails and appeared where they belonged on the ship. The old woman said, "Now, get onto your ship and take on all the men you meet along your way." He went quite a way and met a man who was lying next to a spring. He stopped his ship and asked the man what he was doing there. The man said, "I've drunk up all the water in this spring twice now, and I'm waiting for it to come back again." —"Leave the spring alone," said Little John, "and come with me." —"That's all right with me. I'll be glad to come," said the man. Little John told the man his name, and the man answered, "My name is Bold Drinker."

He went a little farther and saw a man who was licking stones. He said, "What are you doing, friend?" The man answered, "Well, they used to make bread here. These stones were part of an oven seven years ago. I can still taste the bread." —"Well, leave your oven behind," Little John said to him, "and come with me. You might be able to find something better than that." The man said, "My name is Great Eater." They went a little farther and found a man who was blowing across the sea. His cheeks were all puffed out. Little John stopped the boat and asked him, "What are you doing, my friend?" —"I'm turning a mill on the other side of the sea," answered the man. —"Leave your windmill alone and come with me," said Little John. —"I'll be glad to go with you," said the man. "My name is Great Blower."

They went a little farther and came upon a man who was lying down in a field that had just been plowed. "What are you doing, my friend?" asked Little John. —"I'm listening to see if I can hear my oats growing," answered the man. "Leave your oats alone and come with me," Little John said to him. —"It's all the same to me. I'll come with you," answered the man. Then, a little farther on, he met another man who was running behind a rabbit, and this man had millstones tied to his legs, to keep him from running so fast, so that he wouldn't outrun the rabbit. Little John said to him, "What are you doing, good man?" —"Well, I'm trying to catch that rabbit, but I keep running too fast and passing him right by," answered the man. Little John answered, "Well, leave that rabbit be and come with me." —"I'll be glad to go with you," answered the man. "My name is Great Runner."

When they got to the King's house, Little John stopped his ship right on the square in front of his house. He went in to tell the King that he had made the boat that could float on land and on sea and said, "Now will you give me the Princess to marry?" —"No," answered the King. "Not before you find a man who can drink all the liquor I have in my cellar." Little John went back to his ship, angry. Great Drinker asked him, "What's the matter, Little John?" —"Oh, he doesn't want to give me the Princess unless I can find a man who can drink up all the liquor he has in his cellar." —"Well, go tell him that you have found the man. I'll drink up all his old liquor!" So Little John went and told the King that he had found the man. The King said to him, "Bring him here at nine tomorrow morning."

The next morning at nine o'clock, the King had all his barrels of liquor outside in the front yard. Great Drinker began to tap into them. He grabbed them, drank them dry, and then threw the empty barrels away over to the side. When he had drunk the last one, he called to the King to bring him some more. But the King said, "That will be enough for you today." Well, then Little John said to the King, "Now will you give me your daughter to marry?" But the King answered, "Not before you can find me a man who can eat all the food off a table that is set for one hundred persons." Great Eater was standing behind Little John and said, "Well, tell him that you have a man who can do that." Little John said to the King, "I have that man." The King told him, "Bring him here at nine o'clock tomorrow morning."

So the next morning at nine o'clock, the table was all set up. Great Eater ate his way all around that table, and he ate every last crumb. He even ate the tips of the chicken thigh bones. Then he called out to the King, "Bring me some more!" The King answered, "No, that's enough for you today. If that doesn't kill you, we'll do better for you another time." Then, Little John asked the King, "Well, are you going to give me your daughter now?" —"Not before you find me a man who can win her by racing against her," answered the King. "Three miles from here there is a spring. They have to go to the spring to fill their bottles, and the man who will win the Princess has to get back here to the palace before her." Little John said, "I have a man who can run fast." The King answered, "Go get your man."

So Little John came back with Great Runner, and Great Runner and the Princess started their race. Great Runner got to the fountain, filled his bottle of water, and was halfway back before he met the Princess still on her way to the spring. He said to himself, "I think I'll take a little rest," and he lay down. After awhile, Great Eater said to Little John, "Great Runner ought to be back here by now." Great Listener said, "Wait a minute. I'll tell you where he is." He put his ear to the ground and began to listen. "He's lying down asleep. I can hear him snoring. And the Princess has gotten ahead of him." Great Blower said, "Wait a minute. I'll push the Princess back." He puffed up his cheeks and began to blow. The wind got so strong that the Princess had to turn her back to it. It also woke up Great Runner, who looked at the path and saw the Princess's tracks going back to the castle. Great Listener said, "Stop blowing now. He's awake."

In just a few moments, Great Runner had arrived back at the castle. He brought his bottle of water to the old King. It was a long time before the Princess got back too. The King asked her, "What were you doing?" She answered, "Don't ask! I was ahead of him once, but this big wind came up that pushed me halfway back to the spring. That woke up Great Runner who was lying down taking a nap, and he beat me." Then, Little John asked the King, "Well, are you going to give me the Princess now?" —"Yes," answered the King. "I should have given her to you right away. I would have saved my liquor, and all the food that Great Eater devoured. That would have been enough for the wedding feast." So Little John and the Princess got married. Great Drinker, Great Eater, Great Listener, Great Runner, and Great Blower all stayed with Little John and the Princess for the rest of their days.

L'p'tsit bateau qui allait sus mer pis sus terre

C'est bon d'vous dzire eune fouès c'étaient ein vieux pis eune vieille. 'L ontvaient trois garçons. L'vieux rouè avait dzit n'importe qui l'aurait faite ein navire qui allait sus mer pis sus terre i'aurait donné sa princesse en mariage. L'plus vieux des garçons à la vieille dzit: "M'as aller assayer, m'man." I' s'a faite des p'tsites gallettes dans la cenne, pis 'l a partsi sus son ch'min. 'L a arrivé dans l'bois, 'l a rencontré eune vieille grand'mère. A dzit: "Bonjour, mon p'tsit garçon." —"Bonjour," i' dzit, "vieille mille garces!" —"Oùsqu'tsu t'en vas," a dzit, "mon p'tsit garçon?" —"Pas tes affaires," i' dzit, "mais j'm'en vas faire des plats d'bois." —"Plats d'bois, j'te souhaite!" a dzit, "mon p'tsit garçon." 'L a arrivé dans l'bois, pis i'a commencé à bûcher. Tous les écopeaux i' l'vait, ça s'trouvait ein plat d'bois tout faite. 'L a bûche jusqu'à peu près midzi, i' fésait rien qu'des plats d'bois. 'L a pris ein ou deux, les a mis sous son bras, pi 'l a partsi. Arrivé cheux lui, sa mère y'a d'mande quoice qu'il avait faite de ben. —"J'ai fait des plats d'bois," i' dzit.

L'deuxième d'ses enfants i' dzit: "M'as aller assayer d'main matin." L'lend'main matin, il a arrangé son p'tsit dzîner, 'l a partsi comme l'aut'. I'a arrivé dans l'bois, pis i'a rencontré sa vieille grand'mère. "Bonjour, mon p'tsit garçon." I' dzit: "Bonjour, ma vieille mille garces!" —"Oùsqu'tsu t'en vas," a dzit, "mon p'tsit garçon?" —"J'm'en vas faire des micouènes," i' dzit. "Micouènes," a dzit, "j'te souhaite!" 'L a commencé à bûcher, pis tout ça i' bûchait, c'étaient des micouènes. S'a tanné d'faire des micouènes; i'en a pris deux, trois, pis les a 'portées à sa mère. —"T'nez, vous voit quoce j'l'ai faite aujourdz'hui."

L'lend'main matin, l'plus jeune i' dzit: "Moin, m'as aller assayer. J'sais pas quocé j'vas faire, moin." L'lend'main matin, 'l a arrangé son p'tsit dzîner, pis 'l a partsi. Il a rencontré sa vieille grand'mère, lui aussite. "Bonjour, mon p'tsit garçon," a dzit. —"Bonjour, ma grand'mère," i' dzit.

—"Pas de p'tsites galettes à m'donner," a dzit, "mon p'tsit garçon?" —"Ah!" i' dzit, "j'en ai, grand'mère, mais a sont si peu bonnes, j'ai magnière honte d'vous les donner. J'ai fait ça mouè-même dans la cendre à matin." I'a aveindzu son p'tsit sac, pis la vieille grand'mère a en a cassé ein p'tsit morceau d'ane. "Peurnez-en donc tou[t] eune," i' dzit, "ma grand'mère." —"Ah! non," a dzit, "j'voulais ouère justement ton coeur, mon p'tsit garçon. Où qu'tsu t'en vas," a dzit, "mon p'tsit garçon?" —"J'm'en vas essayer à faire ein navire qui va sus mer et sus terre.—" A dzit: "Ein navire qui va sus mer et sus terre, j'te souhaite," a dzit. "Tsu vas l'aouère d'faite avant qu'l'soleil i' s'couche."

Tous les arb's que P'tsit Jean abattait i'étaient équarris, pis mortouèsés, pis mis à leu place. A peu près à trois heures, P'tsit Jean 'l a commencé à eurgarder son navire. "J'crouès bonnement j'l'ai fini' i'a pus rien à faire après." La vieille grand'mère alle a arrivé oùsqu'i' était lui padent 'l était après eurgarder son navire. "T'as fini?" a dzit, "P'tsit Jean." —"J'ouès pus rien qui manque," i' dzit, "ma grand'mère." A dzit: "I' manque pus rien à part qu'les vouèles. On pourra pas rach'ver ça à souère," a dzit, "P'tsit Jean." "Va-t'en," a dzit, "pis va ramasser toutes sortes d'vieux torchons dans la ville. 'Porte tout ça tsu pourras mett' sus ton dos icitte. D'main matin, m'as v'nir t'aider à l'rach'ver."

L'lend'main matin, 'l a porté tous les torchons i' pouvait mett' sus son dos. La vieille grand'mère a v'nu y'aider, pis i' les ont tou[s] ben étendzus. Alle a pris son p'tsit bâton d'magie, alle a cogné sus les torchons, a les a tou[s] eurvirés en beaux ouèles oùsqu'i' appartenaient au navire. "A c't'heure," a dzit, "monte dans ton navire, pis emmène tous les hommes t'as ouère l'long dzu ch'min." 'L a arrivé ein bon boute, 'l a trouvé ein homme qu'était couché au bord d'eune fotaine. I'a arrêté son navire, pis i'a d'mandé quocé i' fésait là. I' dzit: "J'ai bu tout l'eau qu'i' nn'avait dans la fotaine-là deux fouès pis j'sus après attend' qu'a eurvienne encore, qu'a s'remplise." —"Laisse donc ta fotaine tranquille," i' dzit, "pis viens donc avec moin." —"Pas d'dzifférence," i' dzit, "m'as aller." —"Mon nom, c'est 'Tsit Jean," i' dzit. —"Mouè," i' dzit, "c'est Beau Buveur."

Il a été ein p'tsit boute plus loin, pis il a vu ein homme qui était après licher des pierres. I'a dzit: "Quocé tsu fais icitte, vieux?"—"Ben, il[s] ontvaient coutsume d'faire dzu pain; c'était ein vieux four icitte sept ans passés. J'trouve toujours l'goût dzu pain," i' dzit. —"Laisse donc ton vieux four tranquille," i' dzit, "pis viens donc avec moin. Teut' ben, tsu vas trouver queuque chose d'meilleur qu'ça." —I' dzit: "Mon nom, moin, c'est Grand Mangeur." I'a été ein p'tsit boute plus loin, pis i'en a trouvé ein qui était après souffler à travers d'la mer; i'avait ses bajoues tout gonflées. 'L a arrêté, pis i'a d'mandé: "Quoicé tsu fais, mon ami?" —"J'sus après courir ein moulin à vent d'l'aut' côté d'la mer." —"Laisse donc ton moulin à vent tranquille, pis viens donc avec moin." —"Pas d'dzifférence," i' dzit, "m'as aller avec touè. Mon nom," i' dzit, "c'est Beau Souffleur."

Il a marché ein p'tsit boute plus loin, pis il a trouvé ein homme qui était couché dans ein parc qui v'nait d'êt' rabouré. —"Quocé donc tsu fais," i' dzit, "mon ami?" —"J'sus après écouter si j'peux attend' mon aouène l'ver." —"Laisse donc ton aouène tranquille, pis viens donc avec moin." —"Pas d'dzifférence," i' dzit, "m'as aller avec touè." Il a été ein p'tsit boute plus loin, pis 'l a rencontré ein aut' homme; i'était après courir par derrière ein lapin et pis i'amarrait des meules d'moulin après ses jambes à lui pour s'empêcher d'aller si vite, pis i' passait par-d'ssus l'lapin. P'tsit Jean i' dzit: "Quocé qu'tsu fais, mon ami?" —"J'sus après assayer à attraper lapin-là, pis j'passe par-dessus." —"Ah!" i' dzit, "laisse donc lapin-là tranquille, pis viens donc avec moin." —"Ça m'fait pas d'dzifférence. M'as aller avec touè. Mon nom à moin, c'est Beau Coureur."

"The Little Boat That Could Sail on Land and on Sea"

Quand ’l ont arrivé sus l’rouè, ’l a emm’né son navire d’vant sa place d’armes. ’L a été trouver le rouè, i’a dzit qu’il avait faite l’navire qu’i’allait sus mer pis sus terre. “Tsu vas m’donner ta princesse en mariage,” i’ dzit. —“Non,” i’ dzit, “pas avant qu’tsu trouves ein homme qui peut tout bouère la liqueur qu’i’a dans ma cave.” P’tsit Jean i’ s’a rentourné à son navire, bourru, fâché. Beau Buveur y’a d’mandé: “Quocé qu’t’as, P’tsit Jean?” —“Oh!” i’ dzit, “i’ veut pas m’donner sa princesse avant j’peux trouver ein homme qui peut tout bouère la liqueur qu’i’ nn’a dans sa cave.” —“Va donc y dzire qu’tsu l’as; moin, j’vas la bouère,” i’ dzit, “sa vieille liqueur.” I’a été dzire au rouè il avait trouvé son homme. “Emmène-lé,” i’ dzit, “d’main matin à neuf heures.”

L’lend’main matin, à neuf heures, i’ nn’avait tous les barils d’liqueur en dehors d’la cave dans la cour. Beau Buveur i’a commencé à les défoncer; i’ les attrapait, i’ les buvait pis i’ garrochait les barils vides là-bas. Quand il a eu bu l’dernier, i’ nn’a crié au rouè qu’i’ y’en apporte queuques-anes encore. L’rouè i’ dzit: “Ça va t’faire assez pour aujourdz’hui,” —“Ben,” P’tsit Jean i’ dzit, “vous va m’donner vot’ princesse en mariage à c’t’heure.” —“Pas,” i’ dzit, “avant qu’tsu m’trouves ein homme qui peut m’nettèyer eune tab’ qu’est garnie pour cent personnes.” Beau Mangeur i’était planté en errière de P’tsit Jean. “Dzis-yi donc qu’tsu l’as.” I’ dzit au rouè: “J’l’ai votre homme.” —“Amène-lé,” i’ dzit, “à neuf heures d’main matin.”

L’lend’main matin, à neuf heures, la table a était parée. ’L a faite l’tour d’la table, pis l’a nettèyée. I’ mangeait l’boute des ossailles des cuisses de poules. I’a crié au vieux rouè: “ ’Portes-en donc encore ein peu.” —“Non,” i’ dzit, “ça va t’faire pour aujourdz’hui. Si ça t’tsue pas aujourdz’hui, eune aut’ fouès on va t’souègner mieux.” —“Ben,” P’tsit Jean i’ dzit, “vous va m’donner à c’t’heure vot’ princesse en mariage.” —“Pas avant,” i’ dzit, “qu’tsu m’trouves ein homme qui peut la gagner à courir. Trois milles d’icitte, n’a eune fotaine. Faut qu’i’ vonnent à la fotaine emplir leu bouteille, pis i’ faut qu’l’homme qui gagne la princesse eurvienne au palais avant elle.” P’tsit Jean i’ dzit: “J’en ai ane qui peut courir.” L’rouè i’ dzit: “Va qu’ri ton homme.”

Il est eurv’nu avec Beau Coureur, pis ’l ont partsi à la course, Beau Coureur pis la princesse. Beau Coureur ’l a été qu’ri sa bouteille d’eau, lui, pis ’l a rencontré la princesse encore à moquié ch’min; alle était pas rendzue encore à la fotaine. “Ah!” i’ dzit, “j’crouès j’vas m’étend’, pis j’vas m’eurposer ein p’tsit brin.” Taleure, Grand Mangeur i’ dzit: “Beau Coureur i’ devrait être eurvenu.” Beau Ecouteur i’ dzit: “Arrêter, j’vas t’dzire oùsqu’i’ i’est.” ’L a mis son oreille sus la terre, pis i’a commencé à écouter. —“I’est couché après dormir,” i’ dzit. “J’l’attends ronfler, pis,” i’ dzit, “la princesse l’a dépassé.” Beau Souffleur i’ dzit: “Arrête donc, m’as t’la renwèyer, ta princesse.” ’L a commencé à gonfler ses bajoues pis souffler. L’vent ’l est dev’nu assez fort, la princesse a s’a trouvée obligée d’eurvirer son dos au vent. L’vent ’l a réveillé Beau Coureur. ’L a eurgardé dans l’ch’min, pis ’l a vu les pisses d’la princesse; alle était déjà passée. Beau Ecouteur i’ dzit: “Arrête donc d’souffler, il est réveillé.”

Dans ein p’tsit moment d’temps, Beau Coureur était arrivé. ’L a été porter sa bouteille d’eau au vieux rouè. Longtemps après ça, la princesse alle a eursous. L’vieux rouè y’a d’mandé: “Quoi dans l’monde t’as faite?” —“Parlez pas,” a dzit, “j’étais en d’vant d’lui eune fouès, pis i’est v’nu ein vent qui m’a eurpoussée à moquié ch’min en errière. Ça l’a réveillé Beau Coureur qu’i’était étendzu après dormir, pis i’ m’a gagnée.” —“Ben,” P’tsit Jean i’ dzit, “vous va m’donner vot’ princesse?” —“Oui, j’aurais ben dzû la donner tout d’suite, j’aurais sauvé ma liqueur, pis j’aurais ça Grand Mangeur ’l a mangé,” i’ dzit. “Ç’aurait été assez pour les noces,” i’ dzit. Ça fait qu’P’tsit Jean i’ s’est marié avec la princesse. Beau Buveur, Beau Mangeur, Beau Ecouteur, Beau Coureur, Beau Souffleur i’ont tou[s] resté avec P’tsit Jean l’restant d’leus jours.

9.

The Black King, or Fair Ferentine

It's good to tell you that once upon a time there were an old man and an old woman, and they had only one son. These old people ran a store. Their son was getting old enough to help them in the store. One day, his father said to him, "Couldn't you stay in the store while your mother and I go into town to buy some groceries and merchandise? We'll be gone overnight. You could have some friends come and spend the night with you." He gave his son the keys to all the outbuildings there were around the store. When there was no one left around the store, Little John, the son, went around to all the buildings to see what was in there. In one of them, he found a pretty Little Horse. It was hanging from the ceiling by its reins. It was hungry, because it could only grab hold of a piece of hay from time to time. Little John said to the horse, "You're too pitiful like that, I'll cut you down." He cut the reins, and the Little Horse fell back to the ground. Little John fed the horse well.

After a few days, his father and mother came back with lots of merchandise for the store. All the neighbors came in to see what they had brought back. Little John said to himself, "I'll have to try out the Little Horse while they're busy with something else and can't see me." He took his rifle and pretended he was going hunting. He went and saddled up the Little Horse, and they left. When they arrived at the sea, the Little Horse didn't stop but went right over the sea. When they had gotten to the other side, the Little Horse said to Little John, "Well, it's time to take a rest now." Little John was surprised. "What? You can talk, Little Horse?" The Horse answered, "Yes. A horse like me can talk, Little John." Little John asked the Horse, "Where are we going first, my little horse?" —"We're going first to your uncle's place, the Black King," answered the Horse.

After they had rested well, they started out and soon came to a spring. Little John said to his Horse, "I want to drink. You will have to bring me right over by the spring." At the edge of the spring, he found a golden feather. The Little Horse said, "Don't touch that, Little John! If you pick up that feather, you will be swallowed up by the earth." A little way farther, they came to another spring. Here, there was another gold feather, and Little John was about to pick it up when the Horse said, "Don't touch that, Little John. If you pick up that feather, you will sink into the earth." Little John said to himself, "All right, but I bet that if I find another one, I'll take it."

Later on that afternoon, Little John saw another nice spring at some distance away. He left his little horse there and walked to the spring. He had a good drink and picked up the gold feather. Then, he put it into his pocket and came back to the Little Horse. "Ah!" said the Little Horse. "You took the feather, Little John, and you will be punished." — "Well," said Little John, "if I'm going to be punished, I might as well continue on my way for a while, anyway."

He looked up over his head and saw a large eagle, flying and screaming. Looking at the tree, he saw a big snake climbing up toward the eagle's nest. He took his rifle and shot the snake dead. The eagle started flying around Little John, making a loud noise. The Little Horse said to him, "Do you know what the eagle is saying?" Little John answered, "No, I don't. I don't understand eagle language." —"Well," continued the Little Horse, "she's saying that if you ever need her, all you have to do is shout, 'Come to me beautiful eagle,' three times, and she will come help you." —"Well," answered Little John, "if I ever need her, I guess I'll be glad to have her come."

A little farther along, they were traveling along the seacoast, and there was something jumping around on the sand and squeaking. The Horse said to Little John, "Do you know what that little fish is saying, Little John?" —"No," he answered, "I don't understand fish language." —"He's saying that if it is not too much trouble for you to get down and throw him back into the sea, one day he would be glad to be of service to you." So, Little John got off his horse, caught the little fish, and threw it as far into the sea as he could. As Little John was coming back to get on his horse, he heard the fish squeaking at him still. The fish was saying, "Thank you very much, Little John. If you need me, come here to this place and call out three times, 'Come here, O king of the fish!'" —"All right, I'll do that if I ever need you," answered Little John.

So they went on farther down the road and came to a place where there were three giants. Each one was hanging from a branch stuck through his throat. The Little Horse asked, "Do you know what those giants would like you to do, Little John?" —"No," answered Little John. "I can't understand them with those sticks through their throats." —"They're saying that if you would be so kind as to get one of them down, he would be able to get down the other two." —"Wait a minute!" said Little John. "How am I supposed to get them down? They're much too heavy! In any case, I'll need your help, Little Horse. If you set yourself right in front of one of the giants, I'll try to get him down." He did as he said and the freed giant was able to get his two companions unhooked. The first giant said, "Thank you, Little John. When you need me, come to this place and call for the king of the giants, and I will come and help you. If there is ever anything I can do for you, I'll be glad to do it." Little John answered, "Well, that's just fine, King of the Giants."

Little John tosses the fish as far back into the sea as he could.

They went on for another long way and came upon a flock of birds right in the middle of the road. The Little Horse said, "Little John, the king of the birds is marrying off his daughter today, and he wants you to go around the party." —"I'll be glad to do that, Little Horse. In any case, you're the one who'll have to find a path." When they got back on the road after their detour, the king of the birds came flying right up to Little John and said, "Thank you very much for your thoughtfulness. My daughter is getting married today, and it would have been sad to disturb the wedding. If you ever need me, come to this place and call three times for the king of the birds. If there is something that the birds can do for you, we'll be happy to do it."

Then Little John went to the Black King's house. When he got there, the Black King hired him on as a stable hand. The horses began to look good right away, as soon as Little John began to take care of them. The King had some old harnesses, too, that looked shabby. Little John began to clean up the harnesses and oil them. He passed his golden feather over each harness, and they became covered with golden flowers. It was really pretty.

The old Black King was a widower. He went out every week to a different city, looking for another wife. One day, he told Little John to bring his carriage around to the front door, because he was going to go out. When the old King saw his horses, his harness, and his carriage, he didn't recognize them. —"Little John, how in the world did you get my harnesses looking so good?" he asked. Little John answered, "Well, my uncle the king. It's not so hard." The old King walked with a cane. Little John told him, "Give me your cane, and I'll show you." He took the cane and passed his golden feather over it, and it turned into gold. The old King thought the world of Little John.

The King's butler became aware of this and grew jealous. He said to the King one day, "It's really too bad you don't have Fair Ferentine. They say she wants to marry a king." The old King grew interested. "Where is she, this Fair Ferentine?" he asked. —"She's on the other side of the sea," answered the butler. The old King said, "But who can go to the other side of the sea to fetch her?" The old butler answered, "Little John says that he can go and get her." The old King fell in love with just the idea of Fair Ferentine. He said to Little John, "Is it true that you said that you would be able to go and fetch Fair Ferentine?" Little John was surprised and answered, "No, Uncle, I never opened my mouth." —"Well, whether you said it or not," said the old King, "if you don't go get her you will be hanged."

Little John started to cry and went out to find his little horse. The Little Horse asked him what was the matter. —"My uncle the Black King has told me that if I don't go and get Fair Ferentine, he will have me hanged," said Little John. The Horse was sad. "I told you you would get into trouble. Well, go tell the King to give you a bottle of white wine and a loaf of white bread, and we'll go after the princess." After Little John had gotten the wine and bread from the King, he got on his little horse, and they left.

When they got to the sea, the Little Horse kept going just as if he had been on land, and they had soon gotten across. The Horse told Little John, "When we get there, there will be a big ball that evening, and you will be the best dancer there. Tell them that you do dance well, but that your little horse dances even better than you do. They will tell you to come and get me. I'll go and get up on the platform. I'll go around its edge a few times, and then I'll dance. Tell them that I could dance much better yet, if the princess were riding me, behind you. When the princess gets up behind you, you will know what to do."

That evening at the ball, Little John was the best dancer anyone had ever seen. They all began to say how well he danced, but he told them that his little horse danced much better yet than he did. —"Go get him, then," they said to him. When the Little Horse danced around the platform with Little John on his back, everyone was amazed at how well he danced, and the princess admired him like everyone else. "Ah," said Little John. "But he would dance much better yet if the princess would get on behind me." The princess got on the Little Horse behind Little John, and the Horse galloped away as fast as he could.

When they got to the middle of the ocean, Fair Ferentine took her house keys and threw them into the water. She said, "The man who wants to marry me will have to come and get that bunch of keys." They got to the King's house, and he was waiting at the gate. He was so happy! He asked the princess to marry him. —"Yes," she answered, "but not before my castle is sitting right here next to your house." The old King got angry. "Well, why don't you just say that you don't want to get married? Who in the world can bring your castle here right next to my house?" The butler went in and told the King that Little John had been to get the princess, and that he was bragging that he could also go and get her castle. So the King called in Little John. "I hear you were bragging that you could go and get the princess's castle," he said to him. Little John answered, "But, sire, I never opened my mouth!" —"Whether you said it or not, if you don't go and get the castle, I'll have you hanged," replied the King.

Little John, crying, went to find his little horse, who said to him, "Now, what are you crying about?" —"Well, if I don't go and get the princess's castle now, he will have me hanged. He might as well hang me right away and get it over with. I'm finished." The Little Horse said, "Go and tell the King to give you a big ship loaded with meat, and to send it to the seashore where you saw the three giants, and have it unloaded there. If they can't go and get the castle for you, you will just have to hang." So Little John went and got the King to send for a big ship filled with meat and told him where to have it unloaded along the seashore. When Little John got to that place and had the ships unloaded, he called three times for the King of the Giants, and the three giants came running. "Hello, King of the Giants," said Little John. "I heard that you had a real shortage of meat, so I came to visit you, and bring you some, and also ask you to do me a little favor." The giant answered, "Well, Little John, if it's in the giants' power, we'll do it for you." So Little John told the giant about Fair Ferentine, and how, if he didn't get her castle back to where the King's house was, the King was going to have him hanged. The giant answered, "Go back home, Little John, and have a good night's sleep. When you wake up in the morning, the castle will be there, where the King wants it."

The giants ate a big meal of meat and went to get the castle, and Little John went back home. The next morning when the King woke up, the castle, with its golden roof, was sitting right next to his house. The sun was shining so brightly on that roof that he couldn't even look at it. He told the butler to come quickly and to see what had happened. The old King took the princess by the hand and said, "Well, princess, here's your castle!" Fair Ferentine went to the castle and reached into her pocket for the keys, but of course they weren't there. She said, "I won't get married until someone gets me my bunch of keys, which is at the bottom of the sea." The old King got angry again. "Why don't you just say you don't want to get married?" he demanded. "That's not true," she answered. "I will get married just as soon as I get my keys."

When the old King came back into his house in anger, the butler went to tell him that Little John had been bragging that since he had already been to get the princess and her castle, it would be easy for him to get the keys as well. The King called Little John in and said to him, "Little John, you've been bragging that it would be easy for you to get the keys, in the same way as you got the princess and her castle." Little John answered, "Sire, I never opened my mouth." —"Well, whether you said it or not, if you don't go and get the keys, I will have you hanged."

Little John went out crying to his little horse once again and told him about this new threat. The Horse replied, "It looks as though they will hang you. I told you when you took that feather, that the earth would swallow you up. Go tell the King to give you a ship loaded up with small pieces of meat and then take it and go find the king of the fish. He will still be where you threw him when we were on our way here. Then, get a bottle of white wine and a loaf of bread for us to eat while we are out looking for the king of fish and the keys."

When they got to the spot where Little John had thrown the king of the fish back into the water, they unloaded all the little pieces of meat from the ship, and Little John called to the king of fish to come to him. Pretty soon, he began to hear a big noise in the sea, and big waves began to crash against the shore. Finally, the king of the fish appeared and said, "Hey, Little John! I thought you had forgotten me completely, and that you would never come back to see me."

"No, I didn't forget you," answered Little John. "I heard that you were hungry, and I came back to bring you a little something to eat." The king was grateful and answered, "I can assure you, Little John, all of us were really starved. Thank you!" Little John then said, "I also wanted to ask you a little favor." The king replied, "If it is something in the sea that we can do for you, I can tell you that we will be happy to do it." Little John told him about the bunch of keys at the bottom of the sea, and the king of the fish told him that they would be able to find it easily.

Fair Ferentine

So the king of the fish called all the other fish to come to him by beating on a drum in all directions. First, he asked them, "Did anyone find a bunch of keys at the bottom of the ocean?" They all answered that they had not. So the king of the fish turned sadly to Little John and told him that since no one had found the keys, they must not be in the ocean. But then someone remembered Marguerite, the old catfish, who had not yet come. Finally, they saw her coming, and the king of the fish asked her, "What in the world were you doing, Marguerite?" —"Well," she answered, "I'm getting pretty old, and I have to swim slowly. And besides I was far away when I heard your drum, and on my way I found a heavy bunch of keys stuck between two rocks." He saw that she did not have the keys with her and asked her, "Well, old witch, why didn't you bring the keys with you? That's just what we're looking for. Do you think you can find them again?" —"Yes, I can find them again," she answered. So the king of the fish turned to one of his sergeants and told him to follow old Marguerite, and as soon as she had found the keys again, he should take them from her and swim back to shore on the double. The sergeant followed Marguerite the catfish and took the keys from her when she got to them, so that Little John would get them quickly.

"Thank you very much," said Little John. "Thank you very much, too, Little John," said the king of the fish.

Little John brought the keys back to the princess, and the next morning, the King took the princess by the hand and led her to the castle, where he gave her the keys. —"Are you going to tell me now that you don't want to get married?" said the King. Fair Ferentine opened the castle and walked through all the rooms. She came to the granary, and all the grains that were stored there had been jostled around during the castle's moving and had gotten all mixed up together. She said, "Yes, I'll be happy to get married, but not before all these different grains are sorted out again and back in their right places."

The butler went to the King again and told him that Little John had been bragging how easy this would be for him to do. So the King sent for Little John again and asked him about it. Little John protested that he had not opened his mouth at all, but it didn't matter. The King wanted to hang him if he did not sort out all the grain right away.

Little John started to cry harder than ever and went out to find his little horse. "Now what?" said the horse. —"The King now wants me to pick up and sort out all those grains in the princess's castle!" said Little John, crying. —"Well, I told you you'd be sorry when you picked up that feather," said the Horse. —"They might as well hang me now and get it over with," said Little John. "There is no way I can sort out all those little grains."

The horse told Little John what to do. "Go tell the King to give you a big ship filled with grains of wheat, and we'll go find the king of the birds." When Little John arrived at the king of the birds' place, with his ship, he called, "Come to me, king of the birds," three times, and the bird appeared. "King of the birds," said Little John, "I found out that there was a famine in your kingdom, and that the birds did not have enough grain to eat, so I brought you a little something to help out. I'd also like to ask you to do me a little favor." The king of the birds replied, "Well, if it's something in our power to do, Little John, I can tell you that we will be very happy to do it." "Here's what it is," said Little John. "I need to pick up and to sort out all the grain in Fair Ferentine's granary that fell out when her castle was being carried across the sea." "Go back home," said the king of the birds, "and leave that room open tonight and make sure there are no cats roaming about that night, either."

The old King gave orders to keep all cats in the house when Little John told him what would happen. That night, the birds came in and sorted out all the grains so that they were just as they had been before. The next morning, the King took Fair Ferentine by the hand and brought her into the granary. "Now," he said, "you can't say that we won't get married." "Well," said Fair Ferentine, "there is one more thing that I need." The old King was really angry this time. He stamped his foot and shouted, "Well, why not just say that you don't want to get married?" "That's not true," said the princess, "but first of all I need a bottle of beauty water and a bottle of water from Hell." The old King couldn't imagine how anyone could go and get water from Hell, and went away. The butler came and told him once again that Little John had been bragging how easy that would be to do. The King called Little John in and said to him, "I hear you've been bragging again about your power to do this hard job." Little John, crying once again, said, "I never opened my mouth." —"Well," said the King, "whether you said anything about it or not, you will be hanged if you don't go and get me those bottles of water."

When he went back to the Horse, the horse said, "Are you crying again, Little John?" Little John answered, "Yes, this is enough to make anyone cry. Now, I have to go get some beauty water and some water from Hell, or else he will hang me." "Well, Little John," said the Horse, "go and get two little bottles, and we'll go find the eagle. If she can't get you the water, I guess you will just have to be hanged." They left to find the eagle and told her about the two kinds of water. The eagle said, "Well, I think I can find you the beauty water easily enough. But the water from Hell, I wouldn't do it if it hadn't been for the time you killed the snake that was climbing the tree to eat my babies. Stay here and don't get tired of waiting. This is going to take me three days and three nights."

After three days and three nights, the eagle came back, looking a mess. Little John asked her if she had been able to find the water. "Yes," she answered. "The beauty water was not hard to get, but that water from Hell is terribly hot. Look how I've burned my wing tips getting it." —"Well, thank you very much, beautiful eagle," said Little John.

As they were going back home, the Little Horse said to Little John, "Little John, in four more days you are going to forget all about me." "Oh, no!" protested Little John. "I couldn't possibly forget you ever." —"Well, you will," said the Horse, "and you'll forget all the good I've done for you, too."

When they got to the castle, Little John brought the two bottles of water to the old

King. "Be careful," he told the King. "This bottle here is the beauty water, and this hot one here is the water from Hell."

Now the King was sure that Fair Ferentine would marry him, and he brought her the two bottles of water. —"Yes, I will marry you," she said, "but there is just one more thing that has to be done. You must have Little John beheaded." The King said that he couldn't possibly do that to Little John, but the princess just said, "Well, then, I'm not getting married."

Things went on in this way for two or three days, and the butler started getting after the King again, telling him that the princess was the most beautiful one he had ever seen, while Little John didn't really amount to much of anything. So, the King finally decided to have Little John beheaded. When they beheaded Little John, the princess stood by, and as soon as his head rolled off, she uncorked the bottle of beauty water and poured it all over him. Little John came back to life as the most handsome prince anyone had ever seen.

The old King then decided that he wanted his head cut off too, before he got married, so that he could have water poured on him and become handsome too. The princess said, "No, I'm supposed to marry you." But the King said, "No, we'll get married after that, when I've come back to life as handsome as Little John is." The princess shrugged her shoulders and said, "Well, it's up to you, sire." They cut off the old King's head, and the princess poured all over him the water from Hell. He burned up into a little pile of ashes.

"Now, Little John," said the princess, "you and I are going to get married." They did marry each other, and then they took the butler, locked him up, and let him starve to death.

Little John was so happy to be married that he forgot all about his little horse. One day, he was talking with his wife and thought about the Little Horse. He went to see him and found him lying on the ground, all swollen up. Little John began to weep, "Oh, my beautiful little horse! You told me that I would forget you." —"Yes, Little John," said the horse. "Now, I want you to take your knife and cut me in two. That's the only way you can save my life." —"No, Little Horse, I could never cut you in two," said Little John. —"But look at how many times I saved your life, Little John," answered the Horse. —"Well, if that's what I have to do to save your life, I guess I can do it," said Little John, and he cut the Horse with his knife and turned his head. Suddenly a handsome prince appeared before Little John. —"You have married my sister," he said, "and you have delivered me from an evil spell. Now, I'm going to go home with you and have dinner with you and my sister. Then I will go away, and you will never see me again."

Le Rouè nouère ou La Belle Férentsine

C'est bon d'vous dzire eune fouès c'étaient ein vieux pis eune vieille. 'L ontvaient ien qu'ein p'tsit garçon. I' courait ein magasin, vieux-là. Son p'tsit garçon 'l était après commencer à d'venir assez grand pour ben travailler dans l'magasin. Eune journée, l'vieux y'a dzit: "Tsu pourrais pas, touè, rester dans l'magasin padent qu'moin pis ta mère, on va aller dans l'village ach'ter des *groc'ries*, des marchandzises? L'souère," i' dzit, "tsu pourras aouère d'tes p'tsits camarades pour v'nir coucher avec touè." I'a donné les clefs d'tous les p'tsits bâtsiments qu'i' y'avait à l'entour. P'tsit Jean, quand i'avait pas personne au magasin, i'allait ouère dans toutes les cabanes. Dans ane, i'a trouvé ein joli p'tsit ch'fal. I'était pendzu au plancher d'en haut empétré dans des guides. I' nn'avait ien qu'eune paille de foin qu'temps en temps l'p'tsit ch'val i' pouvait attraper. P'tsit Jean i' dzit: "Tsu fais trop piquié, touè, j'te coupe d'là." 'L a coupé d'là." 'L a coupé ses guides, pis l'p'tsit ch'fal 'l a tombé à terre. I' l'a ben souègné.

Ça l'a été comme ça pour plusieurs jours, pis son père pis sa mère sont eurvenus. 'L ontvaient 'porté ein tas des marchandzises quand i' sontaient eurvenus. Tous les ouèsins i' sont v'nus d'alentour pour ouère les marchandzises. P'tsit Jean i' dzit: "Faut que j'vas essayer l'p'tsit ch'val padent i' m'vouèyent pas." 'L a pris son fusil, pis 'l a été ouère comme s'i' s'en allait à la chasse. 'L a été mett' la selle sus son p'tsit ch'fal pis 'l est partsi. Quand son ch'fal 'l a arrivé à la mer, 'l a pas arrêté mais i'a pris en travers sus la mer. Quand il a eu traversé la mer, son p'tsit ch'fal y'a dzit: "Eh ben! on va s'eurposer à c't'heure, P'tsit Jean." P'tsit Jean i' dzit: "Quocé, tsu parles, mon p'tsit ch'fal?" —"Oui," i' dzit, "ein ch'fal comme moin parle, P'tsit Jean." —I' dzit: "Mon p'tsit ch'fal oùsque c'est qu'on va aller d'abord?" —"On va aller," i' dzit, "sus ton onc', l'rouè nouère."

Il[s] ont partsi après qu'il[s] ont été ben eurposés. 'L ont arrivé pas ben loin d'eune fotaine. "J'vas bouère," i' dzit. "I' faudra qu'tsu passes à ras d'la fotaine, mon p'tsit ch'fal." I' nn'avait eune pleume d'or sus l'bord d'la fotaine. Son p'tsit ch'fal y'a dzit: "Touche pas à ça, P'tsit Jean. Si tsu ramasses pleume-là, t'as rentrer dans l'trou." Taleure, 'l a passé là oùsque i'en avait ein autre fotaine. 'L a été pour toucher la pleume d'or pis son p'tsit ch'fal y'a dzit: "Prends pas pleume d'or-là ou tsu vas plonger dans l'trou." P'tsit Jean i' dzit: J'vas gager si j'en trouve eune aut', j'la prends." Tout tard, dans l'après-midzi, P'tsit Jean 'l a eurgardé eune distance autour de lui, pis 'l a vu eune belle fotaine. 'L a laissé son p'tsit ch'fal ein bon boute d'la fotaine. 'L a été bouère, 'l a ramassé la pleume d'or, pis l'a mis dans sa poche. Quand 'l est eurv'nu à son p'tsit ch'fal, "Ah!" i' dzit, "P'tsit Jean, t'as pris la pleume d'or. Tsu vas t'faire pend'," i' dzit. "Vaudra autant qu'i' m'pendent comme êt' après trav'ler comme j'sieus là."

'L a eurgardé par-d'ssus la tête d'ein grand n'arb', pis 'l a vu eune grosse aigle qui l'était après voltiger pis crier. 'L a eurgardé après l'arb', i' nn'avait ein gros serpent qui y'était après monter. 'L a pris son fusil, 'l a tsiré, pis 'l a tsué l'serpent. L'aigle a commencé à tournailler autour de lui, à chanter pis à m'ner son train. Son p'tsit ch'fal i' dzit à lui: "Tsu connais quocé n'aigle-là a dzit?" — "Non," i' dzit, "j'comprends pas l'langage des aigles."—"Ben," i' dzit, "si par cas jamais t'as besoin d'elle, dzis par trois fouès: 'A moin, belle aigle!' a va êt' à ton s'cours." —"Ah! ben," i' dzit, "si j'en ai d'besoin, a purra ben v'nir."

Ein boute plus loin, 'l était après trav'ler l'long d'la mer. I' nn'avait queud' chose qui était après sauter sus l'sable là pis i' m'nait ein p'tsit ramage. Son p'tsit ch'fal i' dzit: "Tsu connais quocé l'p'tsit pouèsson i' dzit, P'tsit Jean?" —"Non," i' dzit, "j'comprends pas l'langage des pouèssons." —"Ben," i' dzit, "si c'était pas trop d'troub' pour touè d'descend', pis le ch'ter dans la mer, queud' jour i' t'rendait ein bon service." P'tsit Jean 'l a descendzu, i'a attrapé l'p'tsit pouèsson, pis i' l'a enwèyé aussi loin qu'il a pu dans l'eau. P'tsit Jean 'l est v'nu pour eurmonter sus son p'tsit ch'fal, 'l a entendzu acore crier après lui. "En t'eurmerciant ben, P'tsit Jean! Si tsu as besoin d'moin, viens icitte pis appelle trois fouès l'rouè des pouèssons." —"Oui, si j'ai besoin d'touè."

I'a partsi en trav'lant. 'L a arrivé oùsqu'i' nn'avait trois giants. I'avait chaquin eune branche dans l'gavion. Son p'tsit ch'fal i' dzit à P'tsit Jean: "Tsu connais quocé les giants-là i' te d'mandent?" —"Non," i' dzit. "j'peux pas les comprend' avec ça i'ont dans la guieule." —"I' dzisent si, par cas, tsu veux en dépend' ein d'eux aut's, i' pourra dépend' les aut's." —"Ben," i' dzit, "comment m'as faire pour dépend' ça? C'est trop grand, ça. En tous cas, ça, c'est laissé à touè, mon p'tsit ch'fal. Si tsu veux t'placer drètte à ras d'ane des giants-là, m'as n'en dépend' eune." Après ça, l'aut' 'l a débarrassé les deux aut's. L'vieux giant y'a dzit: "Ben merci, P'tsit Jean. Quand t'as d'besoin d'moin, viens icitte, appelle pour l'rouè des giants, m'as êt' à ton s'cours, pis s'i' nn'aqueque chose j'peux faire pour touè, j'vas l'faire." —"Ben," i' dzit, "c'est bon, l'rouè des giants."

'L a arrivé ein bon boute plus loin. 'L avait eune grande bande d'zouéseaux drètte dans l'milieu dzu ch'min. Son p'tsit ch'fal i' dzit: "P'tsit Jean, l'rouè des zouéseaux i'est après marier sa fille aujourdz'hui. I' te d'mande qu'tsu faises l'tour." I' dzit: "M'as l'faire; mon p'tsit ch'fal, c'est laissé à touè, ça." Quand P'tsit Jean 'l a eurvenu frapper l'ch'min, l'rouè des zouéseaux 'l est v'nu voltiger drètte à ras d'lui. "En t'eurmerciant," i' dzit, "ben des fouès, P'tsit Jean, d'ta politesse! J'sus après marier ma fille aujourdz'hui," i' dzit. "Si jamais t'as d'besoin d'moin, viens icitte, pis appelle trois fouès au rouè des zouéseaux, pis," i' dzit, "si c'est queuque chose qu'les zouéseaux peuvent faire, on va l'faire."

P'tsit Jean, lui, i' s'en va trouver l'rouè nouère à c't'heure. 'L a mis P'tsit Jean à avouère soin des ch'faux. P'tsit Jean 'l a commencé à avouère soin des ch'faux, pis 'l ont commencé à eurgarder ben tout d'suite. L'vieux rouè 'l avait des vieux 'harnouès qui eurgardaient pas ben. P'tsit Jean 'l a commencé à nettèyer ben les 'harnouès-là, à les graisser. I' peurnait sa pleume d'or, i' la passait en plein sus les 'harnouès-là, i' la passait en plein sus les 'harnouès-là, pis i'avait tout des fleurs d'or' c'était beau. L'vieux rouè nouère 'l était veuf. I'allait s'prom'ner tous les s'maines à ras des villes pour eurgarder pour eune autre femme. Eune journée, i' dzit à P'tsit Jean qu'i'emmène son carrosse d'vant sa porte, i'aurait été s'prom'ner. Quand l'vieux rouè 'l a vu ses ch'faux, ses carrosses, ses 'harnouès, i' les eurconnaissait pas. "Ah! P'tsit Jean, comment dans l'monde vous peut faire pour mett' mes 'harnouès de même?" —"Eh ben! mon onc' l'rouè," i' dzit, "c'est pas malaisé." L'vieux rouè i' marchait avec eune canne. "Donnez-mouè donc vot' canne icitte, m'as vous montrer." 'L a pris sa canne, il a pris pleume-là, i' l'a passée plein en d'ssus; c'était tout doré.

L'vieux rouè i' crouèyait la terre d'P'tsit Jean. L'vieux maît' d'hôtel i' s'est aperçu d'ça. I'a commencé à êt' jaloux. I'a dzit au rouè: "C'est dommage vous l'a pas la Belle Férentsine. I' dzisent qu'a veut s'marier avec ein rouè." —"Ben," l'vieux rouè i' dzit, "oùsqu'alle est la Belle Férentsine?" —"Alle est là-bas l'aut' bord d'la mer." L'vieux rouè i' dzit: "Quis qui va aller qu'ri la Belle Férentsine l'aut' bord d'la mer?" L'vieux maît' d'hôtel i' dzit: "P'tsit Jean a dzit i' pourra aller la qu'ri." L'vieux rouè 'l a commencé à êt' anmourachée. Il a dzit à P'tsit Jean: "C'est-i' vrai t'as dzit tsu peux aller qu'ri la Belle Férentsine?" —"Non, mon onc'," i' dzit, "j'ai jamais desserré les dents." —"Qu'tsu l'ayes dzit, qu'tsu l'ayes pas dzit," i' dzit, "si tsi vas pas la qu'ri, tsu vas êt' pendzu."

P'tsit Jean s'en a été trouver son p'tsit ch'fal en braillant. Son p'tsit ch'fal y'a d'mandé quocé c'était son troub'. "Mon onc' l'rouè nouère, il a dzit qu'si j'allais pas qu'ri la Belle Férentsine," i' dzit, "i' m'aurait pendzu." —"J't'ai dzit, P'tsit Jean, qu't'allais rentrer dans l'troub'. Va dzire au vieux rouè qu'i' t'donne eune bouteille d'vin blanc pis ein pain blanc, pis on va aller la charcer princess-là." Il

" The Black King, or Fair Ferentine "

a été pis i'a dzit au rouè qu'i' voulait eune bouteille d'vin blanc pis ein pain blanc, pis 'l aurait sa princesse. Il est eurvenu. 'L a monté sus l'dos d'son p'tsit ch'fal, pis 'l ont partsi. Quand 'l ont arrivé à la mer, son p'tsit ch'fal i'allait aussi ben sus l'eau comme sus la terre. 'L ont traversé la mer. Son p'tsit ch'fal i'a dzit à P'tsit Jean: "Quand on va arriver là à souère, i' va y avouère ein bal, eune danse, pis tsu vas êt' l'meilleur danseur qui va êt' là. Tsu vas leu dzire qu'tsu danses ben, mais qu't'as ein p'tsit ch'fal qui danse mieux qu'touè. I' vont t'enwèyer m'qu'ri," i' dzit. "J'vas monter sus l'plancher, j'vas faire queuques tours à l'entour, pis m'as danser. T'as leur dzire que j'pourrais danser beaucoup mieux si j'avais la princesse en croupe derrière moin." I' dzit: "Après qu'tsu vas aouère la princesse derrière touè, tsu vas connaît' quoi faire."

P'tsit Jean 'l a arrivé là souèrée-là. C'était l'meilleur danseur 'l ontvaient jamais vu. I'ont tou[s] commencé à dzire comment ben i' dansait. "Oui, mais," i' dzit, "j'ai ein p'tsit ch'fal qui danse beaucoup mieux qu'moin." —"Va donc l'qu'ri," i' dzisent, "pour qu'on le ouè danser." L'p'tsit ch'fal à P'tsit Jean 'l a fait queuques tours sus l'plancher. I' dzisent: "Comme ton p'tsit ch'fal i' danse ben!" La princesse a l'a eurconnu, elle, l'p'tsit ch'fal. "Ah! mais," i' dzit, "i' dans'rait beaucoup mieux si i'avait la princesse en croupe derrière moin." La princesse 'l a monté pis i s'a sauvé avec elle.

Quand 'l ont arrivé au milieu d'la mer, alle avait ein paquet d'ses clefs d'maisonne avec elle, la Belle Férentsine. Alle les a pris pis alle les a j'tées dans la mer, pis alle a dzit: "Celui qui voudra m'marier, i' faudra qu'i' vienne qu'ri paquet d'clefs-là." Alle a arrivé sus l'vieux rouè. L'vieux rouè 'l a été la rencontrer à la barrière. Ah! i' était fier. 'L a d'mandé la princesse si a s'aurait mariée. —"Ah! oui," a dzit, "m'as m'marier, mais pas avant qu'j'aye mon château d'vant vot' place d'armes icitte." L'vieux rouè 'l a partsi fâché. "Dzisez donc qu'vous veut pas s'marier. Quis qui dans l'monde peut porter vot' château icitte d'vant ma place d'armes?" L'maît' d'hôtel 'l a été dzire au rouè que P'tsit Jean 'l avait été qu'ri la princesse, pis qu'i' s'était vanté qu'i' pouvait aller qu'ri son château. L'vieux rouè 'l a app'lé P'tsit Jean. "T'es vanté qu'tsu étais allé qu'ri la princesse et qu'tsu pouvais aller qu'ri son château," i' dzit. "Sire," i' dzit, "j'en ai jamais desserré les dents." —"Qu'tsu l'ayes dzit ou qu'tsu l'ayes pas dzit, si tsu vas pas qu'ri l'château, tsu vas êt' pendzu."

'L a été trouver son p'tsit ch'fal en braillant encore. "Qu'est-ce que t'as," i' dzit, "P'tsit Jean, à brailler encore?" —"Ben," i' dzit, "si j'vas pas qu'ri l'château d'la princesse, à c't'heure, i' va m'pend'. I' peut ben m'pend' tout d'suite, j'aurai fini." —"Vat'en dzire au rouè qu'i' t'donne ein bâtsiment charzé avec d'la viande, pis qu'i' l'faise décharzer sus l'bord d'la mer, oùsque c'est t'as vu tes trois giants. Eux aut's, s'i' peuvent pas aller l'qu'ri," i' dzit, "P'tsit Jean, i' faudra qu'tsu sèyes pendzu." I'a été dzire au vieux rouè qu'i' y donne ein bâtsiment charzé d'viande grasse, qu'i' l'décharze à telle et telle place l'long d'la mer. Quand 'l a arrivé oùsque c'est 'l avait débarrassé ses giants, 'l a fait décharzer ses bâtsiments d'viande. Pis après qu'ses bâtsiments 'l ont été eurpartsis, 'l a appelé trois fouès: "A moin, l'rouè des giants!" Les giants sont v'nus à toute course. "Ben," i' dzit, "l'rouè des giants, j'ai attendzu dzire qu't'étais dans la dzisette pour d'la viande. J'sus v'nu t'rend' eune p'tsite visite pis en meme temps t'demander ein p'tsit service." —"Ben," i' dzit, "P'tsit Jean, si c'est au pouwère des giants, on va l'faire." —"Ben," i' dzit, "j'ai été qu'ri la Belle Férentsine, pis à c't'heure mon onc', l'rouè nouère, i'a dzit qu'si j'allais pas qu'ri son château, pis l'porter sus sa place d'armes, i' m'aurait pendzu." —"Ben, va-t'en," i' dzit, "P'tsit Jean, pis dors tranquille; d'main matin, l'château i' va êt' là."

L'rouè des giants 'l a ben empli tous ses ongues d'la viande. I' s'en vonnent qu'ri l'château, les giants, pis P'tsit Jean s'en va cheux eux. L'lend'main quand l'vieux rouè i' s'a l'vé, la couvertsure dzu château à la Belle Férentsine, c'était tout d'l'or. L'soleil i' paraissait sus couvertsure-là, pis ça aveuglait l'vieux rouè quand i'a sortsi. 'L a crié après l'grand vizir pour qu'i' vienne vite, vite, ouère quocé c'était. L'vieux rouè 'l a pris la princesse par la main, pis y'a dzit: "Eh ben! princesse, v'là vot'

"Ben," i' dzit, "belle aigle, t'as trouvé ton eau?" —"Oui," a dzit, "P'tsit Jean, j't'en réponds, j'l'ai trouvé l'eau d'beauté," a dzit. "Elle, c'est pas malaisé à trouver, mais l'eau d'l'enfer, c'est terriblement chaud! Eurgarde donc, j'ai tout brûlé l'boute d'mes ailes." —"Ben," i' dzit, "en t'eurmerciant, belle aigle!" —"En t'eurmerciant ben, touè aussite, P'tsit Jean!" L'p'tsit ch'fal y'a dzit en allant: "P'tsit Jean, tsu vas m'oblier avant quat' jours." —"Ah! non," i' dzit, "mon p'tsit ch'fal, j'pourrai jamais t'oublier." —"Ah! oui," i' dzit, "tsu vas m'oblier pis tout l'bien que j't'ai faite." Quand 'l ont arrivé, i'a été porter l'eau au vieux rouè. "Faisez ben attention," i' dzit, "à c't'heure. Ça icitte, c'est d'l'eau d'beauté; ça là, c'est d'l'eau d'l'enfer." L'vieux rouè i'a été trouver la princesse pour ouère si a s'aurait mariée. "Ah! oui, mais pas hormis qu'on coupe l'cou au P'tsit Jean sus ein billot." L'vieux rouè i' dzit i'aurait pas coupé l'cou au P'tsit Jean. "Ben," a dzit, "moin, je m'marie pas."

Ça l'a resté comme ça deux, trois jours, pis l'vieux maît' d'hôtel i'a commencé après l'rouè; i'a commencé à y dzire qu'c'était la plus belle princesse i'avait jamais vue, tandi[s] qu'P'tsit Jean i' montait pas à grand'chose. L'vieux rouè leu-z-a dzit qu'i' yi faisent couper l'cou sus ein billot. La princesse a été là quand i'ont eu coupé l'cou au P'tsit Jean. Alle a vidé d'l'eau d'beauté sus P'tsit Jean; i'était l'plus beau prince l'vieux rouè 'l avait jamais vu. L'vieux rouè i' dzit qu'i' fallait qu'i' faise couper son cou à lui aussite avant de s'marier. La princesse a dzit: "Non, on va s'marier, moin pis vous." — "Ah!" i' dzit, "on va s'marier après ça, quand m'as êt' eurvenu joli comme P'tsit Jean." La princesse a dzit: "C'est laissé à vous, Sire." 'L ont coupé l'cou dzu vieux rouè. La princesse 'l a vidé d'l'eau d'l'enfer d'ssus l'vieux rouè. I'a tout brûlé en cend'. "A c't'heure," a dzit, "P'tsit Jean, moin pis touè, on va s'marier." Elle pis P'tsit Jean i' s'ont mariés. 'L ont pris l'vieux maît' d'hôtel-là, l'ont mis ent' quat' murailles; i' l'ont quitté crever d'faim.

P'tsit Jean i'était si fier d'êt' marié il a oblié son p'tsit ch'fal à net. Eune journée, i'était après charrer avec sa princesse; 'l a pensé à son p'tsit ch'fal. Quand 'l a été ouère son p'tsit ch'fal, 'l était à terre, 'l était enflé en haut, gonflé. P'tsit Jean a commencé à s'lamenter. "Ah! beau p'tsit ch'fal!" i' dzit. "Hèye, mon p'tsit ch'fal, tsu m'avais dzit j't'aurais oblié." —"Oui," i' dzit, "P'tsit Jean, prends ton couteau, pis fends-moin," i' dzit. "C'est la seule magnière tsu vas m'sauver la vie." —"Non," i' dzit, "mon p'tsit ch'val, j'te fends pas en deux." —"Mais," i' dzit, "P'tsit Jean, eurgarde donc combien d'fouès, moin, j't'ai sauvé la vie." —"Ben," i' dzit, "si c'est pour t'sauver la vie, j'vas t'fend' en deux." 'L a attrapé son couteau, pis i'a donné ein coup d'couteau, pis 'l a eurviré sa tête. I' s'est trouvé ein beau prince d'vant P'tsit Jean. —"T'as marié ma soeur," i' dzit, "P'tsit Jean, pis tsu m'as delivré, moin en esclavage. A c't'heure," i' dzit, "j'vas aller dzîner avec touè pis ta femme, pis j'vas m'en aller, pis tu m'eurvouerras jamais."

10.

The Girl with Golden Hair

It's good to tell you that once upon a time there were an old King and an old Queen, and they had three sons. The old man had heard about the spring that belonged to the beautiful lady with golden hair. When someone would wash his eyes in its water, that person would regain the good eyesight he had at the age of fifteen years. He said to his children that whichever one of them would bring back to him some water from the beautiful lady's spring would receive the crown. So the oldest son left to find the spring. He told his father that he was going out, and the old man gave him a ship. He sailed across the sea and anchored the vessel when he got to the other side. He found an inn where he asked for a room. After supper, the Innkeeper challenged the young prince to a game of cards. The Innkeeper won all the gold and silver the young man wagered, and he lost all that he had. When his money was gone, he bet his clothes, and when the Innkeeper had won those, he wagered the value of his body. The Innkeeper won that time, too, and put burlap sacks on the prince, and threw him in the cellar.

After awhile, when no one had gotten any news from the oldest son, the second son said to his father, "I'm going to go out and look for my brother." He left in the ship that his father fitted out for him. When he found his brother's vessel, he recognized it because his father's name was on it. "Well! My brother can't be far from here!" he said. He brought his ship up to the other one and anchored it there. He first went to the inn to obtain a room. The Innkeeper was very pleasant and fed him well. After supper, she asked him if he liked to play cards. "Oh, yes, Ma'am. I love playing cards," he replied. Well, she won all of his gold and silver, his ship, his clothing, and the value of his body. She dressed him in burlap sacks and locked him in the cellar with his brother.

Some time went by, and as he had heard no news of his two sons, the old King was getting worried. Peter, his youngest son, said to his father, "I'm going to go out and find my brothers." The old King did not want to see his only remaining son leave him. But Peter said, "Don't worry, father, I'll be back." So, he left in a ship too. When he got to where his brothers' ships were anchored, he recognized them by his father's name on them. "Well! My brothers must be somewhere around here," he said. So he tied up his boat right next to the others.

He went to get a room at the inn. The Innkeeper welcomed him warmly because he was a handsome prince. After supper, she asked him if he wanted to play a game of cards. She bet all the gold and silver she had, and Peter won it all. He won back everything that his brothers had lost; he even won back the two ships. She wagered the value of her inn, and Peter won that. She bet her horse and the carriage that could climb the mountain where the beautiful woman with golden hair lived. She bet her watch, the only watch that kept time for the beautiful woman with the golden hair. She bet her clothes. Peter won all of these. She wagered the value of her body, and Peter won again. She said to him, "Well, now I belong to you, and everything here belongs to you also." He told her to run the place as she usually did, until he needed her.

Before he left, the Innkeeper said to him, "At this time tomorrow, right at twelve, all the animals that keep guard for the beautiful woman with golden hair will be asleep." So, Peter got on his horse and went up the mountain. When he got there, he found a beautiful Princess asleep in bed. He kissed and caressed the Princess. Then, he saw a bottle of wine on the table. He took a drink, but the bottle stayed full. He took a second drink, but the level of wine in the bottle still did not go down. He put the bottle into his suitcase. "Since I'm a traveler, that's going to come in handy," he said. Then, he found a loaf of bread and cut a slice and then a second slice. But the loaf of bread stayed whole and round. He put that into his suitcase, too. Then, he went down into the garden. There was an eagle sleeping on the edge of the spring. He took his bottle and filled it with water, then he took a feather out of the eagle's right wing. Then he went back into the Princess's room and kissed her some more. He spent quite awhile sitting by the Princess, but then it got to be time for him to leave, as his hour was drawing to a close. As he got to the foot of the mountain, all of the beautiful lady's animals woke up again.

Then, he went and set his two brothers free from their prison in the Innkeeper's basement. He gave them back their clothes, and everything they would need to go back home with him. But the oldest brother was jealous of Peter. He paid attention to the kind of bottle Peter had the magic water in and found one that was similar to trick him with. When they were ready to leave, his brothers asked Peter to tie all three boats together and to return home in the lead ship with them. After awhile, the oldest brother filled his bottle with seawater. He asked Peter if he could see the bottle, which came from the spring, that belonged to the beautiful girl with the golden hair. Peter gave it to him without suspecting anything. But the oldest brother gave Peter back the wrong bottle, the one filled with seawater. After awhile, the oldest brother asked Peter what had happened when he had gotten to the Princess's palace. Peter told him that he had found the beautiful Princess sleeping, but that he had not touched her. He then said that he had found a bottle full of wine, and that every time he took a drink the bottle stayed full. But he said that he had left the bottle there and had not taken it. Then, he said, "There was a loaf of bread. I cut a piece out of it and then another piece, but it stayed whole. But I didn't take that loaf of bread.

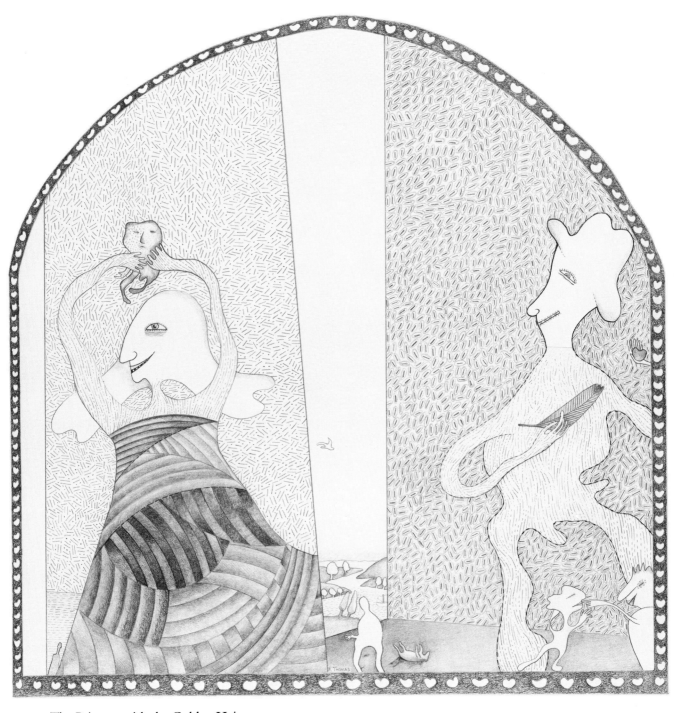

The Princess with the Golden Hair

I left it where it was. I went into the garden to fill my bottle with the magic water, and there was an eagle there sleeping. I took a feather from its left wing. Then, I went back into the Princess's room. She was so beautiful! But I didn't touch her."

When they got to their father's house, the old King was very happy to see his three sons return. He asked them which one of them had gotten to the castle of the Princess with the Golden Hair to get the magic water. Peter said, "It was I, father." The old King said, "Bring me a golden platter." He emptied the water from Peter's bottle into the dish, to wash his eyes in it. But when he had washed his eyes in the salty seawater, they felt worse than ever, and he became angry. Then the oldest son stepped up and said, "I'm the one, father, who went and got the magic water." So the King got another dish, quickly. When he had washed his eyes with the water from the Princess's magic spring, he could see again just as well as he could at the age of fifteen. He said, "Peter, instead of helping me, you wanted to do away with me!" He told his servant to take Peter into the woods to kill him. Then, he said, "Bring me back his heart so I can cook it on the coals and eat it."

Peter and the servant went into the woods. The servant loved Peter and didn't want to kill him. Peter said to him, "Shoot." But the pistol wouldn't shoot. There was a little black dog that had followed them. Peter said to the servant, "Shoot the little black dog." He shot and killed the dog on the first try. "Bring the dog's heart to my father and tell him that it's mine." He put a note in the hood of the servant's coat. "My father is going to need me again. Give him this note when he does. Take good care of my horse and don't let anyone touch it."

So, the servant brought the dog's heart to Peter's father, and the King ate it after roasting it over the coals. Peter went out traveling and came to a big city. He asked for a place to sleep. When they sat down to the supper table, they had a delicious meal, but no liquor. They said it had been years since they had seen any alcohol. Peter said, "Bring me my bag." He took out his bottle of wine and filled all the glasses all around the table. The innkeeper wanted to buy that bottle of wine and offered him a good sum of money for it. Peter sold it to her on the condition that when the beautiful lady with the golden hair should call for it, it had to be given back to her. He sold it, and the next day he set out traveling again.

The next evening, he arrived at another inn and asked for a night's lodgings. He sat down at the table for supper. It was an excellent meal, but they didn't have any bread. The innkeeper told him that there was no bread, that they had had no flour for many years. So, Peter told them to bring in his sack and took out the bread he had gotten from the Princess with the Golden Hair. He cut off all the bread everyone at the table wanted, but the loaf of bread stayed whole. The innkeeper wanted to buy that loaf of bread, and Peter sold her the bread for a good price, on condition that when the Princess with the Golden Hair should call for it, it had to be given back to her.

Peter went out then, traveling far and wide, and finally he came to the palace of another king. He hired himself out to the king, and it wasn't long before everyone in this new kingdom loved Peter. The old king had him work in his store, and everyone who came to trade preferred to deal with Peter rather than with the other employees. Now, while Peter was working in the store, the beautiful girl with the golden hair had a son. She sent word to the old King who had regained his youthful eyesight to send to her the man who had gone and fetched the water for him. "Well," said the King to his oldest son, "you're the one who went to get the water. You'd better go." So, the oldest son left in his ship. When he got to the landing place, he tied up his vessel, and then he had to stoop down on all fours to try to climb the Princess's mountain. The Princess's little son was playing on the porch and said, "Oh, Mama, I see a turkey coming!" —"Be quiet, stupid," she answered. "That's not a turkey. That's a prince."

When the prince got to the top of the mountain, the Princess had him come in. She asked him, "Are you the one who came and got water from my spring?" —"Yes, Princess, I was the one," he answered. She said, "Tell me what you did when you got here." —"Well," he said, "I came in and a beautiful Princess was lying here asleep." —"Did you touch that Princess?" —"Oh, no! I didn't touch her!" —"And after that, what did you do?"—"Well, there was a bottle of wine on the table. When I took a drink from it it stayed full." —"Did you take that bottle?" —"Oh, no, Princess, I didn't take it!"—"And after that, what did you do?" —"There was a loaf of bread on the table, and I cut a slice from it, but it stayed whole." —"Did you take that loaf of bread?" —"Oh, no, Princess, I didn't take it!" —"And then what did you do?" —"Then, I went into the garden, and there was an eagle sleeping on the edge of the spring. I filled my bottle. After that, I took a feather from the left wing of the eagle." —"Well," said the Princess, "you are lying. You're not the one who came. I want you to go back and tell your father that if he doesn't send the one who came here to get water, I'm going to destroy his city."

When his son came back and told the King that he wasn't the one who had really gotten the magic water, but that Peter was the one, the King said, "But I ate Peter's heart roasted in the coals." Then, the servant saw that the King was in trouble and needed Peter, and gave the King the note that he had kept in the hood of his coat. The old King looked at it and said, "What? Peter isn't dead? Then, what heart did I eat?" The servant explained that it had been the heart of the little black dog that had followed him and Peter into the woods.

Not long after that, the King sent word to Peter to come back home. When Peter knew that his father was in trouble, he left for home. He stopped at the inn where he had left the bread and asked for it back, and then he stopped at the other inn and told them that it was time to give the bottle of wine back to the Princess with the Golden Hair. When he got to his father's castle, he asked him what was the problem. The King said that the Princess with the Golden Hair had asked for him to come to her. —"Do you believe now that I was the one who went to get the water at the magic fountain, or do you still think it was my brother?" said Peter. "I'm leaving now to go to the Princess's castle, and when I come back, I don't want to see my two brothers around here any more."

Peter asked the servant to saddle up his horse, and the servant went and got the horse right away. Peter got on and left. The little horse could run on water as well as on land. When he got to the Princess's mountain, which was made out of glass, he started up it on horseback. The Princess's little son was playing on the porch and said to his mother, "Mama, I see a handsome prince coming on horseback."

When he got to the castle, the Princess asked him to come in. When he was sitting comfortably in a chair, she asked him, "Are you really the one who came and got water from my spring?" —"Yes, Princess," answered Peter. —"What time did you come here?" —"Right at noon." —"What did you do?" —"I found a beautiful Princess sleeping." — "Did you touch the Princess?" —"Oh, I certainly did. She was so beautiful I couldn't help kissing and caressing her." —"After that, what did you do?" asked the Princess. —"There was a bottle of wine on the table, and I drank from it but it stayed full." —"Did you take that bottle of wine?" —"Yes, Princess. I took it and put it in my sack."

The beautiful Princess with the Golden Hair was pretty sure now that Peter was the one who had come, but she kept on, just so that there would be no way to make a mistake. —"After that, what did you do?" she said. —"There was a loaf of bread," he answered, "and I cut a slice but the loaf stayed whole." —"Did you take that loaf of bread?" —"Yes, I took it and put it into my bag." —"After that, what did you do?" —"I went into the garden, and there was an eagle sleeping on the edge of your fountain. I filled my bottle with water, then I took a feather from the eagle's right wing." —"Yes," said the Princess, "you're the one who came to get water from my spring. It's time for us to marry each other. Take my horse and carriage and go get your mother and father. Bring them here and we'll get married. But be sure to tell your two brothers not to be anywhere around when we get back to your father's house."

La Belle aux Cheveux d'Or

C'est bon d'vous dzire eune fouès c'étaient ein vieux rouè pis eune vieille reine, pis 'l ontvaient trois enfants, trois garçons. L'vieux 'l a entendzu parler d'l'eau d'la fotaine à la Belle aux Ch'veux d'Or. Eune qui lavait ses yeux dedans, sa vue a eurv'nait aussi bonne qu'à l'âge de quinze ans. Il a dzit à ses enfants qu'lui qui aurait été qu'ri d'l'eau d'la fotaine d'la Belle aux Ch'veux d'Or, i' y'aurait donné la couronne. L'plus vieux 'l a partsi. I'a dzit à son père i'aurait été . L'vieux rouè i' y'a fourni ein bâtsiment, et quand il a trav'lé sus l'eau, quand il a arrivé au bord d'la mer, il a amarré son bâtsiment. Il a été à ein auberge d'mander pour coucher. Après souper, l'aubergisse a attaqué l'beau prince pour jouer aux cartes. Tout l'or pis l'argent qu'i' mettait sus la table, l'aubergisse a l'a gagné; 'l a perdzu tout l'argent 'l avait. 'L a joué son bâtsiment, l'aubergisse a l'a gagné; 'l a joué ses habits, l'aubergisse a les a gagnés. Après ça, 'l a joué son corps pour sa valeur, l'aubergisse a l'a gagné. A y'a mis des sarraux d'touèle sus l'dos pis a l'a mis dans la cave.

Ça s'fait, qu'ça l'a été d'meme plusieurs jours. L'vieux rouè i' entendait pas parler d'son garçon. L'deuxième 'l a dzit à son père: "J'vas y aller vouère à mon frère," et il a partsi dans ein bâtsiment qu'son père y'a fourni. Quand il a arrivé tout près dzu bâtsiment d'son frère, i' l'a eurconnu à cause qu'il avait l'nom d'son père et d'son armée dessus. "Pargué! mon frère n'est pas loin." Il a avancé son bâtsiment tout près d'l'aut' et il l'a amarré. 'L a été à l'auberge d'mandant pour coucher. L'aubergisse l'a ben eurçu. Après souper, a y'a d'mandé à lui aussite s'il aimait la *guime* de cartes. I' y'a répond: "Ah! oui, madame, j'aime beaucoup jouer aux cartes." A y'a gagné tout l'or pis tout l'argent ça 'l avait, pis après a y'a gagné son bâtsiment, son linge, et la valeur d'son corps. A y'a mis des sarraux d'touèle sus l'dos, pis a l'a mis dans la cave avec son frère.

Ça l'a été plusieurs temps, i'entendait pas parler d'ses deux garçons, l'vieux rouè. I'était inquiète, i' s'lamentait. Pierre, l'plus jeune, i'a dzit à son père: "J'vas aller ouère à mes frères." L'vieux rouè i' voulait pas qu'le dernier d'ses enfants i' l'laisse. Pierre y'a dzit: "Craignez eurien, mon père, j'eurviendras." I'a partsi dans son bâtsiment, lui aussite. Et quand il a arrivé tout près des bâtsiments d'ses frères, il les a ben eurconnus par l'nom d'son père et d'son armée qui était d'ssus. "Pargué! mes frères sont pas loin." Il a amarré son bâtsiment tout près des aut's.

Il a été à l'auberge pour coucher. L'aubergisse a l'a ben eurçu parce qu'c'était ein beau prince. Après souper, alle l'a d'mandé pour eune *guime* de cartes. Tout l'or pis l'argent, l'aubergisse a mettait sur la table, Pierre l'a gagné. I'a gagné tout son or et tout son argent à l'aubergisse et tout c'que ses frères 'l avaient perdzu; i'a même eurgagné leus deux bâtsiments. Alle a joué son auberge pour la valeur, Pierre i' l'a gagnée. Alle a joué son j'val et le seul carrosse qui allait sur la montagne à la Belle aux Ch'veux d'Or. Il a gagné sa mont', la seule mont' qui t'nait l'temps à la Belle aux Ch'veux d'Or. Alle a joué ses habits, Pierre les a gagnés. Alle a joué son corps, Pierre i' l'a gagné. Pierre 'l avait gagné l'aubergisse. A dzit: "J'vous apparquiens, Pierre. Tousse que c'est icitte, ça vous apparquient aussite." I'a dzit qu'a coure la place comme d'coutsume jusqu'à il ait besoin d'elle.

Avant qu'i' parte, l'aubergisse a y'a dzit: "A c't'heure, d'main, jusse à douze, tous les bêtailles d'la Belle aux Ch'veux d'Or, i' dorment." Ça s'fait qu'il a monté sus l'ch'val, il a partsi, et i' y'a été. Quand i'a rentré, il a trouvé eune belle princesse d'couchée. 'I a caressé pis 'l a embrassé la princesse. I'a trouvé eune bouteille de vin sur eune table. I' nn'a bu d'dans, a était toujours pleine; i' nn'a bu encore, a était toujours pleine. I' l'a mis d'dans sa valise. "Mouè étant ein trav'leur, ça va v'nir à la main," i' dzit. I' nn'avait ein pain, i' nn'a coupé ein morceau, pis ensuite ein aut', i' était toujours rond; i' l'a mis dans sa valise, lui aussite. Il a été dans l'parterre. I' n'avait ein aigle d'couché sus l'bord d'la fotaine. Il a pris sa bouteille, i' l'a emplie d'eau, pis il a arraché eune pleume sur l'aile drètte d'la belle aigle. Il est eurvenu *beck* dans la chamb' d'la princesse, et ce qu'il a caressé et embrassé la princesse ein bon boute d'temps! Mais i' fallait qu'i' parte, son heure était tout près d'finir. Comme i'a arrivé au pied d'la montagne, les bêtailles s'réveillaient tou[s].

Là, il a été délivré ses deux frères, qui étaient dans la cave en prison. Il les a rendzu l'linge et tout pour s'rentourner cheux eux avec lui. L'plus vieux d'ses frères i'était jaloux cont' lui. Il a faite attention queule sorte d'bouteille il avait et i' s'en a trouvé eune pareille pour la trahison. Quand il[s] ont partsi pour s'en aller, ses frères 'l ont d'mandé à Pierre d'tout amarrer les bâtsiments ensemb' et s'en aller tou[s] dans l'meme. Bêtôt l'plus vieux 'l a empli sa bouteille pleine d'eau d'mer. I'a d'mandé à son frére pour vouère sa bouteille qui v'nait d'la fotaine à la Belle aux Ch'veux d'Or, et Pierre y'a donnée, lui, sans penser à rien. l'a rendzu la mauvaise bouteille, l'eau d'mer. Taleure, l'plus vieux d'ses frères a d'mandé à Pierre quoice qu'il avait faite quand 'l avait arrivé au château d'la Belle aux Ch'veux d'Or. Pierre y'a dzit i'avait trouvé eune belle princesse couchée après dormir, mais il l'avait pas touchée, c'te princesse. l'a dzit qu'i' n'avait eune bouteille de vin, i' nn'avait bu d'dans, a était toujours pleine, l' nn'avait bu acore, a était toujours pleine, mais i'a dzit: "J'l'ai pas pris, c'te bouteille-là, j'l'ai laissée là. l' nn'avait ein pain," i' dzit. "J'en ai coupé ein morceau, pis taleure ein aut', pis il est resté toujours rond. J'l'ai pas pris c'te pain, j'l'ai laissé là. J'ai été dans l'parterre pour emplir ma bouteille, i'avait eune aigle d'couchée et après dormir, j'ai arraché eune pleume sur son aile gauche, et après ça, j'sus eurvenu dans la chamb' d'la princesse. Bougre! C'est eune jolie princesse, mais j'l'ai pas touchée."

Quand 'l ont arrivé sus leur père, l'vieux rouè 'l a été fier d'vouère eurvenir ses trois enfants, ses trois garçons. l' leu-z-a d'mandé queul c'était qu'était aller qu'ri d'l'eau d'la fotaine d'la Belle aux Ch'veux d'Or. Pierre a dzit: "C'est moin, mon père." L'vieux rouè a dzit: "Emporte-moin ein plat d'or." 'L a vidé l'eau-là dans l'plat pour laver ses yeux. Quand il a lavé ses yeux dans l'eau salée-là, ça l'a mis pire qu'tout. l' s'a trouvé fâché. L'plus vieux 'l a dzit: "C'est moin, mon pére, qui a été qu'ri d'l'eau d'la fotaine d'la Belle aux Ch'veux d'Or." L'roué, aprés, 'l a pris ein aut' plat vit-ment. Quand 'l a eu lavé ses yeux avec l'eau d'la fotaine d'la Belle aux Ch'veux d'Or, i' vouèyait aussi ben comme à l'âge d'quinze ans. "Ah!" i' dzit, "Pierre, aulieurs d'me faire dzu bien, vous vouliez m'ôter la vie!" l'a dzit à son domestique d'prend' Pierre et d'l'emm'ner dans l'bois pis d'le tsuer. "Pis," i' dzit, "'porte-moin son coeur pour que j'le fasse cuire sus les braises."

Il[s] ont partsi, pis il[s] ont arrivé dans l'bois. L'domestique, lui, il aimait Pierre, i' voulait pas l'tsuer. Pierre y'a dzit: "Tsire!" L'pistolet 'l a pas voulu partsir. l'avait eune 'tsite chienne nouèr'te qui les suivait. l' dzit au domestique: "Tsire c'te p'tsite chienne-là." 'L a tsiré la p'tsite chienne-là, pis l'a tsuée au premier coup. "Portez l'coeur de c'te p'tsite chienne'là à mon père et dzi[s]-y c'est l'mien." l'a mis ein billet dans la botte d'son capot. "Mon père i' va avouère besoin d'moin encore, donne-y c'billet quand i' va avouère besoin d'moin. Ayez ben soin d'mon j'val, laisse pas personne l'toucher."

L'domestique i'a apporté c'coeur-là à son père à Pierre. Son père i' l'a mangé frit sur les braises. Padent c'temps-là, Pierre s'a mis à trav'ler pis 'l a arrivé à eune grande ville. l'a d'mandé pour coucher. Quand i' s'sont mis à la tab' pour souper l'souère, i'avait eune belle tab', mais pas d'liqueur. l'ont dzit qu'i'avait des années 'l ontvaient pas eu d'liqueur. l' dzit: "Portez-moin ma valise." 'L a pris sa bouteille de vin, 'l a tout empli les gob'lets autour d'la table. L'aubergisse voulait ach'ter la bouteille de vin. Alle a offert à Pierre eune bonne somme d'argent pour sa bouteille. Pierre y'a vendzu sus condzition qu'quand la Belle aux Ch'veux d'Or appel-l'rait pour, i' fallait qu'a y rende. l' l'a vendzue, pis i' s'a rentourné l'lend'main matin; i' trav'lait toujours.

L'lend'main au souère, i'est arrivé à eune aut' auberge, pis 'l a d'mandé à coucher encore. l' s'a assis à la table pour souper: belle table, mais pas d'pain. Pierre a d'mandé pour dzu pain. Ça s'fait qu'i'ont dzit qu'i'avait pas d'pain, qu'i'étaient dans la dzisette depuis ben des années. 'L dzit qu'i' y 'portent sa valise. 'L a pris l'pain d'la Belle aux Ch'veux d'Or. Il a donné tout ça la tab' 'l a voulu user. l'était toujours rond. L'aubergisse voulait ach'ter l'pain avec Pierre. Pierre y'a vendzu l'pain pour eune bonne somme d'argent sus condzition qu'si la Belle aux Ch'veux d'Or alle app'lait pour son pain, fallait qu'a y rende.

Pierre i' s'en va là trav'ler au loin pis i'arrive sus ein rouè. l' s'engage au rouè. 'L a pas été là longtemps qu'tout l'monde l'aimait, Pierre. L'vieux rouè l'a mis dans son magasin à travailler, et tout l'monde qui ach'tait, 'l aimait mieux ach'ter avec Pierre qu'avec les aut's qui travaillaient dans l'magasin. A c't'heure, padent c'temps-là, la Belle aux Ch'veux d'Or alle a trouvé ein p'tsit garçon.

Alle a fait dzire au vieux roué qui était eurvenu à l'âge de quinze ans qu'i' y'envouèye l'homme qui avait été qu'ri d'l'eau d'sa fotaine. "Ah!" i' dzit au plus vieux, "c'était touè qui as été qu'ri d'l'eau d'la fotaine d'la Belle aux Ch'veux d'Or, i' faudra qu'tsu ailles." l'est partsi dans son bâtsiment. Quand 'l a arrivé à la place où est-ce qu'i' arrivent pour *lann'der,* i'a amarré son bâtsiment. Il a partsi en montant la montagne à quat' pattes. Le p'tsit garçon d'la Belle aux Ch'veux d'Or i'était après jouer sus la gal'rie. "Oh! m'man, j'vouès ein coq d'Inde qui s'en vient," —"Tais-touè, p'tsit bêta," a dzit, "c'est pas ein coq d'Inde, c't'ein prince."

Après qu'i' a arrivé, la princesse l'a fait rentrer. A a d'mandé: "C'est vous qui était v'nu qu'ri d'l'eau d'ma fotaine?" —I'a dzit: "Oui, ma princesse, c'était moin." A dzit: "Dzites-moin ça vous avez faite quand vous avez arrivé icitte." —"Eh ben!" i' dzit, "j'ai rentré; i'avait eune belle princesse qui dormait." —"L'avez-vous touchée, c'te princesse-là?" —"Oh! non, j'l'ai pas touchée." —"Après ça, quoi vous l'avez faite?" —"l'avait eune bouteille de vin sus la table. J'en ai bu, a était toujours pleine." —"Est-ce qu'vous avez pris bouteille-là?" —"Oh! non, ma princesse, j'l'ai pas pris." —"Après ça, qu'est-ce qu'vous avez faite?" —"L avait ein pain sur la tab', j'ai coupé ein morceau d'après; i'était toujours rond." —"Vous avez pris c'pain-là?" —"Oh! non, ma princesse, j'l'ai pas pris." —"Après ça, qu'est-ce qu'vous l'avez faite?" —"J'ai été dans l'parterre. I' nn'avait ein aigle d'couché tout près d'la fotaine. J'ai empli ma bouteille; après ça, j'ai arraché eune pleume de d'ssus son aile gauche." —"Mais," a dzit, "t'as mentsi, c'est pas touè qu'es v'nu. Tsu vas t'en aller et tsu vas dzire à ton père qu's'i' enwouèye pas ceul qu'est v'nu qu'ri d'l'eau d'ma fotaine, j'vas engloutsir sa ville."

Quand son garçon 'l est eurvenu et i' y'a dzit qu'c'était pas lui, qu'c'était Pierre qui était allé charcer d'l'eau d'la fotaine d'la Belle aux Ch'veux d'Or, l'vieux roué a dzit: "Pierre, j'ai mangé son coeur frit sus les braises." Ça s'fait quand l'p'tsit domestique a vu l'roué si troublé, i'a donné c'billet qu'i' y'avait dans la botte d'son capot. L'vieux roué a eurgardé ça. "Quocé?" i' dzit, "Pierre i'est pas mort? Queul coeur," i' dzit, "j'ai mangé?" L'domestique y'a dzit qu'c'était l'coeur d'la p'tsite chienne nouèr'te qui l'suivait.

Ça a pas été longtemps avant qu'le vieux roué envouè la parole à Pierre qu'i' s'en eurvienne. Quand Pierre 'l a su qu'son père était dans l'troub', i'a partsi pour s'en eurvenir. l'a passé à eune des auberges où i'a dzit qu'la Belle aux Ch'veux d'Or avait d'mandé son pain; i'a passé à l'aut' auberge, dzisant qu'la Belle aux Ch'veux d'Or avait d'mandé sa bouteille de vin. Quand il a arrivé d'ssus son père, i'a d'mandé à son père quocé c'était son trouble. Son père y'a dzit la Belle aux Ch'veux d'Or l'faisait d'mander, qu'i' vaille. "Aujourdz'hui, vous crouèyez qu'c'est mouè qui a été qu'ri d'l'eau d'la fotaine à la Belle aux Ch'veux d'Or ou ben mon frère?" I' dzit: "Mouè, j'vas au château d'la Belle aux Ch'veux d'Or, pis quand j'vas eurv'nir, j'veux pas trouver mes deux frères icitte," i' dzit à son père.

Pierre a d'mandé à son p'tsit domestique pour son j'val. L'p'tsit domestique 'l a été qu'ri son j'val tout d'suite. Pierre 'l a monté dessus, pis 'l a partsi. Son ch'fal i'allait aussi ben sus l'eau comme sus la terre. Quand i'est arrivé à la montagne, i'est partsi à monter la montagne d'vit' à j'val. L'p'tsit garçon d'la Belle aux Ch'veux d'Or i'était après jouer sus la gal'rie toujours. "Mouman, j'vouès ein beau prince qui s'en vient sus ein beau joual."

Il a arrivé au château, pis la princesse l'a fait rentrer. A y'a donné eune chaise pour qu'i' s'assise. "C'était vous qui était v'nu qu'ri d'l'eau d'ma fotaine?" —"Oui, ma princesse," i' dzit, "c'était moin." —"A queule heure, vous êtes v'nu icitte?" —"Jusse à midzi." —"Quoice que vous avez faite?" —"Trouvé eune belle princesse, après dormir." —"Est-ce qu'vous avez touché c'te princesse-là?" —"Oui, bougre! alle était trop jolite, i' fallait que j'l'embrasse." —"Après ça," a dzit, "quoice qu'vous avez faite?" —"T' nn'avait eune bouteille de vin sus eune tab', j'en ai pris eune gorgée d'dans, alle était toujours pleine." —"Est-ce qu'vous avez pris bouteille-là?" —"Oui, ma princesse, j'l'ai pris et j'l'ai mis dans ma valise."

La Belle aux Ch'veux d'Or alle était certain à c't'heure qu'c'était lui qui était v'nu, mais alle a continué pour qu'i' y'ait pas d'erreur possib'. "Après ça," a dzit, "quocé qu'vous avez faite?" —"N'avait ein pain," i' dzit, "j'en ai coupé ein morceau; i'était toujours rond." —"Vous l'avez pris c'te pain-là?" —"Ah! oui, ma princesse, j'l'ai 'porté avec moin." —"Après ça, quoice qu'vous avez faite?" —"J'ai été d'dans l'parterre. N'avait eune aigle d'couchée près d'ta fotaine. J'ai pris ma bouteille, j'l'ai emplie, pis après ça, j'y ai arraché eune pleume sus son aile drétte." —"Oui," a dzit, "c'est vous qui est v'nu chercher d'l'eau d'ma fotaine. I' faut s'marier. Vous prendra mon j'val pis mon carrosse; vous ira qu'ri vot' père pis vot' mère. Am'nez-lé icitte pis on va s'marier. Souèyez ben sûr d'dzire à vos deux frères qu'i' souèyent pas là quand on va s'rentourner à vot' maisonne."

11.

Prince Green Serpent and La Valeur

It's good to tell you that once upon a time there was an old soldier. He had been one of the king's soldiers for a long time and was getting worn out. One day, he went to ask the king for his discharge. The old king said, "Here, La Valeur, here's twenty-five cents. Go and have a drink." But this solution didn't last long. La Valeur quickly had his drink and, then, came back to ask the king for his discharge. The king said, "Oh, well. I guess I'll let you have your discharge, La Valeur. But don't forget to say good-bye to me before you leave."

La Valeur went to the tailor's and told him that he was leaving the king's army. The tailor said, "Well, La Valeur, why don't you take my turn at guard duty tonight until eleven o'clock. I'll pay you well for your time. I have more work than I can do in here." So, La Valeur took the tailor's turn on guard duty. But when eleven o'clock came and his turn was up, he fired the cannon. It frightened the Grand Vizier, who came to the king asking, "What was that?" —"Oh," said the king. "That was just La Valeur leaving my service and saying good-bye before he leaves."

So the next morning, La Valeur left and went traveling. He stayed on the road until he got tired. He sat down on a log and was complaining to himself that he had no more tobacco, because he would like to have a smoke, when the Log began to move. "Ah!" said La Valeur. "Are you moving?" The Log answered, "Yes, I'm moving. Go get a bunch of hickory switches and come back and use them to beat on this log." La Valeur went and got his bunch of switches and began to beat on the Log with them, until he was exhausted, and his forehead was dripping with sweat. Then he lay down and went to sleep.

When he woke up, there was a saucer next to him, with tobacco, a pipe, and matches in it. He lit the pipe and began to look around. He saw a handsome Prince walking nearby. The Prince said, "Good morning, La Valeur." —"Good morning," answered La Valeur. "I don't know your name." The stranger answered, "My name is Prince Green Serpent. You set me free by beating me with your hickory switches." La Valeur didn't believe this was true, and he said, "Maybe." The stranger said, "La Valeur, come and stay with me. You won't have to do anything except eat. I'll give you all the money you want to spend."

So La Valeur went with the Prince. He stayed with him for quite a while. He spent his days just going here and there and going from one tavern to another drinking. Finally, he got tired of that little village and wanted to leave. So he said to Prince Green Serpent, "I'm going to leave." The Prince answered, "What? Aren't you happy here?" —"Yes, I'm fine, but I'm tired of this place." —"Well, here, take this shirt," answered Prince Green Serpent. "When you put on this shirt you will be invisible, and no one can see you. And here is a sword that will cut fifty feet around you."

Then, La Valeur went out traveling again. He came to another town with another King. He pledged himself to the King to work for him, and the King liked him so much that he made La Valeur his son-in-law. But his daughter didn't like her new husband. She was in love with another king who was her father's enemy. When the other king learned that the girl he loved had been married off to La Valeur, he made war on the girl's father. The morning that he was leaving to go off to battle, La Valeur put on his shirt and asked the King, "Do you see me?" The King answered, "No, I can't see you at all."

So, La Valeur took his sword and left at the head of the army. It took him no time at all to destroy half of the enemy army. He took the enemy king prisoner and brought him in to his father-in-law. La Valeur promised the enemy king that he wouldn't harm him, and he told his father-in-law about this promise he had made. They put the king in prison. La Valeur's wife went to feed him every day and to talk with him. One day, the enemy king told her, "Ask your husband what kind of power he has that he can destroy so many people at the same time. Be nice to him tonight."

When La Valeur came back that night, his wife went to meet him. She acted as though she loved him. That night when they were in bed, she said to him, "La Valeur, my dear husband, tell me how you manage to destroy so many people at one time and so fast." — "Well," he answered, "you know that little box that you kick around every day on the floor? Well, in there I have a shirt that makes me invisible when I put it on. Then I also have a sword that cuts everything in a circle fifty feet wide around me." —"Ah!" answered his wife, "I guess you can destroy a lot of people with those things, all right."

When they got up the next morning, the old King said to La Valeur, "You're the only one of my children who have ever asked me to show them their property." So the next morning, they saddled up horses and set off to visit one city after another, until late in the afternoon. Then, the old King said, "Now it's time to go back home. Tomorrow I'll bring you in another direction." While they were gone, La Valeur's wife went and let the other king that she loved out of prison and gave him La Valeur's shirt to put on. They saddled up their horses and left. The sun was going down, and as La Valeur was returning home, he saw two horses coming toward him at top speed. He said, "We're done for. My wife has let the other king out, and he will kill both of us." La Valeur and his father-in-law got near the other two, and he asked, "Are you going to kill us?" —"Yes, I'm going to kill you," answered the enemy king. La Valeur said, "Well, I would like to ask you just one favor. Cut me in little pieces, put me into my suitcase, and tie the suitcase onto my saddle. Then tie the reins onto my saddle so that the horse can't eat, turn him in the other direction, give

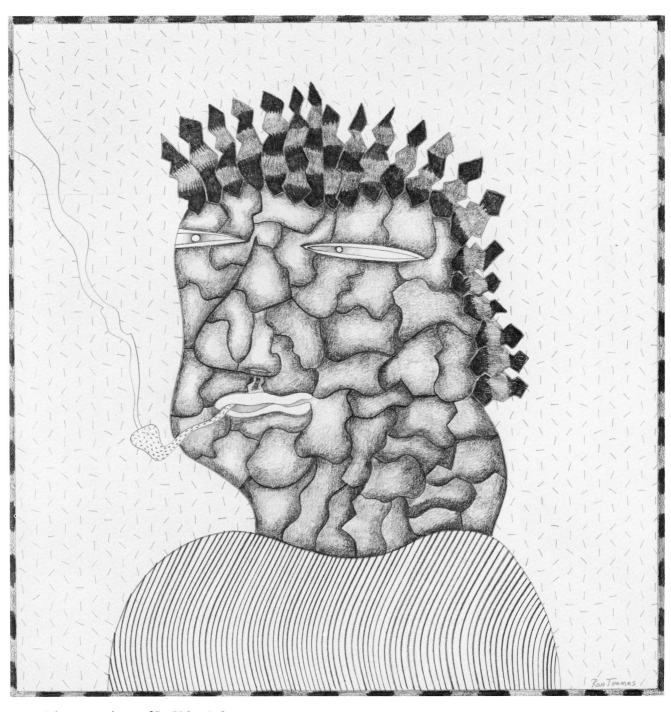

The many pieces of La Valeur's face

It's Good to Tell You

him a blow with your sword on the left flank, and let him go." The King let him go in this way, and then killed the old King too. Then he and La Valeur's widow went back home, and they got married.

One day, Prince Green Serpent's guard said, "I see a horse coming toward us at top speed." The prince said to him, "Open the gate. That's La Valeur." So the guard opened the gate, and the horse came right up on the porch of the Prince's house. Prince Green Serpent took the suitcase into a bedroom and put La Valeur back together again. He rubbed him all over with a kind of salve that he had. La Valeur came back to life but he stayed asleep for a long time afterward. Then one morning, at about nine o'clock, La Valeur woke up, looked all around, and went out to see where he was. Prince Green Serpent was out in his front yard. He asked La Valeur, "How do you feel this morning?" —"Well," answered La Valeur, "I don't feel too good. I feel all broken up." —"How long have you been sleeping, La Valeur?" asked the prince. —"I don't know," answered La Valeur. "I think I've been asleep since last evening." The prince answered, "Well, you've been sleeping for seven years, La Valeur." —"Well, I don't know," answered La Valeur. "I still don't feel very good." La Valeur stayed with Prince Green Serpent for a long time after that.

One day, as La Valeur was sitting by the fire, he was watching these little ants going by and was catching them on the tip of his lance. When he would turn them over on their backs, they would try to take revenge by biting the lance. La Valeur thought this was funny, and he was laughing. Prince Green Serpent asked him, "Why are you laughing?" —"I'm laughing at those little ants taking their revenge on my lance," answered La Valeur. —"What?" said Prince Green Serpent. "Do you want to take your revenge too?" La Valeur answered, "Yes, I do. I'm leaving tomorrow morning."

The next morning, the prince gave a bridle to La Valeur and said to him, "When you arrive near the town, put this bridle into your mouth, and you will turn into the most beautiful horse anyone has even seen. Find the poorest man in the town and let him catch you. He's a water carrier." When he got to the edge of the town, by the spring where the old man got his water, he put on his bridle, and the old man soon came. "What a beautiful horse!" he said. "I must try to catch him." So, he tried to catch the horse gently, by calling to him, "Cup, cup cup!" He caught the horse by the bridle and brought him back to his barn and filled the manger full of hay for the horse to eat.

After awhile, he came back to check on his horse and found that it hadn't eaten anything. He said to the horse, "Is it possible that a horse as beautiful as you doesn't eat hay?" The horse answered, "No, I don't eat hay." The man was surprised. "Can you talk?" he asked. The horse answered, "Yes, I can talk. I want you to get on my back and ride by the king's house. He will ask you where you got such a beautiful horse. Tell him that you bought me. He's going to try to buy me from you. Sell me for one hundred dollars but be sure to keep the bridle."

When the old man rode by the king's house, the king asked, "Where did you find such a beautiful horse?" The old man answered, "It's one that I bought." —"Don't you want to sell it?" asked the king. —"I'll sell it," answered the old man, "if I get my price." The king asked, "What is your price?" —"One hundred dollars," answered the old man. The king said, "Well, all right, bring him into my stable." But the old man forgot to take off the bridle. The king went to get the queen to see the beautiful horse he had bought. When she came and looked at him in the stable, she recognized him. She said, "Yes, indeed, he is a beautiful horse, but I demand that he be killed by a blow through his heart between now and sundown."

The king went away angry. "We can't keep anything nice around here," he grumbled. The little servant girl came out to see the beautiful horse. She asked, "Is it possible that a beautiful horse like you will be killed this evening?" The horse answered, "Yes, but only you can save my life." The little girl answered, "Can you talk, beautiful horse?" —"Yes," he answered. "A beautiful horse like me can talk. They're going to come and kill me this evening. Ask them for the first three drops of my blood. Take those three drops of blood and put them on each side of the door. Tomorrow morning, you will find the three most beautiful trees you have ever seen." The next morning, she went out to look where she had dropped the three drops of blood and found the beautiful trees. Then she went in and told the king to come right away and see the beautiful trees that had grown up next to his door. The old king and queen came, and they found the trees very pretty. But the queen said, "Yes, they are very pretty. But I demand that they be cut down and burned before sundown." The little servant said, "Is it possible for beautiful trees like you to be cut down and burned?" And the trees answered, "Yes, and only you can save our life. Ask them for the first three chips of wood, and this evening throw them into the millpond. Tomorrow morning, you will find the three most beautiful golden ducks you have ever seen."

The little servant girl went down to the pond to look the next morning and found her beautiful golden ducks. She went to tell the king to come with his rifle and see the beautiful ducks. The king did bring his rifle, and as he was sighting along it getting ready to shoot, the ducks flew away to the other end of the pond. They kept doing this until the king was all soaked with the dew. He went back to his house, and his wife said, "Why don't you put on your shirt?" —"Well, I never thought of doing that," he answered. He put on his magic shirt and went back to the pond. He began running from one end of the pond to the other, chasing the ducks, until the shirt was all soaked. He took it off and laid it out on some branches so it would dry out. Then, he went back to the other end of the pond, still chasing the ducks. When the ducks left the other end, they flew right into the shirt. Then La Valeur went and killed the king, and went back to his house, caught his wife, and burned her. He then married the little servant who had saved his life.

L'Prince Serpent Vert pis La Valeur

C'était bon d'vous dzire eune fouès c'était ein vieux soldat. I' nn'avait longtemps qu'i' était soldat pour l'rouè. I' s'a trouvé tanné. Eune journée, i'est allé trouver l'rouè pour sa décharze. L'vieux rouè i' dzit: "Quiens, La Valeur, en v'là vingt-cinq sous icitte, va-t'en bouère l'filet." Ça l'a pas dzuré longtemps; La Valeur 'l a bétôt eu bu. Il a eurtourné vouère l'rouè pour sa décharze. "Ah ben!" i' dzit, "La Valeur, j'vas t'la donner ta décharze, mais oublie pas de m'dzire aguieu avant d't'en aller."

La Valeur 'l a été sus l'tailleur. I'a dzit qu'i' yavait eu sa décharge. Ben, l'tailleur i' dzit à La Valeur: "Garde donc mon quart à souère jusqu'à onze heures. J'vas ben t'payer. J'ai plus d'ouvrage que j'peux faire icitte d'dans." La Valeur 'l a été garder l'quart dzu tailleur. Quand onze heures est v'nu, son temps était fini, 'l a mis l'feu au connon. Grand vizir 'l est v'nu au rouè vit'ment: "Quoice que c'est," i' dzit, "Sire?" —"Ah!" i' dzit, "c'est La Valeur qui a fini son temps là. I' dzit aguieu, i' s'en va, là."

V'là, i' part l'lend'main matin, i' s'en va en trav'lant. 'L a trav'lé jusqu'à temps 'l était lasse. Assis sur eune *logue*, i'était après s'lamenter, i'avait pus d'tabac, 'l aurait aimé d'fumer. La *logue* 'l a commencé à grouiller. "Ah!" i' dzit, "tsu grouilles, touè?" —"Oui," i' dzit, "moin, j'grouille. Va t'qu'ri eune brassée de 'harts d'nouèyer, pis viens tout la user sus *logue*-là." I'a été qu'ri sa brassée de 'harts, pis 'l a commencé à cogner. 'L a cogné jusqu'à temps 'l a été tout trempé d'sueur. I'était lasse; i' s'a couché, i' s'a endormi.

Quand i' s'a reveillé, i'a trouvé eune sicoupe. 'L avait dzu tabac, pis eune pipe pis des *mètches* dedans. 'L a allumé sa pipe pis 'l a commencé à eurgarder à l'entour. 'L a vu ein beau prince qu'i'était après s'prom'ner à l'entour. I' dzit: "Bonjour, La Valeur." —"Bonjour," i' dizit, "j'connais pas ton nom." —"Mon nom," i' dzit, "c'est Prince Serpent Vert. Tsu m'as délivré à user 'harts d'nouèyer-là sus mon dos." La Valeur i' crouéyait pas ça 'l était vrai. I'a dzit: "Ça s'peut!" I' dzit: "Viens donc rester avec moin, La Valeur. Tsu auras eurien à faire à part qu'manger. M'as t'donner tout l'argent tsu vas avouère d'besoin pour dépenser."

La Valeur 'l a été avec lui. 'L a resté avec Prince Serpent Vert eune bonne escousse. I' s'prom'nait icitte pis là-bas, i' buvait d'eune *grocerie* à l'aut'. Il était v'nu tanné d'p'tsit village-là, i' voulait pas rester. 'L a dzit au Prince Serpent Vert: "Moin, j'm'en vas d'icitte." —"Comment ça s'fait?" i' dzit. "T'es pas ben, La Valeur?" —"Oui," i' dzit, "j'sus ben, mais j'sus tanné d'rester icitte." —"Mais quiens, en v'là eune ch'mise que je t'donne. Tsu vas mett' ch'mise-là, tsu vas êt' invisib'. I'aura pas personne qui pourra t'ouère. En v'là icitte," i' dzit, "ein sable qui coupe cinquante pas à l'entour de touè."

Là, 'l a partsi en trav'lant. 'L a été dans ein aut' ville, où 'l avait ein aut' rouè. I' s'a engagé au rouè. L'vieux rouè i' s'a trouvé frappé sus La Valeur. I' l'a marié avec sa fille. Alle aimait pas La Valeur, elle, par exemple. Alle aimait ein aut' rouè qui était ein enn'mi à son père. Quand l'aut' rouè 'l a vu La Valeur était marié à la fille rouè-là, i'a faite la guerre au beau-père à La Valeur. La matsinée i' fallait qu'i' parte pour aller en guerre, i'a pris sa ch'mise, pis i' l'a mis. I'a d'mandé au rouè: "Vous m'ouè?" —"Non," i' dzit, "moin, j'te ouès pas."

La Valeur 'l a pris son sable pis 'l a partsi d'vant l'armée. 'L a été pas auquin temps qu'il a détruit la moquié d'l'armée des enn'mis. 'L a pris l'aut' rouè prisognier, i'a em'né à son beau-père, à son rouè à lui. I'a promis au rouè d'pas y faire dzu mal, lui, La Valeur. Il a dzit à son beau-père 'l avait promis d'pas yi faire dzu mal. I' l'ont mis dans les prisons. La femme à La Valeur alle allait l'souègner tous les jours pis a charrait avec lui. Eune journée, i' dzit à elle; "D'mande donc à ton mari quelle sorte d'pouwère il a pour détruire tant d'monde tout d'ein coup. Fai[s]-y," i' dzit, "bonne mine à souère."

Quand La Valeur 'l a eurvenu, sa famme a été l'rencontrer. A faisait comme si a l'aimait. L'souère après qu'il[s] ont été couchés: —"La Valeur," a dzit, "mon cher mari, dzis-mouè donc comment tsu fais ça pour détruire tant d'monde si vite comme tsu les détruis." —"Ben," i' dzit, "tsu connais p'tsite cassette-là tsu boules à coups d'pieds là tous les jours; ben, là d'dans," i' dzit, "j'ai eune ch'mise. Quand j'la mets," i' dzit, "j'sus invisb'." I' dzit: "J'ai ein sable qui coupe cinquante pas à l'entour d'moin." —"Ah!" a dzit, "j'crouès ben, tsu peux en détruire beaucoup dzu monde avec chose-là, ben sûr!"

Quand i' s'est l'vé matin-là, vieux rouè 'l a dzit à La Valeur: "Vous l'êtes l'seul d'mes enfants qui m'avez jamais d'mandé pour aller ouère vos biens." L'lend'main matin, i' s'ont séllé chaquin ein ch'val, 'l ont partsi à trav'ler d'eune ville à l'aut' jusqu'à tard dans l'après-midzi. L'vieux rouè i'a dzit: "A c't'heure, on va s'rentourner. D'main," i' dzit, "j'vas t'emm'ner sus ein aut' bord." Padent qu'i' sontaient partsis, la femme à La Valeur a été lâcher l'aut' rouè, qu'était en prison pis qu'alle aimait. Il a mis la ch'mise à La Valeur, lui, rouè-là. S'ont séllé chaquin ein ch'val, lui pis la femme à La Valeur. L'soleil i'était après v'nir joliment bas. La Valeur a vu deux ch'vaux qui s'en v'naient en toute course. I' dzit: "On l'est fini. Ma femme alle a lâché l'aut' rouè. I' va nous tsuer tous les deusses." 'L ont arrivé tout près d'l'eux aut's. 'L a dzit au rouè: "Tsu vas m'tsuer." —"Ouais, j'vas t'tsuer." —"Nn'a qu'eune chose que j'te d'mande, eune faveur qu'tsu m'faises. Coupaille-moin tout par morceaux," i' dzit, "mets-moin dans ma valise, amarre ben ma valise après ma corde d'selle, pis," i' dzit, "rêne mon ch'val avec la rêne d'bride ben serré pour qu'i' peut pas manger, eurvire-lé la tête sus l'aut'bord, donne-li ein coup d'sable sur la croupe gauche," i' dzit, "pis laisse-lé aller." Padent i' s'en va, on en parle pus d'lui padent ein bon boute d'temps. 'L ont tsué l'vieux rouè. Ça fait i' s'ont rentournés, pis i' s'ont mariés, eux aut's.

Eune journée, l'gardeur d'barrières au Prince Serpent Vert i' dzit: "J'ouès ein ch'val qui s'en vient à toute course. Ouvre-y la barrière," i' dzit, "c'est La Valeur, ça." L'domestique y'a rouvert la barrière, pis l'ch'val 'l est v'nu drètte sus la gal'rie à la maisonne dzu Prince Serpent Vert. Prince Serpent Vert 'l a pris la valise, 'l a été dans eune chamb', 'l a tout eurmis La Valeur ensemb' encore. I' l'a ben graissé avec eune sorte d'enguent 'l avait. La Valeur 'l est eurvenu en vie, mais 'l est resté endormi longtemps. Ein matin, à peu près à neuf heures, La Valeur i' s'a l'vé, il a eurgardé à l'entour, sortsi pour ouère où 'l était. Prince Serpent Vert 'l était après s'prom'ner dans sa cour, lui. 'L a d'mandé à La Valeur: "Comment qu'tsu *files* à matin?" —"Ah!" i' dzit, "j'*file* pas ben à matin, j'*file* tout cassaillé." —"Comment longtemps qu'tsu dors," i' dzit, "La Valeur?" —I' dzit: "J'connais pas, j'pense que j'dors depuis hier au souère." —"En v'là sept ans," i' dzit, "qu'tsu dors, La Valeur." — "Ah!" i' dzit, "j'connais pas, j'*file* pas ben, toujours." 'L a resté avec Prince Serpent Vert longtemps, La Valeur.

Eune journée, 'l était assis l'long d'la chum'née. I' avait des p'tsites frémilles qui passaient, pis i' les piquait avec sa lance. I' s'eurviraient p'tsites frémilles-là, pis i' s'eurvengeaient, i' mordaient après la lance. Ça faisait rire La Valeur, ça. Prince Serpent Vert i' l'attendait rire pis i' dzit: "Quocé t'as à rire donc, La Valeur?" —"J'chus-t-après rire de p'tsites frémilles-là. I' s'eurvenchent," i' dzit, "c'est c'qui m'fait rire." —"Quocé? T'as envie de t'eurvenger, touè aussite?" —"Oui," i' dzit, "j'vas eurpartsir d'main."

The invisible La Valeur

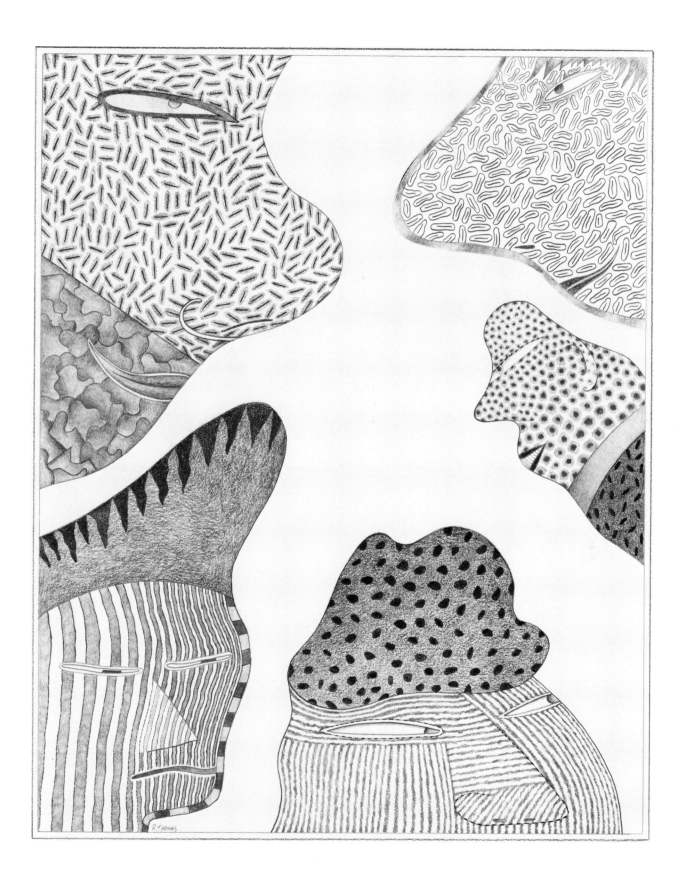

L'lend'main matin, i'a donné eune bride à La Valeur. "Quand tsu vas arriver dans l'bord d'la ville, tsu vas mett' bride-là dans ta guieule, pis tsu vas êt' l'plus beau ch'val tsu l'as jamais vu. Tsu vas t'quitter attraper par l'plus pauvre homme qu'il a dans la ville, ein vieux charrieur d'eau." Quand 'l a arrivé au ras d'la ville, près d'la fotaine où vieux-là pernait son eau, il a mis sa bride, pis l'aut' est v'nu. "Oh! mais queul beau ch'val! I' faut qu'j'assaye à l'attraper." I' commence à assayer à attraper l'ch'val tout douc'ment: "Coppe, coppe, coppe!" Ça fait ein bon coup 'l a mis la main sus la bride. 'L a pris l'ch'val, pis 'l a été l'emm'ner cheux lui dans son écurie; 'l a rempli l'ratelier tout plein d'foin.

'L est eurvenu ouère, pis son ch'val 'l avait pas mangé eune bouchée. "Ah!" i' dzit, "c'est-i' possib' ein beau ch'val comme touè, tsu manges pas l'foin?" —"Non," i' dzit, "ein ch'val comme moin i' mange pas dzu foin." —"Ah!" i' dzit, "beau j'val, tsu parles, touè?" —"Ah! oui," i' dzit, "j'parle, moin." —"Tsu vas monter sus mon dos, tsu vas passer d'vant d'ssus l'rouè, pis i' va te d'mander oùqu't'as pris ton beau j'val. Dzi[s]-y tsu l'as ach'té. I' va assayer à l'ach'ter avec touè. Vends-moin pour cent piasses et réserve la bride."

Quand l'vieux 'l a passé d'vant dessus l'rouè, i'a d'mandé: "Oùsque vous 'l a pris c'beau joual?" —"Ah!" i' dzit, "c'en est ein qu'j'ai ach'té." —"Vous veut pas l'vend'?" i' dzit. —"M'as l'vend'," i' dzit, "si j'ai mon prix." —"Quocé qu'est ton prix?" i' dzit. —"Cent piasses." —"Ben, emmène-lé à mon écurie," i' dzit. I'a oblié dz'y ôter la bride. L'vieux rouè a été qu'ri la reine qu'a vienne ouère c'beau ch'val. Alle est v'nue, pis a l'a eurgardé par la porte; a l'a eurconnu. —"Ouais," a dzit, "c'est ein beau choual, mais j'prétends qu'i' sèye saigné au coeur, entre icitte pis l'soleil couché."

L'rouè a partsi fâché. "On peut rien garder d'beau icitte," i' dzit. La p'tsite servante alle a été ouère à beau choual-là. "C'est-t'i' possib'," a dzit, "ein beau choual comme toué êt' tsué à souère?" Beau choual i' dzit: "Ouais, mais nn'a rien qu'touè qui peux m'sauver la vie." —"Ah!" a dzit, "tsu parles, beau choual?" —"Ouais," i' dzit, "ein beau choual comme moin i' parle. I' vont v'nir pour m'saingner," i' dzit, "à souère. D'mande-leu pour les trois premières gouttes d'mon sang. Pis," i' dzit, "tsu vas prend' les trois gouttes d'sang-là, tsu vas les mett' chaque bord d'la porte à souère, d'main matin, ça va êt' les plus beaux arb's qu'vous 'l a jamais vus." Alle a été ouère d'bon matin. Alle a trouvé les beaux arb's, pis alle a été qu'ri l'vieux rouè pour qu'i' vienne ouère d'bon matin ces beaux arb's d'chaque bord d'sa porte. L'vieux rouè pis la vieille reine i' sont v'nus. Ah! pis i' les trouvaient jolis. La vieille reine a dzit: "Oui, i' sont beaux, mais j'prétends qu'i' souèyent tou[s] coupés pis brûlés entre icitte pis l'soleil couché." La p'tsite servante a dzit: "C'est-t'i' possib' des jolis arb's comme vous aut's i' s'ront coupés pis brûlés?" Ça fait les arb's i' ont dzit: "I' nn'a ien qu'touè qui peux nous sauver la vie. D'mande-leu pour les trois premiers écopeaux, pis à souère va les j'ter dans l'étang dzu moulin. D'main matin, ça va êt' les plus jolis canards dorés qu'vous 'l a jamais vus."

La p'tsite servante alle a été ouère, l'lend'main matin. Alle a trouvé ses beaux canards dorés. A ya été dzire au vieux rouè qu'i' vienne, lui, avec son fusil. L'vieux rouè 'l est v'nu avec son fusil; comme i' s'met en joue pour tsirer, les canards i' voltigeaient à l'aut' boute d'l'étang jusqu'à l'vieux rouè 'l était tout trempe dans la rosée. I'est eurvenue cheux lui. Sa femme a dzit: "Pourquoi qu'tsu mets pas ta ch'mise?" —"Ben," i' dzit, "tsu vouès, j'avais jamais pensé à ça." I' a mis sa ch'mise, pis i'a eurtourné. 'L a commencé à courir d'ein boute à l'aut' d'l'étang jusqu'à temps sa ch'mise a v'nu tout mouillée. Il l'a ôtée, pis i' l'a étendzue sus des p'tsites branches pour qu'a chesse. I'a eurtourné en gagnant l'aut' boute après ses canards encore. Quand les canards 'l ont partsi d'là, 'l ont pris leu volée, i' sont v'nus, pis 'l ont rentré dans la ch'mise. La Valeur 'l a été oùsqu'est l'vieux rouè pis i' l'a tsué. I'a été à sa maisonne, i'a attrapé sa femme, pis i' l'a faite brûler. I' s'a marié avec la p'tsite servante qui y'avait sauvé la vie, là.

It's Good to Tell You

12.

Old Man La Feve

It's good to tell you once upon a time there were an old man and an old woman. They were poor, and all they had to eat every day was beans. Old Man La Feve had sowed beans in his garden. One of the vines went way up in the air, and one day the Old Man decided to climb it to see where it went. When he got to the end of the vine, he was in another world. When he got onto this new earth, he started off walking. He spent the night at an inn and, then, walked some more the next day. Late in the afternoon, he arrived at another house, and he began talking with the old man and woman who lived there. That evening he told them how poor he was. The old woman said, "I'm going to give you a beautiful napkin, and when you want something to eat all you have to do is spread out your napkin and say, 'Beautiful napkin, bring me something to eat and drink.' "

The next evening, he was on his way back home and came to the inn where he had spent the first night. The Innkeeper asked him what he had in his little package. He said, "Oh, it's a beautiful napkin." That night while the Old Man was sleeping, the Innkeeper went in and put an old napkin under his arm in place of the magic one. When the Old Man got back home, he called in his wife and told her to set the table. Then, he spread out his napkin and said, "Beautiful napkin bring me something to eat and drink." He waited awhile, but nothing happened. He said to his wife, "Ah! I was tricked last night!"

The next morning, he left again and climbed back up his beanstalk. He stayed at the inn again that night, and the morning after he set out to find his friends who had given him the napkin. This time, they gave him an old nag. The next morning, he left with his old nag to go back home. He had to stay at the inn that night again, and the Innkeeper asked him about his old horse. "Ah!" he answered. "That old horse makes money." So, the Innkeeper took her own old horse and exchanged it with Old Man La Feve's horse, and the next morning the Old Man left with the wrong horse to go back home. When he got home, he told his wife to spread a good sheet out on the ground. Then he said, "Old horse, I want you to give me gold and silver." After awhile, the old horse made a big pile of manure on the sheet. The old woman was angry with her husband, but he said to her, "I was tricked again last night. I'm going back there tomorrow morning."

So, he went back to find his friends the next day. They said to him, "Why did you come back?" —"I lost my horse," he told them. —"Well, spend the night with us and get rested up," they answered. The next morning, when he was getting ready to leave, they gave him a little bumblebee. They told him, "All you have to say is, 'Little bumblebee, do as God tells you,' and that little bumblebee will do its duty. It knows what to do with that Innkeeper. She's the one who tricked you." That evening, the old man arrived at the inn to spend the night. He put his little bumblebee on the mantel, and the Innkeeper asked him, "What are you putting there?" —"Oh, there?" —"Oh," answered the Old Man, "it's just a little bumblebee." The Innkeeper asked, "what are you doing with that little bumblebee?" —"Oh, nothing," said the Old Man. "You only have to say to it, 'Do what God commands,' and it stings."

Well, that tickled the Innkeeper's fancy. The next morning, she said to her husband, before Old Man La Feve had gotten up, "I just have to go and say to that little bumblebee, 'Do what God commands.'" She tiptoed down to the fireplace and said, "Do what God commands, little bumblebee." The little bumblebee began: Pick! Pack! Zing! all around the Innkeeper's head. She began to holler, "Wake up, Old Man! Your bumblebee is stinging me!" —"That's not my fault!" answered Old Man La Feve. "Didn't I tell you to leave it alone? Give me back my napkin and my horse. Sting her more, little bumblebee!" —"Make it stop!" screamed the Innkeeper, "I'll give them back to you!"

They ate breakfast, and then Old Man La Feve told the Innkeeper it was time to give him back his horse and his napkin. The Innkeeper answered, "I swear to you I don't have them." So Old Man La Feve spoke to his bumblebee again and said, "Do as God commands, until she gives me back my napkin and my horse." The bumblebee began again: Bing! Bing! all around the Innkeeper's old head, as if it were caressing her. She shouted, "Make it stop! I'll give those things back to you!" This time instead of stopping the bee right away, Old Man La Feve said to the Innkeeper, "Go get them and bring them right here to me, and then I'll make the bee stop." So, she went and got the napkin and the horse and brought them to Old Man La Feve and gave them to him. Then, he said to the bee, "Now you can stop, little bumblebee."

He wrapped up his little bumblebee and put it in his pocket and left to go back home. When he got home, he told his wife to set the table and to set it for a big feast. The old woman was angry with him. She told him, "I'm not setting the table for you any more. You're just plain stupid!" He unwrapped his little bumblebee and told it, "Do as God commands, my little bumblebee." The bumblebee attacked the old woman's head: Bing! Bang! —"Make it stop!" shouted the old woman. "I'll set the table." The old man put his beautiful napkin on the table and asked it to bring something to eat and drink. The table was overflowing. After awhile, he brought up the old horse and asked it for gold and silver, and it filled up a whole sheet with gold and silver. The old woman was really happy! And so Old Man La Feve and his wife lived happily for the rest of their days.

It's Good to Tell You

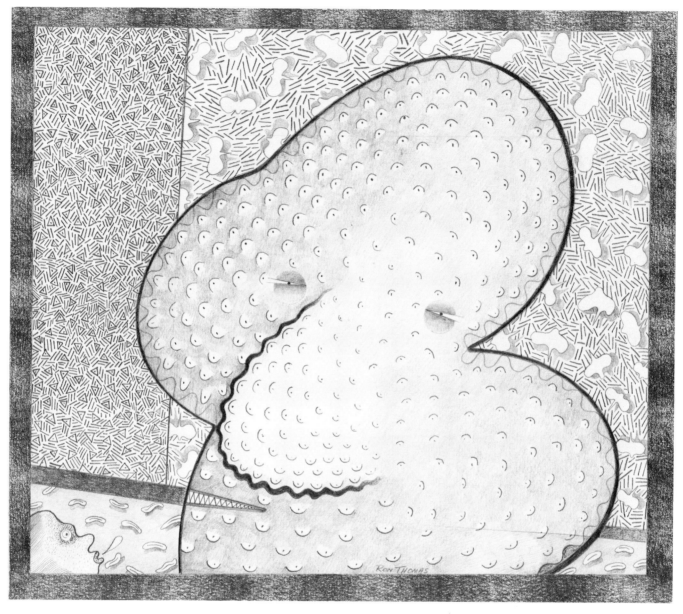

Old Man La Feve and Bumblebees

L'vieux La Fève

C'est bon d'vous dzire eune fouès c'étaient ein vieux pis eune vieille. Sontaient pauv's. I' mangeaient rien des fèves, l'vieux pis la vieille. Il avait s'mé des fèves, l'vieux La Fève. I' nn'a ane qui a ranmé là-bas en l'air. L'vieux 'l a monté eune journée dans sa fève ouère oùsque c'est alle aurait été. Quand il a arrivé au bout' d'la vigne, i'était rendzu sus eune aut' terre. L'vieux La Fève 'l a partsi à marcher quand 'l a frappé la terre. L'souère, i' fallait qu'i' couche à eune auberge. L'lend'main matin 'l a eurpartsi, l'vieux La Fève. Dans l'après-midzi tard, 'l a arrivé à eune aut' maisonne. 'L a commencé à charrer avec l'vieux pis la vieille qui l'étaient là. Souère-là, i' leu dzit comment pauvre 'l était. La vieille a dzit: "M'as t'donner eune belle serviette pis, quand tsu voudras d'quoi manger, tsu auras justement à mett' ta serviette sus la table, pis à dzire: "Belle serviette, apporte-moin donc d'quoi bouère pis d'manger!"

L'souère, i' fallait qu'i' couche à l'aurberge, quand i' s'a enr'v'nu cheux lui. La vieille aubergiste a y'a d'mandé quocé i' portait dans son p'tsit paquet. Il a dzit: "Ah! c'est eune belle serviette qu'i' nn'a là d'dans." Padent l'vieux i' dormait, l'souère, la vieille alle a été, a y'a mis eune vieille serviette sous son bras pis il a partsi. Arrivé cheux lui, i'a crié à sa vieille qu'a mette la table. La vieille alle a mis la tab'; i'a étendzu sa serviette. "Belle serviette," i' dzit, "porte-moin d'quoi bouère pis d'manger!" I'a attendzu, pis i'a rien qu'est v'nu. "Ah!" i' dzit à sa vieille, "j'ai été triché hier."

L'lend'main matin, 'l a eurpartsi, 'l a eurtourné dans sa fève; 'l a couché à l'auberge encore ce souèrée-là. L'lend'main matin, 'l a eurpartsi trouver son vieux pis sa vieille qui y avaient donné la serviette magique la fouès d'avant. Souère-là, i'ont donné ein vieux picaillon. L'lend'main matin, 'l a eurpartsi pour s'enr'v'nir avec son vieux picaillon. I' fallait qu'i' couche à l'auberge encore souèrée-là. La vieille aubergisse a y'a d'mandé quocé qu'c'était son vieux picaillon. "Ah!" i' dzit, "i' fait d'l'argent, mon vieux picaillon." Ça fait la vieille aubergisse a y'a pris son vieux picaillon pis a y'en a rendzu ein autre pareil à la place. L'lend'main matin, l'vieux 'l a eurpartsi avec son picaillon. Quand 'l a arrivé cheux lui, i' dzit à sa vieille qu'alle étende ein drap. I' dzit: "Mon vieux picaillon, fais-moin d'l'or pis d'l'argent!" Taleure son vieux ch'fal i' nn'a faite ein gros tas sus l'drap. La vieille a était fâchée cont' lui. I' dzit à sa vieille: "I' m'ont triché encore hier à souère, j'm'rentourne d'main matin."

I' s'a rentourné trouver son vieux, l'lend'main matin. "Ah!" i' dzit, "mon vieux, tsu t'en eur-viens?" —"Oui," i' dzit, "j'ai perdzu mon vieux picaillon, pis j'm'en eurviens." I' dzit: "Reste à coucher avec nous aut's, tsu vas t'eurposer." L'lend'main matin quand l'vieux 'l a été paré à partsir, i'ont donné ein p'tsit, bourdon. I' dzit: "Tout c'que vous avez à dzire, c'est: Fais c'que Dzieu t'ordonne, pis l'p'tsit bourdon," i' dzit, "va faire son d'vouère, pis i' connaît quocé faire quand tsu vas arriver sus l'aubergisse," i' dzit, "c'est elle qui t'a triché." L'souère, l'vieux 'l a arrêté pour coucher à l'auberge. Quand 'l a serré son p'tsit bourdon sus la corniche, la vieille a dzit: "Quocé vous met là, mon vieux?" —"Ah!" i' dzit, "c'est justement ein p'tsit bourdon." —"Quocé vous faites avec p'tsit bourdon-là?" —"Oh!" i' dzit, "pas rien. On a justement besoin d'dzire: Fais ce que Dzieu t'ordonne, pis i' pique."

Ah! ça chatouillait la vieille aubergisse, ça. L'lend'main matin, d'bon matin, avant qu'le vieux s'réveille, la vieille aubergisse a dzit à son mari: "I' faut que j'vaille dzire à p'tsit bourdon-là qu'i'

La Feve walking through the bean vines

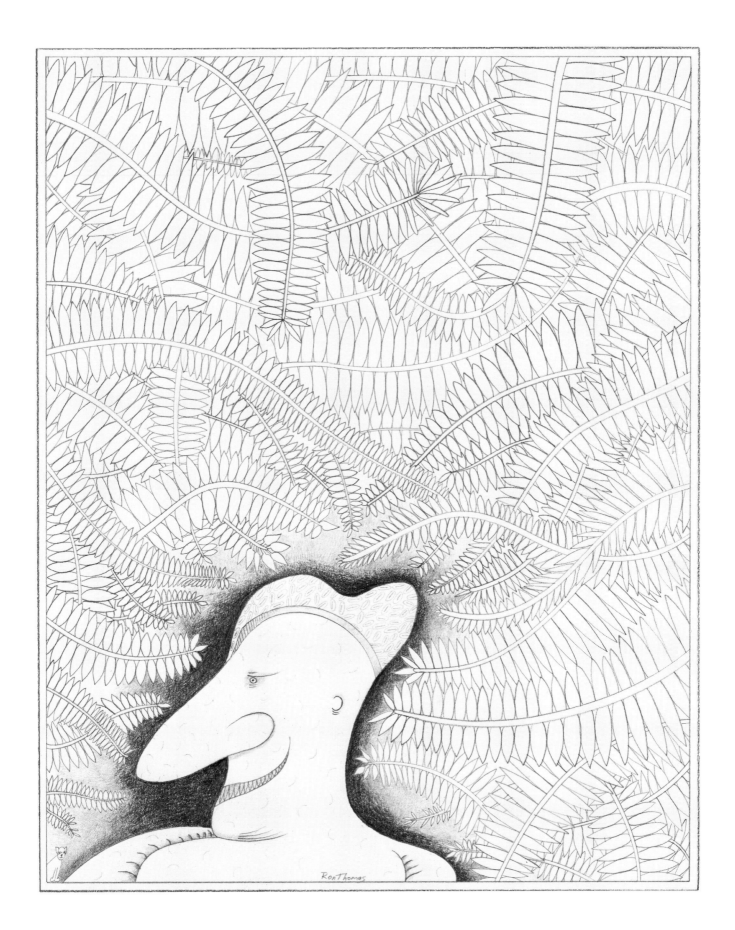

fasse c'que Dzieu yi ordonne." La vieille alle été tout douc'ment, pis alle a dzit: "Fais c'que Dzieu t'ordonne, mon p'tsit bourdon!" L'p'tsit bourdon 'l a commencé: Pique pac, zigne, dans la tête à la vieille aubergisse. Alle a commencé à crier: "Ah! mon bon vieux, réveille-touè donc, mon vieux, l'p'tsit bourdon est après m'piquer." —"C'est pas ma faute, ça," i' dzit. "Moin, j't'avais pas dzit que tsu l'troub's pas?" I' dzit à la vieille aubergisse: "Rends-mouè mon vieux picaillon, pis ma serviette. Pique, pique," i' dzit, "mon p'tsit bourdon, pique-la plus fort." —"Arrête-lé," a dzit, "mon vieux, m'as t'les rendre."

'L ont déjeuné. Après qu'i' yont eu déjeuné, i'a dzit: "J'veux ma serviette, pis mon vieux picaillon à c't'heure." A dzit: "J'l'ai pas, mon vieux. J'te fais mon serment, j'les ai pas pris." —"Fais ce que Dzieu t'ordonne," i' dzit, "mon p'tsit bourdon jusqu'à m'rende ma serviette pis mon vieux picaillon." Bing, Bing, dans sa vieille tête, pis l'p'tsit bourdon 'l était après la caresser. "Arrête-lé," a dzit, "mon vieux, m'as t'les rend'." —"Va m'les qu'ri, pis 'porte-lé dans ma main, pis après ça m'as l'arrêter." Alle a été qu'ri sa serviette pis son vieux picaillon, pis a y'a donnés. "Arrête à c't'heure, mon p'tsit bourdon."

'L a pris son p'tsit bourdon, l'a enveloppé, pis i' l'a mis dans sa poche, pis i'est eurpartsi. 'L a arrivé cheux lui, pis i'a dzit à sa vieille qu'a mette sa table, pis qu'a l'a mette grande. Sa vieille alle était fâchée cont' lui. "Ah!" a dzit, "j'mets pas la table pour touè davantage, t'es ein vieux bêta." 'L a dév'loppé son p'tsit bourdon pis i'a dzit: "Fais c'que Dzieu t'ordonne, mon p'tsit bourdon!" L'p'tsit bourdon 'l a commencé après sa vieille tête: Bing, Bang! "Arrête-lé, mon vieux, pis j'vas t'mett' la tab'." A mis sa belle serviette pis alle a d'mandé pour d'quoi bouère pis manger. Sa table alle était pleine. Taleure, 'l a pris son vieux picaillon, pis i'a faite d'l'or pis d'l'argent plein ein drap. Ah! la vieille alle était ben contente. Pis ça fait l'vieux La Fève pis sa vieille 'l ont vi hureux l'restant d'leus jours après ça.

13.

John and Mary, or the Girl with the Chopped-off Hands

It's good to tell you that once upon a time there were an old man and an old woman who ran a mill down by the river. One morning, the old man went to let water into his pond, and he saw a little box floating on the water. He wanted to see what was in it, so he made it float into his pond. He took the box back home with him. There were a little girl and a little boy in it. He said to his wife, "Let's bring them up." They had them baptized John and Mary. They raised the two children and sent them to school. When they were beginning to grow up, their younger brothers and sisters would tease Mary, and that would get John angry. One evening, Mary said to her father, "Our little brothers and sisters are always teasing us and saying that we are not really related to them." So, the old man told them, "No, you are not really our children. I found you when you were babies, floating on my millpond. I kept you and raised you." So, John said to him, "Well, then, if you don't mind, the two of us would like to leave." The father said, "Well, if you want to leave, all I can give you is a rifle." John thanked his father very much, and they left with their rifle.

As they were walking along that day, John and Mary agreed that neither of them would ever get married but that they would live together for the rest of their lives. They walked far into the woods and found a little hunters' shelter. John asked Mary, "Do you want to live here?" They settled there, and John went hunting every day for a long time. One day, he took off behind a deer and killed it. He put the deer on his back to bring it back, but then he discovered that he was lost. He looked over to the side and saw a village. He forgot all about Mary and said, "Well, I guess I'll go into that village over there." He went into the village carrying his deer over his back. The people went to tell their King that a hunter was passing through the village, and he told them to have him come in.

When John went into the King's house, the King was really happy to see a hunter in his town. He really liked wild meat. So John stayed and hunted every day for the King. The Princess began to fall in love with him, and finally they got married. After they were married, a long time went by when John didn't go hunting. Then one day, he said to his wife, "It's time for me to go hunting again." He went out to the place where he had killed the deer and where he had forgotten Mary, his sister, and suddenly he remembered her again. He said to himself, "I must go and see my poor sister, Mary. I'd forgotten all about her." He got to Mary's little house in the woods and knocked on the door. "Who's there?" she asked. —"It's me, your brother, John," answered John. But Mary replied, "Oh, no, I don't have any more brother." John said, "Of course you do! Open up! It's me, your brother, John!" So, she opened the door, and he went in and began to visit with Mary. He told her that he was married to a Princess who wanted her to go and live with them. She didn't want to, but he said to her, "You can come and build a house right near mine, if you want."

So he went back to his house alone, and that evening his wife could see that he was worried. She asked, "John, what's the matter? Aren't you happy to be married?" —"Yes, I am," he answered, "but my sister lives in a little house in the forest, and she doesn't want to come and live with us." His wife answered, "Well, if she doesn't want to come and stay with us, why can't we make a clearing and build a house for ourselves near hers?" So John went and built a house for him and for his wife near Mary's house. Every morning, he went and got Mary and had her come over to his house for breakfast. He would say to her, "Good morning, Mary, my sister. I hope you spent a good night."

It wasn't long after that that John's wife had a baby. Mary took care of that baby all the time. In the evening, she put its little crib right next to her. John and his wife had a little servant girl who was jealous of Mary, and she began to say to John's wife, "Your husband has two wives." John's wife would answer, "How can it be that my husband has two wives? The other woman involved is his sister, not his wife." The servant girl said then, "Well, I heard him say one morning to her, 'Get up, wife, and come have breakfast with us.'" She was beginning to make John's wife jealous of Mary. She said to John's wife, "Pay attention to what he says to Mary tomorrow." The next morning, his wife clearly heard him say to Mary, "Come, wife, and have breakfast with us." The servant girl offered to get Mary banished from the place. That night, she said, "I'm going to go slit the throat of all his turkeys and then leave the knife with the blood on it in Mary's room."

The next morning, when Mary woke up, she saw the knife on a table, all bloody. John went to get her for breakfast. "Come and have breakfast, Mary, my sister," he said to her. She answered, "John, I'll come and eat, but I can tell you that there is someone who wants my life." John told her, "Mary, don't worry about that. Come and get some breakfast." The servant girl went to the mistress again and said, "I heard him say it again this morning, 'Come and eat breakfast, my wife.' If you want, tonight I'll kill his horse that he loves so much." She did so and brought the knife with the horse's blood on it into Mary's room, just as she had the preceding night. The next morning, when John went in to wake up Mary for breakfast, she was sitting on her bed crying. "What's the matter, Mary?" he asked her. —"Look at that bloody knife on my table again this morning," she answered. John answered, "Oh, come and eat breakfast. Don't worry about that!" The little servant girl went to John's wife again and said, "I'm sure that Mary is his wife. He said it again this morning, 'Come to breakfast, my wife. Don't worry, I love you better than my other wife.'" This really got John's wife angry. Then, the servant girl said, "If you want, tonight I'll go and kill his baby."

When John went into Mary's room the next morning, he found Mary kneeling next to the baby's cradle. He said to her, "Good morning, Mary, my sister. I hope you had a good night." She answered, "Oh, John! I had a very sad night! Look at your baby this morning!" John said, "Come and have breakfast, Mary." But after breakfast, he cut off her two hands at the wrists. "To punish you, I'm banishing you from here with your two hands cut off," he said. He buried Mary's hands in the ground before she left. But when he was on his way back to his house, he stepped on a wooden spike and drove it into his foot by accident. He was limping when he came back. Mary said to him, "What's the matter, my brother, John?" He said, "I got this wooden spike stuck into my foot."—"Well," said Mary, "when I get back my two hands that you cut off, I'll take that wooden spike out of your foot." They put Mary's clothes into a sack on her back, and she went off into the woods.

She walked a long way in the woods and finally came to another country where there was another King. But this King had just died. He had two sons whose names were Joe and Peter. The Queen told her that whoever would bring her the prettiest thing would get the King's crown. Joe didn't care a whole lot, since he really didn't want to be king. Peter didn't care much about it either, but he said to himself, "I'll look around for a while to tease Joe." He went off hunting into the woods, and one day he found Mary. She asked him to put her coat on her. He coaxed her to come back with him. The old Queen found that Mary was the prettiest girl she had ever seen in her life. She cleaned her up and dressed her well. She said to Joe, "I don't think you're going to find me anything prettier than her." Joe said, "No, I don't either. Give the crown to Peter."

So Peter married Mary. When he became king, he had silver hands made for Mary. Peter hadn't been married for long before someone declared war against him. He and Joe had to go off to war. The last thing Peter asked his mother was to take good care of Mary. The messenger that carried letters back and forth between the battlefield and the castle had to sleep on the way, at the house of an old fairy. That fairy was jealous of Mary. She had wanted her own daughter to marry the new king. So every night when the messenger was asleep, she opened the letters and changed them. Peter's wife had two handsome babies, twins. She wrote a letter to Peter and told him that he should see his two handsome sons. But the old witch changed that. She made the letter say that Peter should come and see the two puppies that his wife had had. When Peter got that letter, he showed it to Joe, saying, "Look at this! Our mother wrote to tell us that Mary has had two puppies." So he wrote back to his mother, "Whether they are male or female, keep the puppies until I get home. I want to see them." When the messenger got to the old witch's house with the letter, she changed this one too, to make it say, "Mother, I want you to make a fire and throw my wife and the two babies into it and burn them up."

When the old Queen got this letter, she began to cry. Mary wanted to know what was making her sad. She couldn't keep the secret and showed the letter to Mary. When she had read the letter, Mary said, "Make a fire and burn me in it." But the old Queen said, no, she didn't want to burn Mary. Rather, she would send her back out into the woods. Mary said to her, "Take these hands off me. I don't want anything that he gave me. Tie my prayer book onto my arms and put my babies on my back." She walked a long way into the woods that day, until she came to a little spring where some hunters had been camping, and which they had cleaned out. She put her babies on the ground. They said, "Mama, give us some water to drink." She answered them, "Children, how am I going to give you any water? I don't have any hands!" She heard a voice that said, "Try!" She answered, "I can't try! I don't have any hands!" The voice said again, "Try, I tell you!" So she went and dipped her prayer book into the water, and her two hands were restored. She gave her babies some water to drink. Then a milk goat came along and let Mary milk it to feed her children.

During this time, Peter finished with his war, and he came home to see his wife and the two puppies. When he got home, he asked his mother where Mary was. She answered, "Your wife, my heartless son, what did you tell me to do with her? You told me to burn her up with your two sons. I had sent you a letter to tell you that your wife had had two handsome baby boys." Peter answered, "Well, something's wrong somewhere. Show me your letters." He began to read the letters, and he could see that they had been changed. They asked the messenger where he had spent his nights on the road, and he said, "At the house of old Big Nose." Joe said, "Well, let's go and burn her, with her daughter, and then go look for your wife and sons." They went and shut up old Big Nose in her house with her daughter and burned them both up. They came back to say good-bye to their mother and then went out to look for Peter's wife.

Late one afternoon, they got to the little spring where Mary was staying with her two children. They began to look around, and Joe found their footsteps, little children's footsteps in the dust. They looked around and found a shelter made with branches and bark. Joe said to Peter, "I think that's where your wife is staying with her two children." Mary wasn't in the little cabin. She was out looking for roots to eat, for her and the two children. She came back before too long, and Joe and Peter asked if they could spend the night with her. She told them, "Well, you can do as I do and scrape together a bed of leaves to sleep on." She didn't have any bed to offer them. They went to bed.

Peter was a heavy sleeper, and he fell asleep right away. Mary recognized them. Peter and Joe hadn't recognized her because she had gotten her hands back. When Peter had gone off to the war, she didn't have any hands. She had named her two little boys after their father and uncle, Peter and Joe. When she thought that Peter and Joe were asleep, she called the boys in and said to them, "Go take your old knife and go clean off these boots that belong to your father and your Uncle Joe." The little ones were scraping on the boots, and one of them said, "Mama, Peter is cutting up Uncle Joe's boots." But, Peter then said, "No, it's Joe who's cutting up papa's boots." Joe wasn't asleep, and he turned over on his

Mary with her hand attached

bed of leaves. The little ones dropped the boots and went back to their mother. The next morning, Peter and Joe got up. Joe said to Peter, "It's your wife. Last night I heard her talking to her two sons. She's named them Joe and Peter, like you and me."

So they all visited with each other, and Peter recognized his wife. He asked her where she had found her hands. —"Well," she said, "I found them in the little spring there." They went back to the castle together. Then, Mary said to Peter, "Now I have to go look after my brother, John. I have to take a wooden spike out of his foot that's been in there ever since he cut off my hands. I'm going to pretend I'm a priest, and I want you to pretend to be a doctor. When John hears about a new doctor coming to town, he's going to want you to go and see him. That splinter has taken good advantage of all the time it has spent in John's foot, and it has grown up into a big tree. We're going to tell him that he doesn't have much longer to live, and that he would be wise to confess his sins to a priest as soon as he can. Tell him that there is a new one right near the town where you live."

When John had heard that a new doctor was in town, he sent for him right away. The doctor came and examined John's foot. He said, "My dear friend, I can't do any good for you. You don't have much longer to live, and it would be a good idea for you to see a priest as soon as possible, to confess your sins. There is a new priest in the town next to the one where I live." So, John sent for the new priest right away. As soon as the priest arrived, he began his confession of sins. The priest grabbed hold of that tree growing out of his foot, and it moved a little bit. That was more than anyone else had been able to do. Then the priest said, "Ah, but you still have other sins that you haven't confessed. If you confess all your sins, I'll be able to take that tree out of your foot."

So John confessed other sins, one or two at a time. The priest grabbed the tree and almost pulled it out. He said, "Haven't you ever harmed anyone?" John said, "Well I did cut my sister's hands off once." The priest grabbed hold of the tree and pulled it all the way out of John's foot. Mary said, "John, don't you recognize me?" John said, "No, I don't." —"Don't you remember, John, when I left you, I said that when I got my hands back, I would come and pull that spike out of your foot? Go and look where you buried my hands and see if you can find them." So John went to look, but they weren't there any more. Mary asked him then, "Who do you think it was now who killed your son, me or that servant girl who was here?" John answered, "It wasn't you. It was that servant girl. And my wife wasn't any better." He took his wife and the servant and locked them up at the top of his castle. Then, he lit the castle on fire and burned them both up. He went and stayed with Mary and Peter for the rest of his days.

Jean pis Marie, ou La fille aux mains coupées

C'était bon d'vous dzire eune fouès c'étaient ein vieux pis eune vieille. L'vieux i' courait ein moulin l'long d'la rivière. Eune matsinée, 'l a été virer l'eau dans son étang, pis i' nn'avait eune p'tsite cassette sus l'eau. L'vieux i'était pour vouère quocé c'était; i' l'a faite v'nir à son étang. 'L a pris la p'tsit cassette, pis 'l a partsi chu lui. N'avait eune p'tsite fille pis ein p'tsit garçon dedans. I'a dzit à sa femme: "On va les él'ver." I' les ont faite baptsiser, i' les ont app'lés Jean pis Marie. I' les ont él'vés, i' les ont mis à l'école. Quand 'l ont commencé à v'nir grands, leus p'tsits frères pis leus p'tsites soeurs 'l ont commencé à dzire i' sontaient pas frères et soeurs avec eux aut's. I' faisaient des malices à Marie. Ça faisait fâcher Jean, ça. Alle a dzit ça à son père eune souèrée: "Nos p'tsits frères pis nos p'tsites soeurs sont toujours après nous faire des malices, dzire on l'est pas leu p'tsit frère pis leu p'tsite soeur." —"Ben," l'vieux leu-z-a dzit qu'non: "Vous aut's 'l est pas mes enfants à moin. J'vous ai trouvés quand vous étsiez tout p'tsits sur l'étang d'mon moulin." I' dzit: "J'vous ai él'vés jusqu'à c't'heure." —"Ben," Jean i' dzit, "si ça vous fait pas d'dzifférence, on va laisser, tous les deux." —"Ben," l'vieux i' dzit, "si tsu t'en vas, j'vas t'donner ien qu'ein fusil." 'L a ben eurmercié son père, pis i' sont partsis avec leur fusil.

En marchant journée-là, Pierre pis Marie 'l ont fait ein marché entle eux deux qu'i' s'auraient jamais mariés, qu'i' s'raient restés tous les deux ensemb' tout l'temps d'leu vie. 'L ont trav'lé loin jusque dans l'bois. 'L ont trouvé eune p'tsite maisonne les chasseurs 'l avaient faite. Jean a dzit à Marie: "Si tsu veux, on va rester icitte." Jean i' allait à la chasse tous les jours pendant longtemps. eune journée, 'l a partsi par derrière ein chevreu. Il l'a tsué. Tout d'suite, il a pendzu son chevreu sus son épaule. Quand 'l a l'vé sa tête, i' s'a trouvé perdzu. 'L a eurgardé d'ein bord pis 'l avait ein village. Oblie Marie à net, i' y pensait pus. "Ben, j'vas aller dans village-là." 'L a partsi dans l'village avec l'chevreu sus son dos. 'L ont récité au rouè qu'l'avait ein chasseur qui passait. I' leu-z-a d'mandé à ses hommes qui travaillaient pour lui qu'i' l'faisent rentrer.

Quand Jean 'l a rentré sus l'rouè, l'vieux rouè i'était fier d'vouère ein chasseur dans la ville. 'L aimait beaucoup la viande farouche. I'allait à la chasse tous les jours, Jean. La princesse 'l a commencé à s'anmouracher d'lui. I' s'sont mariés. Après qu'l'ont été mariés, i'a été longtemps qu'i'allait pas à chasse. Eune journée, i' dzit à sa femme: "I' faut qu'j'vas faire ein tour à la chasse." 'L a arrivé oùsqu'il avait tsué son chevreu, oùsqu'il avait oblié Marie, sa soeur. 'L a eurpensé à elle. I' dzit: "I' faut que j'vas vouère à ma soeur, pauv' Marie, j'l'ai oubiée en net." 'L a arrivé à la p'tsite maisonne d'Marie, 'l a cogné à la porte. Marie y a d'mandé qui qu'était là. "C'est moin," i' dzit, "ton frère Jean." —"Oh non," a dzit, "j'en ai pus d'frère." —"Ah si," i' dzit, "Marie, ouvre donc la porte, c'est moin, ton frère." A y'a rouvert la porte, 'l a rentré, pis 'l a commencé à charrer avec Marie. I' a dzit qu'i' était marié avec eune princesse qui voulait qu'a vaille rester avec lui. A pas voulu. "Tsu peux," i' dzit, "v'nir t'faire eune maisonne à ras d'la mienne, si tsu veux."

I' s'a rentourné cheux lui pis l'souère sa femme a vouèyait il était troublé. A d'mande: "Jean, comment ça s'fait, t'es pas satisfait d'êt' marié?" —"Oui," i' dzit, "j'sus ben satisfait. J'ai ma soeur qui reste dans eune p'tsite maisonne dans la forêt, pis a veut pas rester avec nous aut's." Sa femme a dzit: "Si a veut pas rester avec nous aut's, comment ça s'fait on peut pas s'faire nettèyer eune place pis s'faire eune maisonne près d'la sienne?" Jean s'est faite faire eune maisonne à ras d'celle d'Marie. Tous les matins, i'allait qu'ri Marie pis i' l'emm'nait déjeuner. I' yi dzisait: "Bonjour, Marie, ma soeur, comment qu't'as passé la nuit?"

Ça l'a pas été longtemps qu'la femme à Jean 'l a trouvé ein p'tsit bébé. Marie a nn'avait soin de c'p'tsit bébé-là tout l'temps. L'souère, l'mettait à coucher à ras d'elle dans son p'tsit *cribe*. Nn'avait eune p'tsite servante qui s'a mis jalouse cont' Marie. Pis alle a commencé à dzire à sa maîtresse, la femme à Jean: "Vot' mari, il a deux femmes." —"Comment ça," a dzit, "mon mari 'l a deux femmes?" —"L'aut' femme, qui est là d'dans," a dzit, "c'est sa femme, c'est pas sa soeur. J'ai attendzu à matin quand i'a dzit: 'Lève'touè, ma femme, pis viens déjeuner avec nous aut's.' " Alle a commencé à mett' la femme à Jean jalouse. A y'a dzit: "Fais ben attention d'main matin à quoi i' va dzire." L'lend'main a y'a dzit: "J'ai ben attendzu quand i'a dzit: 'Viens déjeuner, ma femme.' Si vous veut, m'as la faire chasser d'icitte. A souère," a dzit, "j'vas aller couper l'cou d'tous ses dindes, pis m'as aller porter l'couteau dans la chamb' à Marie."

L'lend'main matin, Marie, quand a s'a réveillée, alle a vu l'couteau sus eune table plein d'sang. Jean a été la qu'ri pour déjeuner. "Viens déjeuner," i' dzit, "Marie, ma soeur." A dzit: "Jean, j'vas aller déjeuner mais i'en a queuques-ane qui despère d'ma vie." I' y'a dzit: "Ma soeur, fais pas d'cas d'ça, viens-t'en déjeuner." P'tsite servante 'l a dzit à sa maîtresse: "J'ai ben entendzu ça à matin, i'a dzit: 'Viens déjeuner ma femme.' Si tsu veux à souère, j'vas tsuer son ch'val qu'il aime comme lui-même." Alle a porté l'couteau dans la chamb' à Marie la meme chose comme la souèrée d'avant. L'lend'main matin, quand Jean 'l a été pour réveiller Marie, a était assis sus l'bord d'son lite, après brailler. "Qu'est-ce qu't'as," i' dzit, "Marie?" —"Eurgarde donc couteau-là plein d'sang sus ma tab' encore à matin." —"Ah! viens't'en déjeuner," i' dzit, "ma soeur; fais pas d'cas d'ça, laisse pas ça t'troubler." La p'tsite servante a dzit à sa maîtresse: "J'sus ben sûre qu'c'est sa femme. I'a dzit à matin: 'Ma femme, viens déjeuner. Laisse pas ça t'troubler. J't'aime mieux touè qu'l'aut' femme.' " Ça l'a faite fâcher, ça, la femme à Jean. A dzit: "Si vous veut, à souère, j'vas aller tsuer son bébé."

Quand Jean 'l a été dans la chamb' à Marie l'lend'main matin, il a trouvé Marie à g'noux cont' l'berceau dzu bébé. "Bonjour," i' dzit, "Marie, ma soeur, comment-ce qu'tsu as passé la nuit?" —"Ah!" a dzit, "Jean, j'ai passé eune-triste nuit. Eurgarde donc ton enfant à matin." I' dzit: "Viens déjeuner, Marie." Après déjeuner, Jean 'l a coupé les deux mains à Marie au pognet. "Pour ta punition, j'vas t'chasser d'icitte avec les deux mains ôtées." 'L a été enterrer les deux mains à Marie avant qu'a parte. Quand 'l a partsi pour s'en eurvenir, i' s'a enfoncé ein chicot dans l'pied. I'est eurvenue en bouètant. Marie a y'a d'mandé: "Quocé tsu as à bouéter, mon frère Jean?" —"Mais," i' dzit, "j'me sus enfoncé ein chicot dans l'pied." —"Quand j'vas eurtrouver les deux mains tsu m'as ôtées, j'vas v'nir ôter l'chicot dans ton pied." I'ont mis son linge à Marie dans ein sac sus son dos, pis alle a partsi dans l'bois.

Alle a trav'lé loin dans l'bois, en gagnant dans ein aut' pays où i'avait ein aut' rouè, pis, dans pays-là, l'vieux rouè il était mort. I'avait deux garçons qui s'app'laient *Joe* pis Pierre. La vieille reine a leu-z-a dzit lui qui yi aurait 'porté la chose la plus jolite a y'aurait donné la couronne à son père. Ça faisait pas grand dziférence à *Joe* i' voulait pas êt' rouè. "Pour faire des malices à *Joe*," Pierre i' dzit, "j'vas charcer ein peu." Pierre, ça yi faisait pas grand dziférence, non plus. 'L a été à la chasse dans l'bois eune journée, 'l a trouvé Marie. A y'a d'mandé qu'i' jette son capot sus elle. 'L a *coxé* Marie pis l'a emm'née avec lui. La vieille reine 'l a trouvé qu'c'était la plus belle d'mouèselle qu'alle avait vue d'sa vie. A l'a ben lavée, pis a l'a ben chanzée. Alle a dzit à *Joe*: "J'crouès pas qu'tsu peux m'trouver queuque chose d'plus beau qu'ça." —"Non," i' dzit, "donnez la couronne à Pierre."

Pis Pierre i' s'a marié avec Marie. Après qu'il a eu la couronne d'son père, qu'il a été rouè, i'a faite mett' des mains d'argent à Marie. Pierre il était pas marié ben longtemps, i' s'était déclaré eune guerre cont' lui. Fallait qu'lui pis *Joe* vonnent à la guerre. La dernière chose 'l a d'mandée à sa m'man qu'alle aye ben soin d'Marie. I'en avait ane qui portait les nouvelles, les lettres; fallait qu'i' couche en ch'min sus eune vieille fée. Vieille fée-là a était jalouse, a aurait voulu qu'Pierre i'; marisse sa fille.

Pis tous les souères, l'postillon i' couchait là. La vieille fée a rouvert les lett's, pis a les chanzait. La femme à Pierre alle a trouvé deux jolis p'tsits bébés, des bessons. Alle a écrit eune lettre à Pierre, pis a y'a faite dzire i'aurait dzû vouère les deux jolis p'tsits garçons alle avait trouvés. La vieille fée alle a chanzé ça, elle. A y'a faite dzire i'aurait dzû vouère les deux jolis p'tsits chiens sa femme alle avait trouvés. Quand Pierre i'a eu lettre-là, i' l'a montrée à *Joe*. "Eurgarde donc quocé not' mère a nous écrit, ma femme alle a trouvé deux p'tsits chiens." I'a récrit à sa mère; "Qu'ça sèye chiens ou chiennes, gardez-les jusqu'à que je m'rentourne. J'veux les ouère." L'postillon 'l a arrivé sus la vieille fée; i' fallait qu'i' couche là. Alle a chanzé la lett' acore. "Ma mère, peurnez ma femme pis mes deux p'tsits bébés, faisez ein feu, pis brûlez-les tous les trois."

Quand la vieille reine 'l a eurçu lettre-là, a s'a mis à brailler. Marie a voulait savouère quocé alle avait à pleurer. A pouvait pas y quiendre son s'cret caché, fallait qu'a y monte la lett'. Quand Marie alle a eu lu la lett', alle a dzit: "Faisez faire ein feu, pis brûlez-moin." La vieille reine a y'a dzit qu'non, alle l'aurait pas faite brûler. "M'as t'enwèyer," a dzit, "dans l'bois pitôt, dans la forêt." Marie a y'a dzit: "Ôtez ces mains, j'les veux pas, pas rien qu'i' m'a donné. Amarrez mon liv' d'prières après mes bras. Pendez mes deux p'tsits dans mon dos." Alle a trav'lé jusqu'à loin dans la forêt journée-là. Alle a trouvé eune p'tsite fotaine; les chasseurs 'l ontvaient campé là, i' l'ontvaient nettèyée. Alle a mis ses p'tsits à terre. I'ont d'mandé: "M'man, donnez-nous donc d'l'eau." Marie a leu-z-a répond: "Mes chers p'tsits, comment m'as vous donner d'l'eau? J'ai pas d'mains." Alle a attendzu eune vouè qui y a dzit: "Assaye!" Marie a y'a répond: "J'peux pas assayer, j'ai pas d'mains." Vouè-là y'a dzit acore: "Assaye, j'te dzis." 'L a été pour caler son liv' d'prières dans l'eau, alle a eurtrouvé ses deux mains. Alle a donné d'l'eau à ses p'tsits. Eune cabri qui donnait dzu laite, alle a v'nu s'faire tsirer par Marie pour nourrir ses deux p'tsits.

Padent temps-là, Pierre 'l avait fini sa guerre. I' s'en v'nait chez eux pour ouère sa femme et ses deux p'tsits chiens. Quand il est eurv'nu, 'l a d'mandé à sa mère oùsqu'a yétait sa femme. —"Ta femme, mon sans-coeur, quocé qu'tsu m'as faite dzire d'faire de 'helle? Tsu m'as faite dzire d'la brûler elle pis ses deux p'tsits garçons. Moin, j't'avais fait dzire qu'ta femme avait trouvé deux jolis p'tsits garçons." —"Ah! ben," i' dzit, "i'a queuque chose d'pas ben en queuque part. Oùsqu'sont vos lett's?" 'L a commencé à eurgarder les lett's, pis 'l a vu qu'a sontaient tout chanzées. 'L ont d'mandé au postillon oùsqu'i' couchait quand i' portait les lett's. I lé-z-a dzit: "Sus la vieille Grand-nez." —"Ben," *Joe* i' dzit, "si t'es comme moin, on va aller la brûler à c't'heure, elle pis sa fille, pis après ça, on va charcer ta femme pis tes deux p'tsits." 'L ont été renfermer la vieille Grand-nez pis sa fille, pis les ont brûlées. Quand il[s] ont eurvenu, 'l ont dzit aguieu à leu mère. 'L ont partsi pour aller charcer la femme à Pierre.

Ein après-midzi, tout tard, 'l ont arrivé à la p'tsite fotaine oùsque Marie alle était pis ses deux p'tsits. 'L ont commencé à eurgarder à l'entour, pis *Joe* 'l a vu leux pisses, leux p'tsits pieds dans la poussière. 'L ont eurgardé, pis 'l ont vu ein abri d'faite avec des branches pis des écorces. *Joe* 'l a dzit à Pierre: "Tsu vouès, c'est ta femme qui reste là avec ses deux p'tsits." Marie a y'était pas à sa p'tsite cabane. Alle était allée charcer des racines pour manger, elle et ses deux p'tsits. Alle a pas été longtemps avant d'eurvenir. Pierre pis *Joe* i'ont d'mandé pour coucher là. A leu-z-a dzit: "Vous peut faire comme moin, racler ein nic d'feuilles, pis vous coucher là." Alle avait pas d'lite pour les garder. I' s'ont couchés.

Pierre il était dormeur, i' s'est endormi tout d'suite. Alle les a eurconnus. Pierre pis *Joe* eux aut's i' l'ont pas eurconnue par rapporte qu'alle avait deux mains. Quand Pierre il avait partsi pour la guerre, alle avait pas d'mains. Alle avait nommé ses deux p'tsits garçons comme leu père pis leu-z-onc', Pierre pis *Joe*. Après qu'a crouèyait qu'Pierre pis *Joe* i' dormaient a les a dzit: "Vous prendrez vot' vieux couteau pour aller nettèyer les bottes à vot' papa pis à vot' onc' *Joe*." P'tsits-là i' grattaient après les bottes. I'en a ane qui crie: "Oh! m'man, Pierre 'l est après couper les bottes à n'oncle *Joe*." —"Non, c'est *Joe* qui coupe les bottes à papa." *Joe* i' dormait pas lui, i' s'a eurviré dans l'lite. Tcheuc, les p'tsits i' s'ont sauvés cont' leu mère. L'lend'main i' s'ont l'vés. *Joe* 'l a dzit à Pierre: "C'est ta femme, j'ai attendzu hier au souère, alle a nommé ses deux p'tsits comme moin pis touè."

'L ont charré là. Pierre il a eurconnu sa femme. I'a d'mandé oùsqu'alle avait pris ses mains. —"Ben," a dzit, "j'les ai eurtrouvées dans la p'tsite fotaine." I' l'a remm'née avec lui. "A c't'heure," a dzit, "Pierre, i' faudra aller ouère à Jean, mon frère, pour yi ôter ein chicot qu'i' y'a dans l'pied d'pus qu'i' m'a coupé les deux mains. Moin, m'as m'faire passer pour ein curé pis touè pour ein docteur. Quand Jean i' va attend' parler d'ein docteur neu[f] dans la ville, i' voudra vous enwèyer qu'ri. Pis chicot-là i' nn'a profité, i'est ein gros n'arb, dans son pied à c't'heure. On va aller y dzire qu'sa vie alle est courte, i' fait beaucoup mieux d's'avouère ein confesseur aussi vite comme i' pourra. Dzis-yi qu'i' y'en a ein neu[f] dans la ville tout près où vous reste."

Quand Jean 'l a attendzu parler d'ein docteur neu[f] dans la ville, i' l'a enwèyé qu'ri tout d'suite. Docteur-là n'est v'nu, i' a examiné son pied. "Mon cher ami," i' dzit, "j'peux pas vous faire auquin bien. Vous faites ben mieux d'avouère ein confesseur aussi vite qu'vous pourra, vot' vie alle est courte. I'en a ein confesseur neu[f] dans la ville à ras d'moin." Jean il a enwèyé qu'ri tout d'suite l'confesseur. I'a commencé à s'confesser tout d'suite qu'l'confesseur 'l a eu arrivé. L'confesseur il attrapait l'arb' pis il l'grouillait. C'était plus qu'personne d'aut' 'l ontvaient pu faire. "Ah!" i' dzit, "vous a des aut's péchés qu'vous veut pas confesser. si vous confessez tous vos péchés, j'pourras ôter l'arb' dans vot' pied."

I' s'a confessé des aut's p'tsits péchés, eune ou deux à la fouès. 'L a attrapé l'arb' pis l'a arraché quasiment. "Est-ce que vous a jamais faite dzu tort à personne?" —"Coupé les mains à ma soeur," i' dzit, "eune fouès." Il a attrapé l'arb' pis il l'a arraché d'dans son pied. "Tsu m'eurconnais," Marie a dzit, "Jean?" —"Non, j't'eurconnais pas." —"Tsu t'rappelles, Jean, quand j't'ai laissé, j't'ai dzit quand j'aurais eu mes mains ça tsu m'avais ôtees, j'serais eurvenue arracher chicot-là dans ton pied? Va ouère où t'as enterré mains-là si tsu pourras les trouver." Jean 'l a été vouère, mais 'l avait pus d'mains. Marie a y'a d'mandé: "Qui qu'tsu crouès a tsué ton garçon, moin ou la p'tsite fille qui restait icitte?" —"C'est pas touè," i' dzit, "Marie, c'est la p'tsite servante, pis ma femme alle était pas meilleurte." I' les a mis en haut d'son château, les a enfermées en clef dans eune chamb'. 'L a mis l'château en feu, pis les a brûlées, sa femme pis la p'tsite servante. I'a été rester avec Marie pis Pierre l'restant d'ses jours.

14.

Fair Margaret

It's good to tell you once upon a time there were an old man and an old woman. They had only one daughter, whose name was Fair Margaret. One day, when Fair Margaret was out in her front yard, she found a pretty little Snake. She picked up the little Snake and put it into a box. Every day she fed it milk, and it began to grow. She changed the box for a bigger one. But finally the Snake got too big for any box, and she had to let it out on the floor.

One Sunday morning, when her mother and father were at Mass, Fair Margaret was making the dinner, and she heard someone calling her. She looked all around the house and didn't find anyone, so she came back. Then she heard again, "Fair Margaret!" She went inside the house. It was her Snake, which had come out from under her bed. "Fair Margaret," said the Snake. "It's time for me to leave you now. Put your right hand into my mouth right up to the wrist. Now put your left hand into my mouth up as far as the wrist. Anything you touch with your right hand you can turn it into gold, if you want. Whatever you touch with your left hand will be turned into silver if that is what you wish."

They lived in an old log house, and she began to touch the logs and turn them into gold. Then, she made the ceiling all pretty. The Prince of that country was a great hunter. One day, he was passing by that old house, and he saw how nicely it was fixed up. He said to himself, "I'm going to look into that house." He asked Fair Margaret for a glass of water. She brought it to him, and her golden fingerprints were on the glass. When the Prince gave her the glass again, she took it with her left hand, and a set of silver fingerprints appeared on it.

At this point, the Prince was beginning to fall in love with Fair Margaret. The morning of their wedding, Margaret's mother came and said to her, "Fair Margaret, you must go by and visit your Godmother." Fair Margaret's Godmother was an old fairy who was jealous of Margaret. She wanted her own daughter to marry the Prince. When Fair Margaret and the Prince got to her house, she pretended she was happy and welcomed Fair Margaret with open arms. She had them come in and sit down and visit for a while. The Godmother said to Fair Margaret, "If you want some pretty flowers for your wedding, I'll be happy to give you some." She took Margaret with her down into the back garden and tore her eyes

out. She took Margaret's clothes and dressed her own daughter in them. The old fairy's daughter then went and married the Prince, passing for Fair Margaret. They brought Fair Margaret into the woods to die.

There was an old Woodcutter who found Fair Margaret in the woods. He took her back home with him. His wife said to him, "What did you bring that old blind beggar back for?" He answered, "Well, it was better to bring her back here. She was dying of hunger in the woods. We should feed her and give her a little water." She stayed there for quite a while.

One day, the Woodcutter's wife got really tired of having to take care of Fair Margaret, and she locked her up in the smokehouse. Fair Margaret thought of her snake. She said to the old woman, "Please bring me two buckets of water." The old woman had her little sons bring Fair Margaret the buckets of water. Margaret put her right hand into one of the buckets and turned the water to gold. Then, she put her left hand into the other one and turned it to silver. Oh! That old woman sure was happy! She began to call Fair Margaret her grandmother. The Woodcutter came home, and his wife took him out to the smokehouse to see what the blind beggar had done, to change two buckets of water into gold and silver. They fixed her a good dinner and began to take good care of her.

Now Fair Margaret said to the Woodcutter, "You'll have to bring me back into the woods, right where you found me." Oh, no! The Woodcutter didn't want to bring his grandmother back into the woods. He wanted her to stay with him! But he couldn't do anything to keep from having to bring Fair Margaret back into the woods and leave her where he had found her. She told him to bring her supper every evening. After they had gone far into the woods, she called her snake to her. It came through the briars and said, "Fair Margaret, what in the world are you doing out here? Where are your eyes?" She answered, "Oh you don't know, Snake. They tricked me and tore out my eyes." The Snake said, "I'm giving you a basket of pears. When the Woodcutter comes back with your supper, tell him to go into town and trade them for some eyes."

So when the Woodcutter brought Fair Margaret her supper, she asked him to go and trade the basket of pears for some eyes. The man went into town to do as he had been asked. He passed by the old fairy's house, calling, "Pears to trade for eyes!" The servant girl went to tell her mistress, "There's a man passing by with a basket of pears to trade for some eyes." The old fairy told her, "Well, tear out the eyes of the little black dog and go tell him that we'll trade him that pair for his pears."

So the Woodcutter traded his pears for the eyes and went to bring the eyes back to Fair Margaret right away. Then, he went back to his house. Fair Margaret called her snake again. He said, "Ah, Fair Margaret, I don't think those are your eyes." He put one of them

Fair Margaret

in his mouth and rolled it around for a while, then put it into Fair Margaret's eye socket. He asked her, "Can you see?" —"I can see a little," she answered, "but not very well. These aren't my eyes." The Snake then said to her, "Well, here's a basket of grapes. Tell the man to go into the town and trade them for a pair of old eyes."

When the Woodcutter brought her her breakfast the next morning, she asked him to go into the town and trade the basket of grapes for a pair of old eyes. The Woodcutter walked through the town, calling out that he wanted to trade his basket of grapes for a pair of old eyes. No one came out. Then, he said to himself, "Ah, I think I'll go by the house where they traded me the eyes the other day. If they don't have any eyes, I'll just bring the grapes back home and eat them." He called out, "A basket of grapes for a pair of old eyes!" The little servant girl said, "Mistress, why don't you trade Fair Margaret's eyes for that basket of grapes? They look very good." The servant girl brought the Woodcutter Fair Margaret's eyes.

Then, the man went right back to where Fair Margaret was waiting, to bring her the eyes. She called her snake, after the man had been gone for a while. It came as fast as it could. "Ah," it said. "Those are your eyes, Fair Margaret, but I'm afraid they might be too old. I won't be able to help you out if they're too dry." He took one of the eyes and rolled it around in his mouth for a while, until the eye became soft again. Then, he put it into Fair Margaret's eye socket. "Can you see?" he asked her. "Yes!" she answered. "This is my eye, sure enough!" He put the other one in, and Fair Margaret was once again as pretty as she had ever been. "Now," said the Snake, "I'm going to say good-bye, Fair Margaret, and you won't see me ever again."

So then, Fair Margaret left, to go and look for a house. She found an old house in an overgrown field and began to fix it up. She repaired it, and cleaned it, and turned all the porch posts into gold. Now the king was still a hunter. One day, he passed by Fair Margaret's house and said to himself, "My goodness! That reminds me of Fair Margaret's touch. Come to think of it, she has never changed anything into gold or silver since we've been married." That bothered him, and he couldn't keep his mind on his hunting. "I must go back home," he said to himself. He got to his house and asked his wife how come she never changed anything into gold and silver any more, like she used to. She said, "That was just a special gift until I got married."

The Prince wasn't satisfied with this answer. He picked up his rifle and went back to see the old house that Fair Margaret had fixed up to live in. He stopped to visit with her. She told him he could visit with her if he wanted to. He said, "Well, tell me what adventures brought you to this place."—"Well," she answered, "I'll tell you my story. I was getting ready to get married one time, to a Prince. The morning of my wedding, I went to visit my

First version of Fair Margaret

Godmother, and she tricked me. She tore out my eyes and brought me into the woods. Finally, I found my eyes again, and now I'm looking for the Prince that I was going to marry." —"What's your name?" he asked her. —"Well, when I was a girl, they called me Fair Margaret," she answered. He said to her, "Would you recognize that Prince if you saw him again?" —"I think I would," she said. So he told her, "Come with me, Fair Margaret."

He took Fair Margaret to an inn. "Stay here," he told her, "until I come back to get you." Then he went back to his house. He took his wife and brought her to her mother's house. While they were visiting, he set their house on fire and burned them both up. Then, he went back and got Fair Margaret. He said to her, "Now, Fair Margaret, we can get married. Your Godmother won't be able to trick you any more." So they got married and had a big wedding feast.

La Belle Marg'rite

Ben, c'était bon d'vous dzire eune fouès c'étaient ein vieux pis eune vieille. 'L ontvaient ien qu'eune fille. A s'app'lait Belle Marg'rite. Eune journée, Belle Marg'rite a été dans sa cour d'maisonne. Alle a trouvé ein joli p'tsit serpent. Alle a pris l'p'tsit serpent, pis alle l'a mis dans eune p'tsite cassette. Tous les jours a yi donnait dzu laite. I'a commencé à profiter. Alle a échanzé la cassette pour eune plus grande. Taleure, 'l est dev'nu trop gros, i' fallait qu'alle l'mette à terre sus l'plancher.

Ein dzimanche au matin, son père pis sa mère 'l ont été à la messe. Padent qu'alle était après faire son dzîner, elle, la Belle Marg'rite a entendzu crier après elle. Belle Marg'rite a été ouère tout à l'entour d'la maisonne. Alle a eurvenu. Alle a entendzu encore: "Belle Marg'rite!" Alle a été dans la maisonne. C'est son serpent qui était sortsi d'ssous son lite. "Belle Marg'rite," i' dzit, "i' faudra que j'te laisse. Mets ta main drètte dans ma gueule jusqu'à ton pognet. A c't'heure, mets ta main gauche dans ma gueule jusqu'à ton pognet. Ça t'as toucher avec ta main drètte, tsu pourras l'mett' en or si tsu veux; ça t'as toucher avec ta main gauche, tsu pourras l'mett' tou[t] en argent."

I' restaient dans eune vieille maisonne d'bois, pis alle a commencé à toucher les poteaux et à les arranger tout dorés. Alle a arrangé la muraille par en haut tout jolite. Le prince, c'était ein grand chasseur. Eune journée. 'l a passé pis 'l a vu c'te vieille maisonne, comme 'l était tout ben arrangée. "I' faut," i' dzit, "que j'vas ouère à la maisonne." Il a d'mandé à la Belle Marg'rite pour ein verre d'eau. Alle a été yi porter son verre d'eau, pis n'avait l'portrait d'ses douès sus l'gob'let. Pis quand l'prince i'a rendzu l'gob'let, alle l'a pris dans la main gauche. Alle a laissé les apparences d'ses douès d'ssus tou[t] en argent.

A c't'heure, l'prince il a commencé à s'anmouracher d'Belle Marg'rite. La matsinée qu'i'étaient pour s'marier, sa mère yi a dzit: "Belle Marg'rite, i' faut qu'vous passe ouère vot' marraine." Sa marraine, c'était eune vieille fée, pis alle était jalouse cont' Belle Marg'rite. A voulait qu'ça sèye sa fille qui marisse l'prince. Quand Belle Marg'rite pis l'prince sont arrivés, il[s] ont faite comme s'il[s] étaient fièr'tes, 'l ont ben eurçu Belle Marg'rite. 'L ont faite rentrer, assir pis charrer. "Oh! si vous voulez ein joli bouquet pour aller s'marier, m'as vous en donner ein," sa marraine a yi dzit. A l'a emm'née dans son jardin là-bas en errière, loin, pis a y'a arraché les deux yeux. A y'a ôté son linge, alle a chanzé sa fille à elle dans l'linge à Belle Marg'rite. La fille d'la vieille fée a été s'marier avec l'prince. Alle a passé pour Belle Marg'rite. 'L ont emm'né Belle Marg'rite dans l'bois pour qu'a meure.

I' nn'avait ein vieux bûcheur de bois qui a trouvé Belle Marg'rite dans l'bois. I' l'a pris, pis i' l'a emm'née à sa maisonne. La femme à lui, l'vieux bûcher de bois, y'a d'mandé: "Comment ça s'fait qu't'as emm'né c'te vieille borgnasse-là?" I' dzit: "Eh ben, i' fallait mieux que j'l'emmène icitte, alle était après crèver d'faim dans l'bois. Fallait mieux que j'l'emmène icitte pour qu'on la souègne, pour qu'on y donne d'l'eau ein p'tsit brin." Alle a resté là eune bonne grande escousse.

Eune journée, la femme dzu vieux bûcheur a s'a tannée d'en aouère soin, pis a l'a mis dans la boucagnière. Alle a pensé à son serpent, la Belle Marg'rite. A dzit à vieille femme-là: "Fais-mouè donc 'porter deux cuves d'eau icitte." La vieille a y'a faite 'porter par ses p'tsits garçons. Alle a mis sa main drétte dans ane des cuves, alle a eurviré en or; alle a mis sa main gauche dans l'aut', alle a eurviré en argent. Oh! la vieille femme alle était fièr'te! Alle a commencé à l'app'ler sa grand'mère. Vieux bûcheur-là d'bois 'l est eurvenu. Sa femme a l'a emm'né ouère quocé la vieille borgnasse 'l avait faite, comment alle avait chanzé les deux cuves d'eau en or pis en argent, pis 'l ont arrangé ein bon p'tsit dzîner et commencé à la souègner.

A c't'heure, Belle Marg'rite a dzit au vieux bûcheur d'bois: "Faudra qu'tsu viennes me remm'ner drétte oùsque tsu m'as pris." Oh! non, i' voulait pas remm'ner la grand'mère, i' voulait qu'a reste. Mais rien qui faisait, i' fallait qu'i' vienne remm'ner Belle Marg'rite dans l'bois oùsqu'i' l'avait pris. A dzit au vieux qu'i' vienne yi porter son souper l'souère. Après qu'il[s] ont été rendzus ein bon boute, alle a app'lé son serpent. "Mon serpent," a dzit, "viens à moin." I' s'en v'nait en déchirant les fordoches. "Belle Marg'rite," i' dzit, "quoice que dans l'monde tsu fais icitte? Oùsce que sont tes yeux?" i' dzit. —"Oh!" a dzit, "tsu connais pas mon serpent, i' m'ont trahie, i' m'ont arraché mes yeux." —"V'là ein pagnier d'pouères icitte que j'te donne." i' dzit. "Quand vieux-là va v'nir pour porter ton souper, dzis-yi qu'i' va aller *tréder* pour des yeux dans la ville."

Quand l'vieux a v'nu y porter son souper, Belle Marg'rite a y'a d'mandé qu'i' vaille *tréder* son pagnier d'pouères pour des yeux, et l'vieux 'l a été *tréder* ses pouères pour des yeux. 'L ont passé d'vant sus la vieille fée en criant: "Des pouères à *tréder* pour des yeux!" La p'tsite servante alle a été conter à sa maîtresse: "Ein homme qui passe, i' veut *tréder* ein joli pagnier d'pouères pour des yeux." —"Arrachez donc les yeux dzu p'tsit chien nouère, pis on va aller y dzire qu'on va y'en *tréder* eune paire de zyeux pour ses pouères."

Le vieux a v'nu, pis 'l a *tréder* l'pagnier d'pouères, pis quand 'l a eu les yeux, i'a été les porter à Belle Marg'rite tout d'suite, pis i' s'a rentourné à sa maisonne. Belle Marg'rite alle a rapp'lé son serpent. "Ah!" i' dzit, "Belle Marg'rite, j'crouès pas qu'c'est tes yeux à touè, ça." I' nn'a mis eune dans sa gueule, i' l'a ben roulé, pis i' l'a mis dans la tête à Belle Marg'rite. I' dzit: "Tsu vouès?" —"Je ouès, mais pas ben, c'est pas mes yeux à moin." —"Ben," i' dzit, "en v'là ein pagnier d'raisin que j'te donne. Dzi[s]-y qu'tsu vas les *tréder* pour des yeux et qu'tsu veux des vieux yeux."

Quand l'vieux est v'nu y porter son déjeuner l'lend'main matin, a y'a d'mandé qu'i' va *tréder* pagnier d'raisin-là pour des yeux encore, des vieux yeux. I' s'a prom'né en plain dans la ville en criant i' voulait *tréder* ein pagnier d'raisin pour des yeux, des vieux yeux. Personne sortait. "Ah!" i dzit, "j'vas passer d'vant la maisonne où j'ai vu des yeux l'aut' jour. Si j'ai pas d'zyeux là, j'vas 'porter l'raisin à la maisonne et l'manger." I'a crié: "Ein pagnier d'raisin pour des vieux yeux." La p'tsite servante a dzit: "Ma maîtresse, les vieux yeux d'Belle Marg'rite, *trédez*-lé[s]-y donc pour c'pagnier d'raisin, c'en est dzu joli." La p'tsite servante a été y porter les vieux yeux.

Lui, l'vieux 'l a été tout drétte là où était Belle Marg'rite y porter les yeux. Alle a app'lé son serpent après l'vieux homme a été en aller ein bon p'tsit boute d'temps. 'L est v'nu à la course. A y'a montré les yeux. "Ah!" i' dzit, "Belle Marg'rite, ça c'est tex yeux, mais j'ai ben peur i' sont trop vieux. J'pourrai pas en faire rien d'ben pour touè, i' sont secs." I' nn'a pris ane, i' l'a roulé pis l'a mis dans sa gueule jusqu'à qu'l'oeil est eurv'nu mou. Ça s'fait i' l'a mis dans la tête à Belle Marg'rite. I' dzit: "Tsu ouès avec?" —"Ah! oui," a dzit, "j'ouès, ça, c'est mon oeil." I'a posé l'aut'. Belle Marg'rite alle était aussi belle et aussi jolite comme alle avait jamais été. "A c't'heure," i' dzit, "aguieu, Belle Marg'rite, tsu m'eurverras jamais davantage."

La Belle Marg'rite, elle, a part, là, pis a s'a en allée s'charcer ane place. Alle a été làsqu'i'avait eune vieille maisonne dans ein vieux parc. Alle a commencé à arranger sa vieille maisonne, à la réparer, à la nettèyer, pis arranger les poteaux d'gal'rie tout dorés. A c't'heure, en eurv'nant au prince, c'était toujours ein chasseur. Il a passé oùsqu'était la vieille maisonne où la Belle Marg'rite a restait. "Pargué!" i' dzit, "ça m'fait penser à l'ouvrage à Belle Marg'rite,ça, et pis alle a jamais chanzé eurien en argent pis en or depuis alle est mariée." Ça l'troublait, ça, i' pouvait pas chasser. "Faut qu'j'm'en vas à la maisonne." 'L a arrivé cheux lui, pis i'a d'mandé à sa femme comment ça s'faisait a chanzait pus rien en or et en argent comme alle avait coutsume. A dzit: "C'était justement ein souhaut jusqu'à c'que j'me marisse."

Le prince 'l était pas satisfait d'ça. 'L a ramassé son fusil, pis 'l a eurpartsi ouère à sa vieille maisonne où Belle Marg'rite a s'était rentournée viv'. I'a d'mandé pour charrer avec elle. Alle a dzit qu'oui, qu'i' pouvait charrer avec elle s'i' voulait. "Ben," i' dzit, "conte-moin donc par queule aventsure t'es v'nue icitte." —"Ben," a dzit, "j'vas vous la conter. J'étais pour m'marier," a dzit, "avec ein prince eune fouès. La matsinée que j'étais pour m'marier, j'ai passé ouère ma marraine, pis a m'a trahie, a m'a arraché les yeux, pis a m'as emm'née dans l'bois, pis," a dzit, "là, j'ai eurtrouvé mes yeux, pis j'sus-t-après charcer prince-là qu'j'étais pour m'marier avec." —"Quocé qu'c'était vout' nom?" i' dzit. —"Ben, quand j'étais fille, i' m'app'laient Belle Marg'rite." I' dzit: "Vous eurconnaîtrez prince-là si vous le ouèrrez?" —"Oui," a dzit, "j'crouès ça." —"Ben," i' dzit, "v'nez avec moin, Belle Marg'rite."

Il a emm'né Belle Marg'rite à eune auberge. "Restez icitte," i' dzit, "jusqu'à c'que j'viens vous qu'ri." Il a partsi, pis il a été cheux lui. Il a pris sa femme, pis il a été l'emm'ner sus sa mère, la vieille fée. 'L a fermé la porte, ien qu'la fille pis sa mère dans la maisonne. 'L a mis maisonne-là en feu. I' les a brûlées tout les deusses. 'L a été trouver Belle Marg'rite. "A c't'heure," i' dzit, "Belle Marg'rite, on s'mariera. Ta marraine a t'trahira pus." I' s'ont mariés, pis il[s] ont eu des grosses noces.

A close-up of Fair Margaret

15.

Half-Rooster

It's good to tell you that once upon a time there were an old man and an old woman. They were poor and hardly had anything left to eat. All that they had left was an old rooster. One day, the old man said to the old woman, "We'll have to kill the rooster. We'll eat one half today and save the other half for tomorrow." So, the old woman went and got the rooster. She put half of it on the mantel for tomorrow. After awhile, Half-Rooster came down from the mantel and started to scratch in the dirt. He went outside and found a gold coin in the woodpile. A strange man was passing by, and Half-Rooster showed him the gold coin. The man said to Half-Rooster, "That's a gold coin!" The man took the coin and put it into his pocket.

Half-Rooster started running after the man. "Cock-a-doodle-doo! Give me my coin!" Half-Rooster met a Lion, who said to him, "Where are you going, Half-Rooster, calling out, 'cock-a-doodle-doo, give me my coin'?" Half-Rooster answered, "I'm chasing that man who stole my coin." The Lion said, "Let me go with you, Half-Rooster. Get up on my back. You'll go faster." So, Half-Rooster got up on the Lion's back, and they went on their way. A little farther down the road, they met the Wolf, who asked them, "Where are you going, calling out, 'cock-a-doodle-doo, give me my coin'?" Half-Rooster answered, "I'm chasing that man who stole my gold coin." —"I'll come with you, if you want," said the Wolf. —"Come along if you want, Wolf, but walk along behind," Half-Rooster told him. A little farther down the road, they met the Fox. He asked, "Where are you going, Half-Rooster, calling out, 'cock-a-doodle-doo, give me my coin'?" —"I'm chasing after that man who stole my coin," answered Half-Rooster. "You can come with us if you want but walk behind us." After awhile, they crossed the River. The River asked Half-Rooster, "Where are you going, calling out 'cock-a-doodle-doo, give me my coin'?" —"I'm chasing that man who stole my gold coin," answered Half-Rooster. —"Let me go with you," said the River. — "You can come if you want, River," answered Half-Rooster. "But stay behind and don't move too quickly."

When they got to the man's house, Half-Rooster went and perched on the windowsill

Half-Rooster

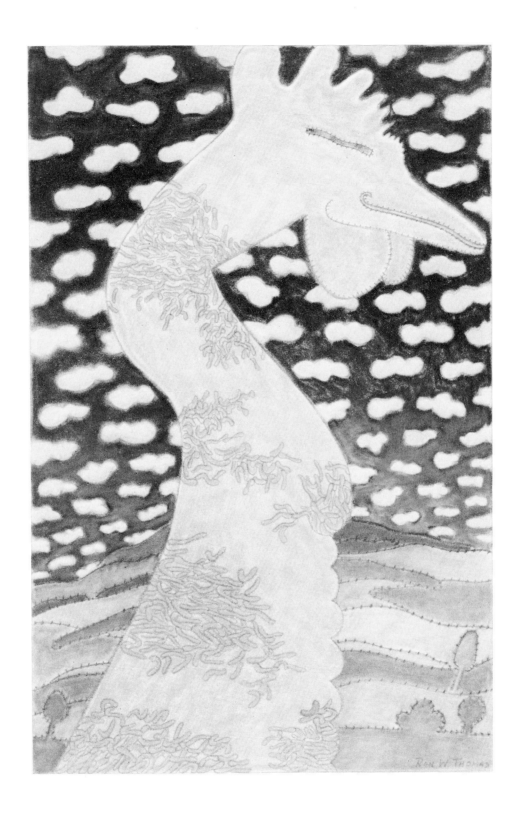

Half-Rooster

and began to crow, "Cock-a-doodle-doo, give me my coin!" The man's wife asked him, "What is that thing on the windowsill?" He answered her, "I was passing by a house today, and there was this Half-Rooster who had found a gold coin. I put the coin into my pocket, and that's what he wants." The wife told him, "Go and throw it into the chicken coop with the other hens. We'll kill it." So, the man took Half-Rooster and locked him up in the chicken coop.

When the man had gone back into his house, Half-Rooster called for the Fox, "Mister Fox! You like chicken so much! Come on in here!" So the Fox went into the chicken coop and killed all the man's hens. Half-Rooster got out and went back onto the windowsill. He sang, "Cock-a-doodle-doo, give me my coin!" The man said to his son, "Take that Half-Rooster and throw him into the stable." So, the little boy took Half-Rooster and went to throw him into the stable. After he was locked up, Half-Rooster called out to the Lion, "Mr. Lion, you like fat meat so much. Come on in here with me. There's lots of good meat." So the Lion went into the stable and killed the horses.

Half-Rooster got out again and went back onto the windowsill. He started crowing again, "Cock-a-doodle-doo, give me my coin." The wife said, "Will you throw that thing in with the hogs. Maybe, they can kill it." So the man took Half-Rooster and went to throw him into the hog pen. When he had left, Half-Rooster called out to the Wolf, "Come here Wolf! You like good meat so much!" So the Wolf went and killed all the hogs. Half-Rooster went back onto his windowsill and started crowing again, "Cock-a-doodle-doo, give me back my coin!" The wife was getting really tired of this, and she shouted to her husband, "Put that thing right into the oven, and we'll roast him now!" So, the man went out and put Half-Rooster into the oven and then came back into the house. Half-Rooster called out, "Oh River! Come and wash this oven quickly! I'm going to burn!" So the River came up and washed out the whole oven. Half-Rooster went back onto the windowsill and began crowing again, "Cock-a-doodle-doo, give me back my coin." The wife said to her husband, "You'd better give that thing back his coin. We'll never be able to sleep with that thing around all night." So, the man gave him back his gold coin. Half-Rooster went back to his house and gave it to his old master so that they would have something to eat for a few days.

The next morning, the man went out feed his horses, but they were all dead. Then, he went to look at the hogs, and they were all dead too. When he went to feed the chickens, they had all been killed and eaten. His wife went to put her bread into the oven, but it was all knocked down. "If I find a Half-Rooster with his coin again, as far as I'm concerned, he can keep it!" said the man. "He killed everything I had on the place. I surely don't know what kind of a creature that was!"

Moquié Coq

C'est bon d'vous dzire eune fouès c'étaient ein vieux pis eune vieille. Il[s] étaient pauv's. I' nn'ontvaient quasiment pus rien d'quoi manger. I' nn'ontvaient pus qu'ein vieux coq qui leu restait. Eune journée, l'vieux i' dzit à sa vieille: "On va tsuer l'coq, pis," i' dzit "on va-n-en manger la moquié aujourdz'hui, pis on va sauver l'aut' moquié pour demain." La vieille alle a été, pis alle en a pris la moquié, pis alle l'a mis sus l'coin d'la chum'née. Taleure Moquié Coq 'l a descendsu de d'ssus sa chumnée, pis i' s'a mis à gratter. 'L a trouvé ein écu dans l'bûcher d'bois. Ein homme étranger i'a passé. Moquié Coq y'a montré son écu. I'a dzit à Moquié Coq: "C'est ein écu, ça." L'homme étranger l'a pris pis i' l'a mis dans sa poche.

Moquié Coq 'l a partsi derrière lui. "Couroucoucou, donne-moin mon écu!" Moquié Coq a rencontré le lion. I' dzit: "Oùsque tsu t'en vas, Moquié Coq, en criant: 'Couroucoucou, donne-moin mon écu?'" I' dzit: "M'en vas par derrière c't homme-là qui m'a volé mon écu." —"Laisse-moin donc aller avec touè, Moquié Coq, pis monte sus mon dos, tsu vas aller plus vite." Moquié Coq 'l a sauté sus l'dos dzu lion, pis 'l a partsi. Ein p'tsit boute plus loin, il[s] ont rencontré l'loup. "Oùsque tsu vas donc, Moquié Coq, en criant: 'Couroucoucou, donne-moin mon écu?'" —"J'm'en vas," i' dzit, "par derrière ein homme qui m'a volé ein écu." —"Tsu veux qu'j'vas avec touè," i' dzit, "Moquié Coq?" —"Ben, si tsu veux, marche derrière, loup." Ein p'tsit boute plus loin, pis 'l ont rencontré l'eurnard. "Oùsqu'tsu t'en vas, Moquié Coq, en criant: 'Couroucoucou, donne-moin mon écu'?" —"J'm'en vas par derrière n'homme-là qui m'a volé mon écu. Viens, si tsu veux," i' dzit, "mais marche derrière." Ein p'tsit boute plus loin, 'l ont traversé la rivière. "Oùsqu'tsu t'en vas, Moquié Coq?" la rivière dzit. —"J'm'en vas par derrière n'homme-là qui m'a volé mon écu." "Laisse-moin donc aller avec touè, Moquié Coq." —"Viens, si tsu veux," i' dzit, "la rivière. Marche derrière, marche pas trop vite."

Quand 'l ont arrivé à la maisonne d'l'homme-là, Moquié Coq 'l a été s'jouquer sus la f'nêt', 'l a commencé à chanter: "Couroucoucou, donne-moin mon écu." La femme à n'homme-là a dzit: "Quocé ça qu'est sus la f'nêt'?" —"J'ai passé eune maisonne aujourdz'hui," i' dzit. " 'L avait ein moquié coq qui avait trouvé ein écu, pis j'l'ai mis dans ma poche. C'est ça i' veut." —"Va donc le ch'ter dans l'poulailler avec les autres poules, on va l'tsuer." 'L a pris Moquié Coq pis 'l a été le ch'ter dans l'poulailler.

Après qu'l'vieux 'l a été rentourné dans sa maisonne, Moquié Coq 'l a crié après l'eurnard. "Oh! l'eurnard, touè qui aimes tant la poule, viens donc icitte d'dans." L'eurnard 'l a été pis i'a tsué tous les poules. Moquié Coq 'l a sortsi, pis 'l a eurtourné sus la f'nêt'. "Couroucoucou, donne-moin mon écu." L'vieux i' dzit à son garçon: "Prends donc Moquié Coq-là, pis va donc le ch'ter dans l'écurie." L'p'tsit garçon 'l a pris Moquié Coq, pis 'l a été le ch'ter dans l'écurie. Moquié Coq 'l a crié après l'lion: "Touè qui aimes la viande grasse, viens donc icitte; i' nn'a ein tas d'bonne viande." L'lion 'l a été pis i' a tsué tous les ch'faux.

Moquié Coq 'l a sortsi. Après ça, 'l est eurtourné sus la f'nêt' pis i'a crié encore: "Couroucoucou, donne-moin mon écu." La femme a dzit: "Prends donc ça, pis va donc ch'ter ça avec les cochons, p'teut' ben eux aut's i' vont tsuer ça." L'vieux 'l a pris Moquié Coq, 'l a partsi, pis i'a été le ch'ter dans la soue des cochons, L'coq 'l a crié après l'loup. "Viens donc icitte, loup," i' dzit, "touè qui aimes la bonne viande." L'loup 'l a été pis i'a tsué tous les cochons. Moquié Coq 'l a eurtourné sus sa f'nêt'. "Couroucoucou, donne-moin mon écu." La femme a dzit au vieux: "Prends donc ça, pis mets-lé dans l'four,, i' va roûtsir." 'L a pris pis l'a mis dans l'four, pis 'l est eurvenu. Moquié Coq 'l a app'lé la rivière. "Oh! la rivière," i' dzit, "viens donc vite laver l'four; m'as brûler." La rivière alle est v'nue pis alle a tout démanché l'four. Moquié Coq 'l est eurtourné sus sa f'nêt' pis 'l a commencé à crier: "Couroucoucou, donne-moin mon écu." —"Tsu devrais y rendre son écu à chose-là, on pourra pas dormir avec c't'affaire-là icitte à souère." L'homme i'a rendzu son écu. Moquié Coq i' s'a rentourné à sa maisonne pis i'a donné ça à son vieux maître pour qu'ça l'quienne en vie queuques jours.

L'lend'main matin, l'homme a été ouère à ses ch'faux, i sontaient tou[s] morts. I'a été pour souègner ses cochons, i' sontaient tou[s] morts. I'a été pour souègner ses poules, a sontaient tout morts pis mangées. Sa femme alle a été pour mett' son pain dans l'four pis i'était tout démanché. "Eune autre fouès, m'as trouver Moquié Coq avec son écu, i' pourra la garder pour ma part. Il a tout tsué ça 'l avait sus ma place. J'connais pas queud' sorte d'bétaille, ça, c'était."

16.

The Rose of Peppermette

It's good to tell you that once upon a time there were an old King and an old Queen. They had three sons and two daughters. The old King was getting ready to go out into the town, and his oldest daughter asked him to bring her back a dress. His youngest daughter, who was the baby of the family, asked him to bring her back a rose.

So the old King went into the village and bought the dress for his older daughter, but he forgot the rose for his baby. He was almost out of the village, when he looked in a window and saw that the room was full of roses. He went in and bought one for his little daughter. The old King called it the Rose of Peppermette. It was the most beautiful rose he had ever seen. On his way back, he had to stop to rest, since he was an old man. He put his little packages on the ground, held the rose in his hand for a moment, and then put it tenderly on one of the packages. But when the old King came back to pick up the rose again, it flew away. He ran after it, but he couldn't catch it. He tried for quite a while and then finally said, "Oh, well, I'm going to have to let it go. It's only a rose."

When he got back home, the oldest daughter came out to meet him and the youngest came too. The older one asked him if he had brought back her dress, and the younger asked about her rose. "Yes," he said. "I did buy your rose, but I lost it. It was the most beautiful rose I have ever seen, that I bought for you." The old King made such a big thing about that rose that the little girl started to cry. The old King told her not to cry, that he would send her brothers to find the rose the next morning.

That evening, he told his sons that the one who could find the rose would inherit his crown. The next morning, all three brothers set out to look for the Rose of Peppermette. They came to a place where the road split into three forks. They agreed to each take one fork and to follow it for three days before coming back. The one who found the rose was the youngest of the three brothers. He came to a place where there was a hillside warmed well by the sun. The rose was in a little rock crevice, warming itself in the sun. The youngest brother walked up to the rose quietly, on tiptoes, and picked it up in his hat. When he had captured the rose, he turned around to go back to the place where the three roads came together.

When it came time to meet, the three brothers came back to the meeting place. The second brother asked the oldest one if he had found the rose. "No," he said. Then, the youngest boy said, "I found it." "You?" asked the oldest brother, all surprised. "Give it to me. I deserve the crown because I'm the oldest." The youngest brother answered, "No, I'm not going to give it to you. I'm the one who found it, and I'm going to bring it back to our father. I don't care about the crown, but I'm going to bring him the rose."

The oldest brother saw that he was not going to get the crown unless he was the one who brought the rose, so he killed his little brother. He told the second brother that if he didn't swear that he wouldn't tell the true story about the rose, he would kill him too. The second brother swore that he would tell the King the oldest brother had found the rose, to save his life. They began by burying their brother in a ditch, with leaves, stones, branches, and all sorts of things, but they could not manage to cover up the tip of one of his little fingers. They even threw big stones on top of it, but that little finger still stuck out. Finally, the oldest brother said, "Well, no one is going to see that, anyway. Let's go." When they got back to their father's house, it was the oldest brother who was carrying the rose, saying that he was the one who had found it. The father gave him the crown, and he became king.

One day, one of the King's shepherds was watching his sheep in the woods. He saw something shining in a pile of stones. He went to see and picked the thing up. It was a little whistle. The shephered said, "That's pretty. I think I'll blow into it." The little whistle began to sing, "Blow, blow, shepherd. You're not the one who killed me in the forest of Verdun for the Rose of Peppermette. I was the one who found it. I was the one who deserved my father's crown." The little shepherd throught that the whistle's song was pretty and blew in it again. It sang the same song again. "I'd better bring this to the old Queen, to see what she thinks of it," said the shepherd to himself.

When he got back to the castle, he went to find the old Queen. "Mistress," he said, "I found this pretty little whistle in the woods today. It sings a very pretty song. Blow into it, to see what it will say to you," he told her. The old Queen blew into the whistle, and it sang, "Blow, blow, my mother. You're not the one who killed me in the forest of Verdun for the Rose of Peppermette. I was the one who found it. I was the one who deserved my father's crown." "Well," said the Queen, "it certainly does sing a pretty song, shepherd."

Then, the old King had to blow into it. The little whistle said the same thing to him. "Blow, blow, my father, you're not the one who killed me in the forest of Verdun for the Rose of Peppermette. I was the one who found it. I was the one who deserved my father's crown."

The old Queen told her oldest son, the king, "Come here and blow into this whistle." —"I'm not going to blow into that thing," said the young king. "I could get poisoned with all the junk the shepherd picks up in the woods." His mother answered, "There's no poison in this. Come and blow into it." The old woman picked up her broom handle and said, "Yes, you are going to blow into it right now." So, he picked up the whistle and blew, and the whistle began to sing, "Blow, blow, my brother. You are the one." The oldest brother took the little whistle and sent it flying against the wall. "I will not blow into that thing,"

Rose of Peppermette

he shouted. "It's poison." The old Queen answered, "You are going to blow into it, or I'll break your head with this stick." The old King said, "You're no better than the rest of us."

So the young king began to blow into the whistle again. The whistle began singing again, "Blow, blow my brother, you are the one who killed me in the forest of Verdun. I was the one who found the Rose of Peppermette. I was the one who deserved my father's crown." The old Queen said, "So! That's why your little brother never came back. You killed him." They set up a gallows in front of the old King's house and they hanged the oldest brother. They went and dug up the little brother who had been killed and washed him and dressed him in fine clothes, and then they put him in brandy so that he would be well preserved and put a crown on his head.

La Rose de Peppermette

C'est bon d'vous dzire eune fouès c'étaient ein vieux rouè pis eune vieille reine. 'L ontvaient trois garçons pis deux filles. L'vieux rouè 'l a partsi pour aller dans l'village, pis la plus vieille d'ses filles a y'a d'mandé qu'i y 'porte eune robe, pis la plus jeune, c'était son bébé, a y'a d'mandé qu'i' yi 'porte eune rose.

L'vieux rouè 'l est allé au village pis il a ach'té la robe à plus vieille d'ses filles, mais a oblié la rose à son bébé. Quand 'l a arrivé quasiment en dehors dzu village, 'l a eurgardé dans eune f'nêt', i'avait ien qu'des roses. I'a été, pis i' s'a ach'té eune rose pour sa p'tsit fille. L'vieux rouè i' l'a nommée la rose d'Peppermette. C'était la plus belle rose 'l avait jamais vue. En eurv'nant, ben, i' fallait i' s'arrête, l'vieux, pour s'eurposer. Il a mis ses p'tsits paquets à terre, il a pris la rose, i' l'a portée dans sa main, pis i' l'a mis sus ein d'ses paquets ben douc'ment. Quand l'vieux rouè 'l est v'nu pour prendre sa rose, alle a partsi à la vole. L'vieux rouè 'l a partsi par derrière la rose, mais i'a pas pu la rattraper. 'L a trav'lé par derrière eune bonne escousse, mais 'l a pas pu l'attraper. "Ah ben!" i' dzit, "m'as la laisser aller, c'est pas plus qu'eune rose."

Quand 'l a arrivé cheux lui, la plus vieille d'ses filles 'l a été l'rencontrer, pis la plus jeune aussite. La plus vieille a y'a d'mandé s'i' y'avait 'porte sa robe; la plus jeune a y'a d'mandé s'i' y'avait 'porté sa rose. "Oui," i' dzit, "j'l'ai ach'tée ta rose, mais j'l'ai perdzue. Ah!" i' dzit, "c'était la plus belle rose qu'j'ai jamais vue que j't'avais ach'tée." L'vieux rouè 'l a fait tant des frais après la rose qu'la p'tsite fille s'est mis à brailler. L'vieux rouè y'a dzit qu'a braille pas, qu'i' yenwerrait ses p'tsits frères la charcer l'lend'main matin.

L'souère, 'l a dzit à ses garçons çu-là i' trouv'rait la rose i' yi donn'rait sa couronne. L'lend'main, 'l ont partsi tous les trois charcer la rose d'Peppermette. 'L ont arrivé à trois fourches d'ch'mins, 'l ont faite l'marché d'tout prend' chaquin leu fourche d'ch'mins, pis d'rester trois jours à charcer avant d'eurvenir. L'plus jeune 'l a trouvé la rose. 'L a arrivé oùsqu'i' y'avait eune place l'long d'eune côte. L'soleil chauffait ben. La rose a était dans ein p'tsit rocher après s'chauffer au soleil. Il a marché tout douc'ment, il a pris son chapeau, pis i' l'a attrapée. I'a partsi pour s'rentourner quand il a eu attrapé sa rose.

Quand la journée 'l est v'nue pour s'rencontrer, i' sont v'nus aux fourches d'chemins, tous les trois ensemb'. L'deuxième 'l a d'mandé au plus vieux pour vouère s'il avait trouvé la rose. "Non," i' dzit. "Touè?" l'plus jeune 'l a dzit: "Moin, j'l'ai trouvée." L'plus vieux i' dzit: "Donne-moin-la. C'est moin qui *déserve* la couronne; j'sus l'plus vieux." I' dzit: "Non, j'te donne pas la rose; c'est moin qui l'a trouvée, c'est moin qui va l'apporter à mon père. Ça fait pas d'dziff18érence pour la couronne, mais," i' dzit, "j'vas 'porter la rose."

L'plus vieux 'l a vu i' pouvait pas avouère la couronne d'autre magnière, pis i'a tsué son p'tsit frère. I'a dzit à l'aut' qu'si i' faisait pas serment à son père qu'c'était lui qui l'avait trouvée i' l'tsuerait, lui aussite. L'aut' pour sauver sa vie a faite l'serment. 'L a commencé pour enterrer son frère dans ein rigolet avec des feuilles, pis des pierres, des branches, toutes sortes de choses, mais i' nn'avait ane d'ses p'tsits douès l'boute i' pouvait pas enterrer. I' j'tait des grosses pierres dessus, p'tsit douè-là i' sortait dessous. "Ah!" i' dzit à son frère, "i' nn'a personne qui va vouère ça. On va s'en aller." Quand 'l a arrivé sus son père, i'a porté la rose, en dzisant c'était, lui, l'plus vieux, qui l'avait trouvée. Son père y'a donné sa couronne. C'est lui qui était rouè.

Eune journée, i'avait ein berger dzu rouè qui était après garder ses moutons dans l'bois. I'a eurgardé, pis i'a vu queuque chose qui éclairait dans tas d'pierre-là. L'berger, 'l a été ouère, pis 'l a attrapé ça; c'était ein p'tsit sifflet. L'berger i' dzit: "C'est joli, i' faut qu'je souffle dedans." L'p'tsit sifflet 'l a commencé à chanter: "Souffle, souffle, berger, ça n'est pas vous qui m'a tsué dans la forêt d'Verdonne pour la rose de Peppermette. J'l'avais trouvée, j'avais ben gagné la couronne d'mon père." L'p'tsit berger i' trouvait qu'ça chantait ben, il a eursoufflé encore. 'L a chanté la même chose encore. "Faut que j'porte ça à la vieille reine pour ouère a va dzire d'ça."

'L a arrivé l'souère, pis 'l a été trouver la reine. "Maîtresse," i' dzit, "j'ai trouvé ein joli p'tsit sifflet dans l'bois aujourdz'hui. I' chante trop joli," i' dzit. "Soufflez donc d'dans," i' dzit, "pour ouère quocé i' va vous dzire à vous." La vieille reine alle soufflé d'dans. L'p'tsit sifflet 'l a chanté: "Soufflez, soufflez, ma mère, ça n'est pas vous qui m'a tsué dans la forêt d'Verdonne pour la rose de Peppermette. J'l'avais trouvée," i' dzit, "j'avais ben gagné la couronne d'mon père." —"Ben, j'ten assure," a dzit, "berger, i' chante joli, ben sûr."

I' fallait qu'le vieux rouè i' souffle dedans. Il a dzit la meme chose l'p'tsit sifflet. Il a dzit: "Soufflez, soufflez, mon père, ça n'est pas vous qui m'a tsué dans la forêt d'Verdonne pour la rose de Peppermette. J'l'avais trouvée," i' dzit, "j'avais ben gagné la couronne d'mon père." 'L a faite l'deuxième garçon souffler là d'dans. Il a dzit la meme chose, l'p'tsit sifflet: "Soufflez, soufflez, mon frère, ça n'est pas vous qui m'a tsué dans la forêt de Verdonne pour la rose de Peppermette. J'l'avais trouvée," i' dzit, "j'avais ben gagné la couronne d'mon père."

La vieille reine 'l a dzit à son garçon, au plus vieux, qu'était rouè: "Viens donc souffler là d'dans, touè." —"J'viens pas souffler là d'dans," i' dzit, "moin. On peut s'empouèsonner avec toutes sortes d'cochonn'ries p'tsit berger-là i'apporte d'dans l'bois." Sa mère a dzit: "I' nn'a pas rien d' pouèson d'dans lui, viens souffler." La vieille 'l a pris sa manche à balai, pis a dzit: "Oui, tsu vas souffler." Il a attrapé l'sifflet, 'l a commencé à chanter: "Soufflez, soufflez, mon frère, c'en est bien vous." Il a pris l'p'tsit sifflet pis i' l'a enwèyé d'flanc cont' la muraille. "J'souffle pas là d'dans, moin," i' dzit, "c'est pouèson." La vieille reine a dzit: "T'as souffler ou ben m'as casser ta tête avec bâton-là." L'vieux rouè i' dzit: "T'es pas plusse qu'nous aut's, touè."

Ça s'fait 'l a eurcommencé à souffler dans l'sifflet encore. L'sifflet 'l a commencé à chanter encore: "Soufflez, soufflez, mon frère, c'en est bien vous qui m'a tsué dans la forêt d'Verdonne. La rose d'Peppermette, j'l'avais trouvée, pis j'avais ben gagné la couronne d'mon père." —"Ah! oui," la vieille reine a dzit, "c'est comme ça ton p'tsit frère 'l est jamais eurvenu, tsu l'as tsué." 'L ont faite planter ein poteau d'vant la place dzu vieux rouè pis l'ont faite pendre. 'L ont été qu'ri l'aut' p'tsit frère qu'était mort, pis i' l'ont ben lavé pis ben chanzé; l'ont mis dans l'*brandzi* pour qu'i' s'conserve, pis i'ont mis la couronne.

17.

Fair Magdelon, or the Knight of the Keys

It's good to tell you that once upon a time there were an old king and an old queen. They had only one son. The old king took him out to see all his villages, and after awhile the king was getting tired, and said, "I'm going to have to go back home." The Prince said, "All right, Father, I'll go back home with you." After he got back home, he went out into the village and had a tailor make him a suit out of skins. Then, he went and said to his father, "Father, I'm going to go by myself and see that pretty little village you told me about before we had to come back home."

So the Prince left. When he got to that town, he went to the best inn and asked for the best room that the Innkeeper had. She said, "Well, my friend. I don't know if you have enough money to pay for my best room!" —"If I didn't feel I could pay for it, I wouldn't ask you for it," answered the Prince. That evening, some sailors were staying at that inn, and they sat down to supper at the same table as the Prince. The captain said to the Prince, "My friend, you are the most handsome man I've ever seen. It's too bad you can't marry the princess that they call Fair Magdelon." The Prince said, "Could you bring me a picture of that princess? I'll stay here until you come back."

A week later, the captain's ship came back to that town, and the captain had the picture of the princess. When the Prince saw the picture, he fell in love with her right away. He asked the captain to bring him to Naples, where the princess lived. The captain said to him, "Ah, my young man, you know that the King of Naples and the King of France are enemies, and they're at war with each other. But I'll try to bring you there. Tomorrow afternoon, we'll set sail. When my ship is all loaded up, stay right near to it. I'm going to let my men go for a half-hour to get a last drink. During that time, I'll hide you in a little cabin, and then when we get to Naples, you stay there quietly until I come to get you."

When they got to Naples, the captain let his men go to drink for a while. Then he went and got the Prince and showed him a little chapel where the princess went to Mass every morning. He showed him an inn where he could stay. The Prince went and got a room at the inn, and then the next morning he went to wait for the princess in front of the little chapel. The princess came, with her two ladies-in-waiting. She had a heavy veil covering her face. When she was going into church, the Prince dipped his fingers into the holy water and held out his hand to her so that she could take some and bless herself. She kind of turned her head toward him.

The next morning, he went back and waited for her again in front of the little chapel. He put his finger in the holy water again and gave it to her. She sort of lifted up her veil, so that he could see her face. The third morning, he went back to meet her again at the same place in front of the little chapel. That morning, before going into the chapel, she pushed her veil all the way back, and the Prince gave her the holy water on his finger so she could use it to bless herself. After that, he went back to his inn and told the Innkeeper that he was a Frenchman. —"Ah," she said. "If you're a Frenchman, I can't keep you here." She sent word to the King that a Frenchman was staying at her inn. The King said, "A Frenchman? Bring him here so I can see him."

So the Prince left and went to see the King. The King asked him how he had come there, and he said, "I'll tell you why I came here. I was doing all kinds of brave deeds for the King of France, and I was still just a soldier. Other people who just did ordinary brave deeds were getting to be high officers. I got tired of that, and I decided to come here and fight under your banner instead." The King said to him, "Good. I'm happy to have you. Do you want a job?" —"Yes, that's what I'm looking for!" answered the Frenchman. — "Well," answered the King. "I'm putting you in charge of my gardens." The princess began to talk with him, but she wasn't able to see him much out in the garden, and she wasn't happy with that. So, she said to her father, "Why don't you promote the Frenchman, papa, from the garden to the stable, where he can take care of the horses. You know that working in the garden is too unexciting for a man. That's what killed our last gardener. There just wasn't enough excitement." The King said, "I'll do as you say. Come here, gardener! Being in the garden is too calm for you. I'm going to promote you to taking care of the horses!" The Frenchman said, "Thank you very much, king. I like taking care of horses very much."

It wasn't long before the Frenchman and the princess were going out for long carriage drives. The princess said, "How in the world is it that you don't give that man a name? Frenchman isn't any kind of a name!" The King said, "Well, what shall we call him?" — "Why not Knight of the Keys?" So the King said, "Frenchman, come over here! We just call you 'Frenchman' all the time, and that's not any kind of a name. From now on, we're going to call you 'Knight of the Keys.' " The new "knight" answered, "Oh! Thank you very much, sire." So things went along quietly for a while, until the princess said to her father one day, "Why don't you give the word to all the guards at your gates that when they hear the name 'Knight of the Keys,' they should immediately open up all the gates, so that he won't need to have a pass." The King did as she suggested, and now when she and the King were out riding with the Knight of the Keys, and they could pass through all the checkpoints without stopping, the King said to himself that Fair Magdelon was right, and it was handy not to have to stop so often.

Things were quiet for a while, and Magdelon and the Knight of the Keys rode together all over the town. One day, the princess told the Knight of the Keys, "I want you to have two horses shoed backwards, and tonight we'll leave." They left that night and rode all

night long. The next morning, the old King went looking for his daughter. No princess! All the horse tracks were coming toward the town. There weren't any that were leaving. The next morning, when Fair Magdelon and the Knight of the Keys arrived at the seashore, they stopped to rest. The princess was wearing a beautiful rose on the front of her dress. She lay down and put her head on the Knight's lap, to rest, and while she was sleeping, a bird flew down and stole the rose. The Knight of the Keys put the princess's head down on the ground very gently and took off after the bird, to catch it and get the rose back.

As he was chasing after the bird, he got lost. The princess woke up and started calling the Knight of the Keys, but she got no answer. Finally, she started looking for his tracks. It so happened that there were some ships that were landing there to take on fresh water. Fair Magdelon thought that the Knight of the Keys had gotten drowned, and since one of the ships was French, she got on it, and it took her back to France. The Knight of the Keys finally found his way back to the place where he had left his love, and he began to look all around. Finally, he found her footprints that went up to the edge of the sea. He thought she was drowned and mourned for her. Another ship stopped there, and he got on it and went to another town where there was another king.

When he got there, another princess fell in love with him. He was nice to the princess, but he really didn't love her. He hadn't forgotten Magdelon. He became one of the old king's great hunters and stayed there for a good while. But he still couldn't forget Fair Magdelon. One day, he got on another ship and went back to where he had lost Magdelon. He said, "I want to find some bones, or some other evidence, if you really did die here." He got off the ship and stayed there on the beach. But before he had left to come back to this place, he had sent two barrels of salt to the King of France, from the place where he had been staying. Fair Magdelon, after she had arrived in France, had set up a hospice and an inn. She took care of all the sick and wounded who came off the French vessels. When the old King had gotten the two barrels of salt, he said, "We'll bring those to the hospice down there, and that way all the sick people will have salt for free."

One day, the people at the hospice ran out of salt. The princess told her servant girl to go into the cellar, where there were two barrels of salt. She went down and opened up one of the barrels but found that there was another lid under the first one that she couldn't open up. She went and told this to the innkeeper, who said, "I'll go down and look myself." When she went down and looked, she found that the two barrels were full of silver and gold. She said to herself, "This is the work of the Knight of the Keys."

The Knight, meanwhile, had looked and looked for Fair Magdelon along the beach, until he got so weak that he could no longer raise up his head. A ship that was passing by there was coming to France. It stopped to take on fresh water, and a sailor passed by where

Fair Magdelon loses her nose

the Knight was lying. He said, "I think he's dead." Another sailor came by and kicked the Knight in the back. He yawned. So, they said to each other, "He's not dead after all. Let's put him on board the ship, and we'll bring him to the hospice." So, they brought him to the hospice and left him there. They took care of him very tenderly there, and after about ten days, he was able to get up and sit on the edge of his bed. He spent his days sitting on the bed and mourning for his beautiful princess that he had lost on the seashore.

There was a little servant girl who brought him his meals. When she got to his door, she heard his lament and listened to what he was saying. When the little servant girl opened the door, he was quiet. The servant went and told her mistress what she had overheard. She said, "There's a man in one of your rooms who's really pitiful." —"Why?" asked the innkeeper. —"He keeps talking about this princess that he lost along the seashore," answered the little servant. —"Did he say the princess's name?" asked the innkeeper. —"Oh yes, he names her every five words. He calls her Fair Magdelon." The innkeeper said to the servant then, "All right. I want you to pay close attention to what he says when you bring him his meal tonight." The servant got close to his door, and he was lamenting over his lost princess again. He was saying, "Not tomorrow, but the day after, I'll be strong enough to get out of here, and then I'll go as far and as long as the earth will hold me until I find either the remains of Fair Magdelon, or Fair Magdelon herself."

The little servant went back and told her mistress what she had heard. The innkeeper said, "Tell that man, when you bring him his dinner tonight, that he shouldn't leave here tomorrow. That princess will come and see him right at nine o'clock." The next morning, just as the clock was striking nine o'clock, the knob of the Knight's door turned, and the princess went in. "Do you recognize me?" she asked. —"Yes, I recognize you," answered the Knight. "You're prettier than ever. I've been looking for you for a long time." She said, "Yes, I've been looking for you for a long time, too." So, they went to his father's house, and they got married. Then, they let the King of Naples know that his daughter had married the son of the King of France, and the two kings became good friends again.

Failli, Chevalier des Clefs

C'est bon d'vous dzire eune fouès c'étaient ein vieux rouè pis eune vieille reine. 'L ontvaient rien qu'ein garçon. L'vieux rouè 'l a été l'emm'ner ouère ses places, les villages. Ça l'avait partsi à trav'ler ça, l'prince. L'vieux rouè i' s'a trouvé tanné et lasse, i'a dzit: "I' faut que j'm'en vaille." — "Ben," i' dzit, "mon père, j'vas m'rentourner avec vous, vous allez me remm'ner." Ça fait qu'après il est eurv'nu cheux eux, il a été dans l'village, pis i' s'a faite faire ein habit tout d'peau, pis i'a dzit à son père: "J'vas aller vouère jolie p'tsite ville-là vous m'a parlé." L'vieux rouè y'avait dzit d'eune jolie ville, mais i'était trop fatigué, lui, l'vieux, i' fallait qu'i' s'en eurvienne cheux lui.

L'prince 'l a partsi. Quand 'l a arrivé à ville-là, 'l a été à l'auberge plus 'haute qu'i' nn'avait dans la ville, pis 'l a d'mandé à l'aubergiste pour rester là. —"Ouais," i' dzit i' pouvait eurgarder. —"J'veux la chamb' la plus haute vous 'l a." —"Ah!" i' dzit, "mon ami, j'connais pas si vos mouèyens vous permettent aouère la chambre plus haute." —"Si j'me sentsirais pas capab'," i' dzit, "j'appell'rais pas pour." L'souère n'a des matelots qu'est v'nu là. I' s'ont mis à la tab' pour souper à la même tab' que l'prince. L'capitaine y'a dzit: "Mon ami, vous êtes l'plus joli homme qu'j'ai jamais vu. C'est ben dommage," i' dzit, "vous peut pas s'accoupler avec la princesse on appelle la belle Magdelonne." I' dzit: "Est-ce vous peut pas m'porter l'portrait princesse-là?" Ça fait l'capitaine 'l a répond: "Oui, j'peux t'en 'porter eune." —"Ben," i' dzit, "j'vas rester icitte jusque vous eurvienne."

Au boute d'huit jours, l'bâtsiment 'l est eurv'nu. L'capitaine y'a porté l'portrait à la princesse. Quand 'l a vu la princesse, lui, i' s'est trouvé frappé sus elle tout d'suite, l'prince. I'a d'mandé au capitaine si i' pouvait pas l'am'ner en Naples. "Ah!" i' dzit, "mon jeune homme, vous savez l'rouè des Naples pis l'rouè d'France i' sont pas amis, i' s'aiment pas, i' sont en guerre, là." "Mais," i' dzit, "j'vas assayer à vous l'emm'ner. D'main aprèsmidzi," i' dzit, "on va partsir. Quand m'as avouère mon bâtsiment tout charzé, t'nez-vous tout près," i' dzit, "dzu bâtsiment. J'vas lâcher mes hommes eune d'mi-heure pour qu'i' vonnent bouère leu filet, pis dans c'temps-là, j'vous mettras dans eune p'tsite chambre, pis quand on va arriver en Naples, restez ben tranquille jusqu'à temps j'vaille vous qu'ri."

Quand 'l ont arrivé en Naples, 'l a lâché ses hommes pour qu'i' vonnent bouère l'filet eune d'mi-heure. 'L a été qu'ri l'prince, pis 'l a été montrer oùsque 'l avait eune p'tsite chapelle où la princesse allait à la messe tous les matins. I'a montré ein auberge oùsque c'est 'l aurait pu aller coucher. 'L a été coucher à l'auberge, pis l'lend'main matin, 'l a été attend' la princesse à la p'tsite chapelle. La princesse alle est arrivée. A était condzuit par deux filles de chambre. Alle avait ein grand vouèle par-d-ssus sa figure, la princesse. Quand alle a entré dans l'église, l'prince i'a mis son douè dans l'eau bénite, pis i'a présenté pour qu'a faise l'signe d'la crouè. Alle a magnière eurviré sa tête.

L'lend'main matin, i'a eurtourné l'attend' dans la p'tsite chapelle encore. I'a eurmis son douè dans l'eau bénite encore, pis i'a présenté. Alle a l'vé son vouèle, quasiment ôté de d'ssus sa figure en net. Troisième matsinée, 'l a eurtourné la rencontrer dans la meme place, dans la p'tsite chapelle. Matsinée-là, avant d'rentrer dans la p'tsite chapelle, alle a poussé son vouèle bas en errière, ôté de d'ssus sa figure en net. L'prince y'a présenté son douè avec d'l'eau bénite pour qu'a faise l'signe d'la crouè. I' s'a enr'tourné à son auberge après ça, l'prince. I'a dzit à l'aubergiste qu'i'était ein Français. —"Ah!" a dzit, "si vous êtes ein Français, i' faudra qu'vous s'en va." Alle a enwèyé dzire au rouè qu'elle, l'aubergiste, avait là ein Français. L'rouè i' dzit: "Ein Français? Dzis-yi qu'i' vienne icitte, j'veux l'ouère."

'L a partsi, pis 'l a été trouver l'rouè. L'rouè y'a d'mandé comment ça s'fait i'était v'nu là. "Ben," i' dzit, "j'vas vous dzire pourquoi j'sus v'nu icitte. J'faisais des grands coups d'noble sus l'rouè d'France, pis j'étais toujours simple soldat. Les autres i' faisaient justement des tout p'tsits coups d'nobles, i' les fésait grands officiers. J'm'ai tanné d'ça," i' dzit. "J'pensais v'nir, pis m'attacher sous vot' pavillon." A c't'heure, l'vieux rouè i' dzit: "Bon, j'sus fier d'vous ouère. Est-ce qu'vous veut d'l'ouvrage?" —"Ah! ouais," i' dzit, "c'est ça j'charce, d'l'ouvrage." —"Eh ben!" i' dzit, "j'vas vous mettre jardigneur." La princesse alle a commencé à charrer avec lui, mais alle avait pas grand chance dans l'jardin. Ça yi plaisait pas, ça, à la princesse. A dzit à son père: "Comment ça s'fait, papa, vous ôte pas Français de d'dans l'jardin pour l'mett' à avouère soin des ch'faux?" A dzit: "Vous savez, c'est trop tranquille pour ein homme dans l'jardin. C'est ça qui a tsué not' vieux jardigneur, c'est trop tranquille." —"Ah! ben, c'est comme vous va dzire." I'a crié: "Français, viens icitte. Jardigneur," i' dzit, "c'est trop tranquille pour touè, Français. J'vas t'mettre gardeur d'ch'faux." —"Ah!" i' dzit, "j'vous eurmercie ben, rouè. J'aime beaucoup à garder les ch'faux."

Ça l'a pas été longtemps lui et la princesse 'l ont commencé à s'prom'ner en carrosse. La princesse a dzit: "Comment ça s'fait dans l'monde vous donne pas ein nom à n'homme-là? Français, tout l'temps, ce n'est pas ein nom." —"Ben," i' dzit, "quoice qu'on va l'app'ler?" —"Pourquoi pas Ch'valier des Clefs?" —"Français," i' dzit, "viens icitte. On t'appelle Français tout l'temps, c'n'est pas ein nom, ça," i' dzit. "On va t'app'ler Ch'valier des Clefs." —"Ah! ben," i' dzit, "Sire, j'vous eurmercie ben." 'L a été d'meme plusieurs temps. 'L a d'mandé à son père: "Comment ça s'fait vous laisse pas la parole à tous les guétteurs d'barrières qu'quand i' vont entendre nommer l'nom Ch'valier des Clefs qu'i' rouvrent la barrière, qu'i' yaurait pas besoin d'passe?" —"Ah!" l'vieux rouè i'allait s'prom'ner en carrosse avec Ch'valier des Clefs pis la reine. Les gardes i' entendaient nommer Ch'valier des Clefs, les barrières s'rouvraient. L'vieux rouè i' dzit: "Belle Magdelonne avait ben raison. C'est ben en main quand i' faut pas arrêter aux barrières."

Ça l'a été plusieurs temps d'meme, la princesse pis l'Ch'valier des Clefs i' s'prom'naient partout dans la ville. Eune journée, la princesse a y'a dzit à Ch'valier des Clefs: "Vous allez faire ferrer deux ch'faux les crampons en errière, pis à souère on va partsir." L'souère, 'l ont partsi, trav'lé toute la nuit. L'lend'main matin, l'vieux rouè i' charçait pour la princesse. Pas d'princesse! Tous les pisses d'ch'faux i' rentraient dans la ville, i'en avait pas qui sortaient. L'lend'main matin, quand la belle Magdelonne pis l'Ch'valier des Clefs 'l ont arrivé l'long d'la mer, 'l ont arrêté là pour s'eurposer. La princesse alle avait eune belle rose sus son estomac à elle. Alle a mis sa tête sus les g'noux d'Ch'valier des Clefs pour s'eurposer, pis a s'a endormie. Ein zouéseau est v'nu, pis 'l a volé rose-là. Ch'valier des Clefs 'l a mis la tête d'la princesse à terre ben aisé, pis 'l a partsi par derrière le zouéseau. I' dzit: "C'est ein péché, i' faut que j't'attrape."

I' s'a perdzu à courir par derrière l'zouéseau. La princesse a s'a réveillée, alle a commencé à crier au Ch'valier des Clefs. Pas d'réponse. Après ça, alle a commencé à eurgarder pour ses pisses. Ça s'a adonné i' nn'avait des bâtsiments qui v'naient là pour prendre d'l'eau clairte. Belle Magdelonne crouèyait Ch'valier des Clefs nèyé, et pis i' nn'a ein bâtsiment d'la France qui était v'nu pour prend' d'l'eau clairte, là. Alle a monté dans l'bâtsiment pis i' l'ont emm'née en France. L'Ch'valier des Clefs i'était eurv'nu trouver sa place oùsqu'i'avait laissé sa maîtresse. I'a commencé à eurgarder à l'entour, l'Ch'valier des Clefs. I' vouèyait ses pisses où alle avait été sus l'bord d'la mer. I' s'lamentait pour sa princesse. I' nn'a ein bâtsiment qui passait pis s'en allait dans eune aut' place, pis i' l'a ramassé lui pis l'a emm'né dans ein aut' ville où i' nn'avait ein aut' rouè.

Arrivé là, ein aut' princesse s'a anmourachée d'lui. I' faisait bonne mine à la princesse, mais en même temps i' l'aimait pas. I'avait pas oblié Magdelonne. I'a travaillé pour l'vieux rouè; i'était ein d'ses grands veneurs. Il a resté là eune bonne escousse. Mais i' pouvait pas oblier Belle Magdelonne. Eune journé, 'l a partsi sus ein aut' bâtsiment, pis 'l a eurtourné oùsque c'est 'l avait perdzu Magdelonne. I' dzit: "J'veux trouver d'tes apparences ou d'tes ossailles d'queuque manière, si t'es morte icitte." I'a descendzu d'dans l'bâtsiment, pis i'a resté là, lui, l'Ch'valier des Clefs. Lui, avant d'partsir d'cheux lui, de d'ssus l'vieux rouè, 'l avait enwèyé deux barils d'sel au roué d'France. La belle Magdelonne, après qu'alle a arrivé en France, s'a faite faire ein auberge, pis ein hôpital. Tous les blessés pis tous les malades qu'arrivaient sus les bâtsiments-là, a les faisait 'porter à son auberge ou ben à son hôpital. L'vieux rouè, lui, quand il eurtiré les deux barils d'sel-là, i' dzit: "On va aller porter ça à l'auberge-là en bas, ça coûte pas rien pour mettre tous nos malades là d'dans," i' dzit.

Eune journée, il[s] ont couru ennehors d'sel. La princesse alle a dzit à la p'tsite servante qu'a vaille dans la cave, i' nn'avait deux barils d'sel, là. La p'tsite servante alle a été, pis alle a défoncé ane

It's Good to Tell You

des barils. A a gratté, pis a ya touché à ein aut' fond. A été dzire ça à l'aubergisse. A dzit: "M'as aller mouè-meme." Alle a été vouère, pis les barils-là i' sontaient pleins d'or pis d'argent. "Ah!" a dzit, "ça, c'est des ouvrages à Ch'valier des Clefs." Lui, i'avait charcé Belle Magdelonne jusqu'à 'l était assez faible i' pouvait pus l'ver sa tête.

I' nn'a ein bâtsiment qui a passé qui s'en v'nait en France. I'a arrêté pour prend' d'l'eau, là. I' nn'a ein mat'lot qui a passé oùsqu'i'était, lui. —"J'crouès il est mort, lui," i' dzit. Ein aut' 'l a passé oùsqu'i'était, lui, pis y'a donné ein p'tsit coup d'pied dans l'dos. L'Chevalier des Clefs 'l a baillé. I' s'ont dzit l'ein et l'aut': "I'est pas mort. Va donc l'mettre sus l'bâtsiment. On va aller l'porter à l'aubergisse." I' l'ont porté à l'auberge, pis i' l'ont emm'né dans l'hôpital après. 'L ont commencé à n'avouère soin, à l'souègner tout douc'ment. Eune dzizaine de jours, Ch'valier des Clefs a commencé êt' capable de s'lever sus l'bord d'son lite. I' s'assisait sus l'bord d'son lite, pis i' s'lamentait pour sa belle princesse il avait perdzue l'long d'la mer.

I' nn'a eune p'tsite servante qu'a été y porter son manger. Quand alle a arrivé à la porte, a l'a attendzu s'lamenter, pis alle a écouté quocé i' dzisait. I' s'lamentait pour sa belle Magdelonne. Quand la 'tsite servante a rouvert la porte, i' s'a tait. La p'tsite servante a s'a rentournée raconter ça à sa maîtresse. A dzit: "Vous l'a ein homme dans eune des chambres qui fait piquié." —"Quocé," a dzit, "il a?" A dzit: "Ah! i' parle d'eune princesse 'l a perdzue l'long d'la mer." —"Tsu l'as pas attendzu nommer princesse-là?" —"Ah! ouais," a dzit, "il la nomme à tous les paroles. I' l'appelle la belle Magdelonne." —"Ben," a dzit, "à souère quand tsu vas aller l'souègner, fais ben attention quoi i' dzit." La p'tsite servante alle a arrivé à la porte, pis i'était à s'lamenter pour la belle Magdelonne encore. "Pas d'main, mais après-d'main," i' dzit, "m'as être assez fort pour sortsir d'icitte d'dans." I' dzit: "M'as trav'ler tant qu'la terre a va m'porter oùsque j'trouve des apparences d'la belle Magdelonne ou j'la trouve, elle."

La p'tsite servante a s'a rentournée, alle a raconté ça à sa maîtresse. A dzit: "D'main matin, quand tsu vas aller souègner n'homme-là, dzis-yi qu'i' parte pas d'main. Princesse-là a va aller l'vouère jusse à neuf heures d'main." Jusse à neuf heures, comme l'horloge alle a sonné neuf, la serrure d'porte alle a tourné. A dzit: "Tsu m'connais?" —"Oui, j't'eurconnais. T'es plus jolite qu'jamais. I'a longtemps qu'j'sus après t'charcer." —"I' nn'avait longtemps, mouè, j'sus après t'charcer," a y'a dzit, elle. 'L a été sus son père pis i' s'ont mariés. 'L ont laissé acconaître au rouè des Naples l'garçon dzu rouè d'France avait marié sa fille. I' sont eurvenus grands amis, les deux rouès.

18.

Beausoleil

It's good to tell you that once upon a time there were an old King and an old Queen. They had three sons, and the youngest was called Beausoleil. They were nearing manhood, all three of them, but they were still playing in the ashes and making popcorn. One day, the old King said to them, "Three princes, not one of you has had the courage to go out to see the world!" Beausoleil answered, "If that's what you want us to do, father, I'll leave tomorrow morning." So the next morning, they bought a nice suit of clothes for Beausoleil and gave him all the money he needed, and Beausoleil left. Beausoleil didn't let on he was rich, but instead made believe he was poor.

He kept walking till he got to another city that had another king. He went to see the king to sign on as a soldier. The king was happy to have Beausoleil in his army, and Beausoleil was well liked by everyone. One day, he wrote to his father that he had been promoted sergeant. His mother was so happy when she read his letter! She said to his two brothers, "Look at this! Your brother has become a sergeant! A sergeant deserves to have some money. We'll send him five dollars." But Beausoleil wasted all the money on liquor, in no time at all. After awhile, he said to himself, "Maybe I should write and tell them that I've been promoted to colonel." He sent the letter to his parents, saying that he had been promoted again. When the old Queen got this letter, she showed it to his brothers. "Look at this!" she said to them. "Beausoleil has only been gone a year and already he's a colonel! The two of you are still wasting your time playing in the ashes! You should be ashamed of yourselves!" The two brothers hung their heads and said nothing. They didn't do anything either. Their mother went on, "A colonel needs a lot of money." She sent him more money in a letter, but Beausoleil quickly wasted all the money that his mother had sent him on liquor. One day, Beausoleil began to think: "I wrote to my father that I was a sergeant, and I really wasn't. Then I lied again and said that I was a colonel, when I was still just a soldier. I think I'd better go find the king and get my discharge and get out of here." So he went to get his discharge papers from the king. The king gave Beausoleil twenty-five cents instead and told him, "Why don't you go enjoy yourself at the tavern?" But that didn't satisfy Beausoleil, and the next day he went back to see the king again. This time the king gave him his discharge papers and said to him, "Say good-bye to me before you leave." There was a tailor in that town who had a lot of work, and he asked Beausoleil to go and take his place on guard duty that evening. Beausoleil said to him, "But I'm leaving." —"I'll pay you well, Beausoleil, if you'll go and do it," said the tailor. So Beausoleil went, and when he had finished his turn, he fired the cannons. The Grand Vizier went to see the king to find out what all the shooting was about. The king said, "Don't worry, it's just Beausoleil who is leaving, and that's his way of saying good-bye."

So Beausoleil left and walked for a long time. Late in the afternoon, he got to another king's town and asked that king if he could spend the night there. The king said, "I'm really sorry, my friend, but all my rooms are full." It was cold and rainy, since it was late in the fall. Rather than see him have to find another place to sleep, the king said to Beausoleil, "There's a nice castle over there where you can sleep. It's true that no one who has ever slept there has ever come out the next morning. But I'll give you a good supper before you go over there." Beausoleil answered, "Well, if you give a me a good supper, at least if I die in there tonight I'll have a full belly."

So after Beausoleil had his supper, he went over to the castle. He lighted his candle and began to read his prayer book. Ten o'clock came, and he hadn't seen anything unusual yet. Beausoleil said to himself, "I'll wait for a while yet, and then if I don't see anything I'm going to go to bed. I'm tired." After awhile, Beausoleil said his prayers, and at about eleven o'clock, he began to hear doors closing, in the distance. The more they closed, the closer they came, until a tall man all dressed in white came into the room where he was. He was carrying a tall candle. He went over and lighted his candle from Beausoleil's candle. Then, he went and stood over on one side of the room. Then, eleven men just like him came in. When the eleventh man came in and took his place, Beausoleil went and stood next to the last one, with his candle too. The one who was in the front turned around to leave and signaled Beausoleil with his finger that he should come too. He went with them as far as the door and then said, "My friends, I've come this far with you, but now you'll have to excuse me. I'm tired, and it's time for me to go to bed." But the one in the front was still signaling him to follow behind. Beausoleil said, "I think I'll go and tear off your finger!" But he went, and when they got to a tunnel, they all went in. They walked into the tunnel for a while and came to a place where there was a big stone. One of the men said to Beausoleil, "Lift up that big stone." Beausoleil picked up the stone and found all kinds of silver and counterfeit money that had been stolen. The man said to Beausoleil, "All this money has been stolen. Tell the king to give it back to the people who own it, and his castle will never be disturbed again. We are eleven kings like him, and we can't get into Paradise because of all this money here. You can go to bed now, Beausoleil, and we won't bother you any more tonight. You'll have a good night's sleep. I'm going to give you a little bottle of drops. Do you see all these little bumps on the ground? Those are all people who have been changed. Put one drop on each little bump, and the people will come back to life."

Beausoleil went back to his room and went to bed. He slept until eight o'clock the

next morning. The old king sent his servant boy pretty early in the morning to see if Beausoleil was up yet. The boy went as far as the gate and didn't see anyone. He went back and told the king that he hadn't seen Beausoleil. At nine o'clock, the king sent the boy back to the castle to look for Beausoleil again. Beausoleil was out on the front porch, and he told the boy to go tell the king to come over, because he wanted to see him. When the king got this news, he told the boy to go back and tell Beausoleil that the whole castle and everything in it belonged to him, to Beausoleil. The little boy went back and told Beausoleil, "Sire, the king says that he is giving you this castle and everything that is in it." Beausoleil answered, "Go tell the king that I don't want the castle or anything that is inside it. I just want him to come over here."

The king answered that he wouldn't go. He didn't want to have anything to do with that castle. Beausoleil said to the boy, "Go tell the king that if he doesn't come, I'll open fire on him." He went down into the tunnel and began to pour drops on the little bumps in the ground, and all the men came out like flies. He put a man at each cannon. When the old king saw this, he said, "It doesn't make any difference which way I die. I guess I'll go over." When he got to the gate, the king said to Beausoleil, "Beausoleil, I don't want to have anything to do with this castle. I give it to you, with everything that is in it." Beausoleil answered, "I don't want your castle, or anything in it. I just want you to come with me. Nothing happened to me last night, and nothing will happen to you today, either." So the old king went, but he was walking backwards. When they got to the entrance to the tunnel, the king wanted to leave. Beausoleil said to him, "No, no, sire! You don't need to be afraid. Nothing will happen to you." When Beausoleil arrived where the hidden money was, he showed it to the king and said, "Sire, they were eleven kings like you. This is all the money they stole, and the counterfeit bills they made, and this is what was keeping them from getting into Paradise. Give all this back to whoever it belongs to, and your castle will never be bothered again." The king said, "Well, come on over and eat breakfast, Beausoleil."

While they were eating breakfast, Beausoleil was telling them how he had been traveling the earth looking for an experience that would make him afraid. The Princess asked him to stay and have dinner with her. He told the Princess that he would. She caught a live crow and rolled it up in a piece of pie dough. When their dinner was almost finished, she asked Beausoleil to pass her the plate with the dough. She said, "This is my favorite dish!" She asked him to cut her a piece. He began to cut into it, and the crow started to crow loudly and to flap its wings. Beausoleil dropped the piece of dough on the table. The Princess said to him, "You can't tell me that that didn't scare you!" He answered, "Yes, Princess, I was scared." So the Princess suggested that they get married. Beausoleil went to tell the king

Beausoleil

and told him that he didn't need to be afraid for his daughter, because he, Beausoleil, was a prince, as his daughter was a princess.

They had been married for a while, and one day Beausoleil was sitting on his front porch, thinking. His wife asked him, "Beausoleil, what are you thinking about? Aren't you happy to be married?" He answered, "Oh yes, Princess! I'm very happy to be married. But I'm thinking about my parents." After awhile, he said, "If you don't mind, I'm going to leave tomorrow to go visit them." The Princess gave orders to one of her servant boys to pay close attention to everything that he would do on the trip and to come back and tell it all to her. Beausoleil left with the boy. Late one night, they came to an inn, and Beausoleil said to the boy, "We'll stay here tonight." They went in and got a room from the innkeeper. She put their horse in the stable and fed it well. When Beausoleil and the boy came down for supper, instead of two places at the table there were six. When the clock struck the hour, four gamblers came in. During supper, one said to the other, "This one looks rich!" When supper was finished, they challenged Beausoleil to a game of cards. They began to drink and gamble, and after awhile they won everything that Beausoleil had, including the clothes on his back. They put burlap on his back and wooden shoes on his feet. The next morning, Beausoleil was ashamed. He told his servant boy to go and tell his wife what had happened. "As for me," he said, "I started out to go visit my parents, and that's where I'm going."

The servant went back to tell the story to the Princess, and Beausoleil left with his burlap bags on his back to go see his mother. He arrived at his father's house late in the evening, after sunset. He recognized the guard who was at the gate and said, "Open the gate, guard!" —"I don't open the gate for anyone after sunset," answered the guard. Beausoleil insisted, "Open the gate, guard. It's me, Beausoleil." The guard answered, "No, my mistress doesn't have any children who wear burlap sacks for clothes or wooden shoes on their feet. I won't open the gate before I go and ask." So the guard went in to the old Queen and told her that there was a man at the gate who said he was Beausoleil, but he was wearing burlap sacks and wooden shoes. She said to him, "Well, have him come in so I can see him." Beausoleil came in and his mother saw him. "You sure look like a sergeant," she said. "And you look even more like a colonel! For your punishment, I'm making you colonel over my hogs, with my old servant Mary Jane." They gave Beausoleil some cheap clothes and put him out to keep the hogs with the old Mary Jane.

Meanwhile, the servant boy had told Beausoleil's wife what had happened to his master. She got dressed up like a prince and left with the servant boy. They came to the same inn and slept there that night. When the four gamblers came downstairs for supper, one said to the other, "There's another rich one!" So after supper they challenged this new prince to a game of cards. Oh yes! The handsome prince loved to play cards. They all sat down to the table to play cards together, but the Princess asked them what they though they were doing, all sitting down to play. "I won't play against four," she said. "I'll only play one person at a time. The one of you who thinks he is the best player should stay here, and I'll play with him. The other three should go away into a different room. The only other person I want in here with me is my little servant boy, to get me what I want." So the three other gamblers left, and the one who thought he was the best stayed with the disguised Princess. The little servant had been told to pass the bottle of liquor often. He filled the gambler's glass full but only put a little each time into his mistress's glass. After awhile, the gambler got drunk. Then, the servant boy took a mirror and went and stood behind the gambler. His mistress could then see what he had in his hand. She won back all the gold and silver they had, everything that Beausoleil had lost. After that, she won all their clothes. She dressed them all in burlap sacks, with wooden shoes on their feet, and sent them into the street, kicking them in the rear. "I'll show you how to take advantage of people," she shouted at them.

Then, she left to find Beausoleil. She arrived at his parents' house late in the afternoon. The guard opened up the gate just as soon as he saw this handsome prince coming down the road. The news was passed around that they would have a good dinner for the prince. She came in and visited with the two brothers who were still playing in the ashes. They didn't know how to make a conversation, since they had never left the house. But she didn't see Beausoleil anywhere. She asked the old queen, "Do you only have two sons?" —"No, prince, I have three," answered the Queen. —"Where's the other one? Isn't he here?" —"No," answered the Queen, "let me tell you what he did to us. He left here to go out and see the world. One day, he wrote to tell us that he had become a soldier. We sent him some money right away. Then, he wrote and told us that he was a sergeant; then he told us he was a colonel. A few days ago, he came back here with a burlap bag on his back and wooden shoes on his feet, if I have to tell you." The Princess said to her, "Go send for him. I'd like to see him." The Queen answered, "To give you pleasure I'll send for him. But otherwise I don't want him around the place."

Beausoleil was called and came into the house. He didn't have any problem talking with a strange prince. But the old Queen didn't want him to eat at the same table with everyone else. The prince said, "Well, if he doesn't eat at the same table as the rest of you, I'll eat at the same table with him." So, to please the guest, they let Beausoleil eat at the same table as the King. While they were eating, the two brothers who had never left home were jealous. One aimed a kick under the table at Beausoleil but hit the prince on the leg instead. "Listen here!" she said. "I'm not a dog for you to kick under the table!" So the two brothers left to go make their popcorn in the ashes. That evening, the handsome prince asked if he could sleep in the same room as Beausoleil. The old Queen didn't like that idea at all, but to please her guest, she said yes. That night, when they had gone into their room, the Princess said to Beausoleil, "Do you recognize me?" Beausoleil answered, "No, of course not. I've never seen you before." So the Princess went off into the next room and dressed as she had been dressed the morning that Beausoleil had left her. She came back in and said, "Do you recognize me now?" —"Yes, now I recognize you," answered Beausoleil. "I didn't know I was talking with my wife all day long." —"You don't need to be ashamed,

Beausoleil," she said to him. "The same thing has now happened to those gamblers as happened to you."

The next morning, at about four o'clock, the old Mary Jane came to get Beausoleil to go and look after the hogs with her. She started to shout, "Hey, Beausoleil, come and feed the hogs!" She shouted for him several times, and Beausoleil's wife said to him, "What's making that noise down there?" —"It's the old servant who wants me to go and feed the hogs with her," answered Beausoleil. His wife said, "Let her get up to the door and then punch her one in the face, to show her that you aren't going to feed any hogs with her." The Queen told Mary Jane, "Go up and knock on his door and wake him up, so that he'll go out and help you with the hogs." So Mary Jane went up the stairs, knocked on the door, and said, "Beausoleil, it's time to come and take care of the hogs!" As she was about to open the door, Beausoleil opened it for her and punched her one, and boudoum, boudoum, she fell down the stairs. She said to the Queen, "Go and see for yourself if your Beausoleil looks in any mood to go and feed the hogs!" After awhile, Beausoleil and his wife came down for breakfast. Beausoleil's wife said what she thought of the old Queen. "Whether you like it or not," she said, "makes no difference to me. My mother and father are queen and king like you. I'm a Princess as Beausoleil is a prince. I'm bringing Beausoleil back home with me since he's my husband."

Beausoleil

C'est bon d'vous dzire eune fouès c'étaient ein vieux rouè pis eune vieille reine. 'L ontvaient trois garçons. L'plus jeune, i' s'app'lait Beausoleil. I' sontaient après v'nir hommes, tous les trois. I' jouaient dans la cenne, i' faisaient des tactacs. Eune journée, le vieux rouè i' leu dzisait ça: "Trois princes," i' dzit, "pis jamais ane de vos aut's qui a eu le courage d'partsir pour aller ouère auquin pays!" Beausoleil i' dzit: "Si ça vous plaît, mon père, j'partsiras d'main matin." Le lend'main matin, i' ont ach'té eune belle habit, i'ont donné l'or pis l'argent i' avait d'besoin, pis Beausoleil 'l a partsi. Beausoleil i' s'faisait pas passer par exemple pour ein prince; i' s'faisait passer pour ein pauvre!

'L a trav'lé jusqu'à temps 'l a arrivé dans ein aut' ville sus ein aut' rouè. 'L a été ouère le rouè pour s'engager soldat. Le rouè 'l a pris Beausoleil, il était ben fier d'l'aouère. Beausoleil i s'faisait aimer parmi tout l'monde. Ça fait qu'i'a écrit eune lett' à son père qu'i' était sergent. Ah! la vieille reine, quand alle a lu lettre-là, alle était fièr'te. A dzit: "Ah! eurgardez donc, vot' frère, il est sergent!" "A ein sergent," a dzit, "i' prend d'l'argent. On va y enwéyer cinq piasses." Beausoleil 'l a bu ça, lui, dans ein p'tsit moment d'temps. "Faut que je leur écrise," i' dzit, "que j'sus coronel." 'L a enwéyé eune lettre à son père pis à sa mère qu'il était coronel. Quand la vieille reine alle a eu c'te lettre, alle a montré ça à ses frères. "Eurgardez donc," a dzit, "Monsieur Beausoleil i'est justement partsi i' nn'a ein an, i'est rendzu coronel, pis vous aut's est toujours après jouer dans vos cennes. Vous aut's, vous devrez aouère honte." I' baissaient leu tête eux aut's, i' dzisaient pas rien, mais i' grouillaient pas. "Pour ein coronel," a dzit, "i' prend beaucoup d'argent." Alle a pris eune lettre, pis a y'en a enwèyé. 'L a bu tout son argent ça 'l avait eurçu d'sa mère.

Eune journée, Beausoleil a commencé à jongler: "J'ai écrit à mon popa j'étais sergent, pis j'l'étais pas. Après ça, j'y ai ècrit que j'étais coronel, pis," i' dzit, "j'étais toujours simple soldat. M'as trouver le rouè pour ma décharze, pis j'm'en vas d'icitte." I' va ouère le vieux rouè pour sa décharze. L'vieux rouè 'l a pris vingtcinq sous, 'l a donné à Beausoleil, pis i'a dzit: "Va-t'en donc bouère le filet." Mais ça l'a pas satisfait Beausoleil, ça. L'lend'main, 'l est eurvenu trouver l'rouè pour sa décharze. L'vieux rouè i'a donné sa décharze, pis i'a dzit: "Dzis-moin aguieu avant d'partsir, Beausoleil." I'avait ein tailleur dans la ville qu'avait ein tas d'l'ouvrage, pis 'l a d'mandé à Beausoleil d'aller servir à sa place au quart. "Ben," i' dzit, "m'as aller." —"M'as ben t'payer," i' dzit, "Beausoleil, si tsu veux aller." Ça fait que, quand Beausoleil 'l a eu fini son quart, 'l a mis l'feu aux connons. Grand vizir 'l a été ouère le rouè pour connaître quocé c'tait tous les tsirements-là. "Ah!" i' dzit, "Troub'-touè pas, c'est Beausoleil qui partait, qui m'dzisait aguieu."

Ça fait Beausoleil, lui, i' part à trav'ler à c't'heure. 'L a trav'lé pour longtemps, pis, l'après-midzi tout tard, 'l a arrivé sus ein autre rouè dans ein aut' ville. 'L a d'mandé au rouè pour coucher. L'rouè y'a dzit: "J'sus ben chagrin, mon ami, mais j'ai pas d'place pour touè, tous mes chamb's sont pleines." I' mouillassait, pis i' fésait frètte; c'était dans l'automne, tard. Le rouè y'a dzit plutôt qu'l'ouère coucher dehors: "I' nn'a ein beau château là-bas, tsu pourras coucher là. C'est vrai," i' dzit, "nn'a jamais personne qui a couché là d'dans qu'est eurvenu. Mais," i' dzit, "m'as ben t'souègner, Beausoleil, avant qu'tsu vas dans château-là." Beausoleil i' dzit: "Ben, si tsu m'souègnes ben, pis si j'meurs là d'dans à souère, m'as mourir l'ventre plein."

Après que Beausoleil i'a eu soupé, i' s'a en allé dans son château, 'l allumé sa chandelle, 'l a commencé à lire dans son livre de prières. Dzix heures, i'avait pas rien vu acore. Beausoleil i' dzit: "M'as attend' encore ein escousse, pis si nn'a pas rien qui vient, m'as m'coucher, j'sus lasse." Taleure, 'l a dzit sa prière, Beausoleil; i' s'a mis à genoux, pis 'l a prié. Quasiment onze heures, 'l a commencé à attendre clencher des portes. I' attendait clencher des portes d'au loin; pus ça allait, pus ça l'approchait, jusqu'à temps v'là ein grand homme tou[t] habillé en blanc qu'a rentré. I'avait eune grande chandelle. I'a été l'allumer après la celle à Beausoleil. 'L a été s'planter dans ein bord d'la maisonne, pis i'en a onze comme ça qu'a rentré. Quand le onzième 'l a été rentré, pis planté à sa place, Beausoleil 'l a été pis i' s'a planté à côté dzu dernier, qui s'avait planté avec la chandelle, lui aussite. L'premier qu'était d'vant 'l a partsi; i' faisait signe à Beausoleil avec son douè qu'i' va avec lui. Beausoleil 'l a été avec eux aut's jusqu'à la porte. I' leu-z-a dzit: "Mes amis, j'sus v'nu ça d'loin avec vous aut's," i' dzit, "faudra que vous aut's m'excusent, j'sus lasse, m'as aller m'coucher." Le premier qu'était d'vant i' faisait toujours signe qu'i' va. "Ben," i' dzit, "j'pense que j'vas aller, pis m'as t'arracher ton douè." Quand 'l ont arrivé à ein grand souterrain, 'l ont rentré. 'L ont été là d'dans ein bon grand boute, 'l ont arrivé oùsqu'i' n'avait eune grosse pierre. Ein des aut's a dzit à Beausoleil: "Lève pierre-là." Beausoleil 'l a l'vé la pierre, pis c'était tout d'l'argent pis des faux billets qui étaient d'ssous. I' dzit: "Beausoleil, ça, c'est tout d'l'argent pis des faux billets qui a été volé. Dzis au rouè qu'i' rende ça à les ceuzes ça apparquient, pis son château," i' dzit, "i' s'ra jamais troublé davantage. Nous sommes onze rouès comme lui. Ça qui nous empêche d'aller en paradzis, c'est l'argent qu'i' a icitte, pis," i' dzit, "tsu peux t'en aller t'coucher, Beausoleil, pis tsu s'ras pas troublé d'la nuit, tsu vas dormir ben." I' dzit: "N'en v'là eune p'tsite bouteille de gouttes que j'te donne icitte. Tsu vouès tous les p'tsites buttes-là icitte," i' dzit. "Ben, c'est tout dzu monde en morphose," i' dzit. "Videz-en eune goutte par butte," i' dzit, "pis i' vont tou[s] eurvenir en vie."

Beausoleil i' s'a en allé s'coucher, pis i'a dormi jusqu'à huit heures l'lend'main matin. L'vieux rouè 'l a enwèyé la p'tsit domestique joliment d'bon matin pour ouère si Beausoleil 'l était l'vé. I'a été jusqu'à la barrière, pis i' l'a pas vu. 'L a eurviré, pis i' s'a rentourné dzire au rouè qu'i' avait pas vu Beausoleil. A neuf heures, i' l'a renwèyé ouère acore. Beausoleil était après s'prom'ner sus sa gal'rie. Beausoleil 'l a dzit au p'tsit domestique qu'i' dzise au rouè qu'i' vienne, qu'i' voulait le ouère.

Quand le vieux rouè 'l a eu la nouvelle, 'l a dzit au p'tsit domestique qu'i' dzise à Beausoleil le château pis ça qu'était d'dans, c'était à lui, à Beausoleil. Le p'tsit domestique 'l a été, pis i'a dzit à Beausoleil: "Sire," i' dzit, "le château pis ça qu'est d'dans, c'est à vous." —"Va dzire au rouè," i dzit, "que j'veux pas l'château, j'veux pas ça qu'est d'dans, j'veux que lui i' vienne."

L'rouè i'a dzit qu'i' allait pas, qu'i'avait pas rien à faire avec château-là. Le domestique 'l a dzit à M. Beausoleil l'rouè 'l avait dzit i' voulait pas aouère rien à faire avec château-là, i'allait pas. Beausoleil i' dzit: "T'as dzire au rouè si, par cas, i' vient pas icitte, m'as faire feu sus lui." 'L a descendzu dans son souterrain, 'l a commencé à vider les p'tsites gouttes sus les buttes, pis tous les hommes sortaient de là d'dans comme des mouches. I' nn'a mis ein à tous les connons. Quand l'vieux rouè 'l a vu ça, i'a dzit: "Mourir d'eune magnière ou ben d'l'aut', j'vas," i' dzit. Quand 'l a arrivé à la barrière, l'vieux rouè i'a dzit à Beausoleil: "Beausoleil, j'veux rien aouère à faire avec l'château. J'te l'donne, pis tout ça i'a là d'dans." Beausoleil i' dzit: "J'veux pas l'château ni rien ça i'a d'dans, c'est vous j'veux qu'i' vienne avec moin. I' m'a pas rien arrivé à moin hier au souère, i' va pas rien vous arriver à vous aujourdz'hui." L'vieux rouè 'l a été, mais en arculant. Quand 'l a arrivé pour rentrer dans l'souterrain, l'vieux rouè i' voulait eurvirer. "Non, non," i' dzit, "Sire, vous n'a pas d'besoin d'avouère peur, i' nn'a rien qui va vous troubler." Quand Beausoleil 'l a arrivé oùsque la cache d'argent 'l était, i'a montré, pis i' dzit à c't'heure: "Sire, c'étaient onze rouès comme vous. C'est tout d'l'argent 'l ont volé pis des faux billets 'l ont faites; c'est ça qui les a empéchés d'aller en paradzis, pis," i' dzit, "eurmettez ça à qui ça apparquient, pis vot' château," i' dzit, "s'ra jamais eurtroublé." —"Ben," i' dzit, "viens déjeuner Beausoleil à c't'heure."

Padent Beausoleil 'l était après déjeuner, i' leu-z-a dzit comme ça il aurait trav'lé tant que la terre l'aurait porté jusqu'à il aye à il aye peur. La princesse a y'a d'mandé pour rester à dzîner avec elle. "Ah oui!" i' y'a dzit à la princesse i'aurait dzîné avec elle. Alle a faite attraper ein courbeau vivant, pis 'l a env'loppé dans ein morceau d'pâte pas cuite. Quand 'l ont eu quasiment fini d'dzîner, alle a d'mandé à M. Beausoleil qu'i' y passe la pâte pas cuite. A dzit: "J'aime beaucoup ça, moin." A y'a d'mandé qu'i' y coupe ein morceau. M. Beausoleil 'l a commencé pour couper là d'dans. Le courbeau 'l a faite: couac, couac, pis 'l a battsu des ailes. M. Beausoleil 'l a échappé la pâte pas cuite sus la table. La princesse a dzit: "Vous dzira pas que vous 'l a pas eu peur, M. Beausoleil!" —"Ouais," i' dzit, "ma princesse, j'ai eu peur." —"Faudra s'marier," a dzit, "moin pis vous, d'abord." Ça s'fait que Beausoleil pis la princesse i' s'ont mariés. Beausoleil i'a dzit au vieux rouè i'avait pas besoin d'aouère peur d'lui donner sa princesse par rapporte qu'i' était prince, lui, comme elle, alle était princesse.

Sontaient mariés i' nn'avait plusieurs temps. Eune journée, Beausoleil était assis sus l'bout d'sa gal'rie après jongler. Sa femme a y'a d'mandé quocé 'l avait à jongler. "T'es pas satisfait d'être marié?" a dzit. "Oh si!" i' dzit, "ma princesse, j'sus ben satisfait d'être marié, mais j'sus après jongler à mon père pis à ma mère." Taleure, i' dzit: "Si ça vous plaît, m'as partsir d'main pour aller les ouère." La princesse avait instruit ane d'ses p'tsits domestiques d'faire ben attention tout ça, a dzit, "ton maît' i' va faire, pis t'as m'conter ça quand t'as eurvenir." Beausoleil part avec son p'tsit domestique. Ein souère tard, 'l a arrivé à ein auberge. I' dzit à son p'tsit domestique: "On va coucher icitte à souère." 'L ont rentré pis 'l ont d'mandé à l'aubergisse pour coucher. Alle leu-z-a dzit qu'oui. Alle a faite mettre le choual à l'écurie, ben souègné. Quand Beausoleil pis son p'tsit domestique sont v'nus pour s'mett' à la tab', à la place de deux places, i' nn'avait six. Quand la cloche alle a sonné, i' nn'a quat' *gaimbleurs* qu'a descendzu. Quand i' sontaient après souper, i'en ane qui a dzit à l'aut': "C'en est ein gras, çu-là." Après qu'i'ont eu soupé, i' l'ont attaqué pour eune *guime* de cartes. 'L ont commencé à bouère pis jouer aux cartes. 'L ont tout gagné ça Beausoleil 'l avait, jusqu'à son linge il avait sus son dos. l'ont mis des sarraux d'touèle sus l'dos pis des sabots aux pieds. Le lend'main matin, Beausoleil 'l avait honte. I' dzit à son p'tsit domestique: "Tsu peux t'en aller pis conter à ma femme ça i' m'a arrivé. Moin," i' dzit, "j'ai partsi pour aller sus mon père pis sus ma mère, pis m'as m'rendre."

L'domestique i' s'en va conter son histouère à sa maîtresse, lui. Beausoleil i' part avec son sarrau d'touèle sus l'dos pour s'en aller sus sa mère. Il a arrivé sus son père tard le souère, après l'soleil couché. Le suisse qu'i' était après guétter la barrière, Beausoleil l'a eurconnu. l'a dzit: "Rouv' donc la barrière, suisse." —"J'ouv' pas la barrière après soleil couché à personne." —"Rouv' donc la barrière," i' dzit, "c'est moin qui est Beausoleil, suisse." —"Non," i' dzit, "ma maîtresse a pas des enfants qu'ont des sarraux d'touèle sus l'dos pis des sabots aux pieds. J'rouv' pas la barrière avant dz'y d'mander." Suisse 'l a été pis 'l a dzit à la vieille que 'l avait ein homme là qui avait ein sarrau d'touèle sus l'dos pis des sabots aux pieds: "pis i' s'appelle Beausoleil," i' dzit. —"Ben," a dzit. "fais-lé rentrer pour que j'le ouèye." Beausoleil 'l a rentré, sa mère a l'a vu. "Tsu eursemb's à être sergent," a dzit, "tsu eursemb's à être coronel aussite," a dzit, "j'crouès, comme tsu eurgardes. Pour ta punition, tsu vas êt' coronel d'mes cochons avec ma vieille négresse, la vieille Marie-Jeanne." l'ont donné ein habit ben bon marché, pis i' l'ont mis à garder les cochons avec la vieille négresse Marie-Jeanne.

L'p'tsit domestique 'l avait conté à sa maîtresse quocé 'l était arrivé à son maître. A s'a habillée comme ein prince, 'helle. Elle pis son p'tsit domestique 'l ont partsi, il[s] ont arrivé à la meme auberge, pis il[s] ont couché là eux aussite c'souèrée-là. Quand les quat' *gaimbleurs* 'l ont descendzu pour leu souper, i'en ane qui a dzit à l'aut': "C'en est ein aut' gras, lui." Après souper, l'ont attaqué pour eune *guime* de cartes. Ah oui! l'beau prince 'l aimait beaucoup à jouer aux cartes. I' s'ont tou[s] mis autour d'la tab', pis i'ont tou[s] commencé à jouer ensemb'. A leu-z-a d'mandé quocé i' voulaient faire, s'mettre tou[s] à l'entour d'la table. "J'joueras pas cont' quat'," a dzit, "j'joueras cont' ane. Cetsui-là qui s'crouè l'meilleur joueur, qu'i' reste icitte d'dans, m'as jouer avec lui, pis que les trois i' s'en vonnent dans ein aut' chambre. J'veux pas personne d'aut' icitte d'dans à part que mon p'tsit domestique pour m'servir." Les trois autres i' s'en ont allés, pis celui-là qui s'app'lait l'meilleur il a resté. 'L ont commencé à jouer. L'p'tsit domestique 'l avait été instruit d'passer la bouteille joliment souvent. I' vidait le gob'let dzu *gaimbleur* plein, mais i' en mettait pas beaucoup dans le celle d'sa maîtresse. Taleure, le *gaimbleur* 'l est v'nu saoul. L'p'tsit domestique i' pernait ein mirouère pis i' s'mettait derrière l'*gaimbleur*. Sa maîtresse a pouvait ouère ça il avait dans sa main. Alle a tout gagné l'or pis l'argent 'l ontvaient, tout gagné ça M. Beausoleil 'l avait perdzu. Après ça, alle a gagné leu-z-habits. A la place, a leu-z-a mis des sarraux d'touèle sus l'dos, des sabots aux pieds, des coups d'pieds dans les fesses, pis a les a enwèyés sus la rue. "M'as vous montrer à prend' l'avantage dzu monde, vous autres!"

A c't'heure, a s'en va trouver Beausoleil. Alle a arrivé tard dans l'avant-midzi. Le suisse a rouvert la barrière sitôt comme il a vu l'beau prince arriver. C'étaient des belles alertes; i'allait avouère ein bon dzîner pour l'beau prince. Alle a rentré, pis alle a charré avec les aut's, là, qu'étaient après jouer dans la cenne. I' connaissaient pas charrer, i'avaient jamais grouillé. A ouèyait pas Beausoleil, elle. A y'a d'mandé à la vieille reine: "Est-ce que vous avez rien qu'deux garçons?" —"Mais, non," a dzit, "mon prince, j'en ai trois." —"Oùsqu'est l'aut'?" a dzit. "l'est pas icitte?" —"Non, j'varas vous conter quocé qu'i' nous a faite. l'a partsi d'icitte," a dzit, "pour aller trav'ler pour ouère dzu pays. I' nous a écrit eune journée i'était soldat. A c'coup-là, on y'a enwèyé d'l'argent, tout d'suite. Après, i' nous a écrit i'était sergent; après ça, i' nous a écrit," a dzit, "i' était coronel. Queuques jours passés," a dzit, "i'a eursous icitte avé ein sarrau d'touèle sus l'dos pis des sabots aux pieds, s'i' faut que j'vous dzise." La princesse a dzit: "Enwèyez-lé donc qu'ri, j'aim'rais ben d'le ouère." La vieille reine a dzit: "Pour vous plaire, m'as l'enwỳer qu'ri. Autrement, j'le veux pas sus la place."

Beausoleil 'l a arrivé, 'l a rentré; i' était pas inquiète, lui, d'charrer avec ein prince étranger. La vieille a voulait pas qu'i' mange à la même table qu'eux autres. Le prince étranger i' dzit: "Ben, s'i' mange pas à la meme table que vous autres, m'as manger à la meme table qu'lui, moin." Pour plaire au prince, i' l'ont laissé manger à la meme table que l'vieux rouè. Padent sontaient après dzîner, les deux qui jouaient dans la cend' sontaient jaloux. I'en a ane qui a donné ein coup d' pied à Beausoleil pis i' a frappé l'beau prince étranger sus la jambe. "Ecoute donc icitte," a dzit, "j'sus pas ein chien pour attraper des coups d'pieds sous la tab'." Croup, pis i' s'en allaient faire leur tactac dans la cend'. L'souère, l'beau prince 'l a d'mandé à la vieille reine que Beausoleil couche avec lui. Ah! la vieille reine alle aimait pas ça, mais pour y plaire, alle a dzit qu'oui. Le souère, après qu'l'ont été rentrés dans leu chambre, alle a dzit à Beausoleil: "Tsu m'eurconnais?" —"Non," i' dzit, "ben sûr, j't'eurconnais pas, j't'ai jamais vu avant." La princesse alle a rentré dans ein aut' chambre, pis a s'a habillée comme alle était la matsinée Beausoleil l'avait laissée. Alle a rentré, alle a dzit: "Tsu m'eurconnais à c't'heure?" —"Oui," Beausoleil i' dzit, "j't'eurconnais." I' dzit: "J'crouèyais pas que j'étais après charrer avec ma femme tout la journée." —"T'as pas besoin d'avouère honte," a dzit, "Beausoleil, i' leu-z-en a arrivé autant aux *gaimbleurs* comme à touè."

Le lend'main matin, à à peu près quatre heures, la vieille négresse voulait Beausoleil pour qu'i' garde les cochons avec elle. 'L a commencé à crier: "Ah! Beausoleil, viens garder les cochons." Alle a crié ça plusieurs fouès, la vieille négresse. La femme à Beausoleil a dzit: "Quocé qui geint là en bas?" —"Vieille négresse-là," i' dzit, "qui veut que j'vas garder les cochons avec elle." —"Laisse-la donc v'nir jusqu'à la porte," a dzit, "pis sacres-y-en donc ein bon sur la gueule, ça va y montrer si tsu vas garder les cochons avec elle." La vieille reine y'a dzit: "Va jusqu'à la porte, Marie-Jeanne, réveille-lé, pis mène-lé guétter les cochons." La vieille négresse 'l a partsi en montant les escaliers, dzup, dzup! "Ah! Beausoleil, viens guétter les cochons." Comme alle allait pour rouvert sa porte pour crier, Beausoleil y'a donné ein coup d'poing sus la gueule. Boudoume! boudoume! la vieille négresse alle a tombé en bas. "Ouais," a dzit, "allez ouère vot' Beausoleil, à matin, si i' eursemble à garder des cochons." Taleure, Beausoleil pis sa femme 'l ont descendzu pour l'déjeuner. La femme d'Beausoleil alle a dzit ça a pensait d'la vieille reine. "Que vous aut's l'aiment ou l'aiment pas," a dzit, "ça m'fait pas d'dzifférence. Mon père pis ma mère sont rouè et reine comme vous. Moin, j'sus princesse comme Beausoleil 'l est prince. Moin, j'remmène Beausoleil avec moin, c'est mon mari."

19.

Master Thief

Once upon a time there were an old man and an old woman. They were poor. They had one son. There was also a rich man who had a daughter. He was sort of the lord of the place, under the King. Master Thief and the rich man's daughter went to the same school, and they had been courting since they had been little. When they got big and finished school, Master Thief still saw the girl secretly. Then one day Master Thief wanted to get married. He went to see the rich man to ask him for his daughter in marriage. The rich man said to him, "What? A man with no trade? You don't even know how to put the plow into the earth. Go and learn a trade and then come back, and I'll let you marry my daughter."

So the next morning, he went out to learn a trade. Late that afternoon, he met three men and began to talk with them. One of the men asked him where he was going. —"I'm going to find a place where I can learn a trade," he said. —"Well, why don't you come along with us, and we'll teach you the trade of Master Thief?" they answered. He said, "It doesn't make any difference to me. What is a trade anyway?" So, they began to have him steal a little something here and a little something else over there, and after awhile he could steal almost as well as they could. Finally, one of the thieves said, "We're going to send him over to the King to steal his golden shoes. The King will put him in prison, and then we will be able to get rid of him." So they said to him, "Now, Master Thief, if you can go and steal the King's golden slippers, you have learned your trade well." He answered, "I'll go tomorrow morning."

The next morning, he left to go see the King. He hired on with the King, to bring his papers and letters into his office so he could read them. He bought himself a pair of pants with big pockets. One day, he was bringing in the King's letters, and he saw one with pretty writing on it. He said to the old King, "I'll open that one up. It probably has good news in it." While the king was reading his letter, Master Thief put the golden slippers into his big pockets and left. When he got to their cabin, it was pretty dark, and he started a fire and lit the lamp. The other thieves saw the light as they were getting near the cabin. "That fellow has come back," they said. "I'll bet he doesn't have the golden slippers." But when they opened the door, the golden slippers were shining in the lantern light, so brightly that they blinded the thieves, and they couldn't see. The thieves were jealous of Master Thief,

"Master Thief"

It's Good to Tell You

because he could steal better than they could. They wanted to get rid of him, so they said, "You can go now. We've taught you the trade of Master Thief." The next morning, they filled his pockets with silver and gold and sent him on his way.

He went back to his home and found the rich man and asked him for his daughter in marriage. The rich man asked him what kind of a trade he had learned, and he answered, "The trade of Master Thief." —"Aren't there enough thieves around here already without you going and learning that too?" asked the rich man. "Well, I'll have to test you to see how good you are. I don't want you to steal from me, but I have a neighbor who has a pair of oxen that I've always wanted. I want you to go and get them for me. I don't know how you're going to steal them. He's on his way now to sell them."

The next morning, early, Master Thief went out and hid by the side of the road where the neighbor would have to go by with his oxen. He saw the old man coming and took his gold slipper. He put it in the middle of the road. The old man was taking only one ox at a time, and when he got to the place where the gold slipper was, he said, "Oh, that's beautiful! I'll have to bring it to my wife. But, no, that old witch, if I bring it to her I'll have to buy a mate for it. I'll bury it in the leaves, and when I find another one, I'll come back and get this one and bring them both to my wife." The old man started out again with his ox. Master Thief took the gold slipper that the old man had buried, and hurried ahead of the old man, and put it back in the road. The old man arrived at the new place where the slipper had been put and said, "Well, look at that! There's another gold slipper. I'll tie my ox up here and go get the other slipper I buried. Then, I can bring them both to my wife." Master Thief took the ox when the old man had left to go and get the first slipper. He went and tied up the ox in the woods in a big deep gully. The old man couldn't find the first slipper where he had hidden it. He said to himself, "Well, I'm not going to stew any longer about those golden slippers. I'm going to go and sell my ox." He went back to get his ox, but he couldn't find that either! He looked all around, and when he still couldn't find it he said to himself, "Well, I guess I'll go and get the other ox and go sell that one. Whatever I get for that one, I'll tell my wife that's what I got for the pair." He went and got the second ox, and when he got to the place where he'd lost the first one, Master Thief was hiding by the side of the road, and he began to bellow like an ox. The old man said, "Ah! I hear my ox bellowing! I'm going to tie this one up here and go find the other one. He'll know where I am." So he went off calling the ox, "Soup! Soup!" While he was searching, Master Thief came around the other way and got the second ox. He went and got the first one that he had tied up in the woods before.

Master Thief brought the two oxen back to the rich man. "Now, it's time for you to give me your daughter," he said. The rich man answered, "No, I want to test you again first." Master Thief answered, "What do you want me to steal?" The rich man answered, "I want you to steal the horse out of my stable this evening. But I'll tell you that when you come around here tonight, you're going to get yourself killed. There will be two men on guard, and one of them will have the key to the stable in his wallet in his pocket." Master Thief said, "That's all right. I can steal from you if you want me to."

That night, Master Thief came to get the horse. As he arrived, it was starting to get really dark. Master Thief was dressed up like an old grandfather with a white beard. It was cold, and there was a fine mist in the air. The two guards were playing cards around a little fire. When he got a little way from them, he began to holler, "Hey! Hey!" One of the guards said, "Who's that hollering out there?" The other one looked and said, "It's an old man, don't you see him?" One of the guards asked him what he wanted. "Wouldn't you let me warm myself for a few moments by your fire, my children?" The rich man had told them not to let anyone come near the place, but one said, "Let the old man warm himself. He doesn't look like he could steal a horse, he can't even walk!" So, the guards told the old grandfather to come and warm up by the fire. The old man came near and said, "Don't you ever have anything to drink when you stand guard like this?" —"We'd have a drink if the rich man would let us, but he doesn't want us to drink. Do you have something on you to drink, old grandfather?" The old man answered, "Well I have a little flask in my pocket, but I don't like to let others drink from it. If I give it to you, I might end up freezing tonight." The guards answered, "No, no, grandfather. If you give us your bottle of liquor, we'll make you a big fire, and we'll let you spend the night with us." The old man gave them the bottle of liquor.

They were talking with the old man. The little flask didn't last very long. "Don't you have another one?" they asked the old man. —"I have another one here in my pocket, but I really don't want to give it to you," answered the old man. They replied, "Oh, you don't need to be afraid, grandfather. We'll make you a good fire all night long, and tomorrow morning you can have a good, warm breakfast with us." So, the old man gave them his second little flask. They both drank from it and then fell asleep. The old man put his hand into the pocket of the guard who had the key in his wallet. He took the key and went to get the horse. Then, he put the key back into the guard's pocket and left with the horse.

The next morning, the man went out to look at his horse. He asked the guard for the key and opened up the stable. He said, "Where did my horse go?" The guard said, "Your horse is in the stable." The rich man answered, "He's not in here. Are you sure you didn't see anyone around here last evening?" The guards said that they had seen an old man who came to warm himself by the fire for a few moments. The rich man said, "Well, that was Master Thief, here to steal my horse." The rich man turned around to go back home, and Master Thief called after him, "Wait a minute! I'm coming to bring you back your horse. Now, I want you to give me your daughter in marriage." —"I won't give her to you yet," answered the rich man. "I want to test you one more time." Master Thief asked him, "What do you want me to steal tonight, old man? Do you want me to steal you?" —"If you come around here tonight, you'll get yourself killed," answered the rich man.

Master Thief went away and made a straw man and dressed it in the clothes he had been wearing that morning. That night, the rich man put his two bravest men on guard in a room. "If you two see something out the window tonight, I want you to shoot it. If you're afraid to shoot, come and get me." Master Thief passed in front of the window two or three times, and they saw him. "Do you see that?" asked one of them. Then, Master Thief put his straw man up in front of the window. One of the guards said, "Do you see him? Go ahead and shoot!" —"No! I'm not going to shoot him. You shoot him!" —"No, I'm not going to shoot. Let's go and get the rich man. He said that if we were afraid to shoot we should go and get him." So, they went and got the rich man and said, "He's standing in front of the window downstairs, your Master Thief." The rich man said, "Wait a minute. I'm going to go downstairs and shoot him." He went downstairs and shot, and the straw man fell over.

The rich man said to one of his guards, "Go dig a ditch in the garden," and to the other, "Go get a load of straw, and if the two of you promise me never to tell a soul that I killed him, I'll give you a good pension for the rest of your days." The rich man then went to tell his wife, "I've killed him. Dear woman, don't ever tell a soul about this. If the King finds out, he'll have me hanged. I'm going to go out and make sure that he's buried right in the garden." Master Thief was standing by the door, and as soon as the rich man left the room he came in. "Old woman," he said, "give me your sheet to wrap him up in." —"Wait!" she said. "I'll give you a clean one." —"No!" answered Master Thief. "Don't go to all that trouble. Just give me one of the sheets on your bed." Master Thief got his sheet and left. The old rich man and the two guards worked almost all night to get the straw man buried. When the rich man came back in, his wife asked him, "Did you wrap him up in the sheet?" The rich man answered, "No, I didn't wrap him up at all." "Didn't you come to get a sheet?" she asked. "Yes, you did. You came in and asked for a sheet, and I wanted to give you a clean one. You said, 'Don't go to all that trouble. Just give me a sheet from the the bed.'" The rich man was surprised. "I didn't come in here at all looking for a sheet." The old woman said, "Well, someone did." The rich man answered, "Well, I guess that was him. We didn't kill him at all." The next morning, Master Thief tucked the sheet under his arm and went to the rich man's house. He said, "Good morning, mister rich man. I came to bring you back your sheet. Shall I steal your body tonight?" The rich man answered, "No. Take my daughter and marry her and don't come around here any more."

Fin Voleur ou Les Pantoufles d'Or

C'étaient ein vieux pis eune vieille. Sontaient pauv's. 'L ontvaient ein garçon. N'avait ein riche qu'avait eune fille. C'était comme l'seigneur, 'l était emp'reur d'place-là sous l'rouè. Fin Voleur pis la fille dzu riche i'allaient à la meme école, pis il[s] ontvaient commencé à courtsiser depuis qu'i'étaient tout p'tsits. Et quand 'l ont sortsi d'l'école, i' charrait avec la fille en cachette d'son père à elle. Pis eune journée, Fin Voleur voulait s'marier. I'a été ouère beau riche, i'a été ouère l'homme riche pour qu'i' y donne sa fille en mariage. "Mais quoi ein homme qui connaît pas d'méquier! Tsu connais pas comment enfoncer eune charrue dans la terre! Vas apprend' ein méquier," i' dzit, "pis eurviens, j'vas t'donner ma fille en mariage."

'L a partsi l'lend'man matin pour apprend' ein méquier. Dans l'après-midzi, ein peu tard, 'l a rencontré trois hommes. I'a commencé à charrer avec eux aut's. Ane y'a d'mandé oùsqu'i' s'en allait. —"J'm'en vas charcer à apprendre ein méquier." —"Viens avec nous aut's, on va t'montrer l'méquier d'fin voleur." —"Pas d'dzifférence," i' dzit, "quoi que c'est, moin, d'abord qu'c'est ein *tréde*." 'L ont commencé à y faire voler eune p'tsite artic' icitte pis eune p'tsite artic' là-bas. C'est v'nu i' pouvait voler quasiment aussi ben comme eux aut's. I'a eune qui dzit à l'aut': "On va l'envouèyer sus l'rouè voler ses pantoufles d'or. L'rouè va l'mett' en prison pis on va êt' débarrassé avec lui." Ça s'fait i' y'a dzit: "A c't'heure, Fin Voleur, si tsu peux aller voler les pantouf's d'or dzu rouè, t'as avouère fini ton *tréde*." —"Ben, j'vouèras d'main matin."

L'lend'main, 'l a partsi, 'l a été sus l'rouè. I' s'a eu d'l'ouvrage avec l'rouè. I' portait ses lettres, ses papiers dans son *office* pour qu'i' les lise. I' s'a ach'té eune paire d'quilottes qu'avaient des grandes poches. Eune journée, 'l a été porter les lett' dzu rouè, pis nn'avait eune qui avait d'la jolie écritsure après. 'L a commencé à dzire au vieux rouè: "J'vas ouvrir c'telle-là, c'en est ane qui doué avouère des bonnes nouvelles." Padent l'vieux rouè était après lire sa lett', i'a pris les pantouf's d'or, les a mis dans sa poche, pis i'a sortsi. 'L a arrivé à leu cabane, i' faisait quasiment nouère. Fin Voleur, i'a partsi ein feu, pis i'a allumé sa lampe. Les autres voleurs sont v'nus, pis i'ont vu la clairté. I'a ane qui dzit à l'aut': "Beau gas, i'est eurvenu. J'vas gager il a pas eu les pantouf's d'or." Et quand i'ont rouvert la porte, les pantouf's d'or ont brillé d'vant la lumière d'la lampe. Ça a embrouillé l'vieux, i' pouvait pas ouère clair. I' connaissaient pas comment s'en démett'. I'étaient jaloux ent' eux aut's i'était plus fin qu'eux aut's. I'ont dzit: "A c't'heure, on t'a montré l'méquier d'fin voleur, tsu peux t'en aller, si tsu veux." L'lend'main matin, i'ont donné tout l'argent pis l'or i' pouvait mett' dans ses poches.

'L a partsi pis i' s'a en allé trouver l'riche. I'a d'mandé s'i' y'aurait donné sa fille en mariage. I'a d'mandé queu sorte d'méquier i'avait appris. I' dzit: "L'méquier d'fin voleur." —"Est-ce qu'i' nn'a pas assez d'voleurs dans la ville sans qu'touè tsu vas apprend' ça? Ben, faudra que j't'assaye avant pour ouère, si tsu veux. J'veux pas qu'tsu m'voles, moin, mais i'a ein vieux ouèsin là qui n'a eune paire de boeufs. J'veux les boeufs-là," i' dzit, "pis j'veux pas les ach'ter. J'veux qu'tsu vas m'les qu'ri. J'vouès pas comment t'as faire pour les voler, mais i' s'en va les vend'."

L'lend'main, 'l a partsi d'bon matin, lui, Fin Voleur. I' s'cachait l'long dzu ch'min oùsque l'vieux 'l aurait passé avec ses boeufs. I'a vu v'nir le vieux, i'a pris sa pantouf' d'or pis i' l'a mis dans l'milieu dzu ch'min. L'vieux 'l a arrivé là; i' m'nait rien qu'ein boeu[f] à la fouès. 'L a trouvé c'te pantouf' d'or. "Oh!" i' dzit, "mais comme c'est beau! J'vas la porter à ma vieille," i' dzit, "j'crouès. Mais non, la vieille garce, si j'vas y porter à elle, i' va fallouère qu'j'en achète ein aut'. M'as enterrer elle dans les feuilles, pis si j'en trouve ein aut', m'as eurvenir la qu'ri icitte, pis j'vas aller la porter à ma vieille." L'vieux 'l a eurpartsi avec son boeu[f]. Lui, Fin Voleur, 'l a été qu'ri sa pantouf', pis 'l a été porter là-bas en d'vant dans l'ch'min. L'vieux 'l a arrivé. "Mais eurgarde donc," i' dzit, "en v'là ein aut' pantouf' d'or. M'as aller amarrer mon boeu[f] icitte, m'as aller qu'ri l'aut' pantouf' d'or pis m'as aller les porter à ma vieille." Fin Voleur a pris l'boeu[f], lui. 'L a partsi, pis i'est allé l'amarrer dans l'bois dans eune grande fourche creuse. L'vieux 'l a été charcer sa pantouf' d'or, lui, qu'il avait cachée. Pas pu la trouver. "Ah! j'bavasse pus avec pantoufles d'or-là. M'as aller vend' mon boeu[f]." 'L a été charcer pour l'boeu[f], pis pouvait pas l'trouver. 'L a eurgardé plein à l'entour, pis 'l a pas pu l'trouver. I' dzit: "M'as aller qu'ri l'aut', pis m'as aller vend' lui," i' dzit. "Ça m'as avouère pour lui, m'as faire accreire à ma vieille j'l'ai eu pour les deux." Il a arrivé d'vis-à-vis il avait perdzu son boeu[f] là. Fin Voleur 'l a été sus l'aut' bord dzu ch'min, pis 'l a commencé à beugler comme ein boeu[f]. "Ah!" i dzit, "j'attends mon boeu[f] beugler. M'as amarrer celui-là icitte pis m'as aller qu'ri l'aut'; i' va comprend' où j'chus taleure." 'L a partsi en 'plant: "Soup! Soup!" l'vieux. Fin Voleur 'l a été faire eune grande tournée dans l'bois, lui, pis i'est v'nu, pis 'l a pris l'aut' boeu[f]. 'L a été qu'ri l'aut' 'l avait amarré dans l'bois.

A c't'heure, 'l a été emm'ner les boeufs au riche. "T'as m'donner ta fille," i' dzit, "à c't'heure."—"Non, j'te la donne pas. Faudra que j't'assaye eune aut' fouès avant."—"Quocé qu'tsu veux j'vole?" i' dzit. "Touè-meme?"—"Non," i' dzit, "j'veux qu'tsu vailles voler mon choual qu'est dans mon écurie à souère. Si tsu viens à l'entour," i' dzit, "tsu vas t'faire tsuer à souère. I' nn'a deux hommes sus la garde, pis i' en a ane qui va avouère la clef dans son portefeuille dans sa poche."—"Ça m'fait rien, ça," i' dzit, "j'peux t'voler, touè, si tsu veux," i' dzit. L'souère, l'riche 'l a envouèyé qu'ri l'vieux qui l'avait perdzu ses boeufs pour qu'i' vienne. I'a d'mandé: "T'as vu queuques-anes l'long dzu ch'min quand t'es allé vend' tes boeufs?"—"Non," i' dzit, "j'ai pas vu personne."—"Ben," i' dzit, "tes boeufs sont dans ma grange, C'est Fin Voleur qui les a pris."

L'souère, Fin Voleur 'l est v'nu pour voler son choual. I' commençait à faire ben brin comme 'l est v'nu. I'était habillé comme ein vieux grand-père avec d'la barbe blanche. I' faisait frais pis i' mouillassait d'la p'tsite puie fine. Les deux gardes sontaient après jouer aux cartes, pis il[s] ontvaient ein p'tsit feu. Arrivé ein p'tsit boute d'eux aut's, 'l a commencé à crier: "Hèye! Hèye!" Ane a d'mandé à l'aut': "Quocé qui geint icitte?" I' nn'a eurgardé pis i'a dzit: "C'est ein vieux qu'est là-bas, tsu ouès pas?" Eune des gardes 'l a d'mandé à vieux-là quoi i' voulait. "Vous aut's m'laiss'raient pas chauffer ein p'tsit moment, mes p'tsits enfants?" L'vieux riche i' leu-z-avait dzit pas quitter personne aborder la place. Ane i' dzit à l'aut': "Laisse-lé donc s'chauffer, vieux-là. I' eursemb' à voler ein ch'val, i' peut pas marcher!" I'ont dzit au vieux grand-père qu'i' vienne s'chauffer. I' leu-z-a d'mandé: "Vous aut's, mes p'tsits enfants, bouè jamais quand ane veille d'meme?"—"On bouèrait s'i' voulait nous quitter bouère, riche-là, mais i' veut pas qu'on bouè." Ane qui y'a d'mandé: "Vous nn'a d'quoi bouère, mon vieux grand-père?"—"Ben," i' dzit, "j'en ai eune p'tsite fiole dans ma poche, mais j'aime pas beaucoup la donner. Si j'vous la donne, p't-ben moin, j'vas g'ler à souère."—"Ah!" i' dzisent, "non, non, mon grand-père, si vous donne vot' bouteille d'liqueur, on vous f'ra ein gros feu, on vous quitt'ra passer la nuit avec nous aut's." I'a donné la bouteille d'liqueur.

I' charraient avec mon grand-père. La p'tsite fiole alle a pas dzuré ben, ben longtemps. "Tsu nn'a pas d'aut'" i' dzisent, "mon grand-père?"—"J'en ai eune aut' p'tsite fiole icitte dans ma poche mais ça m'coûte vous la donner, elle."—"Ah!" i' dzisent, "vous a pas besoin d'avouère peur, mon grand-père, on va vous faire ein bon feu tout la nuit, pis d'main matin," i' dzisent, "vous pourra v'nir dèjeuner avec nous aut's. On va vous donner ein bon dèjeuner chaud." Ça fait i' leu-z-a donné sa p'tsite fiole. I' nn'ont pris chaquin ein filet pis i' n'ont tombé endormi tous les deusses. 'L a mis la main dans la poche d'l'homme qui avait la clef dans son portefeuille, i'a pris la clef, i'a été aveind' l'choual, 'l a eurmis la clef dans la poche à l'aut'. I' s'a en allé avec son choual.

L'lend'main matin, l'riche 'l a été ouère pour son choual. "Donne-moin ma clef," i' dzit à la garde. I'a donné sa clef. L'riche 'l a rouvert sa porte d'écurie; i'a d'mandé: "Oùsqu'i' est mon choual?" La garde y'a dzit: "Il est dans ton écurie, ton choual."—"'L est pas icitte d'dans," i' dzit. "T'as pas vu personne," i' dzit, "icitte hier au souère?" Les gardes ont dzit 'l ontvaient vu ein vieux qu'était v'nu s'chauffer ein p'tsit moment. "Ben," i' dzit, "c'tait lui qui a v'nu qu'ri mon choual." L'vieux riche 'l a partsi pour s'rentourner à sa maisonne. Fin Voleur 'l a crié après: "Arrête donc ein p'tsit moment, j'vas t'remm'ner ton choual," i' dzit. "Tsu vas m'donner ta. fille en mariage à c't'heure."— "Pas à c't'heure," i' dzit, "i' faudra que j't'assaye acore eune fouès."—"Quocé qu'tsu veux que j'faise à souère? Tsu veux que j'te vole, touè?" i' dzit, "vieux riche?"—"Ben," i' dzit, "si tsu viens entour d'la maisonne à souère, tsu vas t'faire tsuer."

I' s'a en allé pis i' s'a fait ein bonhomme d'paille, pis il l'a chanzé en l'habit qu'il avait c'te matsinée-là. L'souère, l'riche 'l a mis ses deux hommes les plus braves d'la garde dans eune chambre. "Si vous aut's vouè queud' chose par la f'nêt à souère, vous aut's tsirez, pis si vous 'l a peur d'tsirer, v'nez m'qu'ri, moin." Fin Voleur n'a passé deux ou trois fouès d'vant la f'nêt'. I' l'ont vu. "Tsu l'vouès?" dzit eune des gardes. C'était Fin Voleur. Il a mis son bonhomme planté dans la f'nêt! Eune des gardes dzit à l'aut': "Tsu vouès, tsire donc."—"Non," i' dzit, "moin, j'tsire pas. Tsire donc, touè."—"Non," i' dzit, "allons donc qu'ri beau tsireur. I'a dzit qu'si on l'avait nous aut's, d'aller qu'ri lui pour tsirer." I'ont été qu'ri l'vieux riche, pis i'ont dzit: "I'est planté d'vant la f'nêt' en bas, ton Fin Voleur." I' dzit: "Arrêtez, moin, j'vas aller l'débouler." I'est v'nu, pis l'a tsiré. L'bonhomme 'l a déboulé.

L'vieux riche 'l a dzit à c't'heure aux gardes: "Allez caler eune fosse dans l'jardin, pis l'aut'," i' dzit, "va qu'ri ein vouèyage d'paille, pis si vous m'pronmet d'jamais desserrer les dents que j'l'ai tsué, m'as vous donner chaquin eune bonne pension l'restant d'vos jours." I' s'en va s'lamenter à sa femme à c't'heure. "J'l'ai tsué," i' dzit, "chère enfant, dzis jamais ça à personne! Si l'rouè i' connaît ça, i' va m'faire pend'. M'as aller oùsqu'i' est après caler la fosse dans l'jardin." Fin Voleur 'l était planté à la porte, lui. Quand l'vieux riche 'l a sortsi, lui 'l a rentré. "Ma vieille," i' dzit, "donne-moin donc ton drap pour l'env'lopper."—"Arrête," a dzit, "j'vas t'en donner ein net."—"Non, non," dzit Fin Voleur, "pas tous frais-là. Donne-moin ein drap sus quoi tsu t'es couchée d'ssus." L'Fin Voleur i' s'en va avec son drap, lui. L'vieux riche pis ses deux hommes 'l ont travaillé quasiment tout la nuit dans l'jardin pour enterrer l'bonhomme. Quand l'vieux riche 'l est eurvenu dans sa maisonne, il était assis pis i'était après jongler. Sa femme a y'a d'mandé: "Tsu l'as env'loppé dans mon drap," a dzit, "mon vieux?"—"Ah!" i' dzit, "j'l'ai pas env'loppé en toute."—"T'es pas v'nu qu'ri ein drap icitte? Oui, t'as v'nu qu'ri ein drap. J'voulais t'en donner ein net, pis tsu m'as dzit: Pas tous ces frais-là. T'as dzit: donne-moin ein drap sus quoi tsu t'es couchée d'ssus."—"J'sus pas v'nu qu'ri des draps icitte d'dans en toute," i' dzit. Sa vieille a dzit: "I'a queuques-ane qu'est v'nu en qu'ri."—"Eh ben," i' dzit, "ça, c'est lui, l'beau gas. On l'a pas tsué en toute." L'lend'main, 'l a eursous son drap d'ssour son bras. "Bonjour," i' dzit, "M. l'riche, j'sus v'nu rapporter ton drap. Tsu veux que j'te vole, touè, a souère?"— "Non," i' dzit, "prends ma fille, pis marie-touè, pis eurviens pus à l'entour d'moin."

20.

Carambot

It's good to tell you that once upon a time there were an old man and an old woman, and they had only one daughter, whose name was Mary. Carambot's wife died, and he had a hard time of it until Mary got big enough to cook his meals for him. The poor thing spent all his money, and all he had left was one cow. Mary had to go and work for the King. One day, the King said to Mary, "Go tell your father that if he doesn't keep that cow of his in her pasture, I'll kill her." So, Mary went back home and told her father that the King would kill their cow if she were not kept in her own pasture. Carambot said, "He might as well kill her. She has nothing to eat in our pasture." So the next day when Mary went back to the King's house, he said, "Tell your father to come and take his hide. I killed the cow."

So when she went back home that day, she told her father that the King had killed their cow, and Carambot went and took the hide. He said to Mary, "I want you to stay here alone for a little while, while I go and sell the cowhide." He took the hide and put it in a sack and left. Now Carambot was getting old, and he didn't see too well any more. He walked right up to three men before he saw them. They were thieves, and they were dividing up the money they had stolen. They had their money in a sack. Carambot was scared when he saw them and he began to think. He reached into his own sack quietly and pulled out the cowhide. He put it on his head and back and started walking on his hands and knees. The horns were still on the cowhide. One of the thieves was sitting there facing where Carambot came out of the bushes, and he said, "What does the devil look like?" One of the other thieves answered, "Well I've heard that he has big horns, but of course I've never seen him." Then the first thief said, "Well, he's right behind your back. Turn around and you'll see him."

The three thieves ran as fast as they could, leaving their sack of money behind them. Carambot went and got the sack of money and brought it home with him. He said to Mary, "Now, if you're not afraid to stay alone for a few more minutes, I'm going to go out and bury this cowhide." He took his shovel and went and buried it. The next morning, he said to Mary, "Today when you go to the King's house, I want you to borrow his measure. If he asks you whether I have any money to measure, tell him that you don't know." When Mary got to the King's house, she said, "Good morning, sire."—"What do you want this morning, Mary?" asked the King. She said, "My father sent me to borrow your measure."—"My measure? What does he want with a measure? Where did he get the money?" Mary answered, "I don't know." The King said to his servant, "Put a piece of dough in the bottom of the measure."

Old Carambot measured his money and then hid it in a corner of his house. When he had finished his measuring, he took a twenty-dollar gold piece and stuck it in the dough at the bottom of the measure. He said to Mary, "Go and give this back to the King but give it to him with the bottom up." She went to the King's house, and he said, "Good morning, Mary." Then, she gave him back the measure with the bottom up. The King looked at it and said, "Mary, where did your father get that money?"—"Ah, I don't know," she answered. Things went along for two or three days, and the King was really curious to know where Carambot had gotten the money. Finally, he decided to go visit him to find out.

When the King arrived, Carambot was sitting in a corner, smoking. "Hello, Carambot," said the King. Carambot answered, "Good morning, sire." The King began to visit with Carambot, but Carambot didn't talk much; he acted as if he were half-angry. The King finally asked, "Carambot, are you mad because I killed your cow?" Carambot answered, "No I'm just mad that I didn't have ten cows for you to kill." The King said, "How come, Carambot? Did you get a lot of money for your hide? Tell me how much you got for it." Carambot said, "I got one hundred gold pieces per pound. Don't you see that pile of money I got for my hide?" he asked. The old King said, "Wow! I'm going to kill all my animals and sell all the hides."

So the King had all his animals killed and had all the hides taken off. He said to his men, "Don't sell one of them for less than one hundred gold pieces per skin." They had been gone several days, and when they still hadn't come back, the King began to wonder, "I don't know what they're doing. Maybe, they sold all those skins for one hundred gold pieces each, and now they can't carry all the money." So he hitched up three wagons with big corn beds on them. When he got to town, they hadn't sold a single skin. "You idiots!" the King said to them. "Don't you know how to sell skins? Give me that apron!" He put on the white apron and began to walk up and down the street.

The hide merchants saw that there was a new man there and went to see. They asked him how much he was asking for his hides. He answered, "Great bargain! Great bargain! One hundred gold pieces per skin!" They said, "He's dumber than the others. Let's leave him alone." He stayed there trying to sell his skins for several days, until they began to stink up the town, and he had to leave with them. He threw all the old hides into the woods and came back really angry with Carambot. He said, "I'm going to go get Carambot and have him hanged." Carambot knew that the King would be coming to get him, so the next morning he got up early and heated up some rocks behind his house in a fire. Then, he filled up his kettle with water and chestnuts and started to boil the chestnuts by putting his hot rocks into the water. He saw the King on his way over to get him, and he went to get another big hot rock, and plopped it into the water in his kettle. Then, he took a little whip and began to walk around the kettle, striking it with the whip and whistling.

Carambot dressed in cowskin

When the King arrived, he said, "What in the world are you doing, Carambot?"—"I'm boiling some chestnuts," answered Carambot. The King said, "Yes, but what are you making the water boil with? I don't see any fire." Carambot said, "I don't need any fire. I just make them boil with my little whip. If you don't think they're cooked, all you have to do is taste one, sire." The King said, "Please sell me your little whip, Carambot."—"Oh, no, I can't sell you my whip," said Carambot. "I don't have any wood on my land." The King answered, "I'll give you one hundred dollars for your whip, and all the wood you ever want to burn." So Carambot sold his whip to the King for one hundred dollars.

The King went home with the whip, and the next Thursday he wanted to make a big dinner. But he didn't want any fire anywhere around. He had his servants put all the food in big kettles outside. At around ten o'clock, he gave them his whip and told them to go and start beating the kettles. Of course, they couldn't cook anything that way, and they came back and said to him, "Sire, we can't cook with a whip!" The King said, "You bunch of idiots! You are so ignorant! I'll get the kettles to boil." So, he took the whip and went out and started beating on those kettles and whistling but of course nothing happened. "Tomorrow morning," he said, "I'm going to go down there and kill Carambot right in his own house."

Carambot knew that the King would be coming to get him in the morning. So he took a bag of blood and said to Mary, "When the King comes this morning, he's going to want to hang me. Start talking. I'll tell you to be quiet twice. I'm going to stab this bag of blood under your clothes with my knife. I want you to fall down and make believe you're dead. When I play my little fiddle in your ears, then you can move." So the King came, all angry with Carambot. He said, "Carambot, this morning I'm going to hang you for sure." Carambot answered, "Well, sire, I guess if you're going to hang me you'll just go ahead and do it." Mary began to cry. She wailed, "Papa, he's going to hang you today."—"Be quiet, you," said Carambot.—"But Papa, what am I going to do if he hangs you?" Carambot took out his knife and stabbed Mary, and the blood flew all over the place. The King said, "Now, I really am going to hang you, Carambot. You've killed your daughter."—"Oh, yes, she's dead now, but I'll bring her back to life in a little while," said Carambot.—"Bring her back right away!" said the King. "No," answered Carambot, "let her cool off a little first."

After a little while, Carambot went and got his little fiddle and began to play, "Tigne, Tigne, Tigne," in Mary's ears. She moved a little bit. "Play it louder," said the King. "She moved, Carambot!"—"Take your time, sire. It takes some time to bring someone back from the dead," answered Carambot. A little while later, Carambot turned back to his daughter and began to play again, "Tigne, Tigne, Tigne." Mary got up. The King said, "Please sell me your fiddle, Carambot." Carambot said, "I can't sell you my fiddle, sire, it's the only fiddle I have."—"I'll give you one hundred dollars for your fiddle," said the King. And Carambot sold him the fiddle for one hundred dollars.

The next week, the King's daughter was getting married. After they came back from

Carambot playing the fiddle

the wedding, they went to see the King. He took his pistol and shot them both, "Pow! Pow!" What a big fuss! Everyone was running around shouting and crying! The King said, "Don't worry! I'll bring them back to life in a little while. Let's let them cool off a bit first." So after a while, he went and got the little fiddle and began to play, "Tigne, Tigne, Tigne," in the ears of his daughter and her husband. But they didn't budge. They were dead. The King said, "We're going to bury them." Then, he told two of his men, "Go and take Carambot, put him in a barrel, and bury him in the woods."

The two men went and got old man Carambot, to bury him. Carambot asked them to leave one of his hands sticking out of the ground, and they did. They buried him and the barrel deep in the ground, with one of his hands sticking out, and came back to the King's house. The King asked them if they had buried him well, and they said, "Yes, we buried him deep in sheep country, and he'll never come back." But later that night, when it began to get dark, a big wolf came by and stuck his tail in Carambot's hand. Carambot caught hold of the tail, and you can believe that that wolf pulled hard when he felt Carambot's hand on his tail! He pulled Carambot out of the ground. Old man Carambot took off his belt and fastened it around the wolf's neck and brought him home. He put the wolf in a small shed.

When he came home, he said to Mary, "Go and tell the King what a pretty sheep I brought back from underground." So Mary went and knocked on the King's door. The King asked who was there, and Mary said, "It's me, Mary." The King asked her, "What do you want?" She said, "Well, my father told me to come and tell you about the pretty sheep that he brought back from underground." The old King left right away and went to Carambot's house, and said, "Where is your sheep?" Carambot said, "Ah, he's down in my shed. Do you want to see him?"—"Yes, that's what I came for," said the king. The King looked into the shed and said, "Please sell me your sheep." Carambot said, "I'll sell it to you if you take it back right away tonight." The King said, "I'll give you one hundred dollars if you'll sell me that sheep and bring it over to my place for me." Carambot said, "Oh, I guess I can bring it over for you." Carambot put a leash around the wolf's neck and brought it to the King's barn. "Where do you want it, sire?"—"I want you to put it with the others, so they can get used to each other overnight." So Carambot took the wolf and left it in the barn with the King's sheep, and then he went home to bed. Early the next morning, the King opened his barn door to look at his new sheep. All his sheep were dead, and lying in the corner was a big fat wolf. He said to two of his men, "I want you to go get Carambot, put him in a sack, and bring him and pitch him into the sea."

So the two men went and got a big sack, caught old man Carambot and put him in it, and left. After a while, they got to a little village that had a tavern. One of the men said to the other, "Put down that big ox, and let's go in and get a beer. I'm tired and thirsty." While the men were drinking beer in the tavern, Carambot heard some horse's hoofs approaching. He began to moan, "I don't want to marry the King's daughter! I don't want to marry the

King's daughter! I'm too old, and they're going to take me in this sack and make me marry her!" It was a young shepherd boy riding by, and when he got to where Carambot was on the ground in the sack, he said, "What are you saying?" Carambot repeated, "I don't want to marry the King's daughter! They're taking me in this sack to make me marry her!" The young man said, "I'll marry her!"—"She's a pretty princess," said Carambot. "Untie the sack, and you get in in my place."

So the young man untied the sack, and Carambot crawled out. The young man said, "Do you see that handsome horse? Take it. I'll give it to you." He got into the sack, and Carambot tied the sack back up. Then he said, "Stay quiet, and they'll come and get you in a few minutes." Carambot got on the horse and rode off. He put the horse in his stable and fed it well. After awhile, the two men in the tavern thought about Carambot, and one of them said, "I guess we'd better go and drown that old guy now." One picked him up and they started off with the man in the sack. He was heavier than he'd been before! The young man in the sack was saying, "I'm going to marry the King's daughter!" and the King's men answered, "Yes! Just wait awhile and you can marry her!" When they got to the sea, they threw him in.

After awhile, old man Carambot looked out his door and saw the King's two men coming back. He said to Mary, "Go see the King and tell him that he should come and see the beautiful horse that I brought back from under the sea." So Mary went over to the King's house, and the King said to her, "Mary, what are you going to do now that your father is gone?" She said, "My father came back!" The King said, "What? Your father came back? I sent two men to throw him into the sea this morning." Mary said to the King, "He sent me to tell you to come and see the beautiful horse that he brought back from under the sea!" So the King picked up his hat and left right away, to go to Carambot's house. He said when he came in, "Well, let me see that beautiful horse that you brought back from under the sea."

Carambot showed the horse to the King and said, "I can tell you, it's a pretty one! But there were prettier ones than that in there." The King said to him, "Well, then, how come you didn't bring back a prettier one?" Carambot said, "Sire, you didn't have them throw me far enough in. All the prettier ones were farther away from the shore." The King said, "Carambot, I'm going to get into a sack, and I want you to throw me into the sea. Throw me as far as you can, because I want to get a big, handsome horse." Carambot said to him, "Sire I'll tell you what I'll do for you. If you bring a big sack and walk to the ocean with me, I'll throw you in where the pretty horses are. But I can't carry you, sire. You're too heavy."

So the King left with Carambot, carrying a big sack over his arm. He said, "I want you to throw me out far, Carambot, because I want a big, handsome horse." Carambot said, "Don't worry, sire, I know where the beautiful horses are in there. I've been there myself." So, Carambot brought the King to a place where there was a big rock cliff and said, "From here, I can throw you way out where the beautiful horses are, I promise you." He put the

King into the sack and tied it up well, then he rolled him into the sea. "There!" he said. "Now go and get your horse!"

Carambot

C'est bon d'vous dzire eune fouès c'étaient ein vieux pis eune vieille. 'L ontvaient rien qu'eune p'tsite fille. I' l'app'laient Marie. La vieille à Carambot alle est morte. L'vieux Carambot a eu dzu temps dzur jusqu'à sa p'tsite fille a devienne grande pis a y fasse son manger. 'L avait dépensé tout ça 'l avait, l'pauv' vieux, à part qu'eune vache. C'était tout ça y restait. Fallait qu'Marie a va rendre ses devouères au seigneur; c'était l'rouè. Eune journée, alle a été ouère le seigneur. I'a dzit à Marie: "Dzis à ton père si i' quient pas sa vache dans son parc, m'as la tsuer." Marie alle est eurvenue cheux aut's, pis alle a dzit à son père le seigneur 'l avait dzit que si i' t'nait pas sa vache dans son parc, i' l'aurait tsuée. Carambot dzit: "Faut ben autant qu'i' la tsuse que comme a crève de faim." Le lend'main, Marie a eurtourné ouère le seigneur; i'a dzit: "Tsu vas dzire à ton père qu'i' vient l'ver la peau d'sa vache, j'l'ai tsuée."

Ça fait quand alle est eurvenue, alle a dzit à son père que l'seigneur avait tsué sa vache. Carambot 'l a été l'ver sa peau. I' dzit à Marie: "Tsu peux rester tout seule ein p'tsit moment; m'as aller vend' ma peau." Carambot 'l était après v'nir vieux; 'l a pris sa peau, 'l a mis dans ein sac, pis 'l est partsi. I' ouèyait pus ben clair, l'vieux Carambot. Il est arrivé drètte à ras d'trois hommes avant d'les ouère. C'étaient des voleurs, les hommes-là; i' sontaient après séparer leu-z-argent. I'ontvaient tout leu-z-argent rien qu'dans ein sac. Carambot 'l a eu peur, 'l a commencé à jongler. 'L a aveindzu sa peau d'dans l'sac ben douc'ment. I' l'a mis sus sa tête pis sus son dos. 'l a commencé à marcher sus ses g'noux pis sus ses mains. 'L avait resté les cornes après sa peau. I'en a ane qui était assis la figure en gagnant Carambot, ein des *robeurs*-là. I' dzit à son ami qu'i'avait l'dos en gagnant Carambot: "Comment-ce c'est l'dziab' est faite?"—"Ben, i' m'dzisent il a des grands cornes mais, moin, j'l'ai jamais vu."—"Ben," i' dzit, "il est drètte derrière ton dos. Eurvire-touè, pis t'as l'ouère."

Les trois voleurs i' s'ont sauvés, pis i'ont laissé leu sac d'argent. Carambot 'l a pris l'sac d'argent, pis 'l est v'nu l'porter cheux lui. "A c't'heure," i' dzit à Marie, "si t'as pas peur d'rester tout seule ein p'tsit m'ment, m'as aller enterrer ma peau." Carambot i'a pris sa pelle, 'l est partsi, pis i'a enterré sa peau. L'lend'main matin, i' dzit à Marie: "T'as aller sus l'seigneur empréter sa mesure. Si i' te d'mande si j'ai d'l'argent, dzi[s]-y tsu connais pas." Quand Marie alle a arrivé sus l'seigneur, alle a dzit: "Bonjour, monsieur l'seigneur."—"Quocé tsu charces à matin," i' dzit, "Marie?" A dzit: "Mon papa m'a enwèyée empréter vot' mesure."—"Ma mesure?" i' dzit. "Quocé i' veut avec eune mesure? Oùsque c'est qu'il a pris son argent?"—"Ah!" a dzit, "j'connais pas." I' dzit à sa servante: "Mets ein morceau d'pâte pas cuite dans l'fond d'la mesure."

L'vieux Carambot 'l a mesuré son argent pis i' l'a mis dans ein coin d'sa maisonne, pis quand 'l a eu fini d'mesurer son argent, 'l a pris ein morceau d'or d'vingt piasses, pis l'a collé dans l'morceau d'pâte au fond d'la mesure. "Tsu vas rend' la mesure au seigneur lui-même," i' dzit, "pis tsu vas y rend' le fond en l'air." Quand Marie alle a arrivé, "Bonjour, Monseigneur," a dzit. —"Bonjour," i' dzit, "Marie." A y'a rendzu sa mesure avec le fond en l'air. "Ah!" i' dzit, "oùsque ton père 'l a pris argent-là?" —"Ah!" a dzit, "j'connais pas." Ç'a été comme ça deux, trois jours. Ça chatouillait l'seigneur, ça. L'seigneur i' dzit: "Faut j'vas ouère Carambot oùsqu'il a pris n'argent-là."

Quand 'l a arrivé, Carambot était assis dans ein p'tsit coin après fumer. "Bonjour!" i' dzit, "Carambot." Carambot i' dzit: "Bonjour, l'seigneur." I'a commencé à charrer avec Carambot. Carambot i' parlait pas beaucoup, i' fésait comme si i' était à moquié fâché. "Quocé," i'dzit, "Carambot, t'es fâché parce que j'ai tsué ta vache?" —"Non," i' dzit "j'sus justement chagrin que j'en avais pas dzix de meme." I' dzit: "Comment ça s'fait, Carambot? T'as eu ein bon prix," i' dzit, "pour ta peau, Carambot?" I' dzit: "Comment t'as eu, Carambot?" Carambot i' dzit: "J'ai eu cent écus l'pouèle. Tsu ouès pas c'tas d'argent qu'j'ai eu pour ma peau?" i' dzit. "Ah!" l'vieux seigneur i' dzit, "m'as faire tsuer tous mes animaux, pis m'as vend' tous les peaux."

'L a faite tsuer tous ses animaux, pis 'l a faite l'ver tous les peaux. Il a dzit à ses hommes: "Vendez-en pas ane à moins d'cent écus l'pouèle." I'-z-ont été plusieurs jours i' eurvenaient pas, ses hommes au seigneur. "Ah!" i' dzit, "j'connais quoi 'l ont faite; 'l ont vendzu tous les peaux-là cent écus l'pouèle pis i' peuvent pas porter tout l'argent." Il a faite att'ler deux, trois *waguines* avec des grands *bèdes* à maï[s] dessus. Quand 'l a arrivé, i'avait pas ane peau d'vendzue. "Bande d'bêtas," i' dzit, "vous connaît pas vendre des peaux. Donnez-moin donc tabliyer-là." 'L a mis l'tabliyer blanc d'vant lui, pis 'l a commencé à marcher en montant pis en descendant la rue.

Les marchands d'peaux i' s'ont aperçus qu'i' y'avait ein homme neu[f] là; i'ont été ouère. 'L ont d'mandé quocé i' vendait ses peaux. "Grand marché! grand marché!" i' dzit, "cent écus l'pouèle." Les marchands d'peaux 'l ont dzit: "I'est pus bête qu'les aut's, on va s'en aller." 'L a resté justement queuques jours comme ça, ses peaux 'l ont commencé à puer dans la ville, i' fallait i' s'en va. L'seigneur a tout ch'té ses peaux dans l'bois, pis il est eurvenu fâché cont' Carambot. I' dzit: "M'as aller qu'ri Carambot, pis m'as l'faire pendre." Carambot i' connaissait l'seigneur i' s'rait v'nu l'trouver. L'lend'main matin, i' s'a l'vé d'bon matin, pis 'l a faite chauffer des pierres en arrière d'sa maisonne dans ein feu. 'L a empli sa marmite d'eau pis d'marrons et pis 'l a commencé à faire bouillir les marrons avec des pierres chaudes. Il a vu l'vieux seigneur qui s'en v'nait partsir d'cheux lui. I'a été qu'ri ein aut' grosse pierre ben chaude, pis i' l'a mis dans sa marmite. 'L a pris ein p'tsit fouéte, pis 'l a commencé à marcher à l'entour d'sa marmite; i' cognait, pis i' sifflait.

Quand l'seigneur 'l a arrivé: "Qua dans l'monde tsu fais," i' dzit, "Carambot, à matin?" —"J'sus après m'faire bouillir des marrons," i' dzit. —"Oui," i' dzit, "mais avec quocé tsu les fais bouillir? J'ouès pas d'feu." Carambot i' dzit: "J'ai pas besoin d'feu pour faire bouillir mes marrons, moin. J'les fais bouillir avec mon p'tsit fouéte. Si tsu crouès pas i' sont cuits, goûtes-en ein, seigneur." —"Vends-moin donc ton p'tsit fouéte," i' dzit, "Carambot." —"Ah! non," i' dzit, "j'veux pas t'vend' mon petit fouéte, j'ai pas d'bois sus ma terre," i' dzit, "le seigneur." —"M'as t'donner cent piasses pour ton p'tsit fouéte," i' dzit, "pis tout l'bois tsu voudras brûler, Carambot." Carambot y'a vendzu son p'tsit fouéte pour cent piasses.

L'seigneur i' s'a en allé. L'jeudzi d'ensuite, i'a faite ein gros dzîner mais i' voulait pas d'feu à l'entour. I' s'est faite mett' son manger dans des grandes marmites enne dehors. A à peu près dzix heures, i' leu-z-a donné son p'tsit fouéte, pis i' leu-z-a dzit i' vonnent cogner sus les marmites. I' pouvaient pas faire cuire eurrien, *of course,* avec leu p'tsit fouéte. I' sont v'nus pis i'ont dzit: "Monseigneur, on peut pas faire cuire avec ein fouéte, nous aut's." L'seigneur i' dzit: "Bande d'bêtas, vous connaît pas rien. M'as aller partsir la marmite à bouillir." L'vieux seigneur 'l a partsi, pis 'l a été commencer à cogner avec son p'tsit fouéte, pis siffler, pis i' pouvait pas cuire ça i' y'avait dans la marmite. "D'main matin," i' dzit, "j'm'en vas en bas pis j'tsue Carambot drètte dans sa maisonne."

Carambot i' connaissait l'seigneur i' s'rait v'nu l'lend'main matin. Il a pris eune blague de sang. I' dzit à Marie: "Quand l'seigneur i' va v'nir à matin, i' va voulouère m'pendre et pis commence pour charrer pis m'as t'dzire de t'aire deux, trois fouès. Après ça, m'as t'donner ein coup d'couteau

Carambot

pis ça va casser bosse de sang-là. Tombe," i' dzit, "pis fais comme si tsu s'rais morte," i' dzit. "Quand m'as sonner mon p'tsit violon à tes oreilles, tsu pourras grouiller." L'seigneur 'l a arrivé tout fâché. "Carambot," i' dzit, "j'te pends à matin." —"Eh ben! l'seigneur," i' dzit, "si tsu veux m'pendre, j'pense tsu vas m'pendre." Marie a commencé à brailler. "Papa!" a dzit, "i' va vous pendre aujourdz'hui." —"Tais-touè la gueule, touè," i' dzit, "pis va t'assir." —"Papa," a dzit, "comment m'as faire, moin, si l'seigneur i' vous pend?" Carambot i'a aveindzu son couteau, pis i' donne ein coup d'couteau à Marie. L'sang a volé. "Hum!" i' dzit, "à c't'heure, m'as t'pend', Carambot; t'as tsué ta p'tsit fille." —"Oh! oui," i' dzit, "alle est morte, mais m'as la remm'ner dans ein p'tsit n'ment." —"Ramène-la donc tout d'suite," i' dzit. —"Non," i' dzit, "laisse-la frédzir avant."

Taleure, l'vieux Carambot 'l a été qu'ri son p'tsit violon. 'L a commencé: Tigne, tigne, tigne, dans les oreilles à Marie. Alle a grouillé ein p'tsit brin. "Sonne-lé donc fort," i' dzit, "Carambot, a grouille." —"Prends ton temps, seigneur," i' dzit, "ça prend dzu temps pour remm'ner ane qui est mort." Ein p'tsit m'ment après, Carambot 'l a eurtourné pis i'a commencé encore: Tigne, tigne, tigne. Marie a s'a levée. "Vends-moin donc ton violon," i' dzit, "Carambot." Carambot i' dzit: "J'peux pas t'vend' mon violon, Monseigneur, c'est le seul violon j'ai." —"M'as t'donner cent piasses," i' dzit, "pour ton p'tsit violon." Carambot y'a vendzu son p'tsit violon pour cent piasses.

La s'maine d'après, sa fille au seigneur a s'mariait. Après sont eurvenus de s'marier, i' sont allés ouère l'seigneur. Prend son pistolet. *Bow, bow, bow,* i' les tsue tous les deusses! C'était eune grosse alerte. Tout l'monde i' criait, pis i' braillait. "Restez donc tranquilles," i' dzit, "m'as les remm'ner taleure, laissez-les frédzir avant." Taleure, 'l a été qu'ri son p'tsit violon pis 'l a commencé: Tigne, tigne, tigne, dans les oreilles d'sa fille pis son mari qu'étaient morts. J't'en fous, i' grouillaient pas, sontaient morts. L'seigneur i' dzit: "On va les enterrer, pis," i' dzit à deux d'ses hommes: "Vous autres va prendre Carambot, l'mettre dans ein baril, pis l'enterrer dans l'bois."

Les deux hommes 'l ont été qu'ri l'vieux Carambot pour l'enterrer. Carambot les a d'mandé qu'i' laissent ane d'ses mains sortsir d'la terre. Ça fait il[s] ont laissé la main à Carambot sortsir. 'L ont ben enterré Carambot, 'l ont ben enterré l'baril. I' sont eurvenus. L'seigneur leu-z-a d'mandé si i'avaient ben enterré Carambot. —"Oui," i' dzisent, "on l'a enterré oùsqu'i' eurviendra jamais. On l'a enterré dans l'pays des moutons." Pus tard dans la nuit, quand i'a commencé à faire nouère, i'a ein gros loup qu'est v'nu. I'a passé sa queue dans la main à vieux Carambot. L'vieux Carambot 'l a attrapé queue-là, lui. Tsu peux ben crouère que loup-là a 'halé quand Carambot a attrapé sa queue. Il a 'halé Carambot en dehors d'la terre. 'L a ôté son ceintsuron, le vieux Carambot; l'a mis dans l'cou dzu loup, pis l'a emm'né cheux lui. I' l'a mis dans eune p'tsite cabane.

Il est eurvenu à la maisonne, pis il a dzit à Marie: "Tsu vas aller dzire au seigneur joli mouton qu'j'ai ram'né de d'dans la terre?" Marie alle a partsi, alle été, pis alle a cogné à la porte. L'seigneur y'a d'mandé qui c'est qui était là. "C'est moin," a dzit, "Marie." —"Quocé qu'tsu veux?" i' dzit. —"Ben," a dzit, "mon papa m'a dzit qu'vous vienne ouère joli mouton qu'i'a remm'né de d'dans la terre." L'vieux seigneur 'l a partsi tout d'suite, pis 'l a arrivé sus Carambot. I'a d'mandé: "Oùsqu'il est ton mouton?" —"Ah!" i' dzit, "i'est là-bas dans ma p'tsite cabane. Tsu veux l'ouère?" —"Ah! oui," i' dzit, "c'est pour ça j'sus v'nu." L'seigneur 'l a eurgardé ça. "Vends-moin-lé donc," i' dzit, "ton mouton." —"M'as te l'vend'," i' dzit, "si tsu l'emmènes tout d'suite à souère." L'vieux seigneur i' dzit: "M'as t'donner cent piasses si tsu m'vends ton mouton, pis si tsu viens m'l'emm'ner." —"Oh! ben," Carambot i' dzit, "j'pense j'peux ben t'l'emm'ner."

Carambot 'l a mis eune guide dans l'cou du loup, pis i'a été l'emm'ner dans sa grange. "Oùsqu'tsu veux donc l'mett', Monseigneur?" —"Ah!" i' dzit, "j'veux l'mett' avec les aut's pour qu'i' s'accoutsume avec les aut's le souère." Carambot a pris le loup, pis i' l'a mis dans la grange avec les moutons. L'vieux Carambot i' s'a en allé s'coucher. L'lend'main matin, d'bon matin, l'seigneur il a rouvert sa porte de grange, pis 'l a eurgardé; tous ses moutons sontaient morts. I' nn'avait ein gros loup d'couché dans l'coin. I'a dzit à deux d'ses hommes: "Vous va prend' Carambot, l'mett' dans ein sac, portez-lé," i' dzit, "pis ch'tez-lé dans la mer."

Ça s'fait les deux hommes 'l ont pris ein grand sac, 'l ont attrapé l'vieux Carambot, i' l'ont mis d'dans, pis 'l ont partsi. 'L ont arrivé oùsqu'i'avait ein p'tsit village où i' nn'avait eune *groc'rie*. I'a ane qui dzit à l'aut': "Jette donc vieux chose-là à terre. On va aller bouère d'la bière, j'ai souèf, pis j'ai chaud," i' dzit. Padent sontaient après bouère dans la *groc'rie* eux aut's, l'vieux Carambot a attendzu des pattes d'ch'faux qui s'en v'naient. 'L a commencé à dzire: "J'veux pas marier la fille dzu rouè, moin." C'est ein p'tsit jeune berger qu'était sus le j'val. En passant oùsqu'i'est Carambot, il a attendzu quacé c'était i' dzisait. "Quocé tsu dzis, touè, dans sac-là?" i' dzit. Le vieux Carambot i' dzit: "J'veux pas marier la fille dzu rouè. J'sus trop vieux, pis i' m'portent dans ein sac pour m'emm'ner la marier." Le p'tsit jeune homme i' dzit: "Moin, m'as la marier." —"C'est eune jolie p'tsite princesse," l'vieux Carambot i' dzit. "A c't'heure," i' dzit, "démarre sac-là, pis rent' icitte d'dans."

L'p'tsit jeune homme a demarré l'sac pis Carambot a sortsi. Le jeune homme dzit à Carambot: "Vous ouè beau j'val-là, c'est à moin, peurnez-lé, j'vous l'donne." Il a rentré dans l'sac, pis l'vieux Carambot l'a ben amarré, pis i'a dzit: "Reste ben tranquille, i' vont v'nir le qu'ri taleure." —"Carambot 'l a monté sus le j'val pis i' s'a en allé. 'L a mis son j'val dans l'écurie, i' l'a ben souègné. Taleure, les deux hommes dzu seigneur 'l ont eurpensé à Carambot. I' nn'a ane qui dzit: "J'pense faut mieux aller nèyer vieux-là tout d'suite." Eune l'a ramassé, pis i'a partsi avec. 'L était plus pésant qu'jamais. L'p'tsit jeune homme-là i' dzit: "Moin, m'as marier la fille dzu rouè." I'en a ane des autres-là qui l'portaient qui y'a dzit: "Oui, reste tranquille, tsu pourras la marier." Quand i'ont arrivé à la mer, i' l'ont ch'té d'dans.

Taleure, l'vieux Carambot 'l a eurgardé, 'l a vu les deux hommes qui s'en eurvanaient. I' dzit à Marie: "T'as aller ouère l'seigneur, pis tsu vas y dzire qu'i' vienne vouère c'beau j'val qu'j'ai remm'né de d'dans la mer." Marie alle a partsi, pis alle a été sus l'seigneur. Alle a rentré, pis alle a commencé à charrer avec l'vieux seigneur. "Ben," i' dzit, "Marie, quocé t'as faire à c't'heure que t'as pus d'papa?" A dzit: "Mon papa est eurvenu." —"Ton papa est eurvenu?" i' dzit. "J'ai enwèyé deux hommes le ch'ter dans la mer," i' dzit, "à matin." Marie a dzit au seigneur: "I' m'a dzit d'vous dzire qu'vous vienne ouère c'te beau ch'fal il a remm'né d'dans la mer." Le seigneur 'l a ramassé son chapeau, pis 'l a partsi tout d'suite. 'L a arrivé sus Carambot. I' dzit: "Laisse-moin donc ouère c'te beau ch'fal t'as remm'né de d'dans la mer."

I'a montré le ch'fal il avait remm'né de d'dans la mer. "Ah! j't'en assure, c'en est ein joli." —"Oui," Carambot i' dzit, "c'en est ein joli, mais i'en a des plus jolis qu'ça dans la mer." L'seigneur i' dzit: "Comment ça s'fait que t'en as pas remm'né ein plus joli, Carambot?" —"Eh ben!" i' dzit, "Monseigneur, vous m'a pas ch'té assez loin; les aut's plus jolis i' sontaient plus loin." I' dzit: "M'as rentrer dans ein sac, Carambot, tsu vas m'porter, pis tsu vas m'enwèyer dans la mer. Enwèye-moin loin par rapporte que j'veux ein joli ch'val pis ein gros." Carambot i' dzit: "M'as vous dzire comment m'as faire avec vous, Monseigneur. Si vous s'porte ein bon gros sac pis vous marche jusqu'à la mer, m'as vous mettre dans l'sac, pis m'as vous enwèyer oùsqu'i' n'a des jolis chouaux. Pour moin," i' dzit, "j'peux pas vous porter, Monseigneur, vous êtes trop pésant."

L'seigneur 'l a partsi avec l'vieux Carambot avec ein grand sac sur son bras. I' dzit: "Tsu vas m'enwèyer loin, Carambot, par rapporte qu'j'en veux ein beau pis ein gros." Carambot i' dzit: "Sois pas inquiète, l'seigneur, j'connais où i' sont les beaux ch'faux là d'dans, j'ai été ouère." Carambot a été l'emm'ner oùsqu'i' n'avait ein grand rocher, eune grande écore d'rocher. I' dzit: "Icitte, j'pourras vous enwèyer oùsqu'i' n'a des beaux, j'vous en assure." 'L a mis l'vieux seigneur dans l'sac, pis i' l'a amarré, pis i' l'a roulé dans l'eau. "Quiens," i' dzit, "va t'qu'ri ein j'val, touè, à c't'heure."

21.

Valiant John

It's good to tell you that once upon a time there were an old man and an old woman. They had only one son, whose name was Valiant John. Valiant John's father was dead, and he lived alone with his mother. They were poor. Valiant John had to work hard to earn his living, and he worked cutting firewood. One day, when he was eating his lunch in the woods, he was bothered by flies that came and landed on him. He gave a swat and killed two of them at once. Valiant John was a big strong man, with a good education. He wrote on a piece of paper and put on his hat that he had killed two with one blow. That evening, he went by the King's house, and the King was walking back and forth in front of it. "Is that true, Valiant John," he asked, "what you have written there on your hat?" —"If it weren't true, I wouldn't have put it there," answered Valiant John.

The King began to be afraid of him. The next morning, Valiant John went back into the woods to cut his wood. He waited for several flies to come and land on his leg, and then he gave a swat and killed three. He wrote on a paper to put on his hat that he had killed three with one blow. That evening, he passed by the King's house again. The King asked him, "Is that true, what you have written on your hat?" —"Well, if it weren't true, I wouldn't have put it there." The King said to him, "Come and work for me tomorrow morning, Valiant John." So the next morning, Valiant John went to work for the King. The King said to him, "Valiant John, you are a fearsome man, and terribly strong." Valiant John answered, "Yes, sire, there isn't anything I can't do." —"Well," said the King, "we have a beast here in our forest that I would like you to get rid of for us. All my soldiers are afraid of it." Valiant John said to the King, "I'll go get rid of it. But if it's some little hummingbird, I'll be back here quickly, and you'll have something to holler about." So the king answered, "It's a big animal, Valiant John. It's a lion. It lives somewhere near the old church down in the field."

Valiant John went out, and when he arrived near the old church, he saw the beast lying in the field. It was sunning itself, getting warm. "If I can only get to the old church," thought Valiant John. He sneaked up to the church and climbed up its walls. When the lion saw him up on the bell tower, it went for him, jumping up on the church wall as high as it could. There was a hole in the wall where some bricks had been taken out, and when the beast jumped, it caught its head in that hole. It got stuck in the hole and broke its neck. Valiant John began throwing pieces of shingle down on its back to see if it was dead yet. "I surely hope that it is dead," he said to himself. He climbed down slowly until he got to where the lion was stuck, and it was dead. So then, he climbed back down to the ground and went back to the King.

When he got to the King's house, he was angry, and when the King saw him coming, he got scared. He said to his officers, "He's coming back." One of the officers said, "You don't need to be afraid, he never found it." So the King said to Valiant John, "Well, did you find the beast?" —"Didn't I tell you before I left you," said Valiant John, "that you'd better not be sending me to kill little hummingbirds over by the old church? I caught it by the tail and threw it like this, and its head got caught in a hole on the wall of the old church. If you don't believe me, go and see for yourself. The beast is still there." The old King answered, "For us, that's a big beast, Valiant John." —"Don't talk about it any more," said Valiant John. "If you weren't a king, I'd wring your neck."

The old King was so afraid of Valiant John that he didn't know what to do. So for a long time, Valiant John didn't have any work to do. But after awhile, the old King got word of another beast that was living in his forest, and he said to Valiant John, "There's another big beast in our forest, Valiant John." —"Another little hummingbird!" answered Valiant John. The King said, "No. It's along the river, in a little valley that used to be a field. It's a really terrible beast." —"I'll go," said Valiant John, "but if you're making me go all that way to deal with a hummingbird, I'll come back and break your neck." When Valiant John got to the river, he looked around and saw a big dead tree. "I'd better get up in that tree before the beast sees me," he thought to himself. So, he sneaked over to the tree and began to climb up into it. He had brought some meat with him, and the beast could smell that and started out to find him. When it arrived, it began trying to jump up to him in the tree. There was a fork in the tree, and the beast got its head caught in the fork and broke its neck. After awhile, Valiant John began throwing little pieces of bark down on it to see if it was dead. When he saw that it had stopped moving, he got down.

When he went back to the King, he was angry. "Didn't I tell you not to send me out after hummingbirds? Go see where I put it in that old dead tree near the river." —"Don't get angry, Valiant John," said the King. "For us these are big beasts."

After a little while longer, a war was declared against the King. He asked Valiant John if he would fight. —"I'll go," said Valiant John, "but if I find a bunch of little boys playing, I'm going to come back and break your neck. Give me the best horse that you have." He had his feet tied under the horse's belly and said, "Now, I'm going to go see my mother."

But the horse was such a good war horse that it only wanted to go toward the battlefield and wouldn't go toward the house of Valiant John's mother. He rode through an old cemetery, where there was a big cross. He thought he could grab hold of the cross and get off his horse that way, figuring that the rope holding his feet would break. But the cross was old and wobbly, and it broke off at the foot. As he rode along with the cross in his arms, he put it over his shoulder, and this was the way he arrived on the battlefield, where the enemy army was waiting. The enemy king thought that God himself was riding toward him and ordered his army to get on their knees. Then, he came toward Valiant John and said, "Lord, why did you come here?" —"Why did I come?" asked Valiant John. "I came to tell you to write a promise in your own hand that you will never bother this other king any more and kill all these innocent people for no good reason at all." The enemy king wrote the note right away and gave it to Valiant John.

Valiant John then turned back and went to see his king. He threw the cross away when he got into the woods. When he got to the King's house, he gave him the note, and the King said, "What? Didn't they even fight?" —"Well, read the paper, there," said Valiant John. So the King read it and told his army, "You don't need to go into battle. He's killed them all. We might as well all go back home." Valiant John said to the King, "When we get back home, I'm going to fix you this time. Didn't I tell you not to send me to play with little boys?" The old King begged Valiant John not to do any harm, and he would give him lots of money every month just like a pension, and he wouldn't even have to do any work. There was also a little village on the other side of his kingdom. "I'll give you the village too, Valiant John, if you'll promise not to do me any harm." So Valiant John took his mother and his sister and went to live in his own village. He got married there and lived happily for the rest of his days.

Jean Vaillant

C'est bon d'vous dzire eune fouès c'étaient ein vieux pis eune vieille. 'L ontvaient rien qu'ein garçon. Ils l'app'laient Jean Vaillant. Son père 'l est mort à Jean Vaillant. 'L a resté tout seul avec sa mère. Sontaient pauv's. I' fallait qu'i' travaille fort pour eune vie. Il bûchait dzu bois d'corde. Eune journée, 'l était après manger son dzîner, Jean Vaillant, dans l'bois. Les mouches sont v'nues s'mettre à ras d'lui. I'a donné eune tape pis i'en a tsué deux. Jean Vaillant était ein gros homme fort pis 'l avait eune grosse indzucation. Il a écrit sus ein papier, pis il a mis sus son chapeau qu'i' ya tsué deux hommes d'eune tape. 'L a passé devant d'ssus l'rouè l'souère. L'rouè était après marchailler d'vant son château. "C'est vrai," i' dzit, "Jean Vaillant, ça tsu as sus ton chapeau?" —"Si ç'avait pas été vrai, j'l'aurais pas mis là."

L'vieux rouè 'l a commencé à en aouère peur. L'lend'main, Jean Vaillant 'l a eurtourné bûcher son bois. I'a attendzu qu'i'ait plusieurs mouches qui viennent s'poser sus sa jambe. 'L a donné eune tape pis en a tsué trois. Après qu'i' a eu tsué les trois mouches, 'l a mis ça sus son chapeau qu'l'avait tsué trois hommes d'eune tape. 'L a passé devant d'ssus l'vieux rouè l'souère. L'rouè y'a d'mandé:

"C'est vrai, ça tsu a mis sus ton chapeau?" —"Si ça 'l avait pas été vrai, j'l'aurais pas mis là." —"Viens donc travailler pour moin d'main," i' dzit, "Jean Vaillant." L'lend'main matin, Jean Vaillant 'l a été ouère l'rouè. "Ah!" i' dzit, "Jean Vaillant, t'es ein terrible homme, t'es ein homme fort." —"Oui," i' dzit au rouè, "i' nn'a rien à mon épreuve." —"Ben," i' dzit, "on l'a eune bétaille icitte dans la forêt. J'aim'rais qu'tsu vas la détruitre pour nous aut's. Tous mes hommes i' nn'ont peur," i' dzit. Jean Vaillant a dzit au rouè: "J'vas y i'aller. Mais," i' dzit, "si c'est queuque zouéseau à mouches qu'i'est là, j'vas eurvenir, pis t'es à plaind'!" L'vieux rouè i' dzit: "C'est eune grosse bétaille, c'est ein lion, Jean Vaillant." I' dzit: "A reste entour d'la vieille église dans l'vieux parc, loin, là."

Jean Vaillant 'l a partsi. Quand i'a arrivé à ras d'la vieille église, il a vu la bétaille couchée dans l'parc. I'était après s'chauffer au soleil, lion-là. "Doux Jésus! si j'peux seul'ment m'rendre à la vieille église!" 'L a arrivé à la vieille église, pis 'l a monté d'ssus. Quand la bétaille a l'a vu sus l'clocher d'l'église, alle a partsi pour lui, a sauté après l'église aussi haut qu'a pouvait. I' nn'avait ein trou oùsqui'i y'avait des briques d'ôtées. La bétaille 'l a sauté, pis alle a enfoncé sa tête dans trou-là. Alle a resté pris là, alle a cassé son cou. Jean Vaillant 'l a commencé à j'ter des morceaux d'bardeau sus son dos pour ouère si alle était morte. "Doux Jésus!" i' dzit, "j'espère qu'alle est morte." 'L a descendzu tout douc'ment jusqu'à 'l a arrivé d'ssus la bétaille. 'L a vu la bétaille 'l était morte. 'L a partsi pour s'en eurv'nir sus l'rouè.

Quand 'l a arrivé d'ssus l'rouè, 'l était bourru. Quand l'rouè 'l a vu Jean Vaillant v'nir, 'l avait peur. 'L a dzit à ses officiers: "I' s'en eurvient." Ane d'ses officiers y'a dzit: "Vous avez pas besoin d'avouère peur, i' l'a pas trouvée." L'rouè i' dzit: "Ben, Jean Vaillant, t'as vu la bétaille?" —"J't'avais pas dzit," i' dzit, "touè, avant d'partsir d'icitte qu'tsu m'enwèyes pas tsuer des zouéseaux à mouches à ras d'la vieille église? L'ai attrapée par la queue, l'ai envouèyée en l'air comme ça, sa tête a resté pris dans ein trou dans la vieille église. Si vous veut pas m'crouère, allez ouère, la bétaille alle est là." L'vieux rouè i' dzit: "C'est eune grosse bétaille, ça, pour nous aut's, Jean Vaillant." —"Parle-mouè pus," i' dzit, "si t'étais pas ein rouè, j'te cass'rais l'cou."

L'vieux rouè i'en avait assez peur, i' connaissait pas quoi faire. 'L a été longtemps Jean Vaillant 'l avait rien à faire. Après ça, l'vieux rouè 'l a entendzu parler d'eune aut' bétaille, qui yétait dans sa forêt. I'a dzit à Jean Vaillant: "'L a eune aut' grosse bétaille dans la forêt, Jean Vaillant." —"Ein aut' zouéseau à mouches," i' dzit, "j'pense vous 'l a." —"Non," i' dzit, "c'est l'long d'eune rivière, dans ein p'tsit bas-fond qu'i'avait coutsume d'êt' ein parc; c'est eune terrible bétaille." —"J'vas y aller, mais si vous m'fait marcher pour ein zouéseau à mouches, j'vas eurv'nir, pis j'vas vous casser l'cou." Quand 'l a arrivé au ras d'la rivière, 'l a eurgardé, 'l a vu ein grand n'arbre sec. "Doux Jésus! si j'peux arriver à n'arbre-là avant qu'a m'vouèye!" 'L a arrivé à l'arb', 'l a commencé à l'monter, à grimpiller. I'avait apporté d'la viande avec lui. La bétaille alle a sentsi ça, pis alle a partsi pour lui. Quand alle a arrivé, alle a commencé à sauter après n'arb'-là. L'arb' 'l avait eune fourche. La bétaille 'l a sauté pis alle a pris son cou dans la fourche, pis a s'a cassé l'cou. Jean Vaillant il a commencé à j'ter des écorces dessus pour ouère si alle était morte. "Doux Jésus!" i' dzit, "j'espère qu'alle est morte." Quand i'a vu qu'a grouillait pus, i'est partsi.

I' s'a rentourné sus l'rouè fâché. "J't'ai pas dzit qu'tsu me renwèyes pus tsuer des zouéseaux à mouches, touè? Va ouère oùsque j'l'ai mis dans n'arb' sec-là près d'la rivière." —"Faut pas qu'tsu t'fâches, Jean Vaillant," i' dzit, "c'est des grosses bétailles pour nous aut's, ça." 'L a pas été ben

The beast caught in the fork of the tree.

longtemps i' s'a déclaré eune guerre cont' l'vieux rouè. L'rouè 'l a d'mandé à Jean Vaillant s'il aurait pas été s'batt' pour lui. "M'as aller mais si j'trouve eune bande d'p'tsits garçons après jouer, j'vas eurvenir pis j'vas casser ton cou." 'L a dzit au rouè: "Donnez-mouè l'mmeilleur ch'val de guerre vous 'l a." Il a faite amarrer ses jambes en d'ssur dzu vent' dzu ch'fal avec eune guide. "A c't'heure," i' dzit, "j'vas aller ouère ma mère."

Le ch'fal, c'était ein si bon ch'fal d'guerre i' s'a en allé jusse pour l'champ d'bataille au lieurs d's'en aller oùsque sa mère a restait. 'L a passé dans ein vieux cimiquière oùsque c'est 'l avait eune grande vieille crouè. I' crouèyait s'attraper après ça, pis s'échapper d'son ch'val; i' crouèyait qu'la guide alle aurait cassé. La crouè alle était pourrite, pis alle a cassé au pied. L'a pris, pis l'a mis sus son épaule. 'L a été là-bas en d'vant d'l'armée dzu rouè, pis 'l a arrivé oùsqu'était l'rouè qui faisait la guerre à son rouè là; l'vieux rouè l'a pris pour l'bon Guieu, 'l a commandé à son armée de s'jeter à g'noux. L'vieux rouè 'l a marché à lui: "Mon Seigneur, quoicé c'est vous étsiez v'nu pour?" — "Pourquoi j'sus v'nu?" i' dzit. "J'sus v'nu," i' dzit, "pour qu'tsu m'écrises ein billet d'ta main qu'tsu troubl'ras jamais rouè-là davantage, s'faire tsuer tout ce monde innocent," i' dzit, "pour eurrien!" L'vieux rouè y'a écrit son billet, pis i'a donné.

'L a eurviré, lui, Jean Vaillant, pis i'a été rencontrer son rouè. 'L a j'té sa crouè là-bas quand 'l a arrivé dans l'bois. Quand 'l a rencontré son rouè, i'a donné son billet. L'rouè i' dzit: "Quoi, i' s'ont pas battus?" —"Ah! lis papier-là," i' dzit. L'rouè a dzit à son armée: "C'est pas nécessaire d'aller, i' les a tou[s] tsués. On a autant d'chance d'eurtourner à la maisone." Jean Vaillant i'a dzit au rouè. "Quand m'as arriver cheux touè, j'vas arranger, touè. J'avais dzit d'pas n'enwèyer jouer avec des p'tsits garçons." L'vieux rouè a *bégué* Jean Vaillant d'pas y faire dzu mal, si i' voulait pas y faire dzu mal, i'aurait donné des bonnes grosses gages tous les mois, comme eune pension, i' s'rait pas à la peine d'travailler. Pis i' nn'avait ein p'tsit village loin d'là, d'l'aut' bord d'son rouèyaume. "Pis m'as t'donner p'tsit village-là aussite, si tsu promets d'pas m'faire d'mal." Ça s'fait qu'Jean Vaillant 'l a pris sa mère pis sa soeur, pis i' s'a en allé dans son p'tsit village; i' s'a marié dans son p'tsit village, pis i'est resté là l'restant d'ses jours.

Part II: Historical Background

I.

An Overview of a Fairy Tale

Man has passed fairy tales from generation to generation and from place to place as a means of entertainment throughout the history of civilization. According to folklorist Linda Dégh, in her article "Folk Narrative" (1972), there are two classifications of oral traditional tales. The first of these is the "complex tale." Included in this category are the märchen, religious, and romantic tales. Märchen (pronounced mair-chen) is a narrative that we generally refer to as the fairy tale or magic tale. The märchen appears to have become established in the Middle Ages and has come down to modern times with its knights, swords, petty kings, and serfs intact. Such a tale, although it contains the social trappings of Christian times, still preserves the religious beliefs of earlier, animist religions. Here, souls can inhabit forms other than the human body. There are witches or sorceresses who have control over spiritual reality and who can use their powers for good or for evil. Good or bad fortune comes from supernatural forces. The number three has a mystical power, as shown by the three trials the hero must usually endure, the three brothers who frequently compete for the beautiful maiden, and sometimes the three different parts of the story. In this collection, "John the Bear" is an excellent example where there are threes within threes within threes. Religious tales, on the other hand, deal with Christian virtue, as shown in "The Rose of Peppermette," while romantic tales talk about real historic people and places, relating adventures based on fate rather than on magic. All three of these tale types are similar because they share the same medieval settings and plots. The tale of Samson, for example, is linked together in the same story as the magic tale of the Seven-Headed Beast.

Dégh's second classification of oral traditional tales is the "simple tale." Contained in this heading are the various kinds of stories that are sequences of episodes involving similar human or animal characters. They deal with the struggle between shrewdness and stupidity rather than with the opposition of good and evil forces. They are characterized by more earthy humor than the complex tale types, at least in this collection of the Old Mines stories. Sometimes they involve an accumulation of helpers as in "Little John and His Animals" and "Half-Rooster." Other times they deal with the inevitable victory of intelligence over idiocy in an escalating series of implausible confrontations. In these stories, as in "Carambot," "Valiant John," "The Little Bull with the Golden Horns," and "Master Thief," it is invariably the character with power—the king or the devil—who is stupid and the ordinary person who is smart.

Alongside the different types of complex and simple tales are the common character types, words, and episodes in the stories. These include the young simpleton who triumphs through magic, fate, virtue, or shrewdness; the evil or stupid individuals against whom the hero struggles; the several trials the hero must endure; and the happy ending. They share a standard formula for the beginning and for the ending. There are almost always an old man and an old woman who have a certain number of children, the youngest of whom is the hero. Of course, in "Half-Rooster," the hero is half a bird, but the idea is the same. The hero has to leave home to grow up by winning his own trials, and his reward is generally a beautiful maiden in the end.

In addition to shared episodes and structure, most of the stories also have in common a similar dialogue. The dialogue can be used several times during the story with minor changes. When characters experience a series of similar situations, they say nearly the same thing each time. Indeed, one of the best ways to tell if someone is really telling a story or only talking about it is to see whether or not the dialogue is being repeated in full each time the story is told. All of these basic story elements serve both to alert the listeners to the fact that they should transfer their thinking from the real world to the story world and to make it easier for storytellers to remember tales, some of which may take as long as a week to tell in their entirety.

The notion of fairy tales that most of us are familiar with from our own childhood are the edited, written tales, not the oral ones. Both Charles Perrault with his edition *Contes de ma Mère l'Oye* (1697) and the Brothers Grimm with their collection of German tales in the nineteenth century edited the tales they had collected. Why? There are several important reasons. First, we expect greater perfection from written materials, and oral tales often have gaps and and repetitions. Secondly, anyone relating a story wants to make it their own. This is true for every storyteller, and it is also true for those who work with stories as editors and translators. In addition, a story told orally is fleeting: once told it is gone. But the written word is permanent, inviting reflection and revision. Therefore, the polishing process used for oral performance is different than the one used for written text. As a result, the stories differ greatly.

Another factor in the differences between oral and written stories is the context. Oral tales are perceived as part of a living situation: a certain person in a specific place and time, talking to listeners, and using a given set of words, gestures, pauses, and intonations. Written tales, however, are essentially words that remain permanent, unchanging. Therefore, most of us are not aware of stories as events, and we do not fully realize the role that the person who is writing or telling the story plays in our experience of it. The story for us just exists out there. By examining oral tales, we can begin to recognize that the tales we read as children were just samples of fairy tales. We can begin to understand the role of the original collector and editor, of the translators, of later editors as intermediaries across time and distance between us and the oral tales that were originally transcribed.

There are various factors that shape an oral tale each time it is told. Who is the storyteller? Why is he or she performing? Who is the audience? Why are they there? How much time is available? Where is the performance taking place? What is the narrator's style, vocabulary, repertoire? What is the cultural context? The answers to these questions can be found in the later chapters; however, in this general discussion of the nature of a fairy tale, it is important to examine some of the more general cultural influences on tales and a few of the ways in which the storyteller also shapes them.

One major feature of story context is literacy. A tale written by an editor for a literate audience will use a greater number of different words, will have longer sentences, will avoid any off-color language or humor, and will often have a moral purpose. Richard Dorson, in his foreword to *Folktales of Germany* (1966, by Kurt Ranke), states that as Grimm worked on the stories more and more, he continually edited and refined them:

> Consequently he abandoned the Volksmärchen or true folktale collected exactly from the lips of the storyteller for the Buchmärchen or literary version shaped by the editor. To perfect stories, he did not scruple to add dialogue, nicknames, homely phrases, whole episodes. This practice robbed the Märchen of their true narrators . . . and substituted the style, the values, and the perspective of the intellectuals for those of the folk.

Other important cultural influences on tales are nationality and region. In different countries and regions, different styles and types prevail. In some places, magic tales are the norm, while in others one might find a predominance of ghost stories or humorous anecdotes. In addition, the same basic tale in one place might abound in physical or psychological details, and in another region the same tale might be told briefly with few particulars. In one place, the storytelling style may be animated, with loud speech and dramatic gestures, while in another it will be a subdued activity, bordering on introspection. English märchen tend to be ethereal, set in an essentially supernatural world of fairies and elves. German tales often seem to present the real world in ominous, threatening tones where magic monsters wait for poor, simple mortals. In French tales, like those in this book, the setting is ordinary and recognizable. Paul Delarue, in his introduction to the *Borzoi Book of French Folktales* (1956), states:

> The French tale unfolds in a . . . varied and familiar world, one that corresponds to the greater diversity of a land in which maritime and continental zones, mountain and plain, forest, cultivated fields, prairies and vineyards are blended into a harmonious whole. The supernatural element is simplified, curtailed, disciplined—it becomes almost reasonable. . . . Fantastic beings, so varied elsewhere, are nearly always either fairies or ogres. The French have a tendency to substitute for an action based on magic forces a dramatic development founded on human emotions, and to eliminate whatever is cruel, bloody, or a survival of barbaric periods.

The stories in this book fit Delarue's description of French magic tales, even though they were told primarily in North America.

A further external influence that marks oral tales is industrialization or the lack of it. Märchen or magic tales are forgotten when rural, self-sufficient communities become integrated into modern cash economies. Tales then shift to more modern forms, such as jokes. In addition to needing cultural continuity, traditional märchen also depend on the preservation of their original language or dialect for their continuance. Most rural dialects and minority languages die out when people are assimilated by more powerful, industrialized communities. When the stories can no longer be told in their original form, some individuals attempt to translate them. Over and over, as I talked about these stories with people from the Old Mines community, they would say, "the stories aren't the same in English. They're better in French." The probable reasons for this are that the translated version is less polished than the traditional one, and none of the familiar and endearing words and phrases remains to reinforce the tales' role as a symbol of cultural unity and continuity. Finally, a major function of traditional oral tales is entertainment. When more glamorous forms of entertainment become available, people choose the greater stimulation these can provide, and the stories lose the social environment they need in order to flourish. A further effect of industrialization is that it interrupts occupational continuity. Traditional songs and tales are generally woven into the work patterns of a community and its patterns of leisure activities. When the work environment is changed or removed, a vital part of the cultural context for traditional tales is destroyed. For example, in Old Mines, many of the individuals who would entertain their families and neighbors with the stories in this book, and others like them, had learned these same stories during the time when mining was the community's major activity. The rest and meal breaks "on the diggings" provided the opportunity for apprentice storytellers to learn the craft, and for master performers to share their talents and to obtain the praise and approval that served as an important motivation.

People who know folktales in a community can be true performers and artists, who take their craft seriously. They can function effectively only in a traditional community that has maintained a cultural, linguistic, and occupational continuity with its past. Others are private storytellers, both in intact communities and in those that have retained memories of the past even though the cultural environment has been diverted from its original channels. As a pastime, these people tell stories to their families and close friends. Most of the time, they are parents or grandparents telling stories to their children and grandchildren. Finally, in a culture where public storytelling no longer exists, it is possible to find individuals who remember the stories from the past and who can tell them more as a part of history than as a true performance. Frequently, these same people were private storytellers in the past. There is a great difference in the same story told by different individuals, depending on their literary and dramatic skill and on their perception of what they are doing when they share a story. The results range from true art to complete depersonalization. A storyteller who has no ongoing opportunity to sharpen skills in a public forum has lost the opportunity to participate in the highest level of importance and sophistication. In discussing active storytellers, Donald MacDonald in his article, "Fieldwork: Collecting Oral Literature" (1972), states that "... in most societies the outstanding tradition-bearer is a literary artist, and even in the most tradition-rich areas, an outstanding few in every generation have been responsible for the greatest share in the process of creating, molding, and passing on the best in oral literature."

How storytellers adapt the tales to the present time is the final aspect of the more complex oral tales. According to the explanation offered by Dégh, "The tale, whether composed of one or many episodes, is always a well-proportioned whole. It is fashioned from stable formulas commonly known to the tellers who adjust them to a basic outline knit together by a frame. . . . Putting the outline into words and embellishing it by the combination of the available formulas is the creative act of individual narrators." Skilled storytellers find way to expand or to compress their tales as the situation demands. When time is limited, the narrator tends to omit details while preserving the story's outline. The repetitive elements in this case might merely be mentioned, rather than performed. When there is need for a longer tale, details flourish and are savored. The second technique of adjusting a story to the demands of time is that of linking several story elements together. Many of the tales in this book contain logical transitional points, where the story could begin or end. For example, "The Seven-Headed Beast" actually contains three different parts, that of Little John and Samson, that of Little John and the Beast, and that of Little John and his dogs. All of these parts can be told separately, or can be combined, as they are in this instance. To make a story last a long time, the narrator would both increase details and dialogue and combine more story elements.

These, then, are some of the features of fairy tales that can help us to better understand and appreciate the tales in this collection. A tale, like a person, changes constantly while it remains organically the same. It is only when it is no longer told that it can be fixed accurately in written form. Indeed, at that point, it can only be preserved at all by being put onto paper. But we are eloquently reminded of the importance of the original storytellers by J. H. Delargy, who had collected many tales in Ireland from storyteller Séan O'Conneil. MacDonald (1972) shares Delargy's comments with us: "When at last my work was done and the last tale was written down, my old friend turned to me and said, 'I suppose you will bring out a book of these stories some day. I have told you all the tales I can remember, and I am glad that they have been written. I hope that they will shorten the night for those who read them or hear them read, and let them not forget me in their prayers, or the old people from whom I myself learned them.' "

As we read these tales, it is important for us to remember that they are a gift to us from the people who once told these stories. To understand the stories, we should indeed remember and understand those to whom they belonged.

II.

The Old Mines Community and Its People

Since context is such an important part of an oral tale, it is important to know the history of the community where these stories lived for so long and of the people who told them. People are often surprised to learn that French is spoken in some areas of Missouri. For this reason, it also seems important to explain in some detail how the French came to be here. The story of the French in Missouri begins with the early history of European immigration and settlement in North America. It is a story that is ignored by most, for the simple reason that our general history books tell the story from an Anglo-American perspective. We learn about the Pilgrims at Plymouth Rock, but not about the French and Spanish groups who colonized other areas of the continent at roughly the same time. At the local level, most histories of the state of Missouri devote a few pages at the beginning to the "French Period," which is treated as a kind of prehistory, with historical events starting in 1803, the year when the Lousiana Purchase gave the United States ownership of this vast territory. Looking at the people who kept the stories in this book alive, and learning something about their history, helps us to understand many details of the stories at the same time that it gives us a new and different perspective of the history of Missouri.

The community where the stories in this book were traditionally told lies on the northern edge of the Missouri Ozarks, in northern Washington County. Rather than being a single town, it is composed of numerous small villages and hamlets. The boundaries of this community are marked by the place-names of Old Mines, Richwoods, Racola, Shibboleth, Cannon Mines, Kingston, Cruise, Tiff, Barytes, Fertile, Bellefontaine, Cadet, and Mineral Point. Most of the people living there today are descendants of the first Europeans who had settled in Missouri, long before it became a state or even a territory.

Missouri was part of "Louisiana," the vast, largely unexplored French territory in the midsection of the North American continent. The French had founded Quebec in 1608, twelve years before the Pilgrims landed at Plymouth. They were from the beginning curious about the vast continent that stretched to the South and West. Explorers and adventurers left Quebec and traveled along the rivers in canoes, meeting with the native Americans along the way, trading with them, learning their languages, and listening to Indian tales about more distant territories. They eventually found their way to the Mississippi River, which they hoped was a water highway to the Pacific Ocean. In 1673, Jacques Marquette made his historic descent of the Mississippi River, past Missouri and Illinois, to the mouth of the Arkansas. He was the first European to have traveled this river and to have recorded his voyage. He knew by the time he returned that the river led not to the Pacific Ocean but South to the Gulf of Mexico. He was also able to give detailed information to other Frenchmen about the tribes, the kinds of trade that would be possible, and the lay of the land. A steady stream of trappers and hunters followed Marquette's route down the Mississippi River, establishing trade relations with the Indians and often living with them for extended periods of time. Having established good relations with certain tribes, they settled permanently in places they thought congenial. One of the richest and most pleasant areas along the whole length of the river was that bottomland opposite the place where the Missouri River flows into the Mississippi. The first two French communities in the mid-Mississippi Valley were founded there: Cahokia in 1699, and Kaskaskia, immediately afterward, in 1700.

Notations began to appear between 1700 and 1710 in correspondence and journals about the rich lead deposits on the Missouri side of the river. Father Gravier, in the *Jesuit Relations* (cited in Carl Sauer, 1920, p. 74), wrote that the ore from a lead mine on the Meramec River "yields three-fourths metal." How he obtained this information is not mentioned, but his comment seems to indicate that some mining may already have been carried out in this area. Sauer also tells us that d'Iberville asked for the exclusive privilege of working the mines on the Meramec in 1702 and that the wording of this petition indicated that lead had been previously mined there. There is no record, however, among the European sources of what might have happened to the lead that was obtained. It is probable that the quantities were small and that the ore produced was used locally.

Another early indication that the French were present in the lead-mining area around the Meramec River is the tradition maintained by scholars that a place called "Cabannage à Renaudière" existed prior to 1720, located somewhere among the tributaries of the Meramec. This area was supposedly a lead-mining site. Louis Houck, in his *History of Missouri* (vol. 1, p. 243), states that Marianne Rondeau, who is mentioned in 1748 in the parish records of Fort de Chartres as a resident in the "Village of the Mines of Missouri," was the daughter of a Frenchman who had lived at Cabannage à Renaudière prior to 1723.

According to the early documents, the Frenchmen began to settle in the Missouri mine country in 1723, with the appearance of Philippe François Renault. Renault was the son of a wealthy iron-master who ran the king's foundries at Cousolre in Picardy, near the Belgian town of Maubeuge. He was appointed the agent for the St. Phillip's Company, a group of wealthy businessmen who had funded the exploitation of the lead mines in Upper Louisiana. Renault left France in 1720 with what must have seemed like an enormous expeditionary force at a time when twenty or thirty soldiers handled whole forts in the remote areas of Louisiana. He was accompanied by two hundred French workers and carried with him all the mining tools and equipment that he thought he needed for his American venture. He even brought thousands of bricks that were stamped with his name with which to build furnaces when he should arrive at the mines. One of these bricks has survived and was found in the 1930s in Old Mines at the site that was believed to have been Renault's furnace.

Renault and his company, after crossing the Atlantic, stopped in Santo Domingo, then a French colony, where he purchased slaves to augment his work force. He then traveled up the Mississippi River with all his men and equipment, arriving at Fort de Chartres, on the east side of the river in 1721. The company remained in Illinois until 1723, preparing for their mining venture. Renault obtained a grant to the land now known as the Old Mines Concession in 1722 and then started exploiting the lead fields in earnest. His two largest furnaces were at Old Mines and at Mine La Motte in St. Francois County, but travelers to the area in the early 1800s repeatedly mentioned that Renault had mined so many sites that the entire region was covered with his lead mines. The lead was melted into horse-collar shapes after being smelted and was packed on horses to be shipped South to New Orleans. There was no town at this shipping site on the west bank of the Mississippi before 1735, the year when Ste. Genevieve was founded. In spite of Renault's obvious energy and ambition, the venture was plagued by such high shipping costs that it was unprofitable. In 1742, the St. Phillip's Company collapsed and Renault, bankrupt, returned to his hometown in France.

By this time, he had been disinherited by his father, and his oldest son had taken his rightful place as forge master. The town history of Cousolre does record that Renault returned after his twenty-two years in America, but no mention is made of what became of him then. It is obvious that his family and acquaintances thought him an irresponsible adventurer for having thus abandoned his family and heritage for so long, although the facts indicate that he was quite possibly a truly heroic and tragic figure. He is remembered heroically in the Missouri community that he had established, where there is a general awareness that Old Mines was founded by Renault in 1723.

One official document that supports the fact that there might have been permanent settlements in the mine areas is the baptismal record of a baby said to be from the "Village of the Mines of Missouri," at Fort de Chartres, in 1748. Pierre Vivarenne, the father of that child, was born in Picardy, France, which indicates that at least a few of Renault's men had probably stayed behind at the mines. The child's mother, as we have already noted, was said to be the daughter of a man who had inhabited the mining area before Renault's expedition. It is extremely difficult to trace the history of this community between Renault's departure in 1742 and the beginning of American control in 1803 due to the lack of a formal government, a formal parish structure, and written records. There are, however, some indications of its development in documents relative to Ste. Genevieve, in parish records of Fort de Chartres and of Ste. Genevieve and in records of French migration from the Illinois settlements after the English took control of the east side of the Mississippi River in 1763. Also, there are several records and eyewitness accounts of the mining area that date from shortly after the onset of American control of Louisiana in the first two decades of the nineteenth century and refer to the long standing of certain sites, practices, and situations.

The mining country was far enough removed from the main French settlements so that most of the early French miners preferred to maintain at least part-time residences in the Illinois communities or in Ste. Genevieve. It is probable that some resolutely backwoods types lived full-time in the area of the mines, but the largest part of what we know about lead mining before the turn of the nineteenth century comes from people who lived in the towns. For them, mining lead was a lucrative way to supplement their income during the months of September to December. During this period of the year, the growing of food was over, the weather was generally dry and mild, and the ground was not yet frozen too hard for it to be worked. Population in the interior probably started to increase in earnest in the 1760s. It was at this time that François Azor, known as "Breton," discovered a prolific deposit of surface lead at the site of the present town of Potosi and set up a mine there. That this was to be a tremendously productive source of ore was predicted by the manner of its discovery, which is recounted to us by Christian Schultz (1810, p. 50) who tells of the hearsay he encountered in his travels through the mining country: "The Mine Le Berton [sic] was discovered about sixty years ago by a Frenchman of that name who being out on a hunt, had built a fire against an odd-looking kind of a root, that projected a small distance out of the earth, and soon discovered itself to be ore by the fusion of those parts immediately acted upon by the fire."

The other major event of the 1760s was the cession of the Illinois country on the eastern side of the Mississippi River to the English by the French king. Spain had also obtained Louisiana, on the western bank of the Mississippi, from the French, but this agreement seems to have been a well-kept secret from the French who were then living in the mid-Mississippi Valley. Religion at this time was still a source of political hatred, and the Catholic French in Illinois feared problems with the Protestant British. Therefore, they moved en masse to the west side, which they believed was still French. They arrived in Missouri relatively destitute, having left the majority of their belongings behind, along with whatever land they had possessed. Many went to St. Louis and to Ste. Genevieve.

It's Good to Tell You

However, one of the biggest opportunities of the time lay in the mines, and a good number of these families also moved into the interior, to the mining country. By 1766, three years after England took over the Illinois country, almost all of the residents of Kaskaskia and Fort de Chartres had moved to the western bank of the Mississippi.

During the years between 1760 and 1800, Spain worked hard to encourage Catholic immigrants from Europe to come to Louisiana but prohibited the Protestant Americans from moving there. Of the Europeans, only the French came in any numbers, and therefore the population of the territory became largely French, with a constant trickle of new immigrants. Extant visas and letters in the possession of families in the Old Mines area show that nineteenth-century migration into the area was almost entirely from the northeastern industrial segments of that country, where mines and mining are well-known mainstays of the economy. It is likely that this was also true in the eighteenth century, although we have no documentary evidence to prove this. However, immigration from France in the nineteenth century was basically residual. It was not specifically encouraged, as it had been throughout the second half of the eighteenth century by Spain, and thus probably represented the continuation of habits and expectations that were generated by the Spanish policy.

In the 1790s, the Spaniards could no longer hold back the pent-up tide of the American westward movement, and American miners began to pour into Louisiana. In 1796, possibly in reaction to the flood of new immigration of outside groups, the landowners in the Old Mines area petitioned the Spanish government to grant them an official concession to the land that they had mined and cultivated since the granting of this claim to Renault by the French government in 1722. It is a matter of record that while many Americans entered the surrounding areas, the Old Mines Concession remained almost entirely French. The concession was not approved formally and immediately by the Spanish government, and the inhabitants had to petition again in 1803 but to the American government. One of the features of territorial life in Louisiana just prior to American control was a great flurry of activity by land speculators who were attempting to obtain falsified land grant documents from the Spanish government, so that they would have to be granted rights to that land by the Americans. The Old Mines claim was accurate and proper, but it got confused with the larger problem of whether or not any of the Spanish grants should be awarded to their apparent holders, and if so, which ones. The Old Mines inhabitants had to wait anxiously until 1836 before they were definitively given the right to hold their own land by the American government. The justice of their claim is corroborated by sources that prompted Sauer to state, "Even at that time this tract was considered ancient. It is likely that some of its concessionaires were descendants of Renault's miners, who first worked that property in 1725–26" (1920, p. 77).

The 1803 census, taken on the occasion of the American accession of Louisiana, recorded that the Old Mines Concession had thirty-one heads of families, seventy-two children, and eighteen slaves. Women were not counted, a reflection more of American values than of French ones, since the census was an official American undertaking. Family names on the Old Mines Concession petition included four Boyers (today's most common family name, by far, in the Old Mines area), three Roberts, two Colemans, and the following names of single French families: Bequette, Patenutte, Thibeault, Guibord, Milhomme, Valle, Lacroix, Rose, Bolyin, Gouvinay, Placet, Belay, Partenay, Maniche, Pratte, Duclos, Boissé, Martin, Portell. Most of these names are represented today in the Old Mines area, along with numerous other French names and a few Irish ones.

The American influence was quickly felt throughout Missouri. Russel L. Gerlach tells us that by 1830 only Ste. Genevieve, Old Mines, and Bonnot's Mills had remained French, while other towns and settlements quickly assimilated the American customs and language (Gerlach, 1976, p. 151). Except in the Old Mines Concession, which stayed largely French by virtue of landownership, by 1830 the mines had large numbers of "Americans"—people of English-speaking, Protestant stock who had migrated there from states farther to the east, particularly Kentucky, Tennessee, and Ohio.

In the years immediately following the transfer of Louisiana from France to the United States, there was a spate of "travelers," gentlemen from England or from the eastern states who came to the lead fields as explorers and chroniclers. From them we have some detailed eyewitness information on what they found in the lead mines. Henry Marie Brackenridge tells us (1814, p. 142): "The miners have a variety of rules among themselves to prevent disputes in diggings. Each one takes a pole and measures off twelve feet in every direction from the edge; the pits seldom exceed eight or ten feet in diameter. He is not permitted to undermine farther than his twelve feet, but must dig a new pit if the ground be not occupied." These appear to be rules that had existed for some time, based on custom. They do not appear in any legal documents. The mining techniques described by Brackenridge continued virtually unchanged from the beginning of lead mining until the end of hand-dug barite mining in the 1940s. They were described further by Christian Schultz (1810, p. 49): "The workmen are ill-provided with instruments, having no other tools than a pick-axe and shovel, with which they open a hole about six or seven feet deep and four or five feet in length and breadth; if they are successful, they enlarge the hole, but if not, they abandon it and open another, either alongside of the former, or in any other spot where their fancy may direct."

The simplicity of being a miner was a key factor in the whole history of the Missouri mining fields. From the start, miners were not hired by the landowners but worked as independent contractors. They could dig where they wanted and would then sell the ore they extracted to the owners of the land, for the going rate. They could sell ore extracted from their own land to whomever they pleased. However, the majority of miners who used mining as their permanent occupation were not landowners, or they owned so little land that they were not able to make a living digging on it. In the early days, before 1800, as mentioned in the accounts of Ste. Genevieve and New Bourbon, many inhabitants of these towns, landowners as well as poorer men, turned to mining during the fall and winter. The important fact to remember here is that the majority of miners had little or no capital to invest in the industry, which can be costly when done at higher levels of our sophisticated technology. The Americans, speaking from a position of greater wealth, were generally disdainful of what seemed to be the backwardness of the French and spoke disparagingly of their primitive smelting methods. Schultz, however, provides some insight into the probable role that money played in this situation (1810, p. 51):

> There is but one regular-built air furnace throughout this country, which is at the Mine Le Berton. The expense of such a building is so great, and the mineral so plenty, that the miners prefer an open furnace, which in all probability cannot cost them more than forty or fifty dollars; whereas a proper air furnace, like the one just mentioned, would cost them five or six thousand dollars.

Moses Austin, the builder of the air furnace that is mentioned by Schultz, was one who disparaged the backwardness of the French in his writings, apparently failing to recognize the higher levels of capital investment that he could afford in comparison with the miners.

What was it like to be a miner of lead or barite? Those who have known hand mining for barite in the twentieth century remember it as an all-consuming enterprise, in which everyone in the family would work daily from dawn to dusk, for a living that was far from adequate. In 1930, when the mining of lead ore was exhausted and surface barite was becoming more and more difficult to obtain, barite miners were being paid only three dollars per ton of ore, before payment of royalties and hauling fees. This represented at least a full day's work, on a lucky day. However, early accounts indicate that initially hand mining was in fact a fairly lucrative occupation, at a time when large amounts of lead ore were still readily available and close to the surface. Bradbury cites the price of lead ore as two dollars per hundred pounds (1819, p. 249), which would add up to forty dollars per ton. Schultz (1810, p. 51) also tells us that the price of lead ore was twenty dollars per thousand pounds, or forty dollars per ton. Austin, in the *American State Papers,* writes, "Every farmer may be a miner and, when unoccupied on his farm, may by a few weeks' labor, almost at his own door, dig as much mineral as will furnish his family with all imported articles" (p. 208). Therefore, we can safely assume that lead mining permitted early miners to live a life of relative ease, and many early travelers noted that the miners had often dug enough by Thursday to provide for their families' needs of the week and, as a result, could spend the next three days sitting comfortably on their front porches.

During the second half of the nineteenth century, it was discovered that the white barite that had been discarded as waste was also useful and valuable. This material, known locally as "tiff" (a word that apparently meant "waste matter"), began to be mined for its own sake in the 1860s, immediately after the Civil War. By around 1900, barite, used in paint, oil-well drilling, and as a source of barium, became the major product of the mining area around Old Mines, since lead ore had been virtually exhausted. The same techniques and customs that had prevailed for lead mining were also employed for the hand mining of barite. Joseph Médard Carrière, visiting the barite mines in 1934 (1937, p. 14), wrote: "A barite miner is theoretically at least, his own master, and works only as much as is needed to obtain the barest necessities of life. Such an occupation has undeniable advantages for people who value leisure and good fellowship more than money, but even under the most favorable circumstances it would seldom lead to economic independence." Carrière was apparently reporting on traditional feelings carried over from earlier, more prosperous times in the mining area. Times had been hard since the early 1900s. The lead companies had bought up large segments of the land, and the price had sunk to only two or three dollars for a ton of "tiff." Families needed all their members out on the "diggings" just to make enough money to subsist, even though the mining companies, as an enticement, offered many of them free housing. The mining companies also owned many of the stores from which the miners bought their necessary supplies and foodstuffs on credit.

In 1905, a law maintaining compulsory schooling was passed in Missouri, and one-room schoolhouses were constructed throughout the mining area. Because of economic conditions, the low price of tiff, and the uncertainty of finding ore on any given day to pay for food, many families found it difficult to send their children to school regularly. Also, some families lived in locations that were too isolated or that presented too many obstacles, such as creeks to ford, for children who went to school on foot. The mining companies used free housing as a way to entice people from other areas who were either out of work or had failed at other occupations and were destitute into the mining areas. As a result of hard times for both old French families and newer "American" immigrants to the area, by the 1930s, the mining area was looked upon by social service and educational officials as a socioeconomic problem area, plagued by poor health conditions, a high rate of infant mortality and illiteracy, low school attendance, and a large number of people on "Relief." In addition, state officials and teachers viewed the French language in the area as a barrier that needed to be overcome in order to assimilate these people, and this was regarded as a necessary first step in eliminating problems that appeared to be inherent in the indigenous French culture.

A majority of the French children who went to school from the Old Mines area between 1905 and 1920 generally knew no English before starting first grade. In spite of the fact that English was not their primary language, they were strictly forbidden to speak their mother tongue while attending school, starting with the first day of classes. This situation was universally remembered as degrading, embarrassing, and difficult by those who experienced it. The lesson they learned was to make English their dominant tongue as rapidly as possible. They still spoke French at home to older relatives who knew little English. However, the process of assimilation was rapidly accelerated in the community. By 1937, after only thirty years of American schooling in the Old Mines area, most adults had become bilingual. J. T. Miles tells us (1937) that "about 90 percent of the people at Old Mines speak both French and English. In the homes it is estimated that about 35 percent speak nothing but French." By 1949, only the older residents whose English was poor spoke French regularly, and by the early 1960s, no one remained who could speak only French, and English was used almost exclusively by everyone.

Since the stories in this book were one of the community's primary forms of entertainment in the 1930s and early 1940s, it is important to examine more closely the social and economic context in which Carrière collected the tales I have translated here. As previously mentioned, during this period, it can be said with some assurance that virtually everyone in the Old Mines area community had something to do with mining, "scrapping," or hauling tiff. Generally, the women and children were the ones who "scrapped" the ore. This meant that they would go through the piles of debris around the shafts and pick up bits of tiff overlooked by the miner. A few women actually donned overalls and dug the ore, but most worked at more peripheral activities. People fortunate enough to own a team of horses or mules and a wagon would spend at least part of their time hauling the tiff to the weighing stations for other miners, for a fee.

Digging at that time was still done with a pick and shovel. The miner would dig a hole at a spot he felt was likely to yield ore. If the hole got deep enough, two people would "dig partners," so that a windlass could be used to haul the ore to the surface. When it was brought to the surface, it was cleaned of excess bits of dirt with a "tiff hatchet," a small hatchetlike tool with a hammer on one side and a point on the other. Then it was polished in a "rattle box." This was a cratelike affair standing on one pair of feet positioned in the center so that the box could be shaken back and forth from one side to the other rapidly in a seesawing motion. The companies would accept only clean, dry tiff that was at least 90 percent pure. In wet weather, the tiff would become discolored and could not be sold, as the companies could not then determine its degree of purity.

The physical appearance of the community of Old Mines appears to have changed little between the early 1800s and the 1930s, according to eyewitness descriptions. Schultz (1810, p. 48) writes, "The first [lead mine] you come to on the route I took are the Old Mines, where you find a small village of fifteen houses or cabins, situated on a small rich bottom, on one of the branches of the Big River." The Old Mines village was similar to the hamlets found at each of the mining sites, as Brackenridge described them for us in 1814 (p. 151): "The appearance of the diggings . . . is like that of small villages, consisting of a collection of little huts or cabins." That Old Mines did not grow, or change dramatically, between 1810 and 1935, is indicated by Dorrance's description, which was written over one hundred years after those of Schultz and Brackenridge (1935, p. 44): "There is the church of St. Joachim, two stores, a tiff mill, and a straggling line of houses." According to Miles (1937): "Old Mines is stretched out for about two miles along both sides of Old Mines Creek. Houses in irregular fashion still sit close beside each other, with their small plots of ground running back . . . giving the impression that in no one place is to be found Old Mines proper. However, the geographical as well as the social and religious center of the community is St. Joachim's Catholic Church." When Schultz and Bradbury visited Old Mines, they in all probability saw a log church there that would have resembled the other log houses. The present brick church was built in 1823, some dozen years after the two early travelers visited the community. Miles's statement is insightful on several points. The church is still the center of life for the whole parish of some 150 square miles, as it was when he observed Old Mines in the 1930s. The fact that there is a vibrant community of several hundred families spread over this wide geographical area is not evident to the casual tourist or traveler who drives through the two-mile-long row of buildings scattered along Highway 21. It is difficult indeed to decide where "Old Mines proper" may be found, because there is no town of any size there that vies for our attention. Instead, we must look at the small villages that are scattered throughout the mining area at various former mines and diggings.

Anglo-American pioneers have always followed an isolated settlement pattern. They would select a likely site all by themselves, with no neighbors visible, clear a spot on the land, and build their cabin. The French, on the other hand, arranged their land in long strips, rather than large rectangles, so that they could build on their own property and still enjoy the neighborliness of village life. This characteristic is still apparent in the Old Mines area and helps to explain the existence of a substantial community where none appears to exist. Mary Boland Taussig (1937, p. 20) states, "Some miners' cabins are isolated, but more often several are grouped together into towns." People today still know the names of these hamlets and use them to describe their places of residence. Within St. Joachim Parish, there are easily forty to fifty commonly known hamlet or village locations. The existence of these villages was one of the physical circumstances that encouraged the ongoing transmission of oral traditions, including French tunes, songs, and stories. People habitually "sat up" with neighbors to socialize, relax, and provide some entertainment for themselves. The hamlets still exist today, but of course the other supporting contexts for the stories have largely disappeared, including the hand mining of tiff, the French language, and the physical isolation due to lack of communications media and poor transportation into the area.

Actually between 1944 and 1950, the whole framework within which the French culture had existed in the Old Mines area since the early 1700s abruptly disappeared, with the universal adoption of mechanical mining techniques. A handful of backhoes and power shovels replaced hundreds of hand miners, severely hampering the community's economic life. In 1949, the rate of unemployment among adult males in Washington County was 75 percent, with that in the Old Mines area approaching 100 percent, as few of the people who had been hand miners found employment in the new tiff mills or in strip-mining operations. It is interesting and encouraging to note that the community survived, and that by the end of the 1950s, ten years later, it had been able to reorganize successfully. Such indicators of financial prosperity as new housing, automobiles, and a cash economy were by that time becoming more and more evident. The majority of the people adjusted by commuting to industrial jobs in St. Louis, De Soto, Festus, Potosi, Herculaneum, Crystal City, and Pea Ridge.

This, then, was the mining community that produced the stories translated in this book. We have no way of knowing how long these stories have been passed down in Missouri, as there is no record of when they arrived here from France or who brought them. Their presence was first noted in writing at the very moment of their imminent disappearance during the 1930s by Dorrance and Carrière. However, we do know that the stories are a part of French oral tradition and have been faithfully preserved through oral transmission both in America and in France. The fact that they were part of the Old Mines tradition and that they appear to have been universally known in the community at the time they were collected indicate that they had existed in this community for at least several generations, if not from its earliest days. The fact that the stories have evolved to include features of the Old Mines area also argues for their long standing in Missouri. The stories as told here describe a landscape dotted with little hamlets composed of log homes, each with its front porch, in an area where people picked up and left when one place no longer gave them what they needed to survive and moved on to the next one. They present a culture that depended mostly on subsistence farming and a noncash economy for survival, coupled with occasional strategies for supplying cash needs. They refer to stores and specify American modern tools, such as hoes, pistols, and wheelbarrows. It is clear that they existed in this community for a sufficient number of years to have grown such strong local roots. In order to recognize many of the allusions in the stories, it is important to be acquainted with the physical and cultural environment of the Old Mines area over its 250-year history.

III.

The Character and Culture of the Missouri French

Oral tales, as we have already seen, are inseparable from the context in which they are told and passed on. Having studied at some length the physical aspects of the Old Mines area, we now need to examine the character of the people and the cultural values that animated their lives. We are fortunate, in this case, to have access to two groups of eyewitness accounts, one that was written in the early 1800s and the other in the 1930s. Through this lapse of over one hundred years between both groups of descriptions, we can get a feeling for the cultural stability that made it possible for the stories to flourish here for so long. Another important aspect of these two sets of descriptions is that each group contained both someone who spoke French and knew French culture and someone who was encountering this cultural group for the first time and seeing it through Anglo-American or British values and prejudices. This factor, too, gives us a more three-dimensional picture of the Missouri French community as a cultural framework for the stories. If we examine all of the available eyewitness accounts in some detail, we should gain a deeper understanding of the emotional tone and inferences that are apparent in the tales and of their long survival as well.

One of the fascinating aspects of the accounts of French-speaking and non-French-speaking visitors is the way in which both groups describe the same characteristics but with different interpretations. After talking with a wide range of people connected with the Old Mines area community and after researching the available historical descriptions, social psychologist Joseph G. Pfeffer (1979, p. 27) confirmed in 1979 that this distinction between insider and outsider views persists even today.

> Tentative and preliminary findings indicate a remarkable consistency in accounts written by outside observers of the character, social life, work habits, adherence to traditional values, and general outlook on life of the Old Mines French. From the early nineteenth century travel writers through to academically trained twentieth century writers . . . a stereotype emerges that has been highly resistant to modification. . . . The perceptions are shared by both outsiders and the Old Mines people themselves. Natives tend to use positively toned terms (warm, friendly, hospitable, artistic, musical, full of life, non-materialistic, easy-going, respectful of tradition), while outsiders use more negative, pejorative terms (unmotivated, lazy, cunning, non-achievement oriented, hedonistic, irrationally tradition-bound, fearful of the outside world, degenerate) for much the same perceived character traits.

Pfeffer's observations are accurate, not only in regard to "insiders and outsiders" but also in regard to each outside observer's approach to the community. Among the early nineteenth-century itinerant writers who recorded their observations of the mining communities in the area at the time, Christian Schultz was an American who looked upon the French there as a sort of cultural curiosity. John Bradbury, an Englishman, came to the area expecting to see fulfilled the nineteenth-century romantic myth about America as the Promised Land and interpreted what he saw in light of that myth.

Both men ignored the fact that different cultures have different values and interpreted what they saw in terms of their own preconceived ideas. Neither one saw the French inhabitants as a very pleasing group. Schultz (1810, p. 53), for example, tells us:

> The mine country is a very unpleasant place of residence, as the continual broils and quarrels among the workmen, as well as the proprietors, keep up a constant scene of warfare. . . . After having seen and examined the Mines, I became very anxious to quit a country whose inhabitants are so disgusting in their manners.

He must indeed have spent as little time as possible in that area, because he has no other entries that directly relate to Old Mines.

However, Schultz was forced by a hard winter and a frozen Mississippi River to spend several weeks against his will in Ste. Genevieve. While he was searching desperately for ways to leave (he eventually had local residents build him a boat so that he could leave at the first sign of a thaw), he described, at some length, in his letters the customs he observed during his seven weeks of living there. To place his comments in a perspective that he obviously did not have at his disposal, it is necessary to realize that he was there in January and February. During this time of the year, it was impossible to work mines and to farm and, as a result, the people had more leisure during the winter months than at any other. During this season, too, the French traditionally celebrated a period of weekly dances and parties linking the joyous festivities of the new year to the beginning of the solemn penitential season of Lent, which begins seven weeks before Easter. It was this social cycle that Schultz described to his friends for several pages (1810, p. 60):

> Ste. Genevieve does not seem to be in want of amusements, if eternal dancing and gambling deserve that name. One ball follows another so close in succession, that I have often wondered how the ladies were enabled to support themselves under this violent exercise, which is here carried to extremes. The balls are generally opened at candlelight, and continue till ten or twelve the next day.

Schultz and other Protestant American observers belonged to a religious tradition in which dancing, gambling, and partying were considered sinful. This outlook on life was not a part of the French Catholic tradition, and the French partied on in the presence of their guests, having a good time and apparently remaining unaware of the visitors' horror at what they saw as license and sin. On page 62 of the same text, Schultz speaks of Sundays in Ste. Genevieve:

> Sunday is much better known in all the French settlements of this country as a day of general amusement, than of worship. It is true, that as they have a chapel and confessor, they must necessarily make some kind of use of them; they therefore have a high mass performed every Sunday morning, which lasts half an hour. . . . You see nothing of that general cessation from labor on this day so common with you. . . . Indeed no kind of work or amusement is suspended on account of the day. There is commonly a ball on Sunday evening; and should the billiards rooms, of which there are three in the town, be closed the whole week, you will always see them open and crowded on Sunday. . . . The French settlers throughout this country generally entertain a very bad opinion of the religion of the Americans, and even go so far as to say they have no religion at all.

Schultz gives the impression that he was horrified by what he perceived as a lack of religion on the part of the French, with their scandalously short Sunday service and the amusements that they pursued for the rest of the day. He also had the grace, however, to admit that the French returned his low opinion of their religion and entertained a similar point of view regarding the religious fervor of their American neighbors. This description is an excellent one of the kind of culture shock that has persisted from the first incursions of the Americans into Missouri up to today, whenever American and French values reach an impasse.

In contrast to Schultz's observations of the Missouri French, we are fortunate to have at least one other traveler's account that was published in 1814, and which presents the "insider's" point of view. It was written by Henry Marie Brackenridge, who spent a large part of his boyhood in Ste. Genevieve, where he had been sent by his father to learn French. As a man, he again passed through the area in 1811, as part of a journey up the Mississippi River. He did not stay long in the area, not having been marooned there as Schultz had been, and his description consists of a few brief sentences. However, even his few remarks tend to make us wonder if he could be talking about the same people as Schultz (1814, p. 135):

> These inhabitants were as remarkable for their tame and peaceable disposition, as the natives of France are for the reverse. Amongst their virtues we may enumerate honesty and punctuality in their dealings, hospitality to strangers, friendship and affection among relatives and neighbors. . . . In opposition to these virtues, it must be said that they are devoid of public spirit, of enterprise or ingenuity, and are indolent and uninformed.

In fact, the word *indolent*, or its equivalent *lazy* is commonly used by observers to describe the French groups of the mining communities and of the mid-Mississippi Valley. Even Bradbury, who mostly confined himself to describing to his correspondents in great detail the flora, fauna, and geology of the region, also made some mention of the inhabitants in this area (1819, p. 259).

> The French are very indolent and so much attached to the manners of their ancestors . . . that although they see their American neighbors, by the application of improved implements and methods, able to cultivate double the quantity of ground in the same time, nothing can induce them to abandon their old practices; and if any one attempts to reason with them on the subject, their constant reply is: "As it was good enough for our forefathers, it is good enough for us." Whence it appears that even veneration for ancestry may become an evil.

Like Schultz, Bradbury too takes the trouble to present another side of the issue. He gives us the impression that life in these communities was pleasant and civilized enough, although he qualifies it with the statement that this is true only because the climate and land were rich enough to allow lazy people to prosper. In fact, other historical sources have compared the diet of the Americans, which contained large amounts of lard and cornmeal, to the varied and well-balanced diets enjoyed by the French in the early territorial days, indicating that the French may have been following the principle of "Work smarter, not harder" rather than simply being lazy and unenterprising. Bradbury comments on page 260:

> They cultivate maize [corn], wheat, oats, barley, beans, pumpkins, water and mushmelons, and tobacco and cotton for their own use. Apples and peaches are very fine; . . . They pay great attention to gardening and have a good assortment of roots and vegetables. Notwithstanding their want of industry, there is an appearance of comfort and independence to their villages as, from the richness of the soil and the fineness of the climate, the labours attendant on agriculture and attention necessary to the cattle are comparatively trivial.

In attributing the French settlers' prosperity to the land and the climate, Bradbury is perpetuating one of the great nineteenth-century European myths about America, namely, that it is such a rich land that work virtually does itself, and that the settlers can sit around all day and do nothing and still can have plenty to eat, have plenty of fine clothes, and good housing. The vast American territory must have appeared this way to the Europeans who were coming from an overcrowded rural economy, in which too many people were trying to draw sustenance from overworked land. America, the land of opportunity, seemed to be the answer to their prayers. Bradbury apparently saw nothing in his travels to dissuade him forcefully from perpetuating that myth. Indeed, as he saw the Missouri French enjoying the pleasures of life, he appears to have seized on them as an example of the myth in reality.

The fact that these European immigrants believed in this myth is supported not only by the advertisements that appeared in European newspapers, which intended to attract new immigrants to specific communities in America, but also in their folk materials. For example, Alan Lomax (1960, p. 88) has transcribed a song sung by Norwegian immigrants in Minnesota, which satirizes the inaccurate information that they had received in Norway to encourage them to emigrate:

> In Oleana, land is free, the wheat and corn just plant themselves.
> Then they grow four feet a day while on the bed you rest yourselves.
> The little pigs they roast themselves, and trot about this lovely land,
> With knives and forks stuck in their backs, inquiring if you'd like some ham.
> The cows and calves do all the work; they milk and churn till the dairy's full.
> The bull keeps herd production high and sends reports to Ole Bull.

The song goes on to extol the sun that shines both night and day, the harvest that comes once a month, the fact that you get paid for doing nothing and become richer the lazier you are, and ends with:

> So if you'd like a happy life, to Oleana you must go.
> The poorest man from the old country, becomes a king in a
> year or so.

Oleana in the song is a pun on the name of Ole Bull, a famous Norwegian musician who was enthralled by the romance of America. He had bought a large tract of land in Pennsylvania and had advertised for Norwegians to emigrate and take up residence there. When they arrived, they found out that the land was rough and rocky, covered with forests, and not ready to be cultivated. In addition, they discovered that the man who had sold the tract to Bull was a swindler who did not even own the land. The song, although a satire on a specific episode, was immortalized on both sides of the Atlantic because it highlighted so well the romantic hopes and dreams of Europeans in the nineteenth century who had immigrated to America. The Briton Bradbury obviously saw in the lives of the French settlers in the mid-Mississippi Valley the fulfillment of that myth and attributed all of the pleasant aspects of life there to the supposed hospitality of the land, and very little to the supposedly unindustrious inhabitants.

Approximately 120 years elapsed between the visits to the Missouri French mining country of these first chroniclers and of the arrival of the second group of visitors who wrote substantial amounts of material about the area and its people. One of the aspects that stands out when one compares both groups of writings is the consistency of the observations made when such a long interval existed between them. The second aspect that is striking is the consistency of negative interpretation coming from those who saw themselves as outsiders and were not acquainted with the language, as opposed to the positive interpretations of the same observations made by those who could claim some cultural and linguistic affinity with the people.

The French mining community of Old Mines again came into scholarly prominence in the mid-1930s, when several academic visitors spent varying lengths of time there and wrote about their experiences. One of them was Mary Boland Taussig, who spent a number of weeks in the community in 1937 and 1938, doing research for her master's thesis (1938, Washington University). She was a sociologist, studying the reasons that may have contributed to the fact that while school attendance in Missouri and nationwide in 1935 was around 85 percent, in the French mining district of Washington County, it was only 46 percent. She studied this French-speaking community from an American point of view. She acknowledges the help of many individuals from Washington County, all of them Anglo-Americans who had political or economic leverage over the French miners: for example, the president of the county's chamber of commerce, officials from the lead companies, county court judges, the local physician, the county farm agent, the county superintendent of schools were all individuals who viewed the French population from an American point of view. The bulk of her essay deals with factual observations; however, her introduction is based on the assumption that the French district presented a problem and that the American solution was the right one. Small observations do slip in on the nature of the people she encountered in her interviews. For instance, she notices (1938, p. 13) the warm welcome that was accorded her even though she was a stranger:

> It was not hard to obtain information because usually the novelty of a visitor was welcomed. In one or two instances, where there was reticence at first, this wore off in the course of the conversation. The harder task was to obtain accurate answers from a people little prone to exactitude.

A few pages further on, she describes the relationship that she observed between the Anglo-American townspeople in Potosi (the county seat) and the French-speaking community immediately to its north (p. 21):

> . . . there are no social relations between the townspeople and the outlying rural areas. . . . The townspeople feel that the majority of the miners are shiftless; picturesque perhaps, but irresponsible. . . . this is a fixed idea in which they have been brought up for generations, and which is held inflexibly. With the same lack of flexibility, the miner tells how he is cheated by his landowner, his merchant, the "company," and the "political ring" around the Courthouse. Since the tiff area of Washington County is comparatively small and its inhabitants are so united in the bonds of a single industry, one wonders that they are not united in a more tolerant understanding of one another.

What Taussig fails to consider in her study of the French community in Missouri is the lack of understanding that often permeates relationships between cultures, because of differing values and deficient communications. Since the first American influx into the French mining area in the 1790s, the Americans with their Protestant work ethic have always considered the French too oriented toward enjoying life and too little concerned with productivity. The French, on the other hand, have always felt equally strong about the Americans' lack of appreciation for the good things of life and their relative lack of civility and warmth. The culture conflict that Taussig observed in the 1930s had been engraving itself into everyone's minds for over 140 years and had reached a point where it was so internalized that the people generally were unaware of it. If one talks today to representatives of government, industry, and social service agencies in this area, one will hear essentially the same Anglo-American judgments pronounced on the "French problem." The officials are often unaware that what they are experiencing flows from a poor understanding of opposing cultural values. Yet these values have not, in the past, been sufficiently described and analyzed to permit either side to act on specific knowledge of details.

Two other scholars also visited the Old Mines area in the 1930s. They both spoke French and were interested in comparing the French language and culture found there to that of France and of other regions in North America. Ward Allison Dorrance was an assistant professor of French at the University of Missouri–Columbia. Joseph Médard Carrière had grown up in French Canada, but at the time of his visit to the Old Mines area, he was professor of French at Northwestern University in Illinois. Both of these men shared a romantic conception of the "French peasant" somehow preserved intact in the midst of twentieth-century America. Dorrance tells us (1935, p. 44): "The residents of the cross-roads hamlet and parish of Old Mines, who are quite typical, may serve to characterize the rest. Here are found the colloquial French peasants, still speaking French and holding to their own ways."

Carrière, although his descriptions are longer and more detailed, echoes essentially the same sentiments (1937, pp. 13–14):

> The French natives of Missouri have always been known for their lack of aggressiveness and ambition, their easygoing disposition, and their unquenchable gaiety. . . . Their frugality has always been such that, among more enterprising people it would be a sure sign of destitution. They have been satisfied with securing for themselves the strictly essential things of life, and have always avoided overexertion. In spite of their inertia, the inhabitants of Old Mines have kept to this very day sterling qualities which tend to disappear elsewhere. Family and community ties are very strong among them. The little they have they are most willing to share with their kin and neighbors. Few people are fonder of conversation and more hospitable. In this they are true to two of the most fundamental traits of French character. . . . Their joyful acceptance of the simple pleasures of life, their unqualified resignation to its necessary hardships, the essential sturdiness and wholesomeness of their views have a heroic touch which wins for these simple folk the lasting sympathy and esteem of the visitor who has become intimately acquainted with them.

The contrast of views between Taussig's analysis of the Anglo-American townsfolks' attitudes toward their French neighbors in the Old Mines area and of the interpretation offered by Carrière and Dorrance of the same traits mirrors almost exactly that which we found earlier between Schultz and Bradbury, on the one hand, and Brackenridge, on the other, between 1800 and 1815. Thus, we can infer that the French people in the Old Mines area were able to preserve many of their chief cultural attitudes and values during this period. We can also infer that the conflict that was beginning to emerge in 1810 between the two cultures hardened during the rest of the century to produce an effective wall of isolation around the French community. These two conditions—a conservative, static culture and isolation from other groups—produced a sort of hothouse environment for the preservation and growth of a rich variety of cultural traditions. They were probably important factors in the preservation of the tales told in this book and in their elaboration and wealth of detail.

The Missouri French culture, in addition to being the environment in which the stories evolved, also provided many elements for the content of the tales. These can be studied by pulling together a list of cultural characteristics that all or most of the eyewitness accounts had highlighted. Most of the historical accounts that were discussed in this section have mentioned that the French enjoyed such amenities of life as dancing, music, card playing, and conversation. We get the idea that it was sometimes more important for them to enjoy themselves than to get ahead in the world. From these accounts, we also see that they devoted a lot of attention to food, gardens and orchards, entertainment, and family and community.

Good food is still a pleasure that is important to the present-day Missouri French. Mention of feasts and of good food is made often in the stories, and it is clear that the growing, preparation, and consumption of food are basic elements of this culture. There is a wide variety of traditional foods that is still grown and prepared in this region today. As in Bradbury's day, almost everyone still cultivates a large garden, growing essentially the same foods he listed. The lore of planting by the moon is still exceptionally well preserved, attesting to the importance of the garden in people's lives. One indicator of the priority that food holds as a source of pleasure in this community is the fact that one favorite kind of party is called by the name of the food that was traditionally served— "bouillon" —an evening of cards and conversation, at which the main refreshments were chicken meat, bouillon, pickles, and crackers. Surprising as this party menu may seem to those unaccustomed to it, it is delicious and satisifying. Among other favorite traditional foods are croqueciolles (pronounced crock-see-oles), which is a crisply fried dough fritter; sauerkraut; various kinds of cookies; an amazing variety of pies, some with multiple crusts; an assortment of jams and jellies, some made with wild berries and fruit; galettes chouazes (pronounced gah-late shwahz), a kind of fried biscuit; chicken and dumplings; and several savory ways of preparing wild foods, including greens, mushrooms, and wild game. In general, it can be said that the Missouri French foods, although different from those of continental France, share with the best French-home-style cooking a real flair for highlighting the best flavor of fresh foods with a minimum of preparation.

In several of the stories, music is also mentioned, especially in connection with fiddle playing. We remember Schultz's despair in 1809 as he discussed the frequent balls. In a much later observation, Taussig (1938, p. 75) cites statistics that show that all of the families she had studied, with the exception of the few that were totally destitute, owned some kind of musical instrument, most frequently a fiddle, banjo, or guitar. She also found some families that had a piano or a harmonica (locally called a French harp):

> Whereas only three out of thirty-seven families of irregular school attendants (eight percent) possessed anything of literary quality, such as books, magazines, or newspapers, forty-six percent of them, almost half, owned some sort of musical instrument which they could play themselves, such as a guitar, violin, etc. . . . This means that every family except those twenty who were completely destitute of possessions, owned a musical instrument on which they could perform. . . . The entire family plays, including father, mother, and children. . . . Violins were highly prized, and often handed down from father to son.

The ability to play a musical instrument is one of the liveliest manifestations of French culture in this region. Musicians are in frequent demand to play for the dances that are still, as they were in Schultz's time, a mainstay of social life in the community. Amazingly large numbers of people will still attend the community dances on the coldest winter evening or in the most torrid summer heat. Dances of this sort, at which modern "rock" numbers alternate with traditional fiddle tunes and square dances, are the modern successors of the neighborhood "setting up" parties and bouillons that had prevailed in the 1930s, at the time that Carrière, Dorrance, and Taussig visited the Old Mines community.

Another component of the Missouri French character that has been repeatedly mentioned by outside visitors is a strong loyalty to family and community. This too is often seen in the stories, as characters either act in the best interests of family or community in preference to their own interests or else suffer the punishments they seem to deserve for not doing so. This value is still strong within the framework of the modern French community in the Old Mines area. Many younger people either establish their households in the area from the time of their marriage or else move back as soon as they can if they have moved away. This is true in spite of the fact that in order to work, almost everyone has to commute somewhere else. For some families, this means that at least one member must commute eighty to one hundred miles one way each day, to Illinois or to the northern suburbs of St. Louis for industrial jobs. In addition, many of the young people who have established households elsewhere within a one-hundred-mile radius come back home frequently on weekends, to be with their families. Pfeffer (1979, pp. 31–32) comments on the value placed on family ties within the Old Mines community:

> Traditional extended family life, an ethic of neighborliness which contrasts with the anomie of city and suburb, the traditionally important and somewhat paternalistic role of the Catholic church in providing an organized social life for the community, and a generally positive attitude toward their "Frenchness," which they feel still makes them distinct from the "Americans" who surround them, are the reasons most often given by informants for actively maintaining their ties to Old Mines.

Another strong factor in the makeup of the Missouri French character—one that has been repeated by almost all of the outside observers—is a sense that enjoying life is at least as important as getting ahead. Spending time visiting with neighbors or relatives or relaxing on the porch (generally called a gallery) have traditionally become essential factors of life. On these occasions, the people would pass the time by talking and often by listening to various kinds of stories. We see both neighborly visiting and relaxation on the gallery frequently in the tales as an integral part of the fabric of life. Dorrance (1935, p. 37) gives us a glowing real-life description of the resulting agreeable pace of living:

> The writer took up residence in this locality, living for months the life of the tiff miners, farmers, and hunters who compose the population, accompanying them to the "diggings," to the corn fields, to the woods, listening and questioning as they talked at work or as they fiddled, sang and told tales at night on the lamp-lit gallery.

Taussig describes similar types of activities in somewhat less lyrical terms (1938, p. 78):

> Cultural opportunities among the miners are largely the ones they create for themselves. They gather in each others' cabins for a round of singing, drinking, or talk. Their circle is not a wide one; it consists of the immediate neighborhood.

It is not the particular activities that are important but the time that has traditionally been reserved in this community for talk, music, good fellowship, good food, lively stories, and a general enjoyment of life. The warmth and fellowship generated by that time spent together are manifested in the stories' general good humor, and they also played an important role in assuring the stories' continuation. As we are reading about Little John, Peter, the King, Carambot, Beausoleil, Master Thief, John and Mary, Fair Margaret, Fair Ferentine, Fair Magdelon, and the other characters from the tales, we can both picture them as the Missouri French characters they became over the generations and can imagine their stories being told during lunchtime on the "diggings," on the gallery, or in front of the woodstove in the evening.

Little John and his friends in the tales lived in French Missouri in log cabins in the woods. For entertainment, they went visiting, sat on the gallery smoking and talking, played the fiddle, which are all pastimes common in the Old Mines area. Their lives, like those of the miners, were paced by the rhythms of nature. They esteemed the ability to reduce the discomforts of work by applying wit and ingenuity to a situation. They looked at life with a lively sense of humor and appreciation for the incongruous and the ridiculous. They portrayed a warm sense of hospitality and mutual support for each other, when they were not involved in some kind of feud. They depicted the rewards of traditional family virtues and the punishments for flouting paternal standards and disregarding the good of the family. In short, the reader who has some knowledge of the culture that produced these tales will experience an increased enjoyment of their subtle interplay of situations and personalities. With this will come a heightened realization of the good-natured humor that they represented in the face of sometimes grim physical realities.

IV.

The Fairy Tales in the 1930s

In the early 1930s, as we have already mentioned, two French scholars became interested in Old Mines and spent a considerable amount of time in the community, recording the dialect and observing aspects of the daily life. Ward Allison Dorrance came into the area to do research for his dissertation, which was subsequently published by the University of Missouri–Columbia in 1935. He focused mainly on the language, and the largest part of his book consisted of a glossary of words that were found only in Old Mines French. In addition, it included a kind of postscript in which he devoted a final chapter to his remarks about Old Mines French folklore as he had observed it. However, these were no more than incidental remarks, illustrated with excerpts from songs and stories. Joseph Médard Carrière, on the other hand, was interested primarily in the folklore, especially folktales. The largest part of his book consists of transcriptions from stories that he had been told by two storytellers in the Old Mines area—Frank Bourisaw and Joseph Ben Coleman. He also talks a little about the language, and gives a brief glossary. However, in Carrière's book, it is the linguistic information that is fragmentary and consigned to a postscript chapter.

The first major task of fieldworkers is to establish a good personal relationship with their informants, one based on mutual trust and liking. Only when this has been established are they likely to share freely in the community life that they want to observe and record. Dorrance mentions (p. 103) this process when he refers to the necessity of "taming" storytellers if one is an outsider to the community. The second major challenge that the fieldworker faces, once he receives information from the people with whom he is talking, is to record it accurately, imposing on it none of his or her own preconceived ideas or feelings. In the case of the stories, both Dorrance and Carrière had to write down exactly what they were hearing, resisting to the end the temptation to edit and improve.

The fact that most people spoke French in the Old Mines community was the single aspect of the area that had the strongest drawing power to both Dorrance and Carrière. The French that is heard in Old Mines is an American dialect that evolved in isolation over more than two hundred years. In 1814, Brackenridge had already noted the following about the language (p. 137):

> Their language, everything considered, is more pure than might be expected; their manner of lengthening the sounds of words, although languid and without the animation which the French generally possess, is by no means disagreeable. They have some new words, and others are in use which in France have become obsolete.

Interestingly enough, both Dorrance and Carrière thought that because of the sizable influx of families from the Illinois country, most of whose ancestors had come from Canada, into Old Mines in the 1760s, Old Mines French was a variety of Canadian French. According to Dorrance (1935, p. 47):

With these exceptions, the body of the Missouri French vocabulary has been brought fairly intact from Canada. The question "What is Missouri French?", then, has been answered by Canadian linguists and historians. Canadian French is a melange of the dialects of the north, west, and center of France, of Old French, and of borrowings from English and the Indian tongues.

However, Dorrance fails to take into account the whole history of immigration into the Old Mines area. The first miners to settle the region, as well as the immigrants who continued to come throughout the eighteenth and nineteenth centuries, were from France, not from Canada. Indeed, their places of origin were mostly in the northeastern part of France rather than the northwest. The large variety of influences on this dialect and the long time during which it evolved in isolation both tend to merit for Missouri French the status of a distinctive dialect of American French. It is different from and related to both Canadian and Louisiana French.

In 1970, Clyde Thogmartin analyzed the dialect in terms of pronunciation, grammar, and vocabulary. He studied tape recordings that he made in conversing with a small group of Old Mines area residents and also brought in data from the folktales transcribed in Old Mines French by Carrière in the 1930s. He pointed out many of the ways in which the Old Mines dialect is unique and independent from both Louisiana and Canadian French. He also demonstrated the extent to which English had interfered with the native French over the years in informal use of the Old Mines dialect.

Interestingly enough, many people in the Old Mines area who were familiar with the dialect thought of it as a sort of degraded patois. Somehow it was considered to be less than "real French." Taussig notes this feeling when she says (1939, p. 19): "The older members of the family speak a version of Canadian French, with a nasal twang and many words totally different from classical French." Carrière (1939, p. 110) talks about the Missouri dialect as a "primitive but picturesque" language. However, Thogmartin's work, along with this study, reinforces Brackenridge's 1814 comment, which was previously cited: all things considered, their language is more pure than might be expected, or for that matter, than the French people themselves in the Old Mines area were accustomed to think.

As already noted elsewhere, both Dorrance and Carrière were attracted to the Old Mines area by a sort of nostalgic romanticism. They both perceived in this community a sort of "magic carpet" opportunity to transport themselves backwards in time and space to personally study in the mid-twentieth century real-live–eighteenth-century French peasants. As a result, they both overlooked the hard times and romanticized the lack of material advantages that the community was experiencing during their visits. Although their descriptions of the people and their way of living tend to make one think of the proverbial "rose-colored glasses," they are nevertheless interesting to study because they do provide an eyewitness account of the framework in which the translated stories were told and collected.

In a later, lyrical work, *We're from Missouri* (1938, p. 14), Dorrance presents a somewhat fictionalized account of the way in which stories might fit into an evening's socializing during his visit to the Old Mines area:

Sometimes we'd find a group of men around a table playing cards. They were glad to stop if the Uncle would tell them tales. The Uncle was a "conteur." Of them all, he remembered the folklore best. He alone got each of the tricky words just right. It was he who knew how to make silence eloquent, how to sadden with a glance, how to convulse with a wink or nod. And he was very touchy about the whole matter. One had to approach him as one sets about photographing wildlife.

Once laugh, once show irreverence—Bah! As well try to lure back the deer frightened by the camera flash at night.

When the cards were pushed back, the Uncle would clear his throat. There would be an instant when we heard the moths thud at the lamp, the creek purling about its rocks beneath the window. Then we would hear of the prince whose magic key was swallowed by a fish, and the princess who roamed the golden wheat on the far side of the moon; of Johnny Greenpea; of the Prince White Pig and the Prince Green Snake; of how the rascal Beausoleil tricked the priest, and how Madame the Vulture got a bald head.

Dorrance in this passage undoubtedly captures one of the main reasons the stories survived for so many years and generations in this community: their power to transform such everyday sights and sounds as a smoky room with card players sitting in front of the wood stove, the multitude of moths attracted to the lantern's light, the creek lapping at stones in the field below into a magic world where fantasy knew no bounds and adventure could be had for the wishing. Carrière captures much the same feeling when he describes in this passage the role of a storyteller (1937, p. 7):

To beguile the monotony of life in small communities . . . the Creoles had a rich treasure of oral traditions, songs, and tales. A good singer or a good "conteur" was an important character, and enjoyed unusual prestige. There was a great demand for his talent, as no wedding celebration, no family gathering, no social function could be a success without his presence. Not long ago, miners still used to stop their work to sing a song in chorus, or hear one of their comrades tell a tale. Oral traditions had a definite social significance in primitive settlements. They took everyone, young and old, to a country of fairyland and dream, where all could forget for the time being the dire poverty, the ceaseless struggle, and the hard routine of their everyday life.

During the time when Carrière and Dorrance were doing their work, there appear to have been at least three publicly acknowledged master storytellers or "conteurs." Dorrance mentions one of these, "Gros Vesse" Portell, and transcribes four of his tales in French in his work on the survival of the French language (1935, pp. 108–120). Carrière mentions two others, who were the sources for all of his stories. He tells us (1937, p. 16) that of the stories presented in this book, Mr. Bourisaw told him "John the Bear," "The Little Bull with the Golden Horns," and "Prince White Hog." He heard the other stories from Mr. Coleman, who told him all but eight of the seventy-three stories in his collection. It is important to realize that numerous other people in the Old Mines area told these stories, many of them very well, to judge by the durability of remembrance accorded to their performances by the family members who heard them decades ago. Most hamlets and most families had at least one person in their midst who could tell several of the tales, and who would do so whenever an obliging audience of children and sometimes adults would gather and request a performance. Dorrance tells (1935, p. 103):

There are special "conteurs" known for their skill. Other people would not have the impertinence to attempt what they do so well. The conteur himself is conscious of the respect due his art, and if he is not sure of smooth delivery he refuses to begin a tale until he has practiced it a few evenings to himself. . . . The tale is a manner of ritual. The incidents must succeed one another in proper order. The vocabulary and turn of sentence must remain as nearly as possible as they were handed down. If the tale contains words no longer clear, they must nevertheless be retained and pronounced as well as possible. On the other hand, the "conteur" and his listeners are very grateful for definitions of such words as "un chateau," "un domestique," "un écu," "une épée," "un cygne."

Dorrance then goes on to describe the way in which the conteur tells his tales (p. 103):

> The conteur speaks in a tone somewhat louder than ordinary. Like the Greek actor wearing the cothurnus, his stature must be greater than life. At times he gesticulates, pantomimes his story. There are winks of understanding, nudges; even his silences are eloquent of meaning. Dialogue is delivered with the intonation of natural conversation.

He then finishes his description by telling us that only interjections expressing the audience's reactions to the text are permitted. No other interruptions are tolerated by the storytellers.

As we turn to Carrière's descriptions of his two main sources of stories, we see Dorrance's descriptions confirmed. This information is important, as it represents eyewitness accounts from two independent sources about something that is no longer possible to experience firsthand: the performance of commonly accepted master storytellers in their habitual public forum within the Old Mines community. In describing Mr. Bourisaw, Carrière tells us (1937, p. 9):

> Mr. Frank Bourisaw . . . told his stories with spirit, and his whole person became animated at the dramatic passages. He learned his repertory from various sources, some from Mrs. Bourisaw, others from an uncle, and a great many at gatherings at his home or at friends' and relatives.

As we read on to Carrière's description of Mr. Coleman, who provided Carrière with most of the stories, we find out more about the concept of "conteur," and what it meant to be an Old Mines master storyteller (p. 9):

> Mr. Joseph Ben Coleman . . . learned most of his stories from his father, who had a most extensive repertory of folk songs and tales. . . . As a story teller he is unusually conscientious. He has a high conception of the dignity of his art. For him, to tell a story is an accomplishment, and only a born "conteur" can ever master the ancient art. Like Mr. Bourisaw, he has an excellent memory; he can stop at any place in a story and usually resume it without difficulty. I have also heard him repeat a folk tale and use the same words, the same pauses, and intonations as the first time.

It is fortunate that Carrière and Dorrance had access to different groups in the community and to different storytellers, because in this way we can obtain a broader perspective on the art of storytelling as it existed in the 1930s during their visits. It is obvious, both from these quotations and from other comments in the reminiscences of older community members in the late 1970s, that the storytellers held a special place in the culture of the Old Mines area. They had an unusual ability to expand the narrow limits of each isolated hamlet or hollow, and because of the importance of what they could do, they were able to command extraordinary respect. When a conteur started to perform, none dared interrupt. He was the center of attention. Carrière's and Dorrance's accounts both substantiate the fact that the storytellers were aware of their power and knew how to use it to their best advantage.

There are many stories that seem to have been universal favorites. Dorrance gives us (p. 108) a list of the fairy tales that he says stand out as favorites in the community. A number of his titles are different from those used by Carrière for the same stories, making it difficult to match his list with Carrière's table of contents. However, there is at least a 95 percent overlapping between the two lists. Dorrance's listing includes: "Teigneux," "Renaud" (this was an extraordinarily long story, and even at that time Dorrance and Carrière both tell us that no one was left who remembered the story all the way through), "Bluebeard," "Cinderella," "Stupid John," "Carambot," "La Malice," "Beausoleil," "Sans Peur," "Prince Green Serpent," "Prince White Hog," "Master Thief," "The

Rabbit and the Woodsman's Daughter," "The Seven-Headed Beast," "John the Bear," "Fair Finette," "Fair Ferentine," and "The Ogre with His Soul in the Egg." All of these except "Renaud" were in Carrière's collection. Most of them were also confirmed as favorites by our participants of the weekly story meetings who remembered the stories they liked best as children. It is interesting to note that in four years of research on the topic we have not turned up more than three or four stories in the community that were not among the seventy-three stories transcribed by Carrière.

The stories presented in this book were singled out by a panel in 1978 as the favorite ones. "Stupid John" was mentioned by the panel, but it was almost impossible to translate this story effectively, because it is essentially a series of puns on French words. "The Rabbit and the Woodsman's Daughter" is called "The Little Rabbit" in Carrière's list. The majority of the stories on Dorrance's list were in fact mentioned as favorites in 1978, and they are included in this study. The exceptions are "Bluebeard," "Cinderella," and "The Little Rabbit." Of course, a few favorites with the modern group were not listed by Dorrance either and these too are included.

If we compare translations of a few paragraphs from the same story written down by Dorrance and Carrière, we shall begin to see how different individuals affect these oral tales by giving to them their own details and their own style of narrative. For example, here are the first few paragraphs from "Beausoleil" as Dorrance wrote it down from Gros Vesse Portell.

Well, it's good to tell you that once upon a time there were a man and a woman who had three sons. One of these boys was named Beausoleil. The old man was saying to the old woman that they had three sons, and all of them were good for nothing. Beausoleil heard him saying this, and the next morning he said to his Papa, "I'm leaving." His father said, "Where are you going?" —"I'm going out to make my fortune," said Beausoleil. So Beausoleil went into town. He didn't have any money, so he went to see his captain, and borrowed ten dollars from him. He was a big drinker and gambler, and when this money was gone, he decided to ask his father for some more. So he wrote to his father, asking him for five hundred dollars. After a while, he wrote to his father again, and told him that he had been in prison, and spent all the money he had been sent. He then asked his father for five hundred dollars more, because he had bought a big theatre. When that money was all spent, Beausoleil went to his captain again, and asked him for a pass to go back home. The captain was willing to give it to him, and also gave him fifty dollars.

The story continues with episodes similar to those recounted to Carrière by Mr. Coleman: Beausoleil finds the castle that everyone is afraid to stay in and tells the King he can stay there. During the night, a ghost comes in and shows him the buried treasure and tells him how to bring all the buried people back to life. The King is impressed with Beausoleil's ability to deal with this netherworld and gives him his daughter in marriage.

Although the small details of this story are different from Carrière's version, the major story elements are the same. Let's examine the same story as told to Carrière by Mr. Coleman:

It's good to tell you that once upon a time there were an old King and an old Queen. They had three sons, and the youngest was called Beausoleil. They were nearing manhood, all three of them, but they were still playing in the ashes and making popcorn. One day, the old King said to them, "Three princes, not one of you has had the courage to go out and see the world!" Beausoleil answered, "If that's what you want us to do, Father, I'll leave tomorrow morning." So the next morning, they bought a nice suit of clothes for Beausoleil and gave him all the money he needed, and Beausoleil left. Beausoleil didn't let on he was rich, but made believe he was poor.

He kept walking until he got to another city that had another king. He went to see the king to sign on as a soldier. The king was happy to have Beausoleil in his army, and Beausoleil was well liked by everyone. One day, he wrote to his father that he had been promoted sergeant. His mother was so happy when she read his letter! She said to his two brothers, "Look at this! Your brother has become a sergeant! A sergeant deserves to have some money. We'll send him one hundred dollars." But Beausoleil wasted all the money on liquor, in no time at all. After awhile he said to himself, "Maybe I should write to them and tell them that I've been promoted colonel." He sent the letter to his parents, saying that he had been promoted again. When the old Queen got this letter, she showed it to his brothers. "Look at this!" she said to them. "Beausoleil has only been gone a year and already he's a colonel! The two of you are still wasting your time playing in the ashes! You should be ashamed of yourselves!" The two brothers hung their heads and said nothing. They didn't do anything either. Their mother went on, "A colonel needs a lot of money." She sent him more money in a letter, but Beausoleil wasted all the money that his mother had sent him on liquor. One day, Beausoleil began to think: "I wrote to my father that I was a sergeant and I really wasn't. Then I lied again and said that I was a colonel, when I was still just a soldier. I think I'd better go find the king, get my discharge, and get out of here.

We can see by comparing these two brief excerpts that Mr. Coleman included much more detail than Mr. Portell. In addition, Mr. Coleman carefully pointed out the motivation behind each episode. He also used much more dialogue than Mr. Portell. Every event is related in terms of what people said and thought to themselves, in addition to the external details of what happened. Furthermore, Mr. Coleman was much more careful than Mr. Portell about the transitions between the different events and parts of the story. Mr. Coleman explains how Beausoleil came to have a captain, for example, where Mr. Portell simply says that Beausoleil asked his captain for a ten-dollar loan. Finally, Mr. Coleman's narrative contains more variety of sentence structure, length, and words than Mr. Portell's. As a result, Mr. Coleman's rendition of the story is more interesting. We can see from this comparison why Carrière thought so highly of his informants and of their storytelling abilities. It is one thing to remember a story's outline and events, and quite another to choose the right words and situations to make these events come to life for the hearer.

Another note of interest about the stories concerns the ways in which the same story line can be developed with different examples. In Mr. Portell's version of the story, Beausoleil was not only a drinker but also a gambler. He asked for five hundred dollars at a time from his parents according to Mr. Portell and also received cash from his captain. In this version, he said he needed the money because he had been in jail and because he had invested in a theater. According to Mr. Coleman, he received two payments of one hundred dollars each from his mother, and he told her falsely that he had been promoted in order to get the cash. The basic story line is the same in both versions: he receives money from his parents under false pretenses and squanders it. But the actual details are almost entirely different in the two versions.

It is also possible for a story to contain totally different episodes in each version. In "Master Thief," for example, according to Carrière, Little John is tested three times by the rich man. On one occasion, he has to steal a certain neighbor's oxen; on another he is challenged to steal the horse out of the rich man's stable; on the third occasion, he is supposed to find a way to steal the rich man's bed sheet. In Dorrance's version of "Master Thief," the episode of the oxen is there, but there is an additional important character, the priest, who is also Master Thief's Godfather. The rich man tells Master Thief in this version that he is to steal all of his Godfather's money. To do so, he dresses up as an angel and rings the church bell in order to get the priest out of bed. He gets the money and puts the priest in a sack, telling him that the Lord is calling him to go to Paradise. Little John gets tired of carrying the priest in the sack, however, and thows him into a poultry house along the road. When the priest wakes up, he looks around and asks if he is in Paradise. The owners of the chicken coop laugh at him and tell him, "Yes, you're in the paradise of geese!" This episode is missing entirely from Carrière's version. Of course, the episodes of the horse and the bed sheet are also missing from the version that Dorrance gives us. It is quite possible that the complete story at one time contained all of these episodes. Selective memory is definitely a factor, along with personal style, in making one storyteller's version of a tale different from the version told by another.

Almost all the stories we heard or heard about during our weekly story meetings, with a few notable exceptions, are included in Dorrance's and Carrière's books, although perhaps not quite in the version that we had heard them. One of the exceptions is "Histoire à Renaud," to which Carrière (1937, p. 16) refers. This story was a tremendously long one. According to our informant, it took two full evenings to tell. Dorrance says it took a week "on the diggings," when presumably the same number of hours were spread out over more days. Length is, of course, variable from one storyteller to another, as we have just discussed. However, it is clear that its long duration was one of this story's outstanding characteristics. We learned from this informant that it was a story about Napoleon, in which various assassination attempts and Napoleon's sometimes startling responses to them were described, along with some of his plans to conquer the world. We were told the following:

> That was a long story, and that old man knew the whole thing. I know it took about six hours to tell it like it should have been. It was a true story for the most part. It was in a foreign country and was about Napoleon, who was a war general. When he'd go to war, he'd take all the places; he had only one more place to take and he'd have the whole territory. But he didn't take it. One time, a priest was going to kill him. There was an old drunkard there and he was going into the confession box. He was a spy. The priest told him that Napoleon was going to communion every morning, with his soldiers. So they put some poison in the oats. The next morning when Napoleon went to communion, he pulled his gun and he made the priest take the oats. So the priest died. That's about all I know about it. I used to know a lot about Napoleon, but I forgot it all. Narcisse Politte could tell a lot of that. Those old people could tell you about Napoleon. We used to go over to our next door neighbor's with my dad and my brother, and they would sit down and talk about it. They'd tell a lot of it.

When we asked this person where he thought this story had come from, he thought that it had been taken from a book. This is plausible, given its obvious nineteenth-century origin and the fact that people who came to Old Mines in the nineteenth century from both France and Canada were generally literate and often owned books in French.

Three other stories of which people told us fragments and which we have not been able to recognize in Carrière and Dorrance also surfaced. One of them is "Royaume des Fees":

> There was a little boy that they gave away to this man. But when he came to get him, the little boy wouldn't go. His father took him and stood him in the sand by the ocean, which was where his godfather was supposed to come and get him. But when the godfather came, the little boy wouldn't go. He showed him all kinds of sticks of candy, all kinds of good things, because he was a magician too. But when the boy wouldn't go, he made the ocean come up and wash him away. After awhile, some woman found him. She told her mother that she had found this little boy and wanted to take care of him. But her mother told her to leave him there. She said, "But he looks so pitiful." So the mother told her to go ahead and take him. The girl's mother's name was "Royaume des Fees." After

the boy grew up, he fell in love with the girl, and they got married. They had all kinds of troubles. She went and told her mother, who said to her, "Well, I told you to leave him alone."

This was all that our storyteller remembered. She thought that Mr. Joseph Ben Coleman had told that story, and that lots of other people also remember it.

A second fairy tale that we could not find in Dorrance or in Carrière is "La Belle Aquénnée." This story was about a beautiful horse of that name, and it was mentioned to us that it was a favorite story that many people liked. A third story fragment that we were told about had lost its name in the intervening years. It was about two brothers and a sister who ended up in a box on a lake or an ocean. When they landed, they stayed together. Some kind of a spell had been cast on their mother and father, and they were looking for them. The first boy went out to look for them and came to an old grandfather sitting with his feet across the path. The boy stepped across the old man's legs, and the old man told him, "Son, I want to say something to you. On your journey, don't look either to the right or the left." But as he went along, there were lions and tigers and all kinds of other noises. As soon as he turned his head the first time, he was turned into a bird. The same thing happened to the second brother. But the sister when she came along, after waiting vainly for her two brothers to come back, was very polite to the old man and told him that she couldn't step across him. She gently moved him to the side of the road. As a reward for her politeness, he told her the way to succeed in getting through all the obstacles and in finding her parents and brothers. This story was told by Mr. Tode Villmer to his grandchildren.

The existence of these story pieces seems to indicate that while Carrière's collection of seventy-three stories is a remarkably complete catalogue of contes or fairy tales that existed, and exist, in the Old Mines community at the time he visited it, there are undoubtedly some other stories that he did not hear and record; the unrecorded ones almost certainly amount to no more than 20 percent of the total stories that were, and are, available.

It is important to be aware of the atmosphere that accompanies the telling of traditional stories, and the purpose that these stories fulfilled. It is also important, as we have seen, to realize the tremendous input that a storyteller has for each story which he or she tells. An oral tale changes with different storytellers, in regard to words, sentences, episodes, and amount and quality of detail. This endless potential for variation is one of the things that keep oral tales fresh and interesting: as an audience we enjoy the dramatic skills of the tale teller as well as the feat of memory that he is sharing with us.

V.

Conclusion

The stories recorded by Carrière and Dorrance still retain a large significance within the Old Mines community. Although they are no longer a primary source of recreation and communication, they are symbolic of the community's historic and cultural continuity and of its ethnic heritage. The continued power of these stories to inspire, terrify, and entertain is still obvious today, as it was in the 1930s and 1940s. They are analogues to the "Jack Tales" told elsewhere in North America, except that they derive from French traditional sources. Many of the same characters and motifs can be found in Canadian French and Louisiana French folklore. One finds in them, as we have seen, an ingenuous blend of pagan traditional motifs and biblical ones, and a mythical world populated by kings who while away their time sitting on the front porch, princesses who retire to log cabins in the woods, and woodsmen threatening these royal personages with shotguns. Many delightful hours were spent during the summer of 1980 both listening to these stories and analyzing them. As a result, our discussions in our weekly story meetings focused on three main points: (1) why the stories were no longer told; (2) who the storytellers were and how they told the tales; and (3) the way in which the stories related to the lives of the people in the Old Mines community.

Although these stories were known, at one time, to just about everyone in the area and were told fluently by a large number of storytellers, no one has told them for years. When we asked our participants for the reasons these stories were not being told, we were usually given the following response: "In those days, they'd tell stories most anytime. In the old days, there was no radio, no television, and no place to go, so they'd stay home and tell stories." Prior to World War II, the Old Mines French community was a close-knit culture that was sharply separated from the surrounding Anglo-American one. However, after the late 1940s, paved roads became common; cars, radios, and television sets became widespread; and virtually everyone acquired electricity and a telephone. Community life, as might be expected, was revolutionized by these changes, and as other options of entertainment became available, the need to tell and hear these stories began to disappear. Another reason is the fact that in addition to having to compete with industrialization, the would-be story-tellers were more often constrained to translate their stories into English, as French was used less often. At our weekly sessions, when a story was not too long and taxing, the storyteller was asked to tell the story twice during the same session, once in French and once in English. It became obvious during this process that it was much easier to tell a story in its traditional language and that the audience enjoyed it more too, when it was told in French. To support this observation, many people had told us, "Those stories just sounded better in French." Everyone present would always agree emphatically whenever this statement was made. However, it proved difficult to analyze what exactly was meant by this statement. It seemed to be a kind of gut-level aesthetic feeling that most people had not analyzed. One comment was made, however, about how some of the words in French were enjoyable because they sounded funny:

When he'd tell funny stories, he'd make them sound funny. Like the word "La bebelle" sounds funny in French, but in American it doesn't even sound interesting. It's a long train. "Sa bebelle alle traine dans la poussiere." (Her train would drag in the dust.) That sounded like a funny word.

This comment is important because it suggests that one of the main reasons for everyone's universal preference for hearing the stories in French is that the storyteller is more skilled in choosing and manipulating words in that language. We pursued this idea further and analyzed the same story told in French and in English by the same storyteller and found that the English version generally sounded like a pale translation. For example, the narrator often had to pause and search for the right word. In addition, there tended to be less animation in voice and in gestures. Finally, the words chosen in English often had less color, feel, or sound than those used at the identical place in the same story told in French. As a result, our informants almost all found it less demanding to read stories to their children from books rather than to engage in the strenuous process of translating from memory. However, it is interesting to note that in a community where a grade school education was a norm when they were growing up, many of our modern informants did *read* many stories to their children, which is indicative (1) that the fairy tales of the past had had some effect on their sense of culture, and (2) that they did, and still do, appreciate the value of a fairy tale.

Why did the stories survive as long as they have? The foremost reason is the fact that everyone shared the occupation of digging tiff. Working together on the diggings on a daily basis enabled different stories to be spread throughout the community. Storytelling was a favorite pastime during lunch and other rest breaks, and the miners, as a result, brought the stories home with them to tell to their families, as can be seen in the statement made by one of our informants:

He'd bring them back home with him, and tell them to us at night. Then he'd learn some more the next day, and he'd say, "Tomorrow night I'm going to tell you some more." We couldn't wait for tomorrow night to come.

The importance of tiff mining in the survival of the stories is further illustrated by the fact that Carrière collected most of his stories on the diggings. According to one of Mr. Coleman's nieces:

My Uncle Ben, he was digging tiff like we all did. While he was on the diggings he'd sit down and rest sometimes and tell a story. This French guy came there and he'd sit on the bank and listen to Uncle Ben tell those stories, and write all that down.

She also told us that Carrière had paid Mr. Coleman a certain amount per story for his time on the diggings. Others have asserted that Carrière paid for the stories not in money but in whiskey. It is debatable, of course, whether or not the whiskey should really be interpreted as a payment or simply as a friendly gift, especially since along with the whiskey for Mr. Coleman Carrière also generally brought candy for the children in the family. In any case, it is obvious that Carrière knew how to make himself a welcome visitor and appreciated the importance of the diggings as a context for the telling and learning of stories. Since many stories were told there, it was an appropriate place for him, too, to learn them. When hand mining came to an abrupt end in the late 1930s, community awareness of the stories also slowly disappeared.

Another important factor responsible for the long survival of these tales, and their ultimate disappearance, is the fact that the tales were only one in many types of stories that were common to our informants as they were growing up and raising their own families. Not all the people who were classified as storytellers told the French contes. At least as many others specialized in various kinds of ghost stories, known as "true stories" to our informants. The similarity of the supernatural elements in the true stories and in the contes is obvious: take for example the cat that lived under the house and howled all night but could not be chased away; the people who were kept awake all night by someone rummaging through all the plates and tableware only to find the next morning that everything was just as they had left it the night before; or the case of the people who supposedly had sold their souls to the devil (they were generally identified by the weird events that people witnessed during these individuals' wakes or funerals). This belief in supernatural forces of good and evil acting in real life was undoubtedly one of the things that enhanced emotional response to the fairy tales and made them such a highlight. However, as modern technology began to change the Old Mines community, the climate in which this willingness to be enticed by tales of the supernatural began to disappear.

A second topic that occupied a large portion of our discussion time was the individual who was a storyteller in the twenties and thirties. There were many people who told stories frequently enough to be remembered as "storytellers." Seven people during the story meetings mentioned a total of twenty-eight different individuals who had told stories. The trait that characterized all these individuals was their avid enjoyment of all kinds of verbal material. Some of the people who told either fairy tales or true stories (tales that deal with strange, scary, supernatural events that were supposed to have really happened to someone in the area) were also prolific tellers of jokes, riddles, and tall tales, and many storytellers also knew a number of songs. In addition, it is interesting to note that many of the storytellers also loved to read. One storyteller, who had never learned to read, loved books so much that he would have his children read to him for hours. We were told by one of his daughters:

> After we grew up, Pop never did tell us stories. But he'd turn around and make us read, when we started learning. He'd make us read all night long. We'd even have to read while he was digging tiff.

We also learned that people not only read newspapers eagerly but also ordered books by mail from catalogues and then circulated them among friends and relatives. One of our modern storytellers told us how she had walked miles to exchange books with a friend and then had taken them out on the diggings with her to read during the lunch hour.

As we talked about these people, we asked what made a storyteller "good." The people in our group were definite in saying that some people had a natural talent for telling stories while others did not. The comments focused both on quantity and on quality. A good storyteller usually did these things: he or she knew a large number of stories, put a lot of life into telling them, and developed a suspenseful story line. All of the really good storytellers could tell many stories. This was one of the most common comments about favorite storytellers, as illustrated in the following quotation about Mr. Bourisaw:

> Do you remember Uncle Frank Bourisaw? They called him Boy Bourisaw. He'd go to Mom's house and start telling a story. We'd sit down at seven or eight o'clock, and he could tell stories that would go on until five o'clock the next morning. He'd just keep on telling all different ones.

The second characteristic of a good storyteller was a lively style of delivery:

> People who were more fun to listen to would put more life in their stories. That old man could make it sound like it was real. He'd act like he was really scared or really seeing something. If he was talking about a hog, he'd pretend like he was shooting the hog. Or for a cow, he'd bawl. He'd always tell us "I remember that, because I was there."

He made the stories interesting by the way he told them. He'd make it sound like you were right there and going through that with him. He made it kind of three dimensional.

We were fortunate to be able to observe a number of different people telling stories in our classes and meetings. Most of the storytellers avoided direct eye contact and they looked at the audience only occasionally. They sounded like they were almost talking to themselves, as though the act of storytelling involves introspection rather than performance. The narrative lines were said somewhat loudly, but in a very matter-of-fact tone of voice. On the other hand, the dialogue was acted out with gestures and said just as though the person were really experiencing the situation. This is one of the most engaging aspects of a storytelling performance, and well-acted lines often provide rich humor that is not apparent in the written story.

The third trait of a gifted storyteller is his or her ability to engage the attention of the audience, both by choosing words that have the power to move, surprise, and delight and by building suspense and detail into the sequence of events. One of our informants compared the effect to that of a detective story:

> Those stories were so interesting. They made them just like a detective story. You know, when you're reading a detective story and you want to find out what happened? That's the way those stories were.

How this is accomplished by the storyteller depends on his insight into the motivations and development of the different characters. We have already seen an example of what effect this kind of understanding has on the story when we compared the stories transcribed by Dorrance and Carrière in an earlier chapter. A less successful storyteller treats the tale only as a series of unmotivated events, whereas the gifted performer is able to bring the characters to life through their actions in the story.

An interesting sidelight on this question of storytelling is the general consensus within our group that the true status of storyteller was accorded mainly to males. When we asked why this was so, two reasons emerged: First, while women, who did not participate in the tiff digging arrangements, would sometimes be the storytellers within the family circle as they grew older, they were admittedly retelling stories they had learned from a man. Only men were ever acknowledged as community-level storytellers. Most often, when asked where the men had learned their stories, people would specify that they had been heard "on the diggings." Secondly, women were less dramatic when telling a story:

> It seemed to me that women didn't take as much interest in it as a man did. A woman couldn't sit still to tell a story like a man could. They'd get distracted.

Further discussion indicated that what was meant by this was that women always had too much to do and could not concentrate on one thing to the exclusion of household and child care duties. Whatever the reason, it was certainly true that the well-known public storytellers were all men, and that the women who knew stories told them only to their children and grandchildren.

A final topic that arose as we discussed the subject of storytellers was the reason these people told stories, aside from the obvious desire to read and to produce verbal materials, which we have already discussed. One major motivation was definitely a desire to "pass the time" in a rewarding way. We have previously considered the lack of opportunity for commercial entertainment. The novelty value of storytelling is also evident in the fact that even in families that had an excellent storyteller, if another storyteller came to visit, everyone would gather around the visitor and listen. The storyteller who lived in the house would defer to the visitor. The sheer pressure of requests from eager children and adults alike undoubtedly kept the storytellers performing. Many of our informants remembered begging for stories when they were children:

> Grandma used to come over, and as soon as she'd get there we'd say to her, "Grandma, tell us a story." She'd say, "Be still." We'd sit around and she'd tell us stories until she'd go to bed that night.

The most extreme example of this kind of friendly badgering was remembered by one person who promised plugs of tobacco to her grandfather in exchange for stories. With the exception of this instance, however, everyone agreed that storytellers did not ordinarily get paid for sharing their talents.

As we proceeded further into our discussion, we began to wonder whether or not competition might have been a factor in motivating storytellers to learn more stories and to tell them more often. If this was an important stimulus, it was well hidden. It appears that in most situations, the best storyteller, or the visitor whose stories had some novelty value, was allowed to monopolize the limelight without any challenge from the other storytellers who were present. This courtesy was extended even to situations where someone in the audience knew the story better than the person who was telling it. It was important to give the performer full credit for his or her effort. Our informants further indicated that while these storytellers were generally popular, it was assumed that everyone knew the stories to some extent, and that the ability to tell them well did not entitle the performer to any special consideration.

However, it seems unlikely that the well-known public storytellers like those recorded by Carrière and Dorrance did not feel some sense of pride in the common recognition of their talents. Certainly Carrière indicates this in the passage we have already quoted about the artistic pride that he saw in his informants as they performed. One way in which storytellers asserted themselves as artists was by insisting that there be no talking or interruptions while a story was being told. Our group was emphatic in remembering this: "When those old people would tell them, they were really interesting, and you wouldn't dare make any noise. Until he got through, we didn't get up." We could also infer that storytelling was regarded as a special skill by the fact that none of our informants could remember any situations in which either fairy tales or true stories were told or enacted by children at play.

The third and final broad topic of our story meeting discussions concerned storytelling situations, and the way in which the stories fitted into the community's life cycle. We have discussed situations in which the storytellers were persuaded to tell stories by their eager listeners, and situations in which it was expected that stories would be told. A final variant on the kind of situation in which stories took place was when the storyteller had the paternal authority in the family and would decide more or less spontaneously when he was ready for a storytelling session. His audience would then gather up immediately and sit quietly while he performed. According to one of our group members, "In wintertime, my dad had some nights when he was feeling good, and he'd tell maybe two or three stories. But then maybe it would be several weeks before he'd do it again. We could hardly wait for him to begin when he said he was going to tell us some." For most of our informants, storytelling was primarily an activity characteristic of family gatherings. Often a parent or grandparent would regularly indulge the family with an evening of storytelling, as we have already seen. Or if relatives came to visit for two or three days, and one of them could tell stories, everyone would look forward to the diversion this would provide: "They'd come and stay two or three days at a time. When they'd come, they'd always bring new stories. I don't know where they got hold of them, but they'd always have new ones."

Good food played an important role during these storytelling sessions. Each family had its customary treat to accompany the stories:

> Whenever it was time for a story, we'd put potatoes in the ashes, or we'd put an ear of corn in there, and we'd roast them, and eat them all night. When they were done you'd take them out and put salt and pepper and butter on them. Sometimes we roasted corn in the oven, or made popcorn. In the fall we'd have blackhaws.

> When he'd go out to work in the morning, he'd say to me, "Have a big bowl of hickory nuts and walnut kernels made tonight." We'd run to see which one was going to do that, because we were wanting those stories.

The fact that the preparation of the treat would begin as soon as the storytelling session was announced shows how important food was as a part of general enjoyment. The primary scene for a storytelling session and for good food was the neighborhood "veillée" (pronounced vay-yay). Two or three times a week, the inhabitants of a little hollow or hamlet would get together at the house of one of the neighbors—in most cases, a storyteller's house. Once there, they would sit around, play cards, and listen to stories, with ample opportunity for other relaxing conversation. However, storytelling sessions were not held at all of the social events. The bouillon, a relatively frequent and informal occurrence, was primarily an evening of music and card playing, while a "bal" (pronounced ball), held weekly during the summer and on special occasions during the winter, was a night of dancing at someone's house.

With all that has been said about the people of the Old Mines community, we can safely assume that they indeed believed that life was to be enjoyed to its fullest. They accomplished this feat by indulging themselves with good music, good food, and, especially, good storytelling sessions. These storytelling sessions were looked upon as a way of relaxation, primarily in the wintertime or when it was rainy and outdoor work was difficult or impossible. With the exception of very old people who could no longer work, and therefore had the leisure to tell stories whenever they had an audience, the storytellers confined their performances to evenings or to days of rest, such as Sunday afternoons. As mentioned earlier in this study, and in this chapter, the main purpose of the stories was to inspire, to terrify, and to entertain. Today they still lend themselves to being read, learned, enjoyed, and performed, and shared in a way that is explicitly described below by one of our informants:

> He'd [father] come home for dinner, and he'd say, "Boy! I've got a good one for you tonight." Well, that was something! We couldn't wait for night. He'd say, "After you're done washing the dishes, I'll tell you one." Well, gosh, we couldn't go fast enough. Then, we'd all sit down and not move. Every night that would continue, and for as long as I wasn't big enough that I got married, I think he was still telling them. I sure enjoyed them!

Bibliography

Alvord, Clarence W. *Cahokia Records, 1778–1790*. Springfield, Ill.: Collections of the Illinois State Historical Library, 1907.

———. *Centennial History of Illinois*, vol. 1, *The Illinois Country, 1673–1818*. Springfield, Ill.: Illinois State Historical Library, 1920.

Ben-Amos, Dan, ed. *Folklore Genres*. Austin: University of Texas Press, 1976.

Bettelheim, Bruno. *The Uses of Enchantment*. New York: Alfred A. Knopf, 1976.

Boyer, Mark G. *History of St. Joachim Parish*. Old Mines, Mo.: 1973. Available from Old Mines Area Historical Society, Rte. 1, Box 300Z, Old Mines, Cadet, Mo. 63630.

Brackenridge, Henry Marie. *Views of Louisiana, Together with a Journal of a Voyage up the Missouri River in 1811*. Pittsburgh: 1814; facsimile reprint, Chicago: Quadrangle Books, 1962.

Bradbury, John. *Travels in the Interior of America in the Years 1809, 1810, and 1811*. 2d ed. London: Sherwood, Neely, and Jones, 1819.

Carrière, Joseph Médard. *Tales from the French Folklore of Missouri*. Evanston, Ill.: Northwestern University Press, 1937.

———. "The Present State of French Folklore Studies in North America." *Southern Folklore Quarterly* 10 (1946): 219–26.

Dégh, Linda. *Folktales and Society*. Bloomington: Indiana University Press, 1969.

———. "Folk Narrative." In *Folklore and Folklife: An Introduction*, edited by Richard M. Dorson, pp. 53–84. Chicago: University of Chicago Press, 1972.

Delarue, Paul, ed. *The Borzoi Book of French Folktales*. New York: Alfred A. Knopf, 1956.

Dorrance, Ward A. *The Survival of French in the Old District of Ste. Genevieve*. University of Missouri Studies 10, no. 2 (1 April 1935).

———. *We're from Missouri*. Richmond, Mo.: Missourian Press, 1938.

Dorson, Richard M. *Buying the Wind: Regional Folklore in the United States*. Chicago: University of Chicago Press, 1964.

———. *American Folklore and the Historian*. Chicago: University of Chicago Press, 1971.

Dorson, Richard M. *Folklore and Folklife: An Introduction*. Chicago: University of Chicago Press, 1972.

Dundes, Alan. *Interpreting Folklore*. Bloomington: Indiana University Press, 1980.

Foley, William. *A History of Missouri, Volume I: 1673–1820*. Columbia: University of Missouri Press, 1971.

Gerlach, Russel L. *Immigrants in the Ozarks: A Study in Ethnic Geography*. Columbia: University of Missouri Press, 1976.

Jennepin, A. *Notice historique sur la commune de Coussolre*. Maubeuge: Beugnes, 1877; reprinted, Bagnères de Bigorre: Editions Pyrénéennes, 1971.

Leach, MacEdward. "Problems of Collecting Oral Literature," *PMLA* 77 (1962): 335–40.

McCormick, E. M. "The Coleman Family History." Undated typescript said to have been written in the 1930s. Available as annotated by Patricia Weeks (1979) from Old Mines Area Historical Society, Rte. 1, Box 300Z, Old Mines, Cadet, Mo. 63630.

MacDonald, Donald A. "Fieldwork: Collecting Oral Literature." In *Folklore and Folklife: An Introduction*, edited by Richard M. Dorson, pp. 407–30. Chicago: University of Chicago Press, 1972.

Massignon, Genevieve. *Folktales of France*. Translated by J. Hyland; foreword by Richard M. Dorson. Chicago: University of Chicago Press, 1968.

Meramec Regional Planning Commission, Map of Washington County, Mo. Available from MRPC, 101 W. 10th St., Rolla, Mo. 65401.

Miles, J. T. "History and Customs of Washington, Iron, St. Francois and Ste. Genevieve Counties." Typescript, 1937. Washington County Library, Potosi, Mo.

Pfeffer, Joseph G. "The Paradox of Strength through Weakness: Traditional Values, Ethnic Identity, and Community Cohesiveness in a Missouri French Community." Typescript, 1979.

Ranke, Kurt, ed. *Folktales of Germany*. Translated by Lotte Baumann; foreword by Richard M. Dorson. Chicago: University of Chicago Press, 1966.

Sauer, Carl. *Geography of the Highland Ozarks of Missouri*. Chicago: University of Chicago Press, 1920.

Schultz, Christian, Jr. *Travels on a Inland Voyage*. New York: Isaac Riley, 1810.

Taussig, Mary Boland. "Factors Influencing School Attendance in the Missouri Barytes Fields." Master's thesis, Washington University, 1938.

Thogmartin, Clyde D., Jr. "The French Dialect of Old Mines, Missouri." Ph.D. dissertation, University of Michigan, 1970.

Thomas, Rosemary Hyde. "Some Aspects of the French Language and Culture of Old Mines, Mo." Ph.D. dissertation, St. Louis University, 1979.

Thomas, Rosemary Hyde; Bergey, Barry; and Pfeffer, Joseph G. "Sociocultural Description of Old Mines French Culture and Language." Interim report, NEH Grant no. PD 33399, 1979.

Thompson, Stith C. *The Folktale*. Berkeley: University of California Press, 1977.

Villmer, Natalie. "250th Anniversary Historical Program Pageant Book of Old Mines, Missouri. 1973." Available from Old Mines Area Historical Society.

Index